"*LIR*-SHAPE IS BORN OF MAGIC, SHAPED OF POWER—

"Close your eyes, Rory, and think of *nothingness*," Keely said. "Lose yourself in emptiness, in the utter absence of self."

Slowly, the line in his brow went away. His breathing was deep and even.

"There is power," Keely said, "much power. And if you know how, you can tap it . . . if you are Cheysuli. If you have the blood. If the power acknowledges you. Power unlike any you have known.

"There is a moment when you are neither man nor animal, nothing more than formlessness, waiting for the shape. But it always comes and you are free, *freed,* to be what you must be. Mountain cat, fox, hawk, wolf, owl, bear.

"You are an eagle, Rory, *the lord of the air*, and there is magic in your blood and power in your bones . . . and you fly, *you fly*, where no one else can go . . . being what no one else can be: born of the earth but not bound to it. And then it ends."

His voice was hoarse. "Why must it end?"

"There always must be an ending, or your true shape can be lost."

"And if I found I preferred the other?"

"Then you would be beast: abomination. A thing of ancient nightmares. . . ."

Jennifer Roberson writes:

'The *Chronicles of the Cheysuli* is a dynastic fantasy, the story of a proud, honorable race brought down by the avarice, evil and sorcery of others – and its own special brand of magic. It's the story of an ancient race blessed by the old gods of their homeland, and cursed by the sorcerers who desire domination over all men. It's a dynasty of good and evil; love and hatred; pride and strength. Most of all it deals with the destiny in every man and his struggle to shape it, follow it, deny it.'

Also by Jennifer Roberson

CHRONICLES OF THE CHEYSULI

and published by Corgi Books

Chronicles of the Cheysuli: Book Six

DAUGHTER OF THE LION

Jennifer Roberson

CORGI BOOKS

DAUGHTER OF THE LION
A CORGI BOOK 0 552 13123 7

First publication in Great Britain

PRINTING HISTORY
Corgi edition published 1990

A portion of this novel appeared in slightly different form as the short story
'Blood of Sorcery' in the DAW Books anthology SWORD AND SORCERESS I,
copyright © 1984 by Marion Zimmer Bradley, editor.

Corgi Books are published by Transworld Publishers
Ltd., 61–63 Uxbridge Road, Ealing, London W5 5SA, in
Australia by Transworld Publishers (Australia) Pty. Ltd.,
15–23 Helles Avenue, Moorebank, NSW 2170, and in New
Zealand by Transworld Publishers (N.Z.) Ltd., Cnr. Moselle
and Waipareira Avenues, Henderson, Auckland.

Printed and bound in Great Britain by
Cox & Wyman Ltd., Reading, Berks.

the Tuhlo Ocean

Valgaard

Atvia

Rondule

Kilore

Andemir

Homana

Mujhara

Erinn

Lestra

the Idrian Ocean

Solinde

Hondarth

the Crystal Isle

·danjokuh 1984·

The Chronicles of the Cheysuli: An Overview

THE PROPHECY OF THE FIRSTBORN:

**"One day a man of all blood shall unite,
in peace, four warring realms
and two magical races."**

Originally a race of shapechangers known as the Cheysuli, descendants of the Firstborn, Homana's original race, held the Lion Throne, but increasing unrest on the part of the Homanans, who lacked magical powers and therefore feared the Cheysuli, threatened to tear the realm apart. The Cheysuli royal dynasty voluntarily gave up the Lion Throne so that Homanans could rule Homana, thereby avoiding fullblown internecine war.

The clans withdrew altogether from Homanan society save for one remaining and binding tradition: each Homanan king, called a Mujhar, must have a Cheysuli liege man as bodyguard, councillor, companion, dedicated to serving the throne and protecting the Mujhar, until such a time as the prophecy is fulfilled and the Firstborn rule again.

This tradition was adhered to without incident for nearly four centuries, until Lindir, the only daughter of Shaine the Mujhar, jilted her prospective bridegroom to elope with Hale, her father's Cheysuli liege man. Because the jilted bridegroom was the heir of a neighboring king, Bellam of Solinde, and because their marriage was meant to seal an alliance after years of bloody war, the elopement resulted in tragic consequences. Shaine concocted a web of lies to salve his obsessive pride, and in so doing laid the groundwork for the annihilation of a race. Declared sorcerers and demons dedicated to the downfall of the Homanan throne, the Cheysuli were summarily outlawed and sentenced to immediate execution if found within Homanan borders.

Shapechangers begins the "Chronicles of the Cheysuli," telling the tale of Alix, daughter of Lindir, once Princess of Homana, and Hale, once Cheysuli liege man to Shaine. Alix is an unknown catalyst bearing the Old Blood of the Firstborn, which gives her the ability to link with all *lir* and assume any animal shape at will. But Alix is raised by a Homanan and has no knowledge of her abilities, until she is kidnapped by Finn, a Cheysuli warrior who is Hale's son by his Cheysuli wife, and therefore Alix's half-brother. Kidnapped with her is Carillon, Prince of Homana. Alix learns the true power in her gifts, the nature of the prophecy which rules all Cheysuli, and eventually marries a warrior, Duncan, to whom she bears a son, Donal, and, much later, a daughter, Bronwyn. But Homana's internal strife weakens her defenses. Bellam of Solinde, with his sorcerous aide, Tynstar the Ihlini, conquers Homana and assumes the Lion Throne.

In *The Song of Homana*, Carillon returns from a five-year exile, faced with the difficult task of gathering an army capable of overcoming Bellam. He is accompanied by Finn, who has assumed the traditional role of liege man. Aided by Cheysuli magic and his own brand of personal power, Carillon is able to win back his realm and restore the Cheysuli to their homeland by ending the purge begun by his uncle, Shaine, Alix's grandfather. He marries Bellam's daughter to seal peace between the lands, but Electra has already cast her lot with Tynstar the Ihlini, and works against her Homanan husband. Carillon's failure to father a son forces him to betroth his only daughter, Aislinn, to Donal, Alix's son, whom he names Prince of Homana. This public approbation of a Cheysuli warrior is the first step in restoring the Lion Throne to the sovereignty of the Cheysuli, required by the prophecy, and sows the seeds of civil unrest.

Legacy of the Sword focuses on Donal's slow assumption of power within Homana, and his personal assumption of his role in the prophecy. Because by clan custom a warrior is free to take both wife and mistress, Donal has started a Cheysuli family even though he will one day have to marry Carillon's daughter to cement his right to the Lion Throne. By his Cheysuli mistress he has two children, Ian and Isolde; by Aislinn, Carillon's daughter, he eventually sires a son who will become his heir. But the marriage is rocky immediately; in addition to the problems caused by a second family, Donal's Homanan wife is also under the magical influence of her mother, Electra, who is mistress to Tynstar. Problems are compounded by the son of Tynstar and Electra, Strahan, who has his father's powers in full measure. On Carillon's death Donal inherits the Lion, naming his legitimate son, Niall, to succeed him. But to further the prophecy he marries his sister, Bronwyn, to Alaric of Atvia, lord of an island kingdom. Bronwyn is later killed by Alaric accidentally while in *lir*-shape, but lives long enough to give birth to a daughter, Gisella, who is mad.

In *Track of the White Wolf*, Donal's son Niall is a young man caught between two worlds. To the Homanans, fearful of Cheysuli power and intentions, he is worthy only of distrust, the focus of their discontent. To the Cheysuli he is an "unblessed" man, because even though far past the age for it, Niall has not linked with his animal. He is therefore a *lirless* man, a warrior with no power, and such a man has no place within the clans. His Cheysuli half-brother is his liege man, fully "blessed," and Ian's abilities serve to add to Niall's feelings of inferiority.

Niall is meant to marry his half-Atvian cousin, Gisella, but falls in love with the princess of a neighboring kingdom, Deirdre of Erinn. *Lirless,* and with Gisella under the influence of Tynstar's Ihlini daughter, Lillith, Niall falls prey to sorcery. Eventually he links with his *lir* and assumes the full range of Cheysuli powers, but he pays for it with an eye. His marriage to Gisella is disastrous, but two sets of twins are born— Brennan and Hart, Corin and Keely—which gives Niall the opportunity to extend his range of influence via betrothal alliances. He banishes Gisella to Atvia after he foils an Ihlini plot involving her, and then settles into life with his mistress, Deirdre of Erinn, who has already borne Maeve, his illegitimate daughter.

A Pride of Princes tells the story of each of Niall's three sons. Brennan, the eldest, will inherit Homana and has been betrothed to Aileen, Deirdre's niece, to add a heretofore unknown bloodline to the prophecy. Brennan's twin, Hart, is Prince of Solinde, a compulsive gambler whose addiction results in a tragic accident involving all three of Niall's sons. Hart is banished to Solinde for a year, and the rebellious youngest son, Corin, to Atvia. Brennan is tricked into siring a child on an Ihlini-Cheysuli woman; Hart loses a hand and nearly his life in a Solindish plot; in Erinn, Corin falls in love with Brennan's bride, Aileen, before going to Atvia. One by one each is captured by Strahan, Tynstar's son, who intends to turn Niall's sons into puppet-kings so he can rule through them. All three manage to escape, but not after each has been made to recognize particular strengths and weaknesses.

PART I

One

I was aware of eyes, watching me. Marking every step, every feint, my every riposte with the sword. Thinking, no doubt, I was mad; or did she wish she were in my place?

She had come before to watch me practice against the arms-master. Saying nothing, sitting quietly on a bench with heavy skirts spilling over her legs.

Before, it had not touched me, because I can be deaf and blind when I choose, so focused on the weapons. But this time it did. It reached out and touched me, and held me, with a new intensity.

In the eyes I saw desperation.

It was enough to pierce my concentration. Enough to get me killed, had it been anything but practice. As it was, Griffon's blade tip slid easily by my guard and lodged itself, but gently, in the buckle of my belt.

"Dead," he said calmly. "On your feet, but dead. And all your royal blood spilling out of those proud Cheysuli veins."

Ordinarily I might have cursed him cheerfully, or retorted in kind, or made him try me again. But I did not, this time, because of the eyes that watched in such mute, distinct despair.

"Dead," I agreed, and left him to gape in surprise as I walked past him to the woman.

She watched me come in silence, saying nothing with her mouth but screaming with her eyes. Green Erinnish eyes, born of an island kingdom very far from my own. But born into similar circumstances; bound by similar rules.

Though foreigners, we were kin. She had married my brother. I would marry hers.

Aileen of Erinn, now Princess of Homana, looked up at me as I stopped. Standing, we are similar in height; Cheysuli are taller than other races, but she comes of the House of Eagles, where men are often giants. But she is red-haired to my tawny, green-eyed to my blue. Equally outspoken, but without knowing the frustration I so often faced, because we wanted different things.

But now, she did not stand. She sat solidly on the bench, as if weighted by stone, with both hands clasped over her belly. Looking at her, I knew.

"By all the gods," I said, "he has you breeding *again!*"

I had not meant it to come out so baldly, not to Aileen, whom I liked, and whom I preferred not to harm with hasty words. But I am not a person who thinks much before speaking, being ruled by temper and tongue; inwardly I cursed myself as I saw the flinch in her eyes.

And then her chin came up. I saw the line of her jaw harden, that strong Erinnish jaw, and knew for all she was wife to the Prince of Homana, he did not precisely rule her.

But then, being Brennan, I knew he would not try.

Aileen smiled a little, though one corner curved down crookedly. "In Erinn, bairns *often* follow the bedding. 'Tis the same in Homana, I think."

I glanced over my shoulder at Griffon, due more honor than I gave him, but I was thinking of Aileen, and of things better kept private. "You may go," I told him. "But come again tomorrow, at the same hour."

Briefly, so briefly, there was a glint of something

in brown eyes, but hidden instantly. I regretted my tone, but did not know what I might say to lessen the insult, since it was already given. He was far more than servant, being my father's personal arms-master, and therefore in service to a king. And he owed no service to me, since only men are trained in the arts of war. He had agreed to train the Mujhar's daughter only because he had lost a wager. In winning it, I had won him, and all that he could teach.

He cleaned his sword, sheathed it, bowed to Aileen and left. Giving her the courtesy he might have given me, had I been deserving of it. But for now, Aileen's welfare was more important than Griffon's feelings.

"He might have waited," I said curtly. "He has a son already, and you nearly dead of *that*." Grimly I caught up a soft cloth, cleaned the blade, drove it home into its sheath. "You have been wed but eighteen months, and a child of it already. Now there will be another?" I shook my head, speaking through my teeth. It was their business, not mine, but I could not help myself; Brennan and I are not, always, friends. "Aileen, he gives you no *time*—"

" 'Twas not entirely up to him," she told me sharply, giving me back my tone but in her Erinnish lilt. "D'ye think I had no say in the matter? D'ye think I'd let him take me against my will, or that he would try?" Aileen rose, absently shaking the rucked up folds out of her skirts. "Are ye forgetting, then, that women can want the bedding, too?"

It silenced me, as she meant it to. Aileen and I are close, nearly *kinspirits*, and she knows how strongly I feel about women being made to do certain things merely because they are women. She knows also I have little interest in bedding, being more concerned with freedom. In body as well as in mind.

"He might have waited," I said again. "And you might have let him."

She smiled. Aileen's smile lights up a hall; it lighted the chamber now. "He might have," she agreed, "and *I* might have, as well. But we were neither of us thinking of anything more than the moment's pleasure . . . 'twill come to you, one day, no matter what you think."

I turned away from her and strode across to a sword rack, put away the sheathed blade. I felt the rigidity in my back; tried to loosen it even as I tried to force my tone into neutrality. "When will it be born?"

"Six months' time," she said. "And 'it' will be a 'they.' "

I jerked around and stared at her. "Two?"

"Aye, so the physicians say." Aileen smiled again, speaking easily. "A family trait, I'm told. First Brennan and Hart, then you and Corin. And now—?" She shrugged. "We'll be seeing what we see."

She did it well, I thought. Only her eyes betrayed her. "Two," I repeated. "You nearly died of Aidan, and he was only one."

Aileen shrugged again. "I'm larger, now, from Aidan. It should be easier this time, and the physicians are telling me twins are always smaller."

I could barely stifle a shout. "By the gods, Aileen, you nearly bled to death! What do the physicians say to that?"

It wiped the forced gaiety from her face. "D'ye think I don't know?" she cried. "D'ye think I *rejoiced* when they told me?" Such white, white flesh set in the frame of brilliant red hair; such green, frightened eyes, now dilated black. " 'Twas all I could do not to vomit from the fear . . . not to disgrace myself before them, even as I saw the looks in their eyes. They are afraid, too . . . but heirs are worth the risk, and Aidan is oversmall and sickly. There's a need for other sons." Fingers clutched the folds of her skirts. "Gods, Keely, what am I to do?"

"Lose it," I said succinctly. Then, more clearly, "Lose *them*."

Aileen nearly gaped. Then closed her mouth and wet her lips with a tongue that shook a little. "Lose them," she echoed.

"There are herbs," I said impatiently. "Herbs to make you miscarry."

Aileen's voice sounded drugged. "You want me to kill my bairns?"

"Better them than you." Sweat was drying on my face, against my scalp, beneath the leathers I wore: leggings baggy at the knees; sleeveless Cheysuli jerkin, belted snug; quilted, longsleeved undertunic, cuffs knotted at my wrists. I needed a bath badly, but this was more important. "Brennan has an heir. He needs a queen as well."

"Oh, *Keely*." With effort, she shook her head. "Oh—Keely—no. *No*. Kill my bairns? How could I? How could you even suggest it?"

"Easily," I told her. "If it is a choice between losing you or keeping you, I would sooner lose the babies."

"If you were a mother—"

I turned my hands palm-up. "But I am not. And, given the choice, I never will be."

Aileen sat down again, hastily. "Why *not*?" she asked in shock. "How can ye not want bairns?"

I peeled sticky hair away from my face and smoothed it back, tucking it into my loosened braid. Not wanting to offend her with my odor—and unable to sit close while discussing something so personal —I eased myself down on the stone floor and leaned against the wall. The room was plain, unadorned, nothing more than what it was intended to be: a practice chamber for war.

"Babies *require* things," I said. "Things such as constant responsibility . . . they steal time and freedom, robbing you of choice. They are parasites of the soul."

"Keely!"

I sighed, knowing how callous it sounded; knowing also I meant it. "All my life I have fought for my freedom. I fight for it every day. And I will lose what I have won the moment I conceive."

" 'Tisn't true!" she cried. "Have I lost *my* freedom?"

"Have you?" I countered. "Before you left Erinn and came here to Homana—before you fell in love with Corin—before you married Brennan . . . what was your life like?"

Aileen said nothing at all, because to speak was to lose the battle.

"On the day you lay down with Brennan, Aidan was conceived," I said. "And from that day you became more than a woman, more than *you*: you became the vessel that housed Homana, because one day that child would be Mujhar. Your value was based solely on that, not on you, not on *Aileen* . . . but on that child—that bairn, as you would say— because babies born into royal houses are more than merely babies." I shrugged. "They are coin to barter with, just as you and I were before we were even born." I pulled my braid over one shoulder and played absently with the ends below the thong. It needed washing, like the rest of me. "I have no affection for babies; I would sooner do without."

"You'll not be saying that once you're wed to Sean."

She sounded so certain. *So* certain, in fact, it fanned unacknowledged resentment into too-hasty speech. "And how does it feel, Aileen, to lie in one man's bed—to bear that man his children—while loving yet another?"

Aileen jumped to her feet. "Ye *skilfin*!" she cried. "Will ye throw that in my face? Will ye speak to me of things ye cannot understand, being but half a woman—" And abruptly, on a strangled cry of shock, she clamped her hands over her mouth. "Oh, Keely . . . oh, Keely, I swear . . . I *swear*—"

"—you did not mean it?" Emptily, I shrugged. "I have heard it said before. To me and about me." I pressed myself up from the floor, brushing off the seat of my training leathers. "If I am considered half a woman simply because I prefer to be myself, not an appendage of a man—nor a mother to his children—then so be it. I am Keely . . . and that is all that counts."

Some of the color had died out of her face. She was pale again, too pale. "Will you be saying all this to Sean?"

"As I have said it to you, I will say it to your brother." I crossed the chamber to the door, which Griffon had pointedly closed. "I am not a liar, Aileen, nor one who admires deception. I was never asked if I wanted to marry, but was betrothed before my birth . . . I was never asked if, being a woman, I wanted to bear children. It was simply *assumed* . . . and that, my lady princess, is what I hate most of all." I paused, my hand on the latch, and turned to face her fully. "But you would know." I spoke more quietly now; it was not Aileen with whom I was angry. "You *should* know, being made to wed the oldest of Niall's sons when you would sooner have the youngest. You would know how it feels to have things arranged *for* you, simply because of your gender."

Straight red brows were lowered over an equally straight nose. She is not a beauty, Aileen, but anyone with half a mind sees past that to her fire. "I am not a slave," she said darkly, "and neither am I a fool. There are things in life we're made to do through no fault of our own, but because of necessity, regardless of gender . . . and that *you* should know, being a Cheysuli." She paused, assessing me; I wondered, as I so often did, if the brother was anything like the sister. "Or are you Homanan today? Ah, no—perhaps Atvian, instead." Aileen stood straight and tall before me, her pride a tangible thing. "It strikes me, my lady princess, that *you* are whatever you want to be whenever it takes your fancy. Whenever 'tis *convenient*."

She meant it, I think, to sting. Instead, it made me laugh. "Aye," I agreed, "whatever I want to be. Woman, warrior, *animal* . . . and I thank the gods for that magic."

"Magic," Aileen repeated. "Aye, I was forgetting that—but so, I'm thinking, are you. Because with the magic that makes you a shapechanger comes the price you'll be having to pay. And someday, you'll be paying it. Your *tahlmorra* will see to that."

I frowned. "What price?"

"Marriage," she said succinctly. "Marriage and motherhood; how else to forge the link the prophecy requires?"

I grinned at her. "Ah, but *you* have done that; you and my oldest *rujholli*. Aidan is the one. Aidan is the link. Aidan will be Mujhar."

Evenly, she said, "Aidan may die by nightfall."

It stopped me cold, as she meant it to. "Aileen—"

Her tone lacked expression. Like me, she masks herself rather than show her concern for things of great importance. "He is not well, Keely. Aidan has never been well, ever since the birth. He may die tonight. He may die next year." She clasped her hands over her belly, swelling gently beneath her skirts. "And so you see, it becomes imperative that I bear Brennan another son." She paused, holding me quite still with the power of her eyes and the knowledge of her duty, of her *value*, by which men too often judge women, especially those they marry. "Two would be even better, I'm thinking, in case they are sickly also."

I thought of Aileen in potentially deadly labor, bringing forth two babies at once, for the sake of her husband's throne. I recalled it from before, with

Aidan's birth; how she had bled and bled and nearly died, recovering so very slowly. And now she faced it again, but this time the threat was compounded.

Fear lurched out of my belly and found its way to my mouth. "Aileen, you could *die*."

Her fingers tightened rigidly, clasping the unborn souls. "Men go to war. Women bear the bairns."

I unlatched the door and shoved it open. But I did not leave at once. "Do you know," I told her, "if I could, I would trade."

"Would you?" Aileen asked. "*Could* you, do you think?"

I paused on the threshold, one shoulder against the wood. "If you are asking me if I could kill a man, then I say aye."

Her face spasmed briefly. "So glib," she said. "I'm thinking *too* glib; that you're not knowing what you can—or cannot—do, and it irritates you. It *frightens* you—"

I overrode her crisply. "I will do what I must do."

Slowly, Aileen smiled. And then she began to laugh as tears welled into her eyes. "So fierce," she said, "so *proud* . . . and so very, very helpless. No less so than I."

Denial, I thought, was futile; I closed the door on her noise.

Two

I itched. I wanted nothing more, at that moment, than to climb into a polished half-cask of steaming water, to soak away dried sweat, stretched muscles, irritation. But even as I gave the order for the bath and went into my chambers, untying the knots of my sweat-soiled undertunic, I was prevented. Because my father came in behind me, silently and without warning, and shut the heavy door.

"So," he said, "you have been learning the sword from Griffon."

For a moment, only a moment, I seriously considered stripping out of my boots and clothing anyway, just to see his reaction. I decided against it because, by the look in his eye, he would not be put off by anything, not even his daughter's nudity, until he had his say.

My hands went to my hips. "Aye," I agreed, saying nothing of Griffon's defection; he was, after all, my father's man, not mine. "I have made no secret of it."

"But neither did you *tell* me."

I thought it obvious, but said it anyway. "I knew you would tell me to stop."

"And so you should." He folded arms across his chest. "And so I do: *stop*."

I pressed fingers against my breastbone, tapping for emphasis. "I am not a fragile, useless female . . . I *know* how to fight. All my *rujholli* have taught me knife and bow . . . why should I not learn the sword?"

He leaned against the door, assuming an attitude

of relaxed, quiet authority; he could order me, I knew, and probably would, but if I could give him a logical argument beyond refute, I might yet win. Sometimes I could. Not often. Not nearly often enough.

I looked at my father's face, seeing what others saw: lines of care and concern bracketing eyes and mouth; the silvering of his hair, mingled still with tawny brown; the leather patch stretched over the emptiness that once had been his right eye.

But I saw more than that. I saw kindness and compassion. Strength of spirit and will. Loyalty and love, honesty and pride, and a tremendous dedication to his personal convictions.

Still, I could not give in so easily. He had taught me that.

He countered my question with one of his own. "Why do you *want* to learn the sword?"

I shrugged. "I do. I want to know them all, all the weapons men use in war . . . not because I desire to *go* to war, but because I have an interest in weapons." Balancing storklike on one leg, I twisted my knee up and tugged on the toe and heel of my left boot to work if off. "Why do you ask me such things, *jehan*? You never ask Deirdre why she weaves that tapestry of lions . . . nor Brennan why he enjoys training and racing his horses. You only ask me, because I care for things you and other men think unseemly to a woman." The boot came off; I dropped it and traded feet, feeling the chill of stone on my now-bare sole. "You are such a stalwart champion of fairness and justice, *jehan*—and yet you are blind to unfairness and injustice under your own roof."

"I hardly think it is unfair to ask my daughter to cease learning the *sword*," he said flatly. "By the gods, Keely, you have known more freedom than any woman born in the last fifty or sixty years . . . you have the gift of *lir*-shape, and you speak freely to all the *lir*. All that, and yet you also insist on tricking my arms-master into teaching you the sword."

I dropped the other boot to the floor, hearing the heel smack sharply against rose-red stone. "It was no trick," I retorted, stung. "Hart taught me how to wager . . . I won Griffon's service from him *fairly*."

He sighed and rubbed wearily at his brow, automatically resetting the leather strap that held the eyepatch in place. "Hart taught you how to wager, Corin how to rebel . . . it would be too much to assume Brennan taught you civility and respect—"

I cut him off even as I moved to stand on a rug. "Do you want to know what Brennan has taught me, *jehan*? He has taught me that a man has no regard for his *cheysula*, thinking only of himself . . . by the gods, *jehan*, Aidan's birth nearly killed Aileen! And now she must go through it again, with *two*?" I shook my head. "Teach Brennan restraint, *jehan*, and then perhaps I will allow him to teach me civility and respect."

Weary good humor dissolved. "That is between Brennan and Aileen, Keely. Your feelings are well known on the subject; I think we will get no objectivity from you."

I yanked the knotted thong out of my braid and began unthreading plaited hair violently. "Oh, and I suppose you think making me put down the sword will transform me into an obedient, compliant woman. One like your beloved Maeve, perhaps, giving in to Teirnan when she knows better . . . or perhaps even Deirdre, born to be a queen and yet forced to be. light woman to a king who will not set aside the *cheysula* who tried to abduct his children." In my anger I felt sweat-crisped hair tearing. "Do you know what they call her, *jehan*? Not light woman. Not even *meijha*, which holds more honor . . . no, *jehan*. They call her whore. Deirdre of Erinn, *whore*."

His face was very white. I had succeeded too well

in turning his mind from me to another matter. Part of me regretted it—I had not meant to go so far— but part of me was too angry to think clearly. Always, *always*, someone comes to tell me what I should and should not be . . . gods, but it makes me angry!

I faced him squarely, waiting. Knowing he was hurt and shocked and angry, at least as angry as I, if for different reasons. But he said nothing of that, having better control. Having learned to shut his mouth. It was something I had not, and probably never would. Though sometimes I wished I could.

Just now, I wished I had. I hated to see him hurt. Gisella was far beyond the ken or control of either of us; that some Homanans spoke of her as the Queen of Homana and claimed she should be by the Mujhar's side instead of banished to Atvia meant nothing to us other than ignorance. They did not understand. They *could* not. For even though she was labeled Mad Gisella, she was also the Mujhar's wife in Homanan law, *cheysula* in Cheysuli, and she had borne three sons for the succession, as well as the prophecy. One and the same, these days; to many, it was all that counted.

And so Deirdre, whom my father loved more than life itself, was made to suffer the insults better ladled onto my mother, who had tried to give her children into Strahan's perverted power.

Her *sons*, that is. Her daughter, a mere girl, had counted for next to nothing. It was boys the Ihlini wanted.

He drew in a very deep breath. And smiled, though there was nothing of humor in it. "Meanwhile, my daughter has learned the sword, when I would prefer her not to."

"Too late," I told him crisply. "Would you have me but half-taught? Dangerous, *jehan* . . . Griffon would do better, now, to finish what was begun."

"And if I order him otherwise?"

I met him, stare for stare. "Does it matter? You will do it anyway." I unhooked the belt snugged around my waist, complete with sheathed knife, and slung it to land on my bed. "And I will find someone else to teach me." I was moving away as I said the last, intending to go into the antechamber where my bath was waiting, but he reached out and caught my arm, with nothing of gentleness in his grasp, and snapped me back around.

I nearly gasped, so startled was I by his demeanor. He was coldly, deadly serious, no more the father half-amused, half-tired of his rebellious daughter's antics. He was now more than father entirely, being Mujhar as well.

Being also Cheysuli warrior, with *lir*-gold on his arms and glittering in his hair. Tawny-silver instead of black, blue-eyed in place of yellow, but still he was Cheysuli. Like others, I often forgot it; he seems more Homanan in habits, until he takes care to remind us that in his veins flows gods-blessed blood as hot as it flows in mine.

"Though it suits you to ignore it—" He spoke very quietly; too quietly, for my peace of mind, "—when I tell you a thing I generally have a good reason for it."

My wrist was still in his grasp. "*What* good—"

"Be silent," he said, "and listen . . . if that is possible for you."

I did not answer the rebuke, having decided finally it was better, for now, to do as he asked, if only to get the confrontation done with. My bath was growing cold, my temper hotter by the moment.

His voice was very quiet. "I will not argue for the Homanans, who expect little more of their women than the obedience and compliance you mentioned, but I *will* argue for the Cheysuli, who give women more honor and respect." His grasp tightened on my wrist. "Has it never crossed your mind that women do not learn the sword because they lack the strength to use it?"

I waited only a moment, to lull him, and then I snapped my wrist free of his big hand with ease. Standing tall, balanced, braced, I cocked both arms up before me for inspection. The untied cuffs fell back, baring sinewy forearms. I could not help it; my hands were fists. "Do I look weak to you?"

He knew better. I am tall, even for a Cheysuli woman, and have not spent my years in idle pursuits. Tough and hard and strong, like a warrior, though without a warrior's bulk. "Lean and lethal," Corin had often called me. He had not, lately, because now he lived in Atvia, hundreds of leagues away. Closer now to Erinn than to Homana; farther from Aileen, whom he loved, or had; I no longer knew how he felt. He said nothing of her in his letters. I said little in mine to him.

"Weak, no," he conceded, "but strong enough? Perhaps. Perhaps not; you have never been in battle." He reached out again, this time with both hands, and took my wrists in a much gentler grasp. "I know, Keely. I have seen men shorter and slighter than you in battle, and they do well enough . . . usually. But matched with a larger, stronger opponent, they die. And even you must admit that most women are considerably smaller and weaker than men, particularly hardened soldiers."

"If they were allowed to do things other than mend clothing, make soap, bear babies . . ." I let it trail off, shrugging. "Who could say, *jehan*? And our history tells us Cheysuli women once fought beside their warriors."

"Aye, in *lir*-shape," he agreed dryly. "There is some difference, I think, between that sort of battle and the ones the unblessed Homanans fight."

I sighed, drawing my arms free again. "I have no wish to go to war, *jehan*, that I promise you . . . but I do wish to learn how to use a sword. All my *rujholli* did. Should I be denied simply because of my sex?"

"Are you *so* unhappy being a woman?" He had never asked it before, though my brothers had. Even Maeve once, my very feminine older sister, who allows body to rule head. "Do you wish that much to be a man?"

I smiled with infinite patience. "No," I told him gently. "I want only to be *me*."

Clearly, he did not understand. No one had, yet, not even twin-born Corin, who knew me better than any.

He sighed. "I will strike a bargain with you, then. Meet Griffon as he should be met: as an opponent in battle, but with wrapped blades. And when you are done with the match, decide *then* if learning the sword is worth the trouble and pain."

He meant well. But all I could do was shake my head. "Anything worth doing is worth the trouble and pain. I am new to neither." I grinned at him lopsidedly. "And now, I think, it is time I took my bath. You have been too polite to mention it, but I am rank as a week-old carcass."

The Mujhar of Homana shut his eye. "I cannot begin to predict what Sean will say when he meets you."

I laughed. "If the gods are on my side, he will say he does not want me."

"And he would be a fool." He turned to open the door. "We have given you time, Keely, much time, and so has Sean . . . but it will come to an end. One day, perhaps tomorrow, the letter from Erinn will come asking the marriage be made."

Lightly, I answered, "Then let us pray for a storm at sea." And I went into the antechamber, calling for more hot water, as my father muttered something about gods and rebellious children.

*　　*　　*

I did not get my bath. Because even as servants came to pour in more hot water while I waited impatiently to strip, there came a commotion outside the door, in the corridor. My father had only just left; likely it was something that concerned the Mujhar.

And then I heard Deirdre's voice raised, and realized it concerned more than merely my father.

Still barefoot, I crossed to the antechamber door and pulled it open, letting the voices spill in more clearly. Aye, it was Deirdre, and speaking urgently. There was fear in her tone.

"—with her history, it may be serious," she was saying. "Bleeding she is, and in pain. The physicians are doing what they can, but it may not be enough. Can you and Ian link to heal her?"

Gods, it was Aileen. And *bleeding* . . . gods, she would lose the bairns she wanted, and probably her life as well.

They knew I was there, if barely, too caught up in their conversation to pay me mind. Deirdre looked badly distracted, as was to be expected. Aileen was kin, close kin, being daughter to Deirdre's brother.

My father shook his head but twice. "Not Ian; Tasha has the cubs. Until she is free of them, he is bound by human standards. No *lir*-shape, no healing . . . I will have to do it alone." He frowned. "Brennan should be told. He will want to know—to be with her—"

"Not here," I said succinctly. "He went to Clankeep early this morning, blowing out one of his colts."

Now I had their full attention. Deirdre's face went whiter yet. My father cursed, briefly and powerfully. "Too far for Serri to reach Sleeta through the *lir*-link, to pass the message to Brennan . . . it will have to be done without him."

"I will go." It seemed obvious to me, and not worth the conversation. I left the doorway, scooped up my boots and tugged them on again, also buckling on my belt, knife sheathed. It took but a moment longer to grab a leather hunting cap from a chest, and I was with them once again. "I will send him home at once. Tell Aileen he is on his way already; it may calm her." Briefly I shook my head, putting on my cap and stuffing loose, braid-rippled hair beneath the crimson-tasseled peak rising above the crown of my head. Then tugged pointed earflaps into place, joggling red tassels. "Although why it should calm her to know the man who caused such pain is on his way—"

"Just go." I have never seen my father's eye so fierce. "Just *go*, Keely, without another word. You waste time and try our patience, and Aileen is worth far better than your scorn."

Aye, so she was. But it was not Aileen for whom I had meant it. "Tell her," I said only, and started down the corridor at a run.

I did not stop running until I was outside, on the massive marble steps of Homana-Mujhar, and there I reached deep into the marrow of my bones, where the magic lies, and changed them. Trading human flesh for raptor's, woman's arms for falcon's wings.

I reached out, stretched, caught air—
—lifted—
Screeching aloud in exultation; in sheer, unbridled ecstasy, born of body and of brain.
—gods, oh gods, what glory—
—what glory it is to *fly*—

Three

He is nothing like our father, being black of hair, dark of skin, yellow of eyes. All Cheysuli, is Brennan, unable to hide behind the fair hair and skin of our Homanan ancestors. But he would never try; nor would any Cheysuli, for the gods have made us what we are, blessing us with the *lir* and all the magic that comes with the bond.

I myself do not share that bond precisely. I have no *lir*, but I do not require it. I am blessed instead with the Old Blood in abundance, the strain of the first clans who, settling in Homana from the Crystal Isle, did not mix with others, and so fixed the gifts. It was only after other clans outmarried that the blood weakened, making the true gifts random, that women lost the magic and only warriors bonded with *lir*. And yet now we are *told* to marry out of the clans, to merge our blood with others, so that the gifts may be regained. I have little understanding of such things, and little interest; I know only that all of this specified marriage, as required by the prophecy, is supposed to give birth to the Firstborn again, the race that sired the Cheysuli. And, some say, the Ihlini.

Brennan, I knew, had his doubts. Honor-bound and dutiful, as are most Cheysuli, he served the prophecy unselfishly and kept his thoughts to himself, unless he shared them with Hart in frequent letters to Solinde. But there were times, looking into his supremely Cheysuli face, I wondered if indeed there might be Ihlini in it as well. Or ever would be, in a different, but similar, face.

He sat inside his pavilion, awash in the meager sunlight I let in through the opened doorflap, and stared at me in shock as I told him of Aileen. Unsympathetic, I watched as the color drained out of his face. On a Homanan, it is bad; on a Cheysuli, worse.

His hands shook. I watched as they shook, holding the cup; watched as they spilled liquor over the rim to splash against his leggings. Brennan did not notice, being too engaged in staring at me. Beyond him lay Sleeta, his mountain cat *lir*, sleek black Sleeta, velvet in coat, sharp as glass in opinion. Though we could converse as easily as she and Brennan, we did not; this was between *rujholla* and *rujholli*.

And then Brennan was up, tossing aside the cup, brushing by me without a single word, nearly knocking me aside, ripping the flap from my hands and calling for his horse. Irritably, I followed him; Sleeta followed me.

It was only after the horse was brought that he turned to me, and I saw something other than shock in his eyes. I saw desperation. "Too far," he said. "I will kill him if I run him all the way to Homana-Mujhar, and reach Aileen too late."

It was a supremely ridiculous statement, in view of his heritage. Dryly, I asked, "Why ride at all?"

Fixedly, he looked at Sleeta, as if rediscovering his *lir* and what she represented. "Aye," he said in surprise, then nodded vaguely. "Oh, aye . . . of course . . ."

"Brennan." I frowned, reaching for the reins he held in slack fingers, before he dropped the leather and lost the horse entirely; he is a mettlesome colt. "The way you are behaving—the way you look . . . are you saying you did not know? Aileen had not told you?"

"Aileen is often—private."

It was, I thought, an interesting way of summing it up. Married eighteen months, yet only because it was required, not freely desired; an arranged marriage, just as mine was. Aileen loved my twin-born *rujholli*, Corin, not the man she had wed. And Brennan? He is proud, my eldest *rujholli*, and stringently honorable. Though Aileen's virtue had been intact, her heart was clearly not. And he had not presumed to mend it. He had merely wedded her, bedded her, got a son upon her; a child for the Lion, and also the prophecy.

And now two more who might not live to be born.

"So," I said, "she is private. Well-matched, I would say; you have offered her nothing since the day you married her. But *she* offers you her life." I jerked my head in the direction of Mujhara. "Go, *rujho*. See to your *cheysula*. I will bring your cherished colt."

There were things he wanted to say, but he said none of them. Another time, perhaps; Brennan and I do not often agree, and our discord is sometimes of the spectacular kind. For now, all he did was turn on his heel and walk purposefully away, ignoring me quite easily, with Sleeta at his side.

But I had seen his face. I had seen his eyes. And realized, in astonishment, my brother loved his wife.

I did not leave at once for Mujhara. Perhaps I should have, but Aileen's travail frightened me. If the gods wanted her, they would take her whether or not I was present; I did not think I could face watching her die, nor have the patience to wait quietly in another chamber for someone to come and tell me she was dead. I would go mad with the waiting, saying things I did not mean, hurting people, probably Brennan; having seen his face, I thought he was deserving, at this moment, of more compassion than I was prepared to give him.

So I did not go. Knowing no matter what happened, no matter what I did, I would hate myself.

And then Maeve gave me the opportunity to focus my mood on someone other than myself; to contradict, as always, a woman who considers her world empty if a man is not present in it.

We are sisters, *rujholla,* separated by three brothers —for Maeve was born first of us all—and equally by convictions. Also by blood; though Niall's daughter, there is nothing of the Old Blood in Maeve, nor even of the newer, thinner blood that limits warriors to a single *lir* and women to no *lir* at all, and nothing at all of the gifts. Deirdre's only child reflects mostly the Erinnish portion of her heritage, blanketing the Cheysuli under brass-blonde hair, green eyes, fair skin . . . and none of the Cheysuli woman's tendency toward independence.

Yet of late she *had* shown a tendency toward living in Clankeep, which baffled all of us. Maeve, much more than myself, fit well into palace life, complementing Deirdre's unofficial reign as chatelaine in Homana-Mujhar with ease. She was the Mujhar's dutiful eldest daughter and, of all his children—it was well-known—his favorite, yet of late she had forsaken his companionship for the company of the clans.

We sat outside a slate-blue pavilion on a thick black bear pelt and tossed the prophecy bones. Not to wager—Maeve is not much for it; it is Hart's vice—but to pass the time, and to ease ourselves into conversation, since ordinarily we have so little in common that there is as little to discuss.

Maeve sighed, scooped bones, let them dribble out of her hand after a half-hearted throw. "Perhaps I *should* go. Mother will be so distracted . . . I could lend her aid—"

"Doing what?" I asked bluntly. "Deirdre will indeed be distracted, with no time for you; you would do better to stay out of the way, as I am."

Her mouth tightened. "You are not staying out of the way, Keely—at least, not in order to help. You are staying here because you are afraid." She smacked her hand flat down on the bones as I moved to scoop them up. "No, listen to me—you *are* afraid, Keely . . . afraid to see what it is a woman goes through to bear a child, knowing you will have to do the same." Maeve laughed, a little, shaking her head. "You are so contradictory, Keely . . . on one hand you are willing to take on any man in a fight, with knife or bow or sword; on the other, you are deathly afraid to lie with a man . . . to give over yourself to the bedding, to the loss of self-control, to the chance to love someone other than yourself—"

I raised my voice over hers. "You know nothing about it, Maeve—all *you* know is that Teirnan had only to clap his hands and you spread your legs for him—"

Maeve's face was corpse-white. "Do you think I have not spent the last year of my life regretting the vow I made to be his *meijha*?" Tears sprang into her eyes; born half of anger, I thought, and half of humiliation. "Do you know what it is like to lie down alone each night knowing the man I love is a traitor to his race? A threat to the Lion itself?"

Guilt cut me deeply; gods, why do we always argue? Why does she force me to walk the edge of the blade and then push me off with such talk? "Maeve—"

She scooped up the translucent, rune-scribed bones and hurled them violently away from us both. "Do you have any idea what it is like knowing you have been *used*, without regard for your own needs and desires, or your loyalties?" She stared at me angrily, tears spilling over. "No. Not you. Never. Never *Keely*. Well, I *do* know what it is like . . . and I have to live

with it. Each day, each night . . . and for the rest of
my life."

I was humbled into silence by her passion, by her
humiliation, which she did not trouble to hide, being
as proud as any of us. It is easy for me to dismiss
Maeve because we are so at odds with loyalties and
convictions, so mutually certain of ourselves. But for
all there is little to bind us, what does exist takes
precedence over threats from outside.

"It will pass," I told her finally. "One day you will
look at yourself and realize that Teir won nothing at
all. He lost, Maeve. He lost you, the clans, the afterworld. *Kin-wrecked*, he has nothing, save his *lir* and
the knowledge that he is a traitor to his heritage."

"What of his child?" she asked bitterly. "What of
the halfling got on the Mujhar's daughter?"

"But there *is* no—" I stopped. "Oh, Maeve—*no*—"

"Aye," she answered curtly. "Why do you think I am
here instead of Homana-Mujhar?" Maeve shredded
bear pelt. Her head was bowed; loose blonde hair
hid most of her face. "Why do you think I cannot
bear to see my father—" And abruptly she pressed
both hands against her face, shutting it away from
me as she fought to hold back the tears. "Oh, gods,
Keely . . . what will he say? What will he say?" Her
words were muffled by her hands. "I broke the vow,
I *did*—and yet Teirnan came later, after he had
freely renounced kin, clan, prophecy . . . he came,
and I went with him . . . I lay down with him again,
and now there will be a child!"

In the silence after her outburst, I heard the echo
of Aileen's words: *"In Erinn, bairns often follow the
bedding. 'Tis the same in Homana, I think."*

I wanted to be patient. I wanted to be compassionate. But other emotions took precedence: frustration, disbelief; an odd, abrupt hostility, that she could
be *so* malleable as to give herself to Teirnan after
renouncing him before Clan Council; that she could

so readily dishonor our customs. "You *knew* what he was—*a'saii*, proscribed by the clan, *kin-wrecked*—and yet you went with him? Bedded with him? *Knowing*—"

"—that I loved him." Her tone was dead. She had taken her hands from her face. "Call me whore, if you like—others will, I am certain—but I was not lying with him for coin. It was for love, for pleasure . . . and for the pain, knowing it would be the last time for us ever; knowing also that the risk was worth it, if only for the moment, for the *doing* . . ." She shook her head. "Maybe I am not so different from Hart after all, chancing risk for the lure of the risk itself . . . all I know is that nothing is left of what we had, nothing at all, now—he said so himself, and *laughed*—except the seed he planted."

I bit my lip on recriminations, finally gaining control. Instead, implying nothing, I asked if Teirnan knew.

Maeve shook her head. "That much, at least, is mine. He does not know, and *will* not. It was to humble me, I think; to prove he could put a leading rein on the Mujhar's daughter and make her do his bidding." Self-loathing pinched her tone. "There was no love in it for him—he is too Cheysuli for it, too much *a'saii*—only power. Only acknowledgment of my weakness, proof that the House of Homana is not immune to manipulation." Bitterness shaped her expression. "And so there will be a child."

I kept my voice neutral. "So there will," I agreed, "unless you take measures to rid yourself of it."

Maeve stared at me, much as Aileen had. "Rid myself—?"

Carefully, I said, "Surely you know the means."

It was a new thought to her. "I have told no one," she said blankly. "No one at all, save you . . . the *last* one I would tell, since you have no compassion, no empathy for anyone save Corin . . ." Maeve shook her head. "But now I *have* told you, and your answer is to say I should rid myself of the child."

Scowling, I got up and went a few paces away, retrieving, one by one, the scattered prophecy bones. "It is *one* solution," I told her. "Did I say you had to do it?"

"A child is a child," she said. "The seed is planted, but the harvest not yet begun . . . who can say what manner of son or daughter it will be?" Maeve's tone, now, was steady. Plainly, I had shocked her, as much as I had Aileen. "Should I measure it by the father? Should I make it proxy for Teirnan's sins, accepting his punishment?"

I wanted to throw the bones back at her. "Putting words in my mouth, Maeve? Trying to make me feel guilty? Well, you will not . . . I am not foolish enough to say it is the only answer, nor even the best. I know our history well, Maeve . . . it was not *that* many years ago that Cheysuli warriors stole Homanan women in order to get children on them, because the clans were being destroyed by Shaine's *qu'mahlin*." I sighed, finished picking up the bones, spoke quietly; fool or not, she was my sister, and under the circumstances deserving of more than my derision. "Children are valued within the clans, *rujholla* . . . no matter who the *jehan*, your baby will be welcomed."

"He will hate me," she said hollowly.

"Teir?" I stared. "Do you really care—?" But I broke it off, realizing she did not refer to our cousin. "Oh, Maeve—no, no . . . of course he will not hate you. How could he? You are his favorite. You are Deirdre's daughter."

"The bastard gotten on his whore," she said tonelessly. "Who will herself now bear a bastard, begotten by a Cheysuli who has renounced everything of his race but the magic in his veins."

"Oh, no," I said dryly, "not everything. It is *for* his race he does it, Maeve. That is what they all say, the *a'saii*, as they renounce kin and clan and king." I sighed, kneeling again on the pelt, pouring rattling bones from one hand to the other. "Teir has been jealous of us all since birth, because of his *jehan*, who raised him on bitterness and greed, and lust . . . lust for power, lust for domination; even, I think, for the Lion. In the name of the Cheysuli, Teir and the *a'saii* fight to turn back the decades, the centuries, to the time Cheysuli held dominance, without outside interference."

Maeve's eyes were anxious. "Do you think it is true, Keely? He says fulfillment of the prophecy will give Homana to the Ihlini, destroying everything the Cheysuli have lived for since the gods put them here. He says the only way the Cheysuli can survive is to destroy the prophecy, and then turn to destroying the Ihlini."

"They" and "them." Only rarely does Maeve refer to Cheysuli as we or us. I wondered if she felt *so* apart from the rest of Niall's children that she perceived herself entirely Erinnish and Homanan, not Cheysuli at all, regardless of paternity. If so, it was no surprise Teirnan had held such a powerful sway over her.

"The only way we can survive," I said clearly, "is to make certain the prophecy survives, and to serve it. It is what the gods intended when they made it."

"Ah," Maeve said sweetly, "then we can expect an announcement of your marriage to Sean of Erinn any day."

The thrust went home cleanly, as she intended it to. In answer I dumped the bones into her skirt-swathed lap—Maeve would never wear *leggings!*—and stood. "As to that, it remains my decision, my say-so. Nothing so trivial resides in the prophecy of the Firstborn; I will do as I please in the matter of my marriage."

Maeve's brows arched up. "Nothing so trivial? An

odd thing to say . . . 'tis common knowledge the best way of merging bloodlines is through children, and the prophecy is quite specific about merging those bloodlines. All that's left now is Erinn, Keely . . . and the only way Homana will get Erinn is through marriage—yours to Sean. I hardly think Liam or Sean would *give* Erinn to Homana merely to serve a Cheysuli prophecy; that will be for your son to do, when he is born." She paused. "The son who bears every necessary bloodline save that of the Ihlini."

From my belt I took my hunter's cap and tugged it on, stuffing hair into it. "If I bear that son—*if* I bear that son, ever—it will be of my own choice, not a directive from the prophecy."

Maeve shook her head. "You can't be having it two ways, Keely . . . either you serve the prophecy, or you don't. Either you are of the faithful, as is our father, our uncle, and our brothers, or you are of the *a'saii*." She did not so much as blink. "Just like Teirnan."

I glanced at Brennan's restless colt, tied to a nearby tree. I wanted to fly, not ride, but I had promised to return the horse to Homana-Mujhar. "So," I said finally, "am I to believe it was the prophecy that led you on a leading rein into Teirnan's bed? Into the arms of an *a'saii*?" I shook my head before she could answer, tugging my cap on more securely. "No, *rujholla*, of course not. It was your decision, your *desire* . . . and so now the decision falls to me, as does my desire to be free to make my own choices."

Maeve's expression was bleak. "We are none of us free," she told me. "No matter who we are."

"But I am *Keely*," I said lightly. "A free Cheysuli woman, with magic in her bones."

Maeve sighed and shook her head. "You are as bad as Teir."

"Well, we *are* cousins." I untied Brennan's colt, briefly judged his temper, mounted carefully. "Maeve, if you want to come home, come home." The horse danced a little, ducking head and swishing tail; I cursed him beneath my breath, tightened reins, twisted my head to look back at Maeve. She stared after me blindly, tears swimming in her eyes. "Come home," I told her gently. "*Jehan* could never hate you. That I promise you."

Slowly, my sister nodded. "Tomorrow," she said. "Tomorrow."

Four

Brennan's colt was a fine animal indeed, a leggy chestnut with deep chest, long shoulders, powerful hindquarters. I could feel the speed living in him, and a bright, burning spirit, but it was raw, so raw, as yet uncut and unpolished. He was young, just shy of three—Brennan refused to race at two, saying it broke down leg bones not fully formed—and very green, wary of my touch. He did not know me at all, which left him confused and also clumsy, watching too much of me on his back and not enough of the track that stretched westward in front of his nose.

My task was to get him back to Homana-Mujhar without blemish, but he was making it difficult. He wanted to lunge, he wanted to spin, he wanted to bolt and run: all and yet none of those things. He was too distracted for any, merely teasing me with his nerves. It made my own stretch thin, along with my meager patience.

"Gods," I muttered aloud. "It will be *nightfall* before we are back."

It was, at best, late afternoon, judging by the low-hanging sun. If I let him run we would undoubtedly be home before it set, but I dared not let him go, even though he was begging to be set loose. I knew better. I also knew what Brennan would say—and precisely how he would say it—if I ruined his colt's conditioning.

I considered briefly turning back to Clankeep, to stay the night and go home in the morning, but I

was nearly halfway to Mujhara already. All it wanted
was a little time, a greater store of patience—

"*Hold,*" someone said.

Startled, the colt shied violently sideways, then attempted to run away. He did not, but only because I
jerked his head around to the left, dragging nose
up to my knee. Twisted so, he could not free his
head to bolt; it gave me time to regain control.

I said all manner of soothing, silly things to the
frightened colt, most of them nonsense but effective
because of my tone. When at last his trembling stilled
I loosed his head again, but carefully, slowly, letting
him know I was alert to any tricks.

I glanced at either side of the track, hugged by a
tunnel of trees and close-grown foliage, but saw no
one, only shadows. Still, it did not prevent me from
speaking. With forced lightness—keeping in mind
the colt's touchy temper—I spoke to no one in particular, knowing he would, nevertheless, hear. "Who-
ever you are, you *ku'reshtin,* have a care for my
horse . . . *if* you have a care for your life."

I heard soft laughter, the hiss and rustle of leaves,
the subtle sibilance of boot against deadfall. A man
stepped out of the trees, out of the shadows, into
waning sunlight gilding birch and beech and elm.

The colt saw him, snorted noisily, pinned ears and
rolled eyes. I soothed him with soft words and gentle
hands, thinking it odd contrast to the quickening of
hostility in my heart. For the stranger was more than
merely a man, he also was Cheysuli. More, even,
than that: my *kin-wrecked* cousin, Teirnan.

I looked at his face but saw Maeve's instead, twisted
by anguish and self-derision, washed by tears of
humiliation.

I looked at his face and saw a consummate Cheysuli:
proud, unyielding, determined; as fierce in defense
of loyalties asked, given and secured as any king
could require, for he was bound by sacred oaths. So

like all of us, my cousin, and yet like so very few. His oaths were to himself and to the *a'saii*, demanding a service in direct opposition to the sort freely offered, as Maeve had said, by my father, uncle, brothers.

And, as for my own?

I stared down at Teir from atop Brennan's mettle-some colt, thinking of my sister and the child yet unborn. Then leaned pointedly to one side and spat onto the ground.

"So tactful, as always . . ." He grinned mockingly, twisting his mobile mouth. "Niall should make you an envoy."

"*Ku'reshtin*," I said again. "What are you doing here? What do you want with me?" I looked past him for other warriors. "Where are the rest of your malcontents, Teir?—or have they grown weary of your preaching and pettiness and gone home at last to their clans?"

My cousin shrugged. "*This* is home," he said, "every inch of Homana—every pebble, leaf, raindrop—as was always intended. We have made a new clan out of the old, with warriors and women more cognizant of how things were, how they should be, how they will be again." He lifted one shoulder, dropped it; eloquent negligence. "A clan lacking in prophecy, perhaps, but with an abundance of free will."

"What do you want?" I asked again, more curtly than before. "Have you come to trouble Maeve?"

Teirnan shook his head, folding bare bronzed arms across his chest. *Lir*-gold gleamed; the repeated pattern encircling heavy bands was the profile of a boar, with curving tusks, interlocked within the symmetry. All Cheysuli, Teir, though his *jehana* had been part Homanan, and sister to the Mujhar. "If I wanted to trouble Maeve, I would at least know where to find her." Now he did not smile. "No. I wanted you."

"I have nothing to say to you."

"Nor do I care," he answered equably. "I came to

talk, not listen . . . and you have never been known for a sweet tongue, Keely. A man could spend his time on better things than listening to you."

I shut my teeth on the answer I longed to give, *and* its emphasis. The colt was too nervous already, shouting would send him flying. Quietly, I suggested, "I could say the same of you."

"And will, given the chance." Teir's face, similar to Brennan's, was formed of sharper bones lying but shallowly beneath characteristically dark flesh. It lent him the look of a predator more so than anyone else of our House; I found it ironically appropriate. "Come down from that horse and hear what we have to say."

"We?" I glanced around pointedly. "I see only you, Teir—and no, I am not blind to other warriors, I am Cheysuli myself." A quick link-search gave me the means to smile in scorn. "Nor are there any *lir* nearby save your own, hiding in the shadows; say '*we*' again, Teir, and see if I am foolish enough to bite."

It wiped the amusement from his face and the irony from his tone. We have never been close, Teir and I, and undoubtedly he had forgotten I could converse with his *lir* and that of any other warrior. It made a difference; I could see it plainly. He was reassessing me.

The mask was stripped away and cast aside. Teirnan showed me the face beneath it, naked and feral, with the conviction of a zealot. He was *a'saii*, deserving of nothing from me but renunciation. And, perhaps, my pity; he had cut himself off from his race.

But from none of his heritage. For now he was little more than a troublesome gnat nipping at the Lion, but I sensed he could in time make a danger-ous enemy.

"Keely." His tone was flat, uninflected, yet compel-ling in its own way, underscoring his change in mood. "I came alone because I thought you might prefer it,

being honorable in your own way—*and* me in mine."
He did not so much as blink, speaking so easily
about banished honor. "What I have to say could
affect your own *tahlmorra*, and that is a thing best left
between bloodkin, even among the clans."

I laughed at him outright. "You, Teir, speaking of
my *tahlmorra*? I thought you renounced such things
last year."

He took a single step forward, halted as he saw it
made the colt sidle and snort. He was angry, *angry*,
though he kept it carefully in check, which made it
all the more evident.

"You," he said coldly, "know nothing of what made
me do what I did, *nothing at all*—" Teir stopped
short, clenched his teeth briefly, fought some inner
battle. It only took a moment; he was not the sort of
zealot controlled by ignorant passions, but by cold
efficiency, a personal conviction. "And until you
understand—until I have taken the time to explain it
clearly to you—I suggest you do me the courtesy of
holding your tongue." He paused, then smiled coolly,
under perfect control again. Showing nothing of the
anger that had flared so very brightly, if so very
briefly. "And do yourself the service of not betraying
your ignorance with such naive forcefulness."

"Ignorant, am I?" I flung back. "Naive?" I shook
my head. "I think not, Teir . . . I know very well
what you did, and why. You are a small, petty man,
fed on the bitterness of your *jehan*—" The colt sidled
again, restively slashing his tail as he responded to
my tone. "Because of Ceinn's jealousy and your selfish ambition, you turn your back on our honor and
try to create your own." I shook my head. "You are
no different from Strahan, serving his noxious
Seker—*he* wants power . . . *he* wants control . . . *he*
wants the Lion Throne—" I fought the colt automatically, twisting my head this way and that as I tried to
stare down my cousin. "Renounce everything you

like, Teir, but know it will buy you nothing of what you desire, nothing of what you expect—" I leaned forward in the saddle, holding the colt with reins; holding Teir with will. "If you truly want to destroy the prophecy, why not go to the Ihlini? Go to the Gate of Asar-Suti and trade your manhood for Strahan's pleasure!"

He called me a foul name in explicit and eloquent Old Tongue. In response, I laughed. But then he jumped to catch the colt's bridle, my arm; to pull me down from the saddle. It was no more a laughing matter.

"*Teir—*"

But the colt had had enough. He tore himself free and ran.

How he could run, Brennan's colt . . . how he could bunch and stretch and *fly* in the fluent, fluid language of a horse bred only to race. I knew better than to attempt to curb his flight so soon. The track was clear, level, firm, though layered by crushed leaves. It was best simply to let him run a bit, wearing down the fear. He was doing what he was born for, though transcending human desires. Even Cheysuli ones.

I hunched in the saddle, leaning forward, and began to gather the reins. And then felt my cap loosen, threatening to fly off. One-handed, I caught it, crushed it against my head, one by one tugged the tasseled earflaps to snug it down again.

Too late I saw the rope stretched across the track. Black and taut, dividing the sunset, each end tied to trees; an invisible, treacherous trap. And I fell into it.

On a man, it would hit shoulders, scraping him out of the saddle. On me it hit my neck.

I landed hard on head and shoulders, bent in half like a toymaker's puppet, then completed the somersault and sprawled belly-down on the track.

At first I could not breathe. When I could, whooping

and gulping spasmodically, I inhaled dirt, leaves,
blood.

   Oh, gods. Brennan's colt.

   Oh, *gods,* my head.

   —agh, gods—my *throat*—

Five

Hands tore me from the ground. I was stood on my feet, held firmly on either side—and gaped at. Like a motley-fool at a Summerfair.

Three men, dirty of teeth, hair, habits. And patently astonished by what their trap had caught. But not so surprised as to loosen their grasp of my arms.

Inwardly, I swore; outwardly, I coughed. Gods, but my throat hurt!

The men were thieves, plainly, and plainly intending to ply their trade by cutting my coin-pouch free of my belt. Except there was none. I had left it in my chambers prior to weapons practice, and had exited Homana-Mujhar too quickly to retrieve it.

Two of them held me easily, one on either side. The third faced me squarely, scowling horrifically and chewing the inside of one cheek. He was my height, pock-marked, gray of hair and eyes.

"A *woman*," said the man at my right: young, younger than I, smelling of too many days and nights spent drinking and whoring without bath or change of clothing.

The one on my left shook his head. He smelled little better. "We've no call to rob a *woman*."

Promising, I thought, until the third one spoke. "Woman or not, she's worth coin." He paused. "*Or* better yet."

*Un*promising; he was unlikely to drop his guard simply because of my gender.

Instead, he would drop his trews.

Still, the two who held me were clearly uncertain of their behavior, and it might just be enough.

I was half blinded by pain, in head and neck and throat. But I have never been one to let physical, discomfort have its way until there is time for it; at the moment there was not. And so I swayed against the two men who held me, feigning weakness, and felt their instinctive attempt to right me. Smoothly I altered stance and balance—rolling hips, bunching thigh and buttock muscle—and cow-kicked out with my right foot toward the man who stood so invitingly flat-footed before me.

Full extension—I caught him square on the right knee and snapped it backward. He screamed and went down even as I wrenched free of his companions.

Like me, they had knives. But no swords, thank the gods; it gave me a decent chance. Perhaps better, if they were only indifferent with their weapons. But I thought not. Thieves are rarely unversed in fighting and weaponry.

I ran. Off the track and into the trees, into the twilight of early sundown, where the shadows lay thick and deep with nothing of light about them. *Lir*-shape, I knew, would provide a swifter escape, but I hurt so badly from my fall that the shapechange would require more concentration than usual, consequently more time. I knew better than to hope for the latter, and probably could not manage the former. I had caught them off-guard and put one of them down, but my store of tricks was gone. If they ran me to ground, I would have to fight them.

Behind me, I heard shouting interlaced with shrieks of pain. Also the telltale crashing of bodies through the brush. The quarry had been flushed, now pursuit was begun.

I swore aloud breathlessly, then wished I had not. My throat was afire with pain, inside as well as with-

out. The rough rope had scraped me raw, shredding
the flesh of my neck while also half-throttling me. I
was lucky to breathe at all; it might have broken my
neck.

My hunter's cap caught, came off, was left; I dared
not stop for it. Now hair came tumbling down, snag-
ging boughs and brambles, cluttering itself with leaves
and twigs, growing sticky with juices and sap. Fear-
sweat stung my armpits; breasts ached from nerves.

The shadows grew deeper as day shapechanged
into evening. I fell, rose, staggered, tore vine-ropes
out of my way. Wished myself, vainly, elsewhere, or
at least a sword in my hand.

But mostly I wished for *lir*-shape; for wings in
place of arms.

If I stopped running, perhaps I could summon the
magic. But *if* I stopped running to try it, I chanced
losing the lead I had. And all of my kin had taught
me to treasure advantages, no matter how large or
small; never to spend them foolishly, nor ever surrender them.

I crashed through brush into clearing, staggered
to a halt. Facing me were men. Kneeling, squatting,
hunching, all gathered around a new fire. All listening to another who held a sword in his hands.

The firelight blurred before me, glinting off knives
and in eyes; from the accoutrements of rank. I
blinked, fighting off weakness, clung to the nearest
tree. They were, I thought, king's men; they had
that look about them.

"*Leijhana tu'sai!*" I gasped. "Let me have that sword!"

As one they turned and stared, showing knives,
swords and startled eyes, and hard, strange faces.
Some were bearded, some were not; all wore foreign
clothes.

I put out my hand. "The sword." But it was more
a question than command.

The man with the weapon smiled. There was little

of it I could see in the rich red bush of his beard, so at odds with the blond of his hair. "Sword, is it?" he asked. "And you but a bit of a lass!"

Erinnish, I knew instantly, by the lilt of Aileen and Deirdre.

Cursing was loud behind me, accompanied by crashing. I spun, dragged free my knife, braced to meet the thieves. They broke free into the clearing, saw me, saw *them*, stopped short. And uneasily counted the numbers of the men who stood at my back. Even *Hart* would lay no wager; I unlocked my jaw from itself.

The red-bearded man strode forward, nearly knocking me aside as he brushed a shoulder purposely. "Have ye business?" he asked of the thieves. "Or have ye come for the fun?" He made a sweeping gesture of his left arm as if to invite them in. At the end of it his hand touched me on the chest and pushed me back a step. "A bonny lass, aye, but she'll be serving us first. You'll have to wait your turn." He eyed them assessively. "Unless, of course, you'd sooner play the part of the maid yourself . . . we've just arrived from Erinn and we're not particular whom we rape. 'Tis been a long journey."

As he intended them to, the thieves backed away and ran. Now it was my turn to flee, though I chose another direction.

Two steps only; he caught me by the hair. "Lass, lass, don't go . . . don't you know the sound of a lie?"

I sliced his wrist with my knife. "I know the sound of a threat—let me go, *ku'reshtin!*"

He did so, with alacrity. I saw shock in long-lashed eyes. "*Lass—*"

In clipped, fluent Erinnish, I told him to shut his mouth.

He stared, but he did. And then brought up the sword and knocked the knife from my hand. "*Now*, lass," he said, "d'ye think ye might listen to us?"

"No," I answered promptly, and summoned the magic to me.

Tried to summon the magic . . . the Erinnishman clamped a hand on my right arm and the pain of it nearly sent me out of my senses. I bit into my lip to beat off the swoon and inwardly cursed my weakness.

"Lass," he said, "you're hurt. There's blood all over your neck—" Abruptly, he took his hand from me, "—as well as on your arm. Lass—"

Gods, but I *hurt*. "Let me go," I rasped.

He put up his swordless hand in surrender and took a backward step. "Then go," he said clearly, "though you'll get no farther than a step or two, I'm thinking."

My laugh was mostly a croak. "Who says I will *walk*?"

But the magic would not come. In dismay, I stared at him, then looked down at my arm. From shoulder to elbow the quilted undertunic was shredded, showing rope-burned flesh beneath. Watery blood spread across the fabric. The pain was increasing, not fading; no matter how hard I tried, I could not distance myself from it.

What kind of Cheysuli are you, to let pain take precedence over magic? Old Blood, have you? More like ancient blood, and therefore all used up—

Dizzily, I looked up at him. He was a huge man, larger even than my father. Blond of hair, red of beard, warmly brown of eyes. He put out a hand and touched me, clasping my left shoulder, and turned me toward the fire. "Lass," he said gently, "you're safe with us, I promise. Any woman who speaks gutter Erinnish as fluently as you deserves nothing but our respect; that, and our liquor. Will ye share a cup with us?"

He said nothing else of neck or arm or blood, merely guiding me toward the fire. I thought of protesting—he could very well be lying, no matter what he claimed—but I hurt too much to speak. Reaction was sweeping in; it was all I could do to stand.

He sat me down on a stump of wood, said something briefly to four of his men about warding the wood against thieves, then motioned to a fifth. A full cup was put into my hands. The smell was powerfully pungent.

He gestured again. Quickly cups were brought out from under leather doublets or untied from belts. I heard the gurgle of liquor poured, saw the cups passed around. Tried again to protest, found all I could do was shake.

"To the *cileann*," he said, "and to our bonny lass, though she be foul of tongue and appearance.

"You *ku'reshtin*—" I was up, slopping liquor, then firmly pressed down again.

"Drink," he advised. " 'Tis a compliment, my lass. Are we so very much better?"

No, they were not. Not so filthy as I, perhaps, but not so very much better. Hard-faced, hard-eyed men, watching me intently, with pewter in their hands and steel at their belts.

"Who are you?" I asked.

He lifted one shoulder in a shrug. "What I told the others."

Still I did not drink, though the cup was at my mouth. "Erinnishmen," I muttered.

Blond brows rose. "You're knowing that already."

Suspicion briefly smothered pain. "Who *are* you?" I repeated. "Why have you come to Homana? What are you doing *here*?"

I saw glances exchanged, the masking of faces, the tautening of lips.

"King's men," I said flatly. "Or are you sent from Sean?"

It shocked them, each and every one, even the red-bearded man, who stared hard at me with a burning in his eyes, a fierce bright light that competed with the fire, with the glint of the sword in his hands. He did not hold a cup. He did not drink to me.

"From Sean," he echoed.

With meticulous effort, I rose. This time I remained standing. "Aye," I said clearly. "From Sean, Prince of Erinn. Liam's only son. Aileen's only brother. Do you know the man I mean?"

Plainly my irony stung him. But he said nothing in response, merely sheathed the sword at last. Slid it home with a hiss and click as he rose to face me standing.

I opened my mouth to speak again, but he forestalled me with a curtly silencing hand. "Do I know the man you mean? Aye, lass, I do—is there an Erinnishman who doesn't?"

"Well, then—" I began.

"*Well*, then," he echoed.

"Answer me," I said. "Have you come from Sean? I have a reason to ask."

"Reason," he muttered, "*reason!* So grand as ours, I wonder? So demanding a thing as our own?" He stared down his bold nose at me, arrogant as my brothers. Proud as a Cheysuli, and with at least a little of our honor. "And who are *you* to ask?"

Fair question, I thought. But I dared not give him the truth. "My father is Griffon, arms-master to the Mujhar."

"I didn't ask *his* name, lass."

Carefully, I swallowed. "Keely," I said blandly. "I was named for the Mujhar's daughter."

There was a stirring among the men. No one said a word, but I saw them speak nonetheless.

"Drink," I was told. And then, as I did not, he reached out and took the cup from me, drank half the contents down, gave it back into my hands. "There, lass . . . 'tis not drugged, I promise. But your color is going quickly, and I think 'twill help a bit."

I shivered. Blinked. Drank. It put tears into my eyes and set a fire in my belly. With a second generous swallow, followed by a third, some of the pain diminished.

"Better," he said softly.

Over the cup, I looked up at him. "Your answer," I croaked. "*Are* you sent from Sean?"

He looked at the others. Then down at me once more. "Aye," he said at last. "but not in the way you're thinking."

"No? How do you know what I think?"

"I can see it in your eyes, lass . . . and if you're of the castle, you'd know the girl you're named for. Likely you'd know how she'd feel."

It took me a moment to untangle his references. "If you mean the princess royal, aye—we have met. But as to how she would feel—?"

"If she knew why we were here."

I shrugged a single shoulder; the other was too painful. "She would think you sent from Sean to fetch her to her wedding."

"And would it be pleasing to her?"

I nearly laughed. "Probably not." Then modulated my tone. "She is a stubborn girl, the lady . . . she wants no part of Sean."

He nodded. "I have heard the same."

"*You* have heard—" I stopped. "He *did* send you, then!"

"Not in the way you're thinking." His voice was very steady. "I am not here as the prince's proxy . . . I am here as his murderer."

Six

I dropped my cup. "Sean is *dead?*"

Masked again and mute, he stared at me with eyes throwing back the firelight. I saw shame, guilt and an odd vulnerability, as if he wished he could have said otherwise; especially to me.

All I could do was stare, was *gape*, like that motley-fool at the Summerfair, faced with an unknown thing. I heard again the words he had said, naming himself murderer, and wondered at my emptiness; at the lack of grief or distress. Shock aplenty, aye, but little more than that.

He watched me closely, assessively, waiting for my response. Undoubtedly expecting censure, or some other form of hostility, something to mark what I thought.

What I thought was unfair: *If Sean is dead, I am free.*

Shame flooded me with heat and set my nerves atingle, dancing inside my flesh. I turned unsteadily and walked away from the fire, from the men, unable to show them what I felt, to the edges of the clearing where the wood encroached again.

Thinking yet again: *If Sean is dead, I am free.*

And then I thought of Aileen, his sister; of Liam, his father, and of the others who loved him more than I was able, knowing nothing at all of the man.

I shut off my thoughts and swung back to face the fire. Saw the murderer and his men exchanging glances, telling secrets in silence, and it occurred to me to wonder if they knew precisely who I was, regardless of what I claimed.

Sean is dead, he says. He has killed the Prince of Erinn, and likely himself as well.

"How?" I asked curtly. "And why are you still alive?"

He sighed, stripping thick, unruly hair back from his bearded face. " 'Tis a long story, lass . . . have you the wits to listen?" Unspoken was the question: *"And do you really care?"*

Oh, aye, I cared. And indeed, my wits were failing. But I recaptured them with effort, fixed blurring eyes on the man. "You are, you have said, a murderer—"

"We're not knowing for *sure*."

I blinked. "But—you just said—"

" 'Tis *possible*," he said flatly. "He was sore hurt, aye, with a broken head, and bleeding . . . but I left before the truth was known."

In other words, he fled. My face showed what I thought.

He did not look pleased by his admission. A brief sideways glance at the others showed him men clutching pewter cups but not so much as sipping, none of them, as if too ashamed of their part in this tale. Color stood high in his face, in what I could see of his cheeks between eyes and the edge of his beard.

There was a look, a *presence* to him—"King's men," I said plainly. "And you, I think, their captain."

The flesh by his eyes twitched. "Aye," he said, "we *were*."

I looked again at his men. I have seen their like in Homana-Mujhar, gathered in the baileys, lounging in the guardrooms, on furlough in Mujhara. Only four of them now; four had gone into the wood, making certain the thieves were gone. Every face was masked to me, showing me only what they intended, and that being little enough. Young men all, twenty-five to thirty, but each with that selfsame presence, that quiet *confidence;* all of them ageless in experience, in the knowledge of what they faced.

If he had killed the Prince of Erinn, what he faced was death. What *they* faced, I thought, was exile.

I was tired, so very tired, and the liquor had fuddled my tongue. At best I am often tactless; now I was nothing short of rude, though I hardly meant it to come out so plainly. "So," I said thickly, "you and those men who were with you sailed for Homana, just in case he *did* die, to avoid sentencing." I paused, sucking in a hiss of reawakened pain; I had absently scratched at my shredded neck. "Liam would have had you executed for killing his only son, his *heir*—" I broke it off; it needed no more embellishment. Clearly, he knew what it meant.

" 'Twasn't an easy choice." He stroked into place the heavy mustaches interlacing themselves with beard. So much hair on the man, head and face: bright blond and brilliant red. "Ye see, lass, 'twas only a bit of a thing, this fight between me and Sean . . . hardly enough for *dying*—" He sighed, looking unexpectedly weary. " 'Twas only over a lass."

Dull anger flared and died. "Only" over a lass; I scowled at him blearily. "It seems to me you have an uncommon familiarity with your lord's *name*, Erinnish, rather than his title."

He grinned, but with little humor. "Och, aye, Sean— *Prince* Sean, if you like, but there's little reason for it . . . we're pups of the same sire, though born of different bitches."

My wandering wits snapped back. "Liam is your father?"

He arched an arrogant eyebrow beneath a forelock beginning to curl in damp night air. "I could say something of *you*, lass, using names in place of titles . . . but aye, 'tis all of it true: Liam is my father." He

paused. "The Lord of Erinn, if you prefer, *and* of
the Idrian Isles."

The latter was due, in part, to Corin, who did not
contest the title. His own was Lord of Atvia; he had
told me it was enough.

Gods, I am so tired . . . I roused myself with effort.
"Did Sean know you were his brother?"

Something flickered in brown eyes. "Liam freely
acknowledged me at birth, making no secret of it.
Sean and I were childhood playmates—there's but
thirteen months between us—and later, when Liam
made me a captain in his Guard, boon companions."
He looked away from me. "We often went drinking
together."

I said nothing at all, merely staring at the man
who may—or may *not*—have killed his brother in a
tavern brawl over a pretty wine-girl. It was not, I
knew, unheard of; my own brothers had battled the
odds in such places, and over women of like employ-
ment. They had even begun a fight that became far
more, accounting, in the end, for the deaths of thirty-
two people.

But that was another, older tale. This one still cut
deep; the man, I saw, was bleeding, though perhaps
he did not know it.

Then again, perhaps he did. Abruptly he was strid-
ing away from the fire, as I had, as if he could not
bear to face it, or himself. He paused but a few paces
from me, head bowed, fists on sword-belted hips;
stared bleakly groundward, then frowned and bent
to pick something up. My knife, I saw, and flinched
at my forgetfulness.

Then froze. It was more than merely a knife.
Cheysuli long-knives are particularly valued because
only rarely does one go out of Cheysuli hands. A
student of weaponry knows the design, the style, the
difference; even, I thought, in Erinn.

And if the style of weapon did not give away its

origins—*and* those of its owner—the hilt design might. Rampant lion with rubies for the eyes: the device of the House of Homana.

If he knew it, he knew me.

"You fought," I said lightly, hoping to distract him.

"We fought," he agreed, "to see who would win the lass. We have done it before, but this time, *this* time—" He turned and looked at me. "I was in my cups. So was he. It was wanting little more than that and a bonny lass." He shrugged lopsidedly. "Liam bred true; our tastes are much the same when it comes to bedding the lasses."

"But this time it went too far." I refused to look at the weapon.

"Too far," he agreed, turning it in his hands. "No blades, but we needed none—we are effective enough without."

Aye, so they would be, if Sean shared his brother's size. And Aileen's description of the Prince of Erinn led me to believe he was in every way a match for his bastard brother.

To myself, I shook my head, seeing it too well: two young bulls fighting with the heifer there to watch, and too much liquor in them. "Fools, both of you."

He looked from the knife to me. The blade glinted in his hands, such large, strong hands. "Fools," he echoed, "aye. And now I have paid the price."

Unexpectedly, it stung. "*Have* you?" I asked. "Have you, then, you and your men, living now in Homana . . . while your murdered prince—and kinsman—is walking the halls of the *cileann*?"

It was his turn to gape. I had succeeded at last in drawing his attention from the knife. "What do you know of the oldfolk?" he asked. "A Homanan lass like you, with no ken of Erinnish magic!"

Not of Erinnish, perhaps, but my own share of Cheysuli. Yet I could say nothing of that to him. "A little," I answered evenly. "I have heard the Princess of Homana speak of the *cileann*, as well as the Mujhar's *meijha*."

He frowned. " 'Tis a strange word, that. And not Homanan, I'm thinking."

I cursed myself for the slip. But among those of us who share blood, it is how we referred to Deirdre. It connotes honor, since she holds no Homanan rank. "Old Tongue," I told him truthfully. "Are you forgetting the House of Homana is Cheysuli?"

He grimaced. "Shapechangers."

"Better than murderers."

His hand gripped my knife. "Aye, so they are." He walked the three steps, gave the knife back to me with nary a word of the device. "Well, lass, I'm thinking I'm remiss in my manners, having left most of them behind. Will you stay the night with us? Share our supper with us? The liquor you've already tasted." He grinned. "Or it's tasted *you*, by the black look of your eyes."

I closed a fist over the telltale hilt. "Why Homana?" I asked. "Why not Atvia or Solinde?"

"Atvia is our enemy."

"Was," I said plainly. "Alaric has been dead two years. Corin rules now."

He shrugged. "But a lad, is Corin, and unschooled yet in ruling. 'Twill take time, and he may not have it . . . not with the Ihlini witch on his doorstep and Mad Gisella in his castle."

It made me angry that he could so easily discount my brother. "He is the rightful lord of Atvia—"

"Right has nothing to do with it," he snapped. " 'Twill be who is strongest that holds the throne . . . oh, aye, Corin means well, of that I'm having no doubt, but 'tis early yet to predict who will win. Might be Lillith yet, and Strahan with her . . . no, no, Liam makes no judgments, nor Sean—" He broke it off, as if recalling Sean might never again make judgments.

"Then what of Solinde?" I asked. "Solinde and Erinn have never been enemies—that portion has been Homana's—so why not go there? It is closer to your homes."

His tone was elaborately even, but his eyes gave it away. "We have no homes, lass. As for Homana?" He shrugged. "No particular reason, I'm thinking, only—" But he stopped short. "No, lass, 'tis a liar I am. There *was* a reason, aye . . . but I lack the courage to do what I intended, what I *hoped*—" He sighed, giving it up. "What Sean asked me to do, once, if anything befell him."

I swallowed painfully. "Which was?"

He was backlit by firelight. It set a nimbus around his head, at the edges of his beard. Quietly, he said, "To go myself to the lady and beg her forgiveness and understanding."

I stared. "Beg—? Why? What need is there of forgiveness *or* understanding?"

"For leaving her a widow."

Sluggishly, I shook my head. "But—how can she be a widow if they were never married?"

He frowned. "In Erinn, a betrothal is much like a wedding, and as binding. In Erinnish eyes, the lass would be Sean's widow even without the wedding." He shrugged. " 'Tis customary, lass, especially in royal houses when the heirs are but wee bairns, to make certain the betrothals hold."

It did make sense, though in Homana it is different. Kings barter children in exchange for all manner of treaties and accords; without the betrothal holding weight, the same child could be offered again and again, at the king's convenience.

But I did not like the practice. Widowed before the wedding? Married without the vows? I found the latter most disturbing; it consigned me to the buyer without a trace of courtesy, nor respect for Cheysuli customs.

Between my teeth, I said, "I am sure she would give her forgiveness, if not her understanding."

He looked at my knife, hilt still clasped in my fist. And then he took it back before I could speak, replacing it with his own. "We'll be hearth-friends, then."

In shock, I stared after my knife. "What?"

"An Erinnish custom for wayfarers in need of a fire and a place to sleep. Strangers are welcomed in to sup before the hearth, to sleep in the host's own bed." Teeth glinted as he grinned. "No, lass, I promise—the bed is empty of host."

I was not afraid of him or his dishonored men. Mostly, I was exhausted, stiff with crusting rope burns and bruised from the awkward landing. *Lir*-shape, I knew, was futile; even if I gained it, the shape would not last. What I needed was food and rest.

I refused to glance at my knife or say anything of it, for fear of making him curious. With effort, I looked into his shadowed face. "King's man," I said, "have you a real name?"

He hesitated a moment, as if he feared to tell me; as if I could give him away. "Rory," he said at last. "but also known as Redbeard."

"Rory Redbeard," I muttered, "remember I have a knife."

" 'Tis *my* knife, lass . . . and remember, I have yours."

I looked again at the blade in his hand, aglint with royal rubies. Shut my mouth on an answer and went slowly to the fire.

Seven

One might think the Cheysuli, a race so steeped in honor, are blind to dishonor in others, to deception and subterfuge, believing all men are as they themselves are. Once, perhaps, but no longer, nor has it been so for time out of mind. Contact with the Ihlini, who share some of the Firstborn's power but nothing of their wisdom, has educated the Cheysuli to what unchecked avarice and ambition, augmented by twisted sorcery, can do to a race.

As had Shaine's *qu'mahlin*, the war of annihilation leveled against us by my kinsman, my great-great-grandsire on the Homanan side, nearly a hundred years ago.

So no longer do we trust, nor blind ourselves to betrayal, deception and subterfuge. We have learned to judge, to weigh, to measure, knowing very well that to a people reluctant to show strong emotions to those who are unblessed, the feelings and convictions of other races are often ludicrously transparent.

Men are easy to read. Even Erinnish exiles.

Rory Redbeard was kind in his own rough way, and solicitous of my well-being. In the morning he fed me journey-bread and venison stew spiced with thyme and wild onions, eating what all of them ate, and poured me a cup of water. I ate, drank, felt better, but wished I had my knife.

"Lass," he said quietly, "will ye not let me tend your scrapes?"

"No time," I said briefly, chewing the last tough bite of bread. "I must get back to Homana-Mujhar."

His tone was idly kind. "Surely you can wait *that* long, lass . . . I see how they're hurting you."

Well, they were. Abraded flesh had seeped fluid and watery blood, then crusted as I slept. Movement had broken open the beginnings of fragile, puckered scabs. I could barely turn my head and forbore to use my right arm.

"I must get back," I repeated, thinking of Aileen. But I quailed from it, afraid; quailed also from the acknowledgment I would have to tell Brennan *something*. I had lost his prize colt; how, by the gods, *could* I tell him?

And how would I get back? *Lir*-shape was out of the question. As a bird, I would lack a wing. As anything else, I would lack a foreleg, much limited in speed.

Walking would be faster.

"I have a horse," Rory said, and I looked at him so sharply it cracked a knot in my neck. I winced.

A glint crept into his eyes. By daylight he was a different man: younger in face—what I could see of it above and beneath the beard—though weathered by Erinn's sea-clime; in clothing and accoutrements more obviously a man denied his homeland, as well as the trappings of normal life. Like the others, he was travel-stained and shabby, though knives and swords were well tended.

Aye, they would be. For by knives and swords— and cunning—new lives would have to be forged.

I drew in a deep breath. "My father—" Stricken, I cut it off, then rapidly reshaped it. "My father, the Mujhar's arms-master, would give you no welcome, nor would his master, if they knew."

Rory Redbeard laughed. It was but a short bark of sound, underscored with the knowledge of ironic futility. "Would he not? And *why* not, I'm wondering? In killing Sean—if I have—I've stolen a husband from his lass. 'Tis a serious thing, that, and worth contemplation by men who are merely fathers in addition to Mujhars." Absently he stroked ruddy mustaches into neatness, though all of him wanted washing. "Niall and Liam are friends as well as allies . . . your father's master will have no more love for me than Liam, should news come that Sean is dead."

My father's master . . . with effort, I made the adjustment. I wanted nothing more than to throw off my own subterfuge so I could speak freely again. Never in my life have I *lied* to anyone regarding my heritage; there has been no need for it.

"If the Mujhar learned you were here—"

"But he won't be learning, will he?" He paused significantly. "Unless you're for telling him." A friendly man, was Rory, on the outside of his skin, but willing enough to show steel around the edges when he felt it required of him.

It irritated me. "What would you *have* me tell him?"

Rory shrugged. "Don't lie, lass, save for telling my heritage . . . tell him the truth of everything but that, as you can. Tell him, if you like, there are brigands in Homana—I doubt 'tis anything he doesn't know already, judging by the men who chased you to my fire." He rose, turning away on some errand, then abruptly swung back to face me. His expression was, yet again, masked. "Tell him what you will, lass . . . for when the Mujhar sends men to find us, we'll be in another place." Then, casually cruel, "D'ye think I'm so daft as to trust you?"

It stung. But I gave him a glimpse of my teeth in return. "Nor I to trust *you*."

Rory smiled, then laughed. "Agreed, then! Come, lass, we'll be saddling my horse. 'Tis a long ride, I'm told, to Mujhara . . . we'd best be setting about it."

I stood, gritting my teeth against the aches and stiffness, and followed him from the fire into a thicket. "How would *you* know how far it is to Mujhara?"

He laughed explosively. "We're here for a reason, lass: the road. I'm told it goes from Mujhara clear to Ellas."

Frowning, I nodded.

"Then so does trade, my lass . . . as well as wealthy merchants."

I stopped. "A *thief!*"

He paused, half-turning, putting out a hand to screening foliage, but hesitated to draw it aside. "Become one," he agreed. "Can I be presenting myself to the Mujhar, asking for a place in his service?" His tone was cool. "I'm thinking not, lass . . . not with Aileen there, who knows me. I'm thinking the best way for me to feed myself and what's left of my command is to acquire a bit of the wealth others have in plenty."

"A thief," I said again, thinking of the others; of the man whose knee I had bent—or broken—and the companions who had chased me, intending revenge and rape.

"Aye," he said evenly, and drew aside the foliage.

I started. "Brennan's *colt!*"

Blond brows arched. "Yours, then; I was thinking so, when they brought him to me last night after you fell asleep." His mouth hooked down in a wry smile. "I'm for keeping him, lass."

"But—no . . . not *him*." I pushed past Rory, threading my way through foliage, and went to the chestnut colt. Tied up short, he could barely turn his head. "Not him," I said again, cupping chin and muzzle, thinking of my brother. "He belongs to the Prince of Homana."

"He belongs to Rory Redbeard."

I turned on him angrily. "What right have you to *steal*? This colt belongs—"

"—to me." Rory moved to the colt, deftly shunting me aside. " 'Tis what thievery *is*, lass . . . and that 'right' you speak of is right of conquest, or requirements." He saddled the chestnut easily, tightening girth, snugging buckles. "I'm thinking the Prince of Homana has more than this bright lad in his stable."

"Aye, of course—but—"

"Then he'll do as well without him. 'Twill give him time to ride the others." He turned the colt, swung up, reached down to clasp my hand. "Will ye be coming, lass?"

"You were a *king's* man, once—"

"Once," he said quietly. "Now I may be the cause of my brother's death . . . d'ye think stealing matters to me? Or who I steal *from*?"

It silenced me easily, as he intended it to. I wanted nothing more than to denounce him, but there was nothing left to say. Nothing left to *do*; I clasped his hand, let him pull me up, settled a careful leg on the colt's sleek rump and slid slowly into place.

Thinking violent thoughts.

By the time we reached the outskirts of Mujhara, I was near to tumbling off Brennan's mettlesome colt. That we had arrived at all was nothing short of a god-gift; the colt was bred for speed, not for carrying a man the size of Rory nor the additional weight of a second rider. It had taken all of Rory's strength and skill—and my determination not to be thrown—to tip the colt out of rebellion into a grudging surrender. He had brought us to Mujhara, but not precisely unscathed. Rory complained the saddle was too small— for him, it was—and the long ride had set my head and neck to aching again, as well as breaking open once more the thin crusts on throat and arm.

We were nearly to the gates when I roused from my half-stupor with a stifled curse. "No!" I said sharply. Then, more quietly, "Stop here, Erinnish. No need in going farther."

No indeed, no need: the guards on the city gates knew me too well. I was less willing than ever to admit my true identity, because of Rory Redbeard's link to the House of Eagles. He was in no position now, in exile, to do anything about it, but should Sean prove to be alive rather than dead, I wanted no brother—bastard or no—telling tales of me to the man who intended to name me his wife before we were even wed.

"Stop *here*," I said plainly, bracing to slide off it Rory did nothing to halt the colt.

But he did halt him, all of twenty paces from the Eastern gate with its archivolted barbican. The walls themselves are gray, penning up the city proper in a huge, soft-cornered rectangle. But Mujhara has grown, as cities do; too fast, too far, without regard to the future. Now there was a second city clustered outside the walls, though built of less permanent materials than stone—mostly haphazard, flimsy wooden structures, or soiled canvas tents bearing no resemblance to the jewel-dyed and *lir*-painted pavilions of Clankeep.

Inside, warded by a webwork of narrow, twisting streets and a curtain wall thick as three men lying head to toe, nestles Homana-Mujhar herself, breasting above baileys and sentry-walks, wearing banners for her gown and torchlight for her jewelry. Rose-red in the light of day, bloodied-gray by night. The place I knew as home.

Twenty paces is not too far for a keen-eyed gate guard to see a person clearly, even at night, so long as he has torchlight. But my leathers were badly soiled, and one sleeve of my quilted undertunic shredded nearly into nonexistence. My hair, free of cap or braid, was a mass of tangles sculpted by dirt and tree sap; I doubted sincerely anyone would recognize *me*.

But they might recognize the colt.

I slid off painfully, ignoring Rory's hand. The landing was awkward and jarred my head; I gritted teeth and turned to look up at the Erinnish brigand, putting my back to the gate. The street, unpaved and thick with dust, was thronged with people going this way and that, even now, after sundown. It was possible, if not probable, a passerby might recognize me if I did not act soon to detach myself from Rory Redbeard.

"My thanks for the food and drink," I told him. "My thanks for your aid against the thieves—" I paused "—the *other* thieves—" I ignored the glint in his eyes, "—but I will not give you my gratitude for stealing Brennan's horse."

He pursed lips—and beard—thoughtfully. Thick brows drew down, met, knitted, then slanted back up again as he tilted his head to one side. "Is that the way of it, lass?"

"What?" I frowned. "Is *what* the way of it? What are you talking about?"

"Brennan," he said, "and you."

Dumbfounded, all I could do was blink.

Slowly, distinctly, he nodded. "Aye, I thought so—always Brennan this, Brennan that . . . never the Prince of Homana. Never "my lord," though you'd be having it from me, and for my own brother." He shrugged a little. "Well, I'm not judging ye, lass . . . I'm born myself of a bedding between a prince and a bonny lass—"

I was astounded. "Are you saying you think Brennan and *I*—"

"No shame in it, lass . . . at least, not so much as to ruin your prospects." He grinned. "He'll leave you wealthy, being a prince . . . you could do worse than the heir to the throne of Homana." The glint was more pronounced. "Once he's cast you off, *I* might even consider—"

I smiled up at him insincerely. "Take your stolen horse and go, before I bring the guard down on you."

Laughing, he reined the colt around. "Or your Cheysuli prince?" And laughed more loudly as I mustered elaborate curses. "Lass, lass . . . you'll be getting no censure from *me*—d'ye think I'm so daft as to throw mud at my own reflection?"

I swallowed laughter, not wishing to show my amusement to Rory Redbeard, and put shielding fingers across my lips. With great effort I managed a frown. "Just go," I choked.

Rory nodded, but his share of amusement faded. He worked his mouth thoughtfully, absently soothing the colt with a gentle hand on his neck.

"Lass," he said finally, "there's a thing I must ask you to do."

Wary, I frowned. "Me?"

"Aye." His face was pensive. "Say nothing of it to Deirdre or Aileen, this thing of Sean and me. We're neither of us knowing if he's alive or dead—I'm thinking it might be better left to Liam to give them the truth of the matter." Uneasily, he eyed me. "Lass, will you promise? 'Tis a thing of the House of Eagles—I may be only a bastard, but still kinborn . . . 'twould be better, I'm thinking, not to tell them a thing that might not be true, giving them a grief they may not need to suffer."

"Or may," I said quietly.

He looked over my head at the barbican gate, thinking private thoughts. "Aye," he said finally, "or may."

I owed him nothing . . . except, perhaps, my life. Certainly my virtue.

In pensive silence, I nodded. That much I would give him.

Rory Redbeard leaned down out of the saddle and set a hand to the top of my head, tousling filthy hair. "*There's* my good lass," he said.

And rode away, laughing, before I could summon an answer.

Eight

I went at once to Aileen's apartments, to her bed-chamber. The heavy door was shut. I put out my hand to push it open, knowing she would give me welcome no matter what my state—and stayed the hand even as splayed fingers tensed to push.

I could not face it, could *not*; would not chance walking into a room scented by death and extremity, knowing myself a coward for not returning at once from Clankeep, for staying away to hide from possibilities, from the responsibilities of a *cheysula*.

Oh, gods, how can I deal with this—?

I swung back abruptly, rolling shoulders against the corridor wall, to lean there, teeth gritted, eyes shut tight, skull pressed into stone. Helplessness and futility altered fear into something more, into a wealth of tangled emotions unfamiliar and therefore treacherous, because if I could not name the emotions, neither could I control them.

Under my breath I swore, stringing together every epithet I could apply to myself, for being such a failure as companion, kin, *kinspirit*—

"Keely."

I snapped upright at once, turning stiffly toward him, petitioning the gods to let it be someone else, *anyone* else, so long as it was not my father, who would doubtless take me to task for betraying Aileen when she most needed me, for fleeing responsibilities—knowing if he said none of those things, what he *would* say was that Aileen was dead.

But he said none of those things, because it was *su'fali* in place of *jehan*. Uncle in place of father.

"*Leijhana tu'sai*," I breathed, and relaxed as Ian approached.

"What has *happened*—Keely, are you ill? Are you injured?" His concern was manifest, intensifying my guilt; Aileen was more important. "Keely—"

I shoved back tangled hair. "Aileen," was all I said.

It shut his mouth, but only for a moment. I looked for signs of grief: saw none, only concern and acknowledgment. But then he is not a man for giving things away, my *su'fali*, having suffered grievously for giving away something he treasured more than anything: honor, self-control; for a while, even sanity.

He gave nothing away now, even to me. To no one, I thought, again. Lillith of the Ihlini had taken far too much.

"Alive," he said quietly, wasting no time. "Niall brought her through with the earth magic, *leijhana tu'sai*, though it was much too soon for the babies. But at least Aileen is well." Briefly he sketched a quick gesture I know so well, *too* well: cupped hand turning palm-up, fingers spread.

It was so powerful a relief I could afford to be caustic. I chided my father's brother. "Aileen is not Cheysuli, therefore she has no *tahlmorra*." But my right hand twitched as if it, too, wanted to make the gesture denoting fate and the gods.

Ian's expression did not alter. "She has Brennan. I think it is enough."

Aye, of course: *Brennan*. Truly she was blessed.

And then I thought of the colt lost to Rory Redbeard, and shifted uneasily. "She will recover, then? Fully? She will still be Aileen?"

He frowned. "Of course; what *would* you have her be?"

"Anything but a broodmare." Wearily, I shoved a rebellious lock of hair from my face again. "*Su'fali*, if she goes through this again . . . if she is forced to bear a child—or *two*—simply because Brennan—"

"Keely." He took my arm—the left one, thank the gods—in a firm grasp, turned me away from the door and guided me down the corridor even as I tried to protest. "No—not now, Keely . . . Aileen is resting. Later." He continued to lead me. "You need not worry she will be required to go through this again . . . the physicians say it is unlikely she will ever bear another child." His fingers remained firmly entrenched in my arm. "Now, as to being *forced*—"

I resented being guided, but was too tired, too worn, to do much more than test his grip. "She *was*. She nearly died with Aidan, and yet within a year of his birth she is required to try again, simply to shore up Brennan's claim on the Lion—"

Ian muttered something in Old Tongue under his breath, escorted me ungently to the closest door and pushed it open, pushing *me* in behind it. Then, closing the door by kicking it shut, he guided me over to a chair and plopped me down in it. Only then did he release my arm.

Without preliminaries, my uncle called me a fool, in both languages, to make certain I understood, which I did twice over. And a blind one, as well, twice over again; which did not, particularly, sit well with me.

I stood up. A firm hand on one shoulder pushed me down again. "You *will* listen," he said mildly.

I opened my mouth to protest, shut it to think a moment, glanced around to delay. And frowned. We were in Ian's quarters, which I found unusual; he is very private, my uncle, and keeps parts of himself closed to others, even kinfolk. I had not been in his personal chambers for years, not since I was a child begging him to teach me how to shoot a Cheysuli warbow. No one else would.

Immensely comfortable chambers, filled with Chey-

suli things. In recent years our people have begun
reclaiming some of the crafts *qu'mahlin* and exile
denied, for the threat of extermination leaves little
time for things other than defense. Ian had collected
stoneware sculptures of different *lir*, foremost among
them Tasha, but also his brother's wolf, in addition
to the nubby, round-framed weavings many of the
women do. Across one ironwood table spilled a river
of prophecy bones, but made of silver instead of
ivory; a gift from Hart, I knew, who intended it for
wagering. Our uncle used it instead merely to help
him think, idly throwing patterns.

Something squalled. I glanced around sharply at
the huge bed, draperies hooked up on the bedposts,
and saw Tasha sprawled there with her cubs, all
tangled amidst the bedclothes like knots in Deirdre's
yarn basket. Three young mountain cats, all rich
tawny bronze.

I smiled in delight. *Lovely,* I sent through the link.
*They will make magnificent lir, should the gods give them
the honor.*

Amber-eyed Tasha wasted no time in agreeing,
but before I could say anything else Ian cut me off.

"Not now," he said distinctly. "At this particular
moment I want to make very certain you understand
something clearly."

"*Su'fali—*"

"No," he said firmly. "You are here to listen, Keely,
which is something you should practice more often—
certainly more often than the sword with Griffon.
That you may have mastered; listening you have not."

The meal I had shared with Rory and his men
curdled in my belly. Anger and astonishment evapo-
rated; what I felt was humiliation. Hot-faced, I stared
back at him, wanting to look at the floor but denying
myself the refuge.

He sighed, folding arms across his chest. He is not
much like my father, being thoroughly Cheysuli in

coloring as well as habits, though the black hair is frosting silver. And nothing at all like the Mujhar in temperament, either, being considerably more relaxed and less prone to worry about things. It is sometimes hard to believe they are brothers, although only half; Ian is bastard-born, the son of Donal, my grandsire, and his half-Homanan *meijha*.

"Keely," he said quietly. Too quietly; I know his methods. "Has it never occurred to you that perhaps Brennan and Aileen are content with one another?"

It was the closest *he* would ever come to speaking of love, being so Cheysuli, and therefore characteristically reticent to discuss such things with others, even kin. I have no such qualms; it must be the Homanan in me, which speaks oftener than it should.

"Content." I thrust myself against the back of the chair. "You mean, in their bedding."

"I mean in everything."

I recalled Brennan's behavior, his *eyes*, when I had told of Aileen's condition. Clearly, he was "content." But I also recalled how it had been between them when Aileen had first come to Homana. "But—*Corin*—"

Ian's tone was steady; he knew how I felt about my *rujholli*. "Corin is gone, *has* been gone, for nearly two years."

I shrugged. "What does time matter? You know as well as I Aileen wanted to marry Corin instead of Brennan . . . it was only because of the betrothal to Brennan—*and* the prophecy—that she had to give up Corin. Do you think she would have otherwise? Do you think Corin would have let her?" I sat upright in the chair. "Brennan cares, aye—I have seen it—but what of Aileen? She was forced, *su'fali*, no matter what you say. Forced in marriage, forced in bed . . . forced to bear heirs for Homana." My hands clenched on the chair arms. "Just as *I* will be, one day, if for Erinn instead."

"We are not speaking about you just yet," he said

gently. "We are speaking of Brennan and Aileen, who have had a difficult time reconciling old feelings *and* new ones, with no help from their sharp-tongued *rujholla*."

I disliked intensely being trapped in the chair. It made me want to squirm, like a child; it made me want to jump up and stride around the room, taking solace in activity. But I refused to squirm, and I knew better than to jump up. Ian would only push me down again.

"Aileen and I have talked, it is true," I admitted, "but she has her own mind, *su'fali*. You know that. She is Erinnish. Those born in the House of Eagles know very well how to fly."

"Unless someone puts jesses on them and locks them in the mews."

I stared. "You think *I*—"

"I know." He rose, walked idly around behind me, paused, rested hands on my shoulders. "Keely, you are not a vindictive person, nor one who wishes ill of kinfolk. But you are so strong in your convictions, so *pronounced* in your biases, that you overwhelm other people. Aye, Aileen has her own mind—she is Liam's daughter in that, as Niall says, and Deirdre—but how often do you listen and weigh what she has to say? Have you ever asked her how she feels about Brennan?"

No. Because I knew how she felt about Corin.

Ian's hands tightened. "I do not ask you to betray your loyalty to Corin. He is your twin-born *rujholli*—that is a link no one of a single birth can share, can even *comprehend* . . . but neither should you continue to defend a relationship that ended nearly two years ago."

"How do you know—"

He overrode me easily. "Because *you* prefer not to marry does not mean you should expect every other unwed woman to feel the same, nor a married one to feel guilty if she is content." He paused, squeezing aching shoulders very gently. "Nor should you ridicule them if they do not feel as you do. Their beliefs are as important as your own, and they have as much right to them."

Anger boiled up. *"You* say. *You* say: a man." I sat rigidly in the chair. "What would you know of being forced against your will into a liaison you do not want?"

The hands dug painfully into my shoulders. I thought he did it purposely, to punish me—until I realized what I had asked, and of whom I had asked it.

"Oh, *su'fali*—oh, gods, I *swear*—" I wanted to jump up and turn; to face him, to apologize, but he held me firmly in place, denying me any chance to take back the cruel question. To assuage my guilt, his pain.

"Oh, I know," he said quietly. "I know very well, *harana*. I know what it is to be chattel, to be needed only for the servicing, like a stallion brought to the mare. I know very well what it is to be valued only because of my seed, of the child I can sire . . . and *did*." He sighed wearily. "Not so different, I think, from what many women face. But it need not be what Aileen faces, nor you. She has a chance to be happy with Brennan, as do you with Sean, *if* you will allow it. As for me, well . . . that is a thing I have learned to deal with, after so many years."

I swallowed painfully, clearing the tightness in my throat. "Have you, *su'fali?*"

"Oh, aye—of course."

His tone was too light, his hands too heavy. Slowly I slipped out from beneath those hands, rising, and turned to face him squarely. To look into haunted eyes; so yellow, so *Cheysuli,* beneath the silver forelock.

"Is that why you practice *i'toshaa-ni* every year on the same day, trying to bleed your soul clean of her?" I steadied my voice with effort. "Is that why you never speak of Rhiannon, the daughter you sired on her?" I drew in a breath. "Is that why you take no woman as *meijha* or *cheysula*—because she soiled you?"

"I am not celibate," he said tightly, "nor do I lie with men."

I made a gesture with my hand. "No, no, of course not—but even with a woman in it, your bed is often empty." I felt uncomfortable speaking of such things with him, but I would not stop now. "I heard Deirdre once, with *jehan*—she was saying she thought you were much too hard on yourself for something you could not help. And *jehan* said—" I stopped, seeing the look in his eyes.

Softly, he asked, "What did Niall say?"

I drew in a deep breath, blew it out. "That you believed yourself disgraced. Dishonored. That a dishonored warrior asks clan-rights of no woman."

"No," he said only.

"But, *su'fali*—" I sucked in another breath. "She held your *lir*, your *life* . . . what else was there to do?"

"Then: nothing. Afterward—" He shrugged. "There are ways of expiating dishonor. There is *i'toshaa-ni*—"

"Not *every year*."

"—and there is self-exile from the clans—"

"Not for such as *that*!"

"—and there is the death-ritual."

I stared. "You would *not*!"

Slowly, he shook his head. "I am liege man to the Mujhar."

Words tumbled out. "Is that why—is that the *only*—? Oh, *su'fali*, no—say you would not . . . say *no*—tell me it is a only a jest—a *very* poor jest—"

"Keely, stop. Enough." Ian is older than my father by five years. At this moment, I would have said twenty. "I swear, I have no intention of *kin-wrecking*

myself or giving myself over to the death-ritual; it is
far too late for either. And as for why I ask clan-
rights of no woman—well, that is my concern, not
yours—"

"But *any* woman would have you!"

At last, my uncle smiled. "Would she?" he asked.

"Oh, *aye*, of course! You should hear what they say
of you, *su'fali*." I grinned. "Even before Brennan
married, or Corin and Hart left, it was *you*—"

At last, my uncle laughed, putting up his hands.
"Enough, *enough* . . . all right, Keely, you may sus-
pend your staunch avowals of my appeal." He grinned
and glanced at Tasha, whose affectionate amusement ran through the *lir*-link to us both. "Now, as to
the *original* reason for this discussion—"

"Aye, aye, I know." I waved off the rest with my
hands. "I am too quick to tell others how to conduct
themselves, disregarding their own opinions. I know.
But sometimes—" I cut myself off. "No. No more; I
will try to lock up my tongue."

"But do not choke on it."

I turned resolutely toward the door. Then swung
sharply back. "She *is* all right?" I asked.

"Aileen is, aye . . . but now, as for *you*—"

"No," I said, "no. I must order a bath." And took
myself out of the chamber before he could start on
me.

I soaked in a half-cask until the water was nearly
cold, then dragged myself out with effort. The heat
had dissipated some of the pain, but nearly all of my
energy. Shakily I took up the drying cloth left for
me by the cask and wrapped it tightly around my
body, stepping out with care. I have never been one
to enjoy body-servants hovering, patting me dry and
toweling my hair, and so I had dismissed them before stripping out of my filthy clothing. Now, alone
as I preferred, I discovered an inclination in myself

to simply lie down on the floor. It was too far to walk into the bedchamber, too hard to climb into the bed.

Irresolute, I stood on the damp floor and lost myself in contemplation of my state. Of mind as well as body; there was thinking I had to do, about missing colts and Cheysuli long-knives, and the Erinnish brigand who had them.

Somehow, I will have to get them back, both of them. I cannot let him keep them, either one—

"Keely?" A figure swam into my unfocused gaze, coming through the doorway between bed-and-antechamber. *"Keely,"* she cried sharply. "Oh, gods, Ian said you looked bad—" Deirdre caught my left hand and tugged me through the doorway. "Come with me, my lass, before you fall down where you stand. I'm thinking it might be painful."

The Erinnish lilt, in Deirdre, was far less pronounced than in Aileen, only two years out of Erinn, and certainly less than in Rory Redbeard, so newly arrived. But the "my lass" rocked me; it summoned up his bearded face, his voice, and the tale he had told, of murdered princes and bastard brothers.

As well as reminding me of the promise I had made him.

Sluggishly, I stirred as Deirdre led me into my bedchamber. "No—no, I am well enough . . . only tired."

"And have you looked at your face? Have you heard your voice?" Deirdre pointed to a chair. "There, Keely—and no protests. Here—put this on." Deftly she plucked a folded nightrail from my bed and tossed it to me.

There is no arguing with Deirdre when she sets her mind on a thing. So obligingly I swathed myself in the nightrail, now cloaked in wet hair. I twisted it all into one thick rope, then asked Deirdre for a comb.

She brought it from a table, but as I reached to

take it she jerked it out of my grasp. "Keely—what has *happened*?" Carefully she peeled the collar of the nightrail back from my throat. "Oh, *gods*—this needs salve. I'll send . . ." And went to the door to set a servant to the task, then came back with the much-needed comb. "What else?" she asked evenly. "Be telling no lies, now—I know you, Keely—what else have you done to yourself?"

I sighed, pushing up loose linen sleeve, "Here." I bared my arm. "No worse than the neck."

Deirdre, frowning, inspected it, hissing a little in empathy. "You said nothing of this to Ian . . . you gave him no chance to *ask*."

I shrugged, cocking my right hand up behind my neck so the underside of my upper arm was clearly exposed. Stretched skin stung. "Someone strung a rope across the track. The horse was running; it scraped me off."

Deirdre started to say something more, but a quiet knock at the door forestalled it. She answered it, returned with a stoppered pot and soft linen cloths. " 'Twill sting a little," she warned, "but will help the flesh loosen."

Aye, it stung, and more than a little. I gritted my teeth and sat very still as she worked the salve into the crusty burns on neck and arm. Under her breath she muttered broken sentences in Erinnish, as she did in times of stress or anger. I had even heard her use the whip of her eloquent tongue on my father a time or two; they are surpassing fond of each other, but they do quarrel. Very like playful cats: all noise and flying fur, but claws sheathed for the duration. And always brief, with them.

Twenty-two years together, though neither of them show it, in habits or appearance. Deirdre's hair is still bright blonde, her green eyes direct as ever, her body slim and straight.

So *many* years in Homana . . . and before that—

before Atvia and my mother had intervened, however briefly—a year in Erinn, in the Aerie, learning each other's hearts.

Vaguely, I wondered: *Could it be so for me?*

Until I recalled that, very likely, it could not; possibly Sean was dead.

I tensed as Deirdre finished my neck and moved ministrations to my arm. Ground my teeth as the consequence of such a death became more obvious.

If Sean is dead, jehan will find another . . . he will open the bidding again, to every prince he can think of. I shook my head a little. *Not many realms left, or princes . . . too many rujholli inhabiting foreign thrones . . . he will have to look to Ellas, or Caledon, even Falia—* I frowned. *But never to The Steppes. We have no trade with them, no reason for an alliance—*

"Keely." From the tone of Deirdre's voice, she had said something to me that required comment or answer, and I had given her neither. "Keely, did you see Maeve?"

Maeve. Oh, gods, my half-witted sister, going again into Teirnan's bed. "Aye," I said briefly.

"Did she say aught about coming home?"

Aye, she had. She had said "tomorrow," which now was today. Unless she had changed her mind, which I knew was possible. She was so afraid to hurt our father, whom she loved above all things.

I shrugged slightly, lifting my left shoulder as Maeve's mother worked salve into my arm. "We did not talk about much."

Deirdre sighed, lines settling between her brows. "I worry about her . . . ever since Teirnan showed his true colors and renounced everything the Cheysuli stand for—"

"She will do well enough." I spoke more harshly than I meant to, but Maeve was not a child. She was the oldest of us all, even if, I felt, the most foolish.

Something flickered in Deirdre's green eyes. I had

stung her with my curtness. "One day," she said tightly, "you also will be having a child to worry about. Perhaps even a daughter. *Then* you might understand." She eased my arm from its awkward position, smoothed the linen sleeve back over it. "There. 'Twill require more in the morning, but should be better by midday. As for the hoarseness—"

"It will fade." I put out my hand for the comb.

"No, I'll be doing it . . . just sit here and be silent; give your poor throat a rest." She set the pot and soiled cloth on a table, came to stand beside me, sectioned off my hair and began to work on wet tangles. "You were in the way of being lucky, my lass—had you not put up your arm to block it, the rope might have broken your neck."

"Aye," I said absently, thinking of Rory again. There were things I wanted to ask of him, but did not know how without breaking the promise I had made. I could hardly tell Deirdre he was here in Homana without a proper explanation. She would want to know why, and was persistent enough to work it out of me one way or another. "Deirdre—?"

"Aye?" Deftly, she coaxed hair into neatness again.

I thought rapidly a moment, then drew in a breath. Blandly, I said: "I spoke to *su'fali* earlier."

"Aye, I know—he said you wanted to see Aileen."

"He told me she was resting, and took me away to talk." I chewed my lip a moment. "He never speaks of Rhiannon."

Deirdre paused only a moment, then resumed her combing. "No. 'Tis not something he wishes to recall, that time in Atvia with Lillith and the outcome of it."

"No, but she *is* his daughter . . . and in the clans, bastardy bears no stigma. He could acknowledge her."

" 'Tisn't because she's bastard-born that he won't acknowledge her. 'Tis her mother: Rhiannon's *blood*." Deirdre sighed a little. "Bloodkin to the Ihlini, to Strahan himself—even to Tynstar. A powerful blend,

Keely, and treacherous as well. You know what she did to Brennan, much as her mother did to Ian."

Aye, I did know. Which led me to another line of inquiry. "By now *that* child is nearly two," I said idly. "Yet another Cheysuli-Ihlini bastard. And yet another unacknowledged child." I winced as she hit a snarl. "Brennan, like our *su'fali*, says nothing of his child."

"For much the same reason."

"Not bastardy."

"No, of course not. D'ye think bastardy matters to the father who loves his child?" Gently, she tamed the snarl. "You have only to look at your father to see how it happens. He loves Maeve every bit as much as he loves the children of his marriage."

I sighed. "Kings and princes and bastards." I waited a patient moment. "Is it so with every lord?"

Deirdre's tone was dryly amused. "If this is your way of asking if Sean has any bastards, how am *I* to know? I left Erinn when he was four—much too young to sire children, legitimate or no." Now she laughed. "The eagles may be lusty, but not so potent as *that*!"

I grunted a little. "Sons are often like the father— what of Liam's habits?"

She was silent a very long moment, absently putting my hair to rights. "Aye, well . . . Liam is *mostly* faithful to Ierne—"

"But not always." It was all I could do not to turn and look her in the eye. But to do so would give me away, would underscore the intensity of my interest.

Deirdre sounded troubled. "No, not always . . . Keely, there are times when men turn to other women . . . in sickness, sometimes, or while she carries a child—"

"I know," I said quietly, "I am not questioning his morals." Although I would have liked to, since, by all accounts, Liam loved his wife. "I was only curious. I *do* have reason, Deirdre . . . there is Sean to think about." I would use it as I had to, though not with any pleasure. "As I have said, in the clans bastardy bears no stigma—I would sooner see a bastard acknowledged, as *jehan* acknowledged Maeve, then relegated to oblivion."

"Sean would not be so cruel," she said, "any more than Liam."

Expectantly, I waited.

After a moment, she sighed. "Aye, he has a few. All girls, save for one . . . a boy he named Rory, born thirteen months before Sean."

So. He had not lied.

Oh, gods, if Sean is *dead*—

Nine

With an excess of civility—and more than a trace of reluctance—three of Aileen's ladies turned me away from her bedchamber door in the morning, saying the Princess of Homana still slept, requiring uninterrupted rest. I knew all of the ladies well enough—they had come with her from Erinn—and they knew *me*; clearly, they were afraid I would show them the edge of my tongue.

Which meant, I thought, someone had ordered them to keep me out.

"Then let me see Brennan," I said flatly, neglecting his title and not particularly bothered by it. "He *is* here, is he not?—with Aileen?"

They exchanged glances, the three of them, showing me dismay, regret, hesitation. And, at last, denial.

"Lady, no," one of them—Duana—said. "He has given orders not to be disturbed by anyone."

"*He* has, or has someone else?"

Again the furtive glances. And again, Duana shook her head. "Lady, all we can say is that you will be welcomed another time."

Something akin to desperation welled up inside, stripping diplomacy from my tongue. "By the gods, she is my *kinswoman*! Have you gone mad? What right have you to turn me away?"

"Such rights as they are accustomed to, being in service to the Princess—and therefore the Prince—of Homana." It was Brennan, of course, pulling the door more widely open and dismissing the ladies with a nod. Then he turned to face me squarely, one hand on the edge of the door. "Aye, it is true—I *did* tell them you were not to be admitted. You in particular."

It robbed me of breath. *"Why?"*

"Because Aileen needs time to rest, to recover, without listening to your babble about being forced this way and that, molded into a broodmare for my convenience." There were deep-etched shadows beneath his eyes. The rims themselves were red; clearly, he had sat up with Aileen all night, forgoing sleep entirely. Weariness and worry undermined the customary courtesy in his tone, leaving it raw in sound as well as words. "I know what you will do, Keely— you will come in here with words of sympathy on your tongue, and then it will alter itself into a sword and *cut* her, whether you mean it to or not."

"Oh, *Brennan*—"

He signed to me for silence, though the gesture was mostly half-hearted. "She needs time to understand that her place is secure with me even if there *are* no more children . . . and she will not get it with you jabbering in her ear about her loss of freedom, her lack of *value*—" He broke it off, shut his eyes briefly, threaded splayed fingers through limp black hair and scraped it back from his face. He looked so weary, so *worn*. "Gods, Keely, forgive me for my bluntness—but you know it is true."

I drew in a deep breath. "If it were not for me you would not have known she was in danger. I came to fetch you—"

"*Leijhana tu'sai,*" he said evenly. "But not *now*, Keely—another time." He started to close the door, then pulled it open again. As an afterthought, he said, "You did bring the colt?"

Gods, the colt. "In his stall," I lied.

He nodded vaguely and shut the door, leaving me

staring blindly at studded wood nearly black with age and oil.

I wanted to strike it. I wanted to *kick* it, to cry out that no one, *no one at all*, even Brennan, knew what I thought, what I *felt* ... but I did none of those things, being too angry, too hurt in spirit to dare, for fear I would waken Aileen, or even injure myself more than the fall from the colt had.

Brennan's colt. *Gods*, I was beginning to hate him!

But I went after him nonetheless, and at once, seeking physical diversion. Brennan had made me angry, aye, but he was still my brother, and needed whatever respite from worry I could give him. The gods knew he had more than his share with Aileen.

This time I took bow as well as knife, and full complement of arrows, hanging in a quiver at my saddle. The bow I wore hooked over a shoulder, Cheysuli-fashion. The knife at my belt was Rory's and would be again, once I had forced a trade. I did not dare leave him my Cheysuli long-knife, nor did I want to. It had been a gift from Ian on my twentieth birthday and I wanted it back badly, as much for sentiment as anything else.

The horse I rode was a gelding, one of my own; a long-legged, blaze-faced bay who looked particularly good under a saddle. I thought to give tack and horse to Rory in exchange for Brennan's chestnut, though, when it came down to it, the difference in quality was obvious. But the bay was a good horse, big of heart and willing of spirit. Rory would not lose by him; *I* would. But I had lost Brennan's colt, so it was up to me to sacrifice whatever I was required to in order to get him back.

Now the task at hand was to find the Erinnish brigand. Rory had said he and his men would be gone from where I had found them before, out of concern I might lead guardsmen back to the clearing. I had not bothered to tell him it would be no difficulty for me to find him—in the guise of a bird, a search is ridiculously easy—since to do so would give away my race. But because of the gelding I was limited to normal means, unless I left him tied temporarily along the way while I searched in bird-form, and I had no wish to risk losing yet another royal mount to thieves. So I rode like an unblessed Homanan, hoping for good fortune.

They would be, I knew, somewhere along the road, lying in wait for unwary travelers. I did not look much like a merchant, wealthy or otherwise, nor did I look much like a princess, dressed in Homanan-style hunting leathers, but his men knew me by sight, and I thought perhaps it would not be so hard to flush Rory from cover. He was a man who enjoyed a good jest, and "surprising" me might be one.

Out of meadow into trees, and into the deeper forest. From here to Ellas ran the wood, thick in some places, sparse in others, but always present, shutting out the world while quietly creating another.

It was here in the wood the Cheysuli had settled once Shaine's *qu'mahlin* and resulting exile was over, building the first Keep in thirty years. In time, it had become Clankeep, the largest of them all, and home to so many of us. My own grandsire, Donal, had been born in Clankeep, and raised; it was there he had sired Ian and Isolde on his *meijha* before marrying Aislinn, Carillon's daughter, my Homanan granddame. Where Isolde had died of plague, leaving Teirnan with only a father.

I grimaced in disgust. My warped, embittered cousin, subtly shaped by his father's ambitions. It would have been best if the Mujhar had brought his nephew into Homana-Mujhar after Isolde died, to be raised alongside three princes, but Ceinn still lived, and it is a Cheysuli custom that children, regardless of sex, remain with their parents. There is no fosterage among the clans—except where children are ophaned—as there is in many royal houses. And so Teir had been brought up by an ambitious, avaricious father, bent on putting a son of *his* on the Lion Throne instead of one of Niall's.

Teirnan was no *kinspirit* of mine, being enemy to my House. But he was still bloodkin, my own cousin, and *of* that House, which meant he therefore had a legitimate claim to the Lion—but only if Niall and all his sons were dead.

And so I wondered again, as I had often enough in the past, if Teirnan had seduced Maeve merely because of her link to the Mujhar. How better to irritate your enemy than by taking that enemy's most cherished possession—or child—and making it your own?

He had not succeeded, if he had tried, in reshaping Maeve's opinions to suit his own. He had, however, succeeded in separating her from her beloved father, something Teir in particular would find pleasing. In the time since he had voluntarily renounced the prophecy, his clan-rights and privileges, thereby renouncing his very soul, he had done his best to fracture the clans themselves. By pitting those Cheysuli more dedicated to the old ways against a more liberal faction, he had managed to divide Clan Council more than once, as well as win warriors to his cause. And by stirring up old Cheysuli quarrels—or starting new ones—he quietly diverted Niall's attention from Homana to the Cheysuli. In the Homanan Council there were already mutters of the Mujhar's inattention to matters almost strictly Homanan in nature. Homana's need, they said, was greater; to them, it is not a Cheysuli nation but Homanan, no matter that the gods put us here first.

At that, I laughed aloud. So easily I dismiss the Homanan portion of my heritage, as Aileen had remarked, *and* the Atvian, because it suits me to consider myself almost solely Cheysuli. And more so than most, if the truth be told; I am of the Old Blood, the *oldest* blood. Halfling I may be, or worse, but I still have more power than others. Even *a'saii* like Teirnan.

It was something. And perhaps it was time I used it, to put him in his place.

The gelding snorted, twitching ears forward as he turned his head to intently eye the left side of the track, all aquiver with trepidation. I unhooked the bow, plucked an arrow out of the quiver, nocked it and waited as the gelding halted.

Oddly, I felt relaxed. The odds were different now; Hart would wager on *me*.

The wood was silent. *Too* silent. If they thought they were fooling me—

I laughed aloud, drawing as I raised the bow, and chose my target. Suggesting, in gutter Erinnish, the man give himself up; what would it do to his pride to be pinned to a tree by a woman?

Too much damage, apparently; he slid out of a shadowed copse of elm to stand quietly some ten paces from my gelding, who snorted in noisy alarm but held his ground, thank the gods.

"Aye," I told the man, "you. But then it was not you I was aiming at, but the other man over *there*—" I loosed, sent the arrow thwacking into a trunk, plucked, and nocked a second. "Now, as for *him*—"

It did not take long at all, this time. The second man came around the tree, eyed the arrow askance, grinned, shrugged; pulled it free, unbroken, and brought it to me, presenting it with a flourish as a man might present a woman a long-stemmed flower.

"*Leijhana tu'sai.*" I accepted it, slid it home in the quiver and waited, second arrow still nocked.

They exchanged glances of amusement mingled with rueful consternation.

"Redbeard," I said quietly.

And so they led me to him.

Liam's bastard son sat with his rump on a tree stump, repairing a broken bridle. Deftly he wove leather thong through knife-punched holes, joining the broken halves of a cheek-strap so it was whole again. Beneath fallen blond forelock he frowned; his mouth twisted sideways into his beard as he knotted off the thong, taking care to see it would hold. In his teeth he clenched a piece of leather, working it absently.

Around him others gathered, though none so close as to touch him. Eight men in all, exiled from their homeland. They had the closed-faced look of men who hid a secret, disdaining to show their pain. One man tended a tiny fire, adding wood to the handful of smoking tinder. Another tended his sword, polishing the blade. A third drowsed idly, leaning against a downed log. Yet a fourth threw prophecy bones, or an Erinnish variation.

Rory glanced up from his task as I led the bay into the clearing, with a man on either side. I had put away arrow and bow, since my point was already made, and greeted him empty-handed.

He stopped working the piece of leather in his mouth. Grinned around it, baring teeth, then took it out of his mouth. "Ye see, lass, how we live—reduced to eating leather in place of meat." Sighing dramatically, he shook his head. "Once, there was a time—"

"—when you supped at the lord's own table." I shrugged, unimpressed by his avowal. "And could again, could you not—if Sean survives his broken head?"

He looked at the gnawed piece of leather as if fascinated by it. "I'm doubting it, lass."

"Why? You are Liam's son, and freely acknowledged . . . if all you did was give Sean a headache, no matter how fierce, I hardly think he would want to execute you. He might even take you back."

Rory glanced at his companions. "So we're hoping," he said, "but how are we to know? 'Tis Homana we're in, not Erinn; how many folk here care a whit for the House of Eagles?"

"That, *I* can tell you." And then quickly explained myself. "I mean, I live in Homana-Mujhar. I hear things. If Sean is dead, word will come from Liam. I can pass it to you."

Brows lanced down. "Why would you be doing that? What are we to you?"

"Exiles," I answered quietly. "For twenty-five years the Cheysuli were exiled from Homana, in order to save their own lives during Shaine the Mujhar's purge. I have heard the stories, being privy to many of them within the walls of Homana-Mujhar." I shrugged, glancing briefly at the others, hoping the explanation sound enough. "I know what exile did to the Cheysuli, so long banished from Homana; I would sooner see *you* go home again, than live out your lives here."

Rory gazed at me steadily for a long, uncomfortable moment, scrutinizing my manner. And then he shifted the focus of his stare, looking again at the chewed piece of thong. "We'd be in the way of thanking you, lass, if you could find the truth of the matter."

I pushed the gelding's intrusive muzzle away from my ear. "If Sean is dead, word will come soon enough. The Mujhar will have to be told—"

"—as well as Keely herself." Rory nodded. "No doubt Niall will be looking elsewhere for a husband in order to make an alliance."

"Aye, although he needs Erinnish blood badly—" I broke it off, not wanting to say more than the armsmaster's daughter should know. Although I *could* afford to speak of things other people could not;

Rory himself had lived in the shadow of royalty and would understand how such things come to be known to anyone living within palace walls.

Rory checked knots again. "Erinnish blood, is it? Aye, well, he has it in Aileen, and the son she bore the Prince of Homana. 'Tisn't so necessary that Keely and Sean wed . . . 'twill be little more than redundancy, I'm thinking."

I thought of Aileen, sequestered in her bedchamber with Brennan as her watchdog; of Aidan, their sickly son, who might not live to see another year. And no more sons to come after.

Hollowly I said, "One son is not enough."

" 'Twas all *Liam* had . . . excepting me, of course." Rory shrugged. "But then I'm not in line for the throne, even if Sean should die."

I frowned, listening for the sound of Teirnan's ambition, for an inflection of thwarted desire. "And it does not matter to you?"

To do him credit, he thought about it. Then slowly shook his head. "I am what the gods have made me."

"And you have no ambition? Not one hint of curiosity about what it would be like to rule?"

He looked at me intently. "Would *you* want to rule, lass?"

But I will, I answered silently. Aloud, I said, "Depending."

Eyebrows shot up. "On what?"

"On expectations, anticipations . . . what people want from me." I pushed the gelding away from me again. "For a woman, things are—different. Difficult. No woman rules by her own right, not in Homana, nor even Solinde; in no land that I know of." I shook my head. "It is not fair, that a woman—princess or queen—be required to marry in order to govern the realm she was born to. A man is not. A man is free to do as he will."

"But a man—prince or king—is required to marry

in order to get sons, *legitimate* sons, to inherit after him." Rory sighed, stroking mustaches. "Not so different, I'm thinking, when he'd rather do his own choosing, of time *and* woman." Brown eyes glinted a little. "Sean had no choice, did he? He was told he would marry Keely."

"Aye," I agreed sourly, "they were pledged before she was born."

Rory grinned, then laughed. "Well now, lass, d'ye see? 'Tis not so bad being who we are after all, is it? We're free to wed or not, as we choose, and *who* . . . no one binds our wills by royal whim or prophecy." More quietly, he said, "We're free people, my lass, bound by nothing but ourselves."

For all of our lives Corin and I had held conversations concerning the privileges of rank, of race, of heritage, so certain of our own. We had discussed the requirements of that rank, the dictates of our *tahlmorras*, what we could offer to the world because of our heritage. We had been insular, arrogant, too certain of our power, believing no one other than a Cheysuli could understand what we felt, because they were *lirless* and therefore unblessed, trapped in a lifespan lacking the magic of the *lir*-gifts, the power of our heritage.

Now, listening to Rory, I realized it had nothing to do with race. Men are born with eyes and ears; few of them know how to use them.

I drew in a breath, changing the subject. "I have come to make a trade."

Rory grunted, chewing idly at one of his mustaches. "That brown castrated lad in exchange for my fleet-footed boyo? I'm not such a fool as that."

"He is a fine horse—"

"No doubt," he agreed, "but I'm liking the one I have."

I chewed my bottom lip. "And your knife for mine."

He glanced at the knife snugged in the sheath at my belt, then back to my face. "No, I'm thinking not."

I bit back frustration. "And this warbow."

That put the light of interest into his eyes. "Let me see it, lass."

I unhooked and handed it over as he rose. Rory took it, examined it, felt the silk of the wood, the power, the promise of accuracy. Then waggled fingers in crude request for an arrow.

That, too, I handed over. He glanced around quickly, spied a likely target, nocked, pulled, aimed, loosed. The arrow sang its flight and thunked home in the trunk of a beech.

Rory nodded, though mostly to himself. He nodded, caressed the wood, turned back to me. "I've not seen its like before. We have bows in Erinn, but none so compact as this."

"A Cheysuli warbow," I said. "Designed for ease of hunting, perverted by Shaine's *qu'mahlin*." I drew in a calming breath. "For the colt and my knife, I give you the gelding and warbow."

He looked at the bow, the gelding, pursing lips thoughtfully. Lines formed between his brows. Then he shook his head.

"Why *not*?" I cried "By the gods, Erinnish, no man other than a Cheysuli has ever claimed as Cheysuli bow as his own, except for—" I stopped.

Slowly, Rory grinned. "Except?"

I plowed doggedly ahead; it was too late to turn back. "Carillon," I told him. "The man who ended Shaine's purge."

Rory's expression was momentarily blank. Then, vaguely, he nodded. "Oh, aye, I recall the name, I'm thinking . . . Homanan history is not my own." He looked at the bow again. " 'Tis sorry I am, lass, but why should I trouble myself to trade when I can easily take?"

"*Take—*"

"Both horses," he said, "*and* the warbow, lass—are you forgetting I'm a thief?" And he gestured to the man closest me, on the other side of the gelding.

He put out his hand to take the reins, but did not. The Erinnish knife I now carried was sharp as any other; the brigand learned precisely *how* sharp.

I turned, swung up into the saddle, reined the horse into a pivot to send the two closest men dodging, then reined him around again so I could face Rory. He was grinning at me broadly, idly cursing the man I had cut. "Once was enough," I told him, "I learn my lessons quickly. This one stays with me."

And crashed back through to the track, leaving them all behind.

I did not go far. Only far enough to mislead them into believing I really *was* gone. Then I slowed the gelding, turned off the track once again, rode through trees and foliage to a close-grown copse of brushy fir. I jumped off, tied the gelding securely, started back toward Rory's encampment. On foot, this time, with no intention of warning them, or of giving myself away. I would locate them, wait patiently for my chance, slip in and free the colt, stealing Brennan's horse back from thieves—

An arm locked around my throat. A hand plucked my knife free of sheath. Quietly, a familiar voice said, "I want to talk with you."

Ten

I froze in disbelief. "Teir?"

The arm did not relax, forcing up my chin so the back of my skull rested against my shoulders. The rope burn on my neck stung, protesting the pressure. I knew better than to struggle, or to attempt to assume *lir*-shape. He could choke me down too easily, before I could make the change.

"To *talk*," he stressed, "no more. You are my cousin, Keely—do you think I want to harm you?"

My voice was strained from the weight of his arm against my throat. "You may not *want* to harm me, but you would, and quickly enough, if you thought it would aid your cause."

His breath tickled my ear. Teir's tone was dry. "I am not so desperate as that."

I hated my helplessness. Another man I might try, but Teirnan was unpredictable, while easily able to predict *me*. "What do you want, Teir?"

"To talk," he repeated. "I told you so before; I do so again. But this time I have brought allies, so you understand I am serious. This is not a game, Keely .•. . it is the survival of our race."

Staying trapped as I was would do no good. I gave him my acquiescence.

Teirnan released me at once and stepped aside. I swung around, saw how many were with him, did not move again. But inwardly, I grieved.

So many a'saii, so many kin-wrecked Cheysuli—

I did not bother to count them. I knew the number was higher yet, for women and children had gone with them, and none of them were here, only warriors and their *lir*. In nearly two years Teirnan had collected a clan of his own, lured away from others, dividing the Cheysuli over an issue that touched us all.

Striking first was required, or Teir would win the moment. "Is it worth the loss of the afterworld?"

It was what none of them expected, even Teir. Argument, anger, even name-calling. But not a simple question. Not one such as that.

Teirnan stirred. I struck again. "I know you believe what you do is right. But think what it will cost you."

Fifty or sixty of them, and *lir*, melding with the trees. So still, so silent, so calm, gathering in the shadows. In Homanan parlance, perhaps not so very many. But a warrior with his *lir* is worth several of any Homanan; Teirnan had gathered an army.

"Sit," my cousin said, "and I will tell you precisely *what* it shall cost us—if we serve the prophecy."

"Teirnan—"

"*Sit*, Keely. Please."

I sat. Put my back against a tree. Let my kinsman talk.

He was quiet, for Teir. Also distinctly sincere. I had expected dramatics or fanaticism; what he gave me was belief. A pronounced, abiding conviction that his way was the right one; that if we ignored it, we would die.

At first he paced in front of me, working out his words. Clearly he felt how he spoke was as important as what he said, forgoing his usual manner. He was a different man. Oddly, it frightened me.

He stopped pacing, turned to me, knelt down to look into my face. "I have done none of this out of whim," he said. "I have done none of this out of idle envy or jealousy. I am ambitious, aye, to a fault . . . I think I am more suited than Brennan—" he leaned forward intently, "—but I swear, Keely, *I swear*— there is much more to it than that."

Slowly I shook my head. "How can there be, Teir? You have always wanted the Lion. Ceinn made certain of that."

Teirnan nodded intent agreement. "Aye, aye, of *course* he did—do you blame him? His *cheysula* was *rujholla* to the Mujhar, and Ceinn himself is of a purer line of descent than even the House of Homana. The Lion is *Cheysuli*, not Homanan—who better to claim it than a warrior of Ceinn's descent?"

I started to speak, but he cut me off with a raised hand. "And now you have turned me from the track . . . Keely, you must hear me and understand me. There is much more at stake now than the Lion, *far more*—"

"How can there be?" I snapped. "Holding the Lion Throne is part of the prophecy."

Teirnan's eyes caught fire. "Aye, *aye*—and it is wrong. The prophecy itself is wrong; you serve a perverted relic." I had heard this nonsense before. I tried to tell him so, but he easily overrode me. "Keely, you have stronger gifts than any woman of the clans since Alix, our great-granddame. You know what it is to have the freedom, the *power* of *lir*-shape—what it is to fly the skies—what it is to go in cat-shape, or any form you desire—" Again he shifted forward, eyes fixed on my own. "You know better than anyone else *can* what it is to converse with the *lir*, to share in private thoughts, to have the earth magic at your beck—"

I was growing impatient. "Aye, Teir, I *know*—"

His tone hushed itself. "But what if you did not? What if you *could* not—if the power was stripped from you?"

I shook my head. "Not possible, Teir. The *lir*-gifts are gods-given—"

He was close to laughing in frustration at what he perceived as my ignorance. "And what if the *gods* did it? What if they took those gifts away and made you as all the others? An unblessed Homanan woman, with less freedom than ever before."

"Teir, you are a fool—"

He slid forward on his knees, caught my hands, held them against his chest. "I swear by all that I am, I think they *will* do it. When the prophecy is completed, the Firstborn will rule again, uniting four realms and two races, with nothing left over for us." He gripped my hands tightly. "I *swear by my lir*, Keely, this is not a trick. I mean what I say: the gods will take back the gifts and give them to the Firstborn."

It was suddenly painful to swallow. "What *need*, Teir? Why should they do such a thing?"

"Think," he said earnestly, "recall all the lessons, the histories the *shar tahls* taught us when we were growing up. Think of the prophecy itself, and the story of how it was shaped for us."

"Teir—"

"*Think*, Keely! Think back, remember, recall the focus of what we are taught: the Firstborn had all the gifts, men and women alike ... but they grew too inbred, diluting the blood and the magic. And so the gods formed two races out of one, portioning out the gifts; some to the Cheysuli, some to the Ihlini." He paused, jaw set very tight. "In hopes that someday Cheysuli would breed with Ihlini and fix the gifts once more."

"Why would the gods want their children to fight?" I asked. "We are enemies, Teir—"

"Again, I ask you to think." His intensity died away, replaced with quiet appeal. "We are enemies now, aye, but was it always so? Were we *born* enemies, or did something happen to cause a rift, a schism—a bloodfeud that holds even now?" He raised a silencing hand. "Think of the Ihlini and what we have learned of them; what even the Mujhar claims: not all are engaged against us. Not all serve Asar-Suti, but the old Solindish gods not so different from our own." He smiled. "Perhaps the gods are one and the same, just as Ihlini and Cheysuli."

I pulled my hands free of his, dumbfounded by his claims. "You are saying—"

"—that it took an outside influence to plunge Ihlini and Cheysuli into interracial war. That perhaps a few ambitious Ihlini—possibly only one—decided the natural gifts were not enough. To rule he needed more, and turned to the Seker." Teirnan spread his hands. "Thus spawning a *third* race: Strahan and others like him, with power distinctly augmented by the god of the netherworld."

I licked dry lips. "Then, according to you, the prophecy is more than the unification of races and realms, but a joining of power as well."

Slowly Teirnan nodded. "And once that power is unified, dilution is undesirable. Why not take it all and put it into one vessel? It is concentrated, *augmented* —there is no need for dilution. Dilution is undesirable; so are those who dilute."

I stroked hair from my eyes. "But why, if the Firstborn grew so inbred in the first place, do the gods desire to create them again?"

"Because now there is other blood thrown into the cookpot." Teir's eyes were bright. "Foreign spices, Keely, to make the stew taste better . . . to strengthen the heart of it."

"Gods," I said. "If it is true—if all this added blood does *indeed* strengthen the Firstborn—what will they become?"

"Children of the gods."

"But—that is what—"

"—Cheysuli means, aye." Teir nodded. "We came first, Keely: *we* were the Firstborn, until they split us apart. Until they created the Ihlini." He sat back on his heels. "What need will there be for us? What need for the Ihlini? We are both of us sentenced to death."

It shook me. "Gods, Teir, you sound like *Strahan*—"

"—because he is not so wrong."

It was blasphemy. I shuddered once, shook my head vehemently. "He wants all of us *dead!*"

"He wants the prophecy broken." Teirnan sighed. "His methods are violent, aye, and deadly for those of our House, but I understand his reasons. How else do you break the prophecy than by destroying those it involves?"

"And if it *is*—"

"Then we will be free of destruction, Keely ... free to be *free* again!"

His conviction was overwhelming. "You cannot be saying you wish to serve Strahan or the Seker—"

Teir was adamant. "No, only *myself*. Not Strahan, his god; not even *our* gods, Keely ... only to serve myself. To have free will again, not bound by any *tahlmorra;* to be free of such burdensome rituals made to protect our fragile honor—"

"Teirnan, *no!*" I cried. "You are free to renounce your honor as you wish, but I am not so quick."

"No, nor was I." For a moment pain undermined his conviction, muting the fire in him. "It was not—easy. In no way. What we are, each of us—what we become—is shaped from birth to fit prescribed behavior patterns, all bound up in honor codes and rituals, in the name of Cheysuli gods. It becomes a sacred duty, cloaked in the mystery of faith—but as a way of enforcement, a means of *manipulation* ... because if we were given absolute freedom of choice, would we choose to complete the prophecy? Or turn our backs on it, leaving the gods without the First-born?" He was solemn now, clearly cognizant of what he said, and of what he advocated. "Even the afterworld—is there really an afterworld?—is something we are promised since birth." Teirnan shook his head. "But how do we *know*, Keely? How can we be certain? All we know is what we are told, being taught by other Cheysuli who were taught identical things. Is there room for honesty? Or only for superstition?"

"But you renounced *everything*."

"Because I felt I had to." Teir inhaled deeply, as if requiring strength. "Keely—if Strahan came to you one day and demanded all your *lir*-gifts, would you give them up without a fight? Would you make something holy of it?"

All I could do was deny it, knowing full well the ramifications of what he asked, what he implied; knowing also it made sense. A certain symmetry.

I looked beyond him, to the others. I looked at warriors and *lir*, gathered in the shadows, and wondered how anyone could have foreseen this. It was not in the prophecy. So many things are, though many only fragments like overheard conversations distorted by distance and interruption. And so many things are not, almost as if the gods—or the First-born, who wrote the prophecy—had wanted no one to know the full truth. Because, if Teir was right, to know it gave us the freedom to deny it; now, we only served, with unthinking obedience.

I shut my eyes tightly, resting my head on drawn-up knees. *Oh, gods, if Teir is right*—

"What is the difference?" he asked. "Ihlini, Cheysuli, god. They will strip us of our gifts in order to give them to someone else."

I raised my head and looked into the face of certitude, the eyes of a Cheysuli. And knew, looking at him, he had not forfeited his honor. He was as dedicated to the preservation of his race as anyone else I knew.

But Teirnan risked more; in that, he was alone.

I knew what he wanted. And how badly he needed

it. "The difference—" I swallowed. "The difference *is*, you want too much."

"A little thing, Keely."

"The destruction of the prophecy is not a little thing."

"But you will never see it." He was very calm now. "Such things take time, certainly longer than you and I have."

My chest felt tight. "Teir—"

Quietly, he said, "What I ask is what you want."

I stared in disbelief.

Teirnan's tone was gentle. "Refuse the Erinnish prince. Bear him no children, Keely. It will be more than enough."

Oh, gods—

Gods?

Eleven

I sat locked in silence for a long time after Teir and the other *a'saii* faded back into the wood. Alone with my thoughts, my conscience, clutching drawn-up knees and staring at nothing, I pondered the enormity of what Teirnan had told me, considering ramifications. And realized I could not deal with them.

My belly twisted. I felt *dirty* somehow, as if Teir had drawn me into a web of deceit, when all he had done was to tell me what he thought, and why, and how it might affect us. How it might affect me.

Might. He was not—could not *be*—certain; how could he? All he could be was committed to the cause of the *a'saii*: in his new world he was clan-leader, *shar tahl*, prophet; heretic, traitor, *kin-wrecked* in the old one. Heavy words, each of them; heavier implications.

I shut my eyes, driving fingernails into knees. *If what he says is true . . . if the lir do leave us—*

I had no specific *lir*, but the loss of the bond between the *lir* and the Cheysuli as a race was enough to strip me and everyone else of the magic we tapped so unthinkingly. And to consider myself unblessed, like the Homanans, empty of magic, of flight, of *freedom—*

Gods, it was impossible.

Or was it possible Teir was right?

I swore, thrust myself up from the ground, threaded my way back to my gelding, whom Rory would not have in place of Brennan's colt. Well, time for that later. I had no more taste for sneaking into the Erinnish camp and stealing back the chestnut; Teir's words had stripped me of everything save the desire to go home to Homana-Mujhar, where I could think about what he had said.

What he had *suggested*, knowing it might not be my choice after all. That I might aid his cause even against my will. *Because I could not marry a dead man.*

I untied the gelding, swung up, turned him back to the track. Went home at a pace Brennan would decry, not knowing the circumstances, the turmoil in my belly.

Brennan could not even comprehend there existed a choice.

Fleetingly, I thought, *It must be easy for him, knowing his path so well . . . being so certain of his tahlmorra.*

And wishing, not for the first time, that I could be so certain.

This time when I knocked on Aileen's door, I was admitted at once. Brennan was gone; the chamber was full of Erinnish and Homanan ladies. At Aileen's quiet request, they departed, leaving the two of us alone.

She was ensconced in the huge drapery-bedecked bed, weighed down by coverlets. The brilliant red hair was unbound, spilling down either side of her face to form ropes across the silk. There were smudges beneath green eyes, but otherwise her color was not so bad. Clearly, she would survive.

Guilt churned in my belly. I ignored it, retreating into inanities. "Where is Brennan?"

Aileen smiled a little. "I sent him away to sleep. He refused, of course, but I told him his face was enough to be giving me bad dreams. So, in the end, he went."

I nodded, looking at anything but Aileen. Slowly I wandered around the chamber, picking up trinkets and putting them down, rearranging things, drifting eventually to a casement. Outside it was nearly evening. Inside the candles were glowing.

"Keely." Her tone was gentle. " 'Twasn't your fault."

I made no answer, staring blindly out the casement.

"It had begun before, earlier; I was afraid to be telling them. I meant to tell *you*—" But she broke it off.

I swung to face her. "Aye, you meant to tell me, but I refused to listen." Guilt pinched again. "As Ian has pointed out, it is a habit of mine."

"I value your honesty more than I can say, Keely . . . betimes I think there's far too little in the world." She shifted a little in the bed, rearranging bedclothes. "If anyone is for blaming you, send him straight to me. No matter who it is."

"Well then, I am here." I waved her protest away. "No, no, enough of that—how do you fare, Aileen? That is more important."

"How do I fare?" The green eyes dimmed a little. "Well enough in body—the Mujhar has seen to that— but not so well in spirit."

I looked for a stool, found one, hooked it over and sat down. Quietly I suggested, "Perhaps it was for the best."

Her tone was inflexible. "Losing bairns is never for the best, Keely. How could it be?"

I bit back the passion I longed to release, knowing now was not the time. "At least you were not lost as well."

Aileen grimaced. "Aye, so Brennan said . . . but I can't be helping it, Keely. I'm thinking of my poor sickly Aidan. I'm thinking of Homana. I'm thinking of a barren woman who one day will be queen."

I tried to make my tone light. "It is nothing new to Homana; you are hardly the first. Our House is built on fragile foundations. Shaine himself could get no heirs, even on a second *cheysula*. Carillon sired only a

daughter—" Abruptly, I thought of Caro, the deaf-
mute bastard who lived in Solinde, "—at least, on
Electra." I shrugged. "Donal provided two sons, but
only one was legitimate." I smiled crookedly. "Until
my *jehan* and his brood, the Lion was poor in sons."

"And now, more than ever, the Lion is needing
them." Aileen's expression was pensive. "I'm not meaning to sound sorry for myself, nor to blame the gods
for taking the bairns away—" she sighed, "—but I've
been here long enough to know how important the
prophecy is to the Cheysuli. Corin told me much of
it in Erinn—" Aileen broke that off almost at once,
reflexively, flicking a betraying glance at me. Then
continued in a newer, firmer tone. "Brennan, too,
has told me, and the Mujhar himself, how important
it is for this House to hold the Lion. They'd neither
of them claim me a failure, but this must be of
concern. One son for the Prince of Homana? And
he a sickly boy?" Aileen shook her head. "I know
how Niall must fret, though he will say naught of it.
And I know how Brennan feels, though he tries to
hide it away." She grimaced. "He is such a stalwart
defender of the prophecy, of the Cheysuli, of the
tahlmorra so binding on all of you."

"What about *you*?" I asked. "How does Aileen
feel?"

Her voice was very quiet. "I grieve for the bairns;
both boys, they said. And I grieve for my barrenness, knowing no more will be born. But—I'm thinking I also grieve for you."

"Me!" I stared. "Why?"

Aileen's eyes locked on my own. "Because now it
falls to you. Now more than ever, they'll be needing
you wed to Sean. And soon, I'd wager. They'll be
wanting children of you in haste, in case Aidan should
die. To protect the bloodlines, Keely . . . to fulfill the
prophecy."

I stared blankly at Aileen.

Her tone was infinitely gentle. " 'Tis sorry I am," she said. "I know how you feel, Keely. But I'll be promising you again, as I have so many times: Sean is a man worth having."

And if he is dead? I wondered. *Of what worth is he then?*

Or if he lived, and I refused to marry him for fear of losing the *lir* and all the magic of the Cheysuli. Was any man worth that?

I rose. "Rest you well, Aileen. And know that your lost bairns are in the halls of the *cileann*."

For the merest moment she smiled, and then the tears spilled over. I went out the door and closed it, leaving her to her grief.

I ate supper in my chambers, being disinclined to talk with others of my family, and wasted most of the early evening lost in thought, pacing the floor like a caged beast. I weighed Teir's words against those I had been taught by the *shar tahls* as a child, knowing Teir had been taught them as well. It was a wheel turning and turning, raised for repair and going nowhere; spinning, spinning, spinning, made of useless motion, wasted effort, profitless thought.

Again and again I came back to the beginning. If I refused Sean, as Teir desired—as *I* desired—only one child would carry the Erinnish bloodline so necessary to the prophecy. The last bloodline required; we had all of the others, save Ihlini. And even Ihlini, at that, if you counted Brennan's bastard on Rhiannon, or counted Rhiannon herself.

Aidan. The sole offspring of the coupling between a Homanan-Atvian-Solindish-Cheysuli prince, and an Erinnish-Atvian princess. The necessary link. And possibly enough, if he survived to wed and sire children of his own.

But if he did not, it left the Lion without the proper blood. It left the link broken, the prophecy incomplete . . . unless I married Sean and provided the children Aileen and my *rujho* could not.

The wheel turned once more, and came around again to me.

I stopped dead in the center of my chamber. And then went swiftly out of it to visit my brother's son.

The nursery was empty save for Aidan. Ordinarily he was attended night and day, but his woman had, for the moment, slipped out. The room was made of shadows, heavy and deep, born of a single candle. Light crept into the massive cradle and glinted off silver thread, caressed the creamy richness of aged ivory, glistened faintly from smooth-skinned oak.

The cradle was very old. It had housed infants born to the House of Homana for many, many years. The bedding was fine, soft linen, the coverlets of blue-gray silk with the royal lion crest sewn on in silver thread. Altogether too ostentatious for a baby, I thought, but then it was not my place to judge.

Beneath the silk of the coverlet was flesh too pale, thin hair burnished red in the wan candleglow. Blue-veined lids hid yellow eyes; awake, Aidan showed both sides of his heritage. Asleep, he showed only Aileen.

He was small for a baby nearly ten months old. He cried easily, tired quickly, was fractious most of the time. No one knew what ailed him, suggesting only that his protracted birth had somehow affected his health. He caught chills easily even in temperate weather, and seemed unable to fight off the little indispositions that childhood often brings.

I shook my head slightly. Such a little lump beneath the covers. Such a large one in the prophecy; one day he would rule Homana.

Locking hands on the ivory edges of the cradle, I leaned down a little, to make certain he heard me. In his dreams, if nowhere else; it was important that he know. "It comes to you," I told him. "Not to me; to *you.* The Lion will be yours."

Aidan's answer was silence, save for the sound of uneven breathing.

"You are the son of Brennan, Prince of Homana . . . the grandson of Niall the Mujhar . . . great-grandson of Donal, who was the son of Duncan himself." My hands tightened on ancient ivory. "And of your *jehana* you are born of the House of Eagles from the Aerie in Erinn, perched upon the cliffs of Kilore. Liam is in you, and Shea, and all the other lords." I drew in a constricted breath. "So much heritage, little fox . . . so much power in your blood—"

"—and so much weakness in his body?"

I twitched, caught my breath, stared hard into the darkness of a deep, unlighted corner. It was Brennan, of course; I should have known he would be present.

I drew in a calming breath, feeling my heartbeats slow. "Aileen said you were sleeping."

"Earlier, aye—for a little." I could see nothing of his face save its shape, but his tone made it unnecessary. He was worn to the bone, my brother, and in need of more than sleep. "But I dreamed my boy was dead, and the Lion in deadly peril."

In view of the situation, the revelation did not surprise me. "May I light another candle?"

"If you like."

I liked. I lit a second candle, set it into its cup, looked more closely at my brother. The light was not good, but better than before. Now I could see his face. Now I could see his eyes.

I caught my breath up short. Then slowly let it out. "You cannot know," I told him.

"That he will die?" Slumped deeply in a chair, Brennan shrugged raggedly. "No, of course not—but I can fear it. I think every parent does. But I have more cause than most; you have only to look at him, to *hold* him—" He broke it off, pressing fingers against his temples. "—gods—I am tired. Forgive my bad company."

"*Rujho*—"

As always, he did not shirk the truth, nor seek to hide it from me. "There will be no more, Keely. The physicians have confirmed it."

It took me a moment to answer. "I know. Aileen told me."

He pulled his hands away from his head. "Aidan is all there is—all there can *ever* be, now; what happens if he dies?"

I had not expected such bluntness from him, especially in this place, nor at this moment. But he had brought it up, and I was free to say what I would.

Or ask what I could ask.

I turned from the cradle to face him. "What *does* happen, Brennan? There must be a Prince of Homana. There must be an heir to the Lion."

He looked older than twenty-three. More like *forty*-three. "There are—alternatives."

I opened my mouth to ask him what they were, not being versed in all the responsibilities of kingcraft, then shut it again sharply. I knew. Looking at him, I knew. Nothing else would hurt him so. "Such as setting aside a barren *cheysula* and taking another woman."

His tone was flat and empty. "It is the only provision in Homanan law for setting aside a wife."

Carefully, I observed, "Men have done it before. Princes, too; kings in particular, when sons are needed for thrones."

He did not flinch, being Brennan, who faces truths with equal honesty. "Aye, they have," he agreed, "but *this* prince—or king—will not do any such thing."

So. There it was: Brennan's commitment was made. I had expected no other answer, but it is always worth the asking. One can never be certain.

I looked at Aidan again, stirring in his sleep. Delicate, fragile Aidan, meant for too heavy a burden. It might be the killing of him. Steadfastly, I stared at Aidan, refusing to look at Brennan. Not wanting to see the pain. "If he dies, you have no heir. None of your body."

He answered easily. "No. And unlikely to get another."

Now I did look at him. "Next after you is Hart."

Brennan shook his head. "Not now. *Jehan* has made it clear: on the day of his death, Solinde and Atvia no longer owe fealty to Homana. They become autonomous, subject only to their own lords. Hart will have Solinde to rule as he will, just as Corin will have Atvia. I can hardly strip Solinde of her king simply to give Homana a prince." He shook his head slowly. "*Jehan* is right to make it so, but it muddles the line of succession."

"Only because a man must be Mujhar." I lifted a single shoulder as well as single eyebrow. "*I* am left, after all. But Council would never approve."

Brennan sighed wearily: he had heard my tone before. "There is a reason, Keely, that the Lion requires a man—"

"*What* reason?" I asked. "A woman is more likely to keep a land at peace instead of war."

"Possibly," he conceded, "but there is another reason. A more compelling reason—"

"Tradition," I said in derision.

"Childbirth," he countered succinctly.

Frowning, I stared at him. "What?"

Slowly Brennan rose, pushing himself out of his chair. He crossed the room to the cradle, smoothed the coverlet over Aidan, lingered to caress the silk of his hair. "Childbirth," he repeated. "A ruler must beget heirs. As many as possible, to insure the line of succession."

"Aye," I agreed, thinking it obvious; we had been discussing it in depth.

"A woman risks her life each time she bears a child. A woman ruler would risk more than her life ... she would also risk her realm." His tone was gentle. "I know you are strong, Keely, and you would make a fine Mujhar ... but bearing a child every year is no way to rule Homana."

No, it was not. "And yet you willingly pack me off to Erinn so I may give *Sean* his heirs."

"More than that, perhaps." His fingers stroked red hair. "If Aidan dies, there is only you. From your union with Sean will come the next link in the prophecy. Perhaps the final one."

I thought of Rory and Teir. One perhaps a murderer, the other in fact a traitor. And caught between them was Sean, one way or another.

Folding my arms, I turned away. Took three paces, hugging myself; swung back, facing Brennan. "Men die," I said tautly. "What happens if Sean dies?"

Brennan frowned. "I hardly think—"

"Men *die*," I said again. "He is young, aye, and healthy, but men do die. Of illness, injury ... murder." I drew in a deep breath. "What happens if Sean *dies*?"

Brennan stared back at me. At first I thought he would not answer, and then I saw he would. But he hated it. He *hated* it, did Brennan; I saw it in eyes and posture, in the tautness of his mouth.

He answered it with questions. "Who after me is left? What warrior of our blood? What warrior of our *House*?"

Only rarely is Brennan bitter. But I thought he had just cause.

"Teirnan," I said. "Oh—*gods*—"

PART II

One

Lio closed one pale eye as he screwed up his face in ferocious contemplation. It was a good face, young and boldly mobile, and without doubt better served by another expression (or so a few of Aileen's Erinnish ladies had told me once or twice), but he paid little mind to the effect. I had made a request —no, extended an *invitation*—and he was considering.

At length, he sighed and shook his head. "Lady, I should not. The Mujhar himself has forbidden it."

Progress. Lio had said should not, not *can*not. I favored him with an eloquent—and pronounced— assessment, then shook my head in resignation. "One way of protecting your pride, I suppose . . . ah, well, it might have been worth a wager or two." I shrugged, smiling warmly. "Perhaps another time."

Pale eyebrows lanced down. Lio is very blond and fair-complected, with eyes the color of water. Homanan-born and bred, but some say there is Solindish blood in him somewhere, going by his color; Carillon's Solindish wife, Electra, had identical hair and eyes, and Hart's Ilsa is as fair. As far as Lio or anyone else knows he is pure Homanan, but the jest is repeated often merely to ruffle his feathers.

"Protecting my pride?" he asked sharply. "What do you mean?"

I lifted an eloquent shoulder. "Just that one way of making certain you do not lose to me—a *woman*—is not to try at all."

He scowled, chewing bottom lip. Lio and I are

much alike in pride and temperament, which means I know the tricks to winning acquiescence even when he has no wish to give it. At the moment he did not, and for good reason; the Mujhar *had* forbidden it. But I had no intention of letting that stop me.

Now all I had to do was convince Lio not to let it stop *him*.

He sighed, shaking his head. "It would be no true contest," he told me. "I am taller, heavier, stronger—and I have won the Lady's favor two years in a row at Summerfair."

I nodded grave acknowledgment. Deirdre's favor consisted of a length of gold-freighted silk dyed bright Erinnish green; it bought him supper at the High Table in Homana-Mujhar each night for a week during Summerfair, which is a boon all young men in the Mujharan Guard pray for. It is a way of catching the Mujhar's personal interest, so that advancement through the ranks may consequently be hastened.

Lio had indeed won the favor twice, and my father's interest was subsequently piqued. Clearly, Lio had no wish to risk losing royal favor by going against the Mujhar's orders; neither did he wish to lose *my* favor. Because, after all, I too could pique the Mujhar's personal interest. Certainly more often than once a year during Summerfair.

Sometimes entirely *too* often.

I lifted my hands briefly, let them slap down at my sides. "So, we will never know who is better with a blade . . . and you will spend your nights wondering." I grinned, arching brows. "Unless, of course, we contest to see if battle *can* be joined."

Lio frowned. "What do you mean?"

I glanced around the bailey. Mostly empty of people, it nonetheless was filled with possibilities. I swung back to Lio. "A race," I suggested. "To the wall and back." I tapped knuckles lightly against the guardroom door. "Whosoever touches this door first, wins. If it is you, your duty to the Mujhar is satisfied. But if *I* win, you meet me with your sword."

Lio looked at the distant wall. Back to the door. Considered it.

"A simple race," I told him. "Nothing more than to the wall and back."

He stared at me a long assessive moment, then unbuckled his belt and stripped out of his leather doublet, dropping it and the belt to the bench by the door. Off-duty, he had left off the crimson tabard with the black rampant lion sewn into the left breast. Now he faced me in linen undertunic, leather trews, boots. And determination.

We lined up with right legs extended, left heels against the door. "Knock," I suggested. "When it opens, we run."

Lio knocked. After a moment it opened, and we were gone.

The bailey is cobbled. No such surface can be perfectly level, and the bailey is hardly that. Centuries of summer rains and winter snows, boots and iron-shod hooves have worn pockets in the cobbles, crumbled the edges, even cracked a stone or two. But we ignored it all, and ran.

He beat me to the wall, as I expected. And, as I expected, he thrust off and was four strides ahead of me by the time I slapped and spun. But the lead meant nothing to me. In the end, I would win.

Lio was halfway back to the door. Laughing. Wasting his breath. Secure in the knowledge he would not forfeit his duty to the Mujhar to the Mujhar's daughter.

Any of my brothers would have known better. We had played this game before. Hart had invented it.

Five strides off the wall, I traded flesh for feathers. And beat him easily to the door.

Lio slapped wood as I completed the change back

into human form. I folded my arms and leaned against the door. Grinning. "Fetch your sword, soldier."

He was only a little out of breath, and mostly from the shock. "You—you said—" He paused and tried again. "You said a *race*, lady!"

"It was. To the wall and back." I raised disingenuous brows. "No one required it to be on foot."

He sucked in wind to protest again, thought back over what we had said, realized I had caught him. No indeed, no one had specified a *foot*race. Merely a race.

Lio sighed, knowing defeat when it spat in his eye. "I will fetch my sword." And went inside the guardroom.

My own blade, sheathed, lay on the bench beside the door, covered by Lio's doublet. I unearthed it, unsheathed it, admired the clean sleek line of blade in the sunlight. It had been made for me specifically, not ground down from a man's blade, which meant the balance was perfect.

Such a magnificent thing, the sword. I wondered, as I had countless other times, why the Cheysuli disdained it so, refusing to learn its use. Tradition, again; clan-born warriors felt men should fight face to face, and very close, instead of at the greater distance a sword provided. It had something to do with pride and skill; the belief that a man should taste the strength of his opponent, and his blood, in order to make the fight truly honorable. For the same reason the bow had originated for hunting, not battle, but Shaine's *qu'mahlin* had perverted its use.

Yet tradition changed, if slowly. Now Cheysuli born to the House of Homana learned the sword, and had ever since my grandsire, Donal, inherited Carillon's broadsword with its massive pommel ruby. Even though my own father had given the sword to the Womb of the Earth on Donal's death, the legacy survived. My father and my brothers had learned the art of the sword, and its strength. Certainly its beauty. So had I.

And would go on learning it, regardless of my father.

Lio returned with his sword. He saw me with mine, sighed, shut one eye again. "If he learns of this, I will be stripped of my rank."

"You have no rank," I pointed out.

My words put color in his face and prickles in his tone. "If I win the favor again *this* year, the Mujhar must make me an officer. It is well known. The Mujhar rewards excellence—in duty *and* swordskill."

I eyed him sourly. "Then consider this bout practice for Summerfair."

"At Summerfair, we fight *men*." Lio grinned as I muttered imprecations against his parentage. "Now we are even, lady."

I pointed away from the door. "There."

We struck stances, tapped blades, prepared. But before we could properly begin, Lio broke off, staring past my shoulder. He went red, then white, then shut his eyes and muttered something beneath his breath. His blade was no longer at the ready; clearly, someone was approaching. Someone whose mere presence was enough to stop the bout before it even began.

Oh, gods—not jehan—

I turned. No, not *jehan*. But just as bad: Brennan. He calmly crossed the bailey at a pace eloquent in its idleness. Sunlight struck slashes of light from the heavy *lir*-bands on bare arms. He wore Cheysuli leathers dyed black, as he often did; Brennan says he merely prefers unremarkable colors, but *I* think he knows perfectly well the color, on him, is dramatic: black leathers, black hair, dark skin, yellow eyes. He is not Homanan handsome, as Corin is or our father had been before Strahan's hawk had taken an eye, but all Cheysuli, with classic Cheysuli looks.

Some might call such looks too bold, too fierce, too arrogant. Too *feral* for their tastes.

Others might recall the magnificence of a mountain cat in motion; the stoop of a hawk after prey. And know better.

Brennan smiled. I frowned.

"Disobeying *jehan's* orders?" he asked cheerfully. "Aye, well, you would hardly be Keely if you did not."

Lio muttered again. Crossly, I told him to go back inside the guardroom if he could not bear to face the Prince of Homana, who was not precisely his liege lord; not *yet*, and in no imminent danger of becoming so, since the Mujhar was in significantly excellent health . . . which meant, I pointed out, Brennan could hardly censure Lio for transgressions not yet committed, and likely *not* to be committed, now, since Lio was sheathing his sword.

Muttering.

I scowled at Brennan. "*Jehan* sent you."

He smiled. "No."

He was blatantly unconcerned with what our father might think of my behavior, which was unlike him. Brennan had been the dutiful heir for as long as I could recall, even as a child aware of the responsibilities attendant upon his title. Although he had faced, as we all did, parental—and royal—disfavor in younger years, such disfavor for Brennan was rare, and usually the result of actions taken on behalf of Hart or Corin. While not a talebearer, Brennan was hardly reluctant to point out failings in comportment if he thought it warranted.

Lio had not gone inside the guardroom. Probably because Brennan had not given him leave to, although none was required; Lio was ambitious. Also genuinely apprehensive.

"My lord." He inclined his head to Brennan, who smiled at him vaguely and reached out to take my sword from me.

"May I?" Brennan asked.

I gave the sword into his keeping, waiting suspiciously.

Brennan tested the weight, the balance, examined the blade itself. Nodded thoughtfully, then glanced past me to Lio. And gave my sword to him. "Would you sheathe it and tend it for the lady? We are going riding, and have no need of swords."

"Riding! Brennan, wait—"

"*Leijhana tu'sai,*" Brennan said easily as Lio quickly did as asked. Then he put a hand on my arm, turned me away from the guardroom, guided me across the bailey. "Aileen is feeling much better, thank the gods. I am taking her to Joyenne for the summer."

It surprised me. "You will stay away from Mujhara that long?"

He shook his head. "Not I, perhaps—*jehan* will have things for me to do—but I think Aileen will enjoy the time away from the city. Away from—reminders."

I glanced at him sidelong. With Aileen's continued recovery his own spirits revived, but he was still not entirely himself. Not yet. Perhaps the time at Joyenne would do him as much good as Aileen.

"Then you will be leaving Aidan here?"

"For a while . . . he is not at the moment strong enough to travel. Aileen will fret, of course, until he can join us, but Deirdre will tend him, and *jehan*, and all the nurses. I think he will do well enough." Brennan rested a hand on my shoulder. "I thought perhaps you might come with us for a while, to give Aileen company when I am called back to Homana-Mujhar."

"Aye, of course . . . I enjoy Joyenne—" I stopped walking. "Is *that* why you halted the match with Lio?

To ask me this?" I sighed, biting back a stronger
retort. "It might have waited, Brennan . . . or did
you do it in lieu of *jehan*?" Pointedly, I paused. "As
you do so often."

He started me walking again. "I did not stop it
because *jehan* has forbidden it. Such things as your
behavior are your concern, not mine." My brother
smiled blandly. "I came to ask you for your company, at Joyenne and now. I thought we could match
my colt against the new gray filly."

Alarums rang. "Colt," I echoed. "*Which* colt?"

"The chestnut." He shrugged. "It has been days
since you brought him back, and I have yet to ride
him. He will need the work."

Oh, gods, not the colt— I stopped dead in my tracks.
"Brennan—" But I broke it off, unable to tell him.
Not so baldly. Not after so much time. I had lied.
Now it had caught up to me, and I found I could not
admit it.

His brows rose. "Aye?"

I opened my mouth. Shut it. Then shook my head.
"No—I think another time. Not now. I—" I paused.
"There is something else I must do. Another time,
rujho."

"Now." One hand locked around my arm, held me
in place, and he smiled all the while. "Keely, I have
been to the stables. The colt is missing." His tone was
calm, *too* calm. "The grooms say you came back from
Clankeep without him."

Oh, gods. And without inflection, "Aye."

Brennan released my arm. His expression was carefully noncommittal, which made it all the worse.
"You lied to me when I asked about him, Keely . . .
and now, when I give you a chance to explain what
has happened, freely and without prejudice, you ignore the opportunity and create an empty excuse to
leave." His tone hardened, as did his expression. "I

want to know why. What have you done, Keely? What
have you done *now*?"

Oh, gods, I hate *this*— I drew in a deep breath and
told him the truth. "Because I was ashamed."

Brennan was astonished. "Ashamed! Why? What
happened?"

My belly twisted. I felt no better about the loss of
the colt now than I had then. "I was tricked," I told
him curtly, though my displeasure was for me, not
for Brennan, who had a right to know. "Like a fool,
I fell into a trap—first thieves who wanted my coin,
then outlaws who—" I stopped short. I wanted to say
nothing of Rory Redbeard and his Erinnish companions. Not yet. Not with things unresolved.

"Outlaws?" Brennan prodded. "Outlaws *and* thieves?
Are they not one and the same?"

I shook my head. "I tried to get him back, Brennan. I did. I went back for him the next day, but
Teir—"

"Teir!" Brennan caught my arm again. "You saw
Teirnan? Spoke with him? Where? Where is he,
Keely? What did he say to you?"

I saw no profit in keeping my meeting with Teirnan
secret, since I had sworn no promises, nor had he
asked any. And so I told Brennan freely. He listened
intently as I recounted a little of my meeting with
Teirnan, but not all. To Brennan, I could not; he
would not understand. He had no doubts of his
heritage, his duty, his *tahlmorra*. He would not toler-
ate any in me. Certainly he would not understand
how I could even consider that our *a'saii* kinsman
might have a valid point . . . or two, or even three.

Which brought us back to the chestnut colt.

"What thieves?" he asked. "If you went back for
him, you know where they are."

"Where they *were*," I countered. "I doubt they
will be there now."

He shook his head, urging me toward the stables

again. "Take me there anyway . . . we may find a trace—something to tell us where they went."

"Brennan—no." I twisted my arm free. "No. Leave it be. I want nothing to do with those men."

"If you are afraid, we can go in *lir*-shape . . . they will never even know—"

"*No,*" I told him curtly. "I have coin put away—I will buy you another horse."

Brennan's short bark of laughter lacked all humor. "Are you mad? That colt was the last get of a stallion who died the day after the mare was bred—there can *be* no more, Keely! And even if there could be, you would not have the coin to buy him. *I* nearly did not—"

My temper deserted me. "A *horse!*" I shouted. "Not a woman, a child, a *lir* . . . gods, Brennan, you drive me mad—can you think of nothing else save your horses? What about Aileen? What about Aidan? What about *me?*"

"You," he agreed. "Aye, let me think about you; about why you stand here so afraid of showing me where outlaws tried to steal your coin, and perhaps your virtue—" It brought him up short. He stared, going gray around the mouth. "Gods, Keely—they did *not*—"

"No," I said shortly. "No, they did not—do you think I would let them? I had a knife, *rujho* . . . and the Erinnish—"

"*Erinnish!*" Brennan nearly gaped. "They were Erinnish? Keely—"

My hands were fists. "Gods, Brennan, enough! *Enough!* I tried to get the colt back—I did try—but I could not. Does it matter who stole him? He is gone, *gone*—" I clamped hands against my head. "I swear, you will drive me mad—always asking questions!" I swung on my heel and walked away.

"Keely. Keely!"

I ignored him.

Brennan said something very rude in Old Tongue. I swung around, snapped back at him, tried to turn, but he had my arm yet again. "Keely, *wait*—"

But I did not. I twisted free, tapped the earth magic, felt air beneath my wings—

—and the paw that slapped me down.

I lay sprawled on my back on hard cobbles, human again, staring blurrily up at the tawny mountain cat who stood over me, one paw on either side of my neck. He is large, is Brennan, in *lir*-shape, and worthy of attention.

The tail twitched. Lashed. Then whipped down to smack my shin. I gritted teeth as the cat reached out one paw, extended one precise claw, and patted my left cheek. Like a man goading another to fight.

Or a brother warning a sister.

"Get off!" I shouted at him, rolling my head away from the paw. "Or would you have us settle this as cats, and let the tale make the rounds of Mujhara, where some still call us demons?"

The tail thwacked my leg again, and then the cat was moving, changing, flowing aside to alter fur into the flesh of a man. But the eyes were the same, and the anger.

"Aye," he agreed coldly, "let us consider the Homanans. Let us settle it as they do." He reached down, caught a wrist, jerked me to my feet. Took me to the guardroom and banged on the door.

Lio answered it. "My lord?"

"Swords," Brennan said curtly. "Hers, and one for me. Yours will do."

I drew a breath. *"Rujho*—"

"Now," he told Lio, who found my sword and his own with admirable haste, and gave them both to Brennan, who thrust mine into my arms and pointed. "There. Let us see precisely how good you are." He paused. "Or are not."

"Brennan—"

He jerked Lio's blade free and threw the sheath to the bench. "*Now*, Keely. Not ten years from now—if your tongue and temper have not gotten you killed by then. Or, for that matter, by tomorrow."

"*Ku'reshtin*," I said calmly, and stripped my sword naked.

Two

Perversely, I was content. The anger melted away into determination, a cold, quiet calm that lent me the focus I needed. Brennan is not a truly gifted swordsman—I doubt any Cheysuli can be, lacking proper dedication—but he is strong and quick and solidly grounded in technique. I was no less so, since he had taught me what he knew, but it had been nearly two years since we had faced one another and I had improved tremendously.

Over the blade, I grinned. "Well met, *rujho*—"

But Brennan wasted nothing, not even his breath on me. He engaged before I could blink.

Sparring only, but with an element of genuine risk. Blades clashed and hissed, filling the bailey with song. I grunted, caught my breath, expelled it noisily, bit my lip, spat blood, gritted teeth until they ached.

He beat me across the cobbles to the wall Lio and I had slapped. And then turned me, working me back toward the guardroom.

I stopped him, held him, pushed him back three steps. Then he came on again.

I was dimly aware of people gathering in the bailey. Guardsmen, grooms, horse-boys, even passing servants. I heard mutters, comments, wagers being made. Not on me, I hoped; Brennan was clearly winning.

It made me angry. I had expected him to hold back because of my gender. It was not what I *wanted* from an opponent, but I had come to expect it. Come to depend on it; an advantage I enjoyed. But this time, *this* time, Brennan gave me none. He had a point to make, and he was using his to do it.

We were nearly to the guardroom. I caught a heel, went down on my back, dropped my blade, tried to snatch it up again, but Brennan trapped it with the tip of his own and slung it away from me. It rattled and rang on the cobbles.

I rolled onto belly, trying to stretch and catch the hilt, but Brennan's sword tip was at my reaching hand, stinging flesh. I snatched it back, cursing, tried again with the other, suffered another sting. And then the tip was at my throat, pressing me onto my back, guiding me gently down upon the cobbles. I sprawled there, hot-faced and humiliated, and impugned his ability with every epithet I could think of.

Brennan listened, and laughed. He lifted his blade, paused, brought it slashing down.

And stopped it, precisely as he intended, with the edge caressing my throat. Tipped my head back easily with only a single nudge. "So," he said, "now you know."

That I could lose, aye. I had not expected to win. I had expected only to prove I was good enough; instead I had failed. As before, I sprawled on the cobbles, with Brennan over me. This time in human form, but the degradation was the same. With claw or with sword, he had forced his will upon me.

But he was brother, not enemy. We did not fight in truth, only to settle a point.

Another time, I told myself. *There will be another time.*

I shut my eyes. Willed the anger to go. In a moment, so did the sword.

Brennan tapped my boot-toe with his own. "Keely, come up. Here—take my hand."

I took it. He snapped me up, released me, bent

and scooped up my sword. I accepted it with a muttered, *"Leijhana tu'sai."*

Brennan assessed my temper. Then slowly grinned.
"You were better than I expected."

My mouth hooked wryly. "So were you, *rujho.*"

He laughed. Slapped a hand against my back to
brush away the dust and nearly knocked me down.
"Now," he said lightly, "will you tell me about the
outlaws? Erinnish, I think you said?"

I looked past him, focusing abruptly. I did not
answer him, being unable. All I could do was stare.

Ian. Deirdre. *Jehan.* Along with all the others.

Frowning, Brennan turned to follow my gaze. And
stiffened, even as I had, though he had less cause,
being Brennan, who *always* has less cause. Which
meant I was the one who would bear the brunt of
our father's displeasure.

Well, it had happened before.

I sighed, glanced at Brennan, strode across the
cobbles to halt before the Mujhar. "I started it."

Gravely, he nodded. "So I assumed, when Lio came
to tell me my son and daughter were fighting."

I scowled. Lio again; I would speak to him later.
As for now, from my father, there was no sign of
anger. No sign of impending punishment. I waited a
moment for something more; when he did not ap-
pear prepared to say anything else, I frowned a
little. Glanced around at the crowd who had gathered to watch the Mujhar's son and daughter match
strong blades and stronger wills, and realized he
would do or say nothing in front of so many people.

A quick glance at Deirdre showed me apprehension melting away into relief. A look at Ian showed
me a man openly amused and not in the least afraid
to display it even before his royal brother. He nodded a little and grinned at me, which made me feel
better.

"But I lost," I told him.

My father glanced swiftly at Ian to see what had prompted my comment. And frowned, but only a little; he had learned the value of giving nothing away in public.

Brennan came up beside me. "She is not due all the blame," he said. "I suggested the match, *jehan* . . . I thought it was time she learned what it is for a woman to fight a man. Particularly a man unimpressed by her gender, and more than willing to overlook it while wielding a sword against her."

"*Leijhana tu'sai*," I said sourly.

Brennan laughed and touched my shoulder briefly. "You did well enough," he said. "Griffon has improved you."

"But not enough. Not *near* enough; how many times did you break through my guard?" I asked. "How many times did you—"

Our father broke in at that. "*Enough*," he said. "Quite enough, from both of you." His single eye was stern, though his tone was mild in deference to those watching. "I am quite certain you have impressed everyone with your prowess, Keely, and certainly your courage, which means your point has been made. Which means you can put away the sword and think of other things."

I grinned at him, unperturbed; Ian was my ally. And I *had* proved something, though not as well as I might have liked. "Other things, *jehan*? Such as weddings and having babies?"

My father sighed. "It would be best, aye . . . but I know better than to expect it."

I nodded. "Good. I would prefer not to be predictable; it makes a person boring." I glanced again at Ian and saw the laughter in his eyes. It made me grin back, failure diminished, and then I turned to Brennan. "Another time, *rujho*."

"No," our father declared.

Brennan made no answer, which did not in the

least surprise me. I also kept my silence, which our
father accepted as assent, and watched as he took
Deirdre's arm and escorted her back toward the palace entrance.

I looked at Brennan. "Promise me, *rujho*."

He sighed noisily. "Keely, you heard what he said."

"Aye, I heard. But promise me, Brennan. Once
more only. Win or lose, I will be content. Only give
me one more chance."

"What will it hurt?" Ian asked.

Brennan stared at him in surprise. "You support
this madness?"

Ian shrugged. "What is madness, *harani*? She is
refused the chance merely because of her sex. If
Keely were a man, Niall would not say no. It is only
because he thinks Sean may not want a sword-wielding
cheysula that he refuses to let her learn. He is afraid
to risk the union."

Brennan's tone was flat. "Because if Aidan dies, he
needs the blood from other sources."

"Aye," Ian agreed, sparing Brennan nothing. "You
should understand what it is to put so much value on
a union that other feelings no longer matter. Not
even the feelings of your children; you simply do
what must be done. And so, because there is risk to
the prophecy if Aidan dies, Keely's life becomes all
the more precious." His eyes were on me. "The
union is necessary. So is the Mujhar's caution."

I frowned. "But *you* advocate that we fight again."

"Because you will let it gnaw your belly to pieces if
you do not, just as Niall did when he was told not to
do a thing he wanted to do badly. I remember, even
if he does not." Ian, smiling, shrugged. "Once more,
you said. I think it will do no harm."

Brennan sighed again and waved a hand to indi-
cate resigned surrender. "Once more, then. When?"

I shook my head. "Not yet. Later. When I have
learned a little more. I will tell you when." And then,

thinking again of Erinnish brigands and a curious older brother, I made haste to go away. Taking my sword with me.

It was to Ian I went later, rather than to my father. I knew what the Mujhar would say, bound up by paternal duties. But Ian had none of those burdens, which took away the barriers and allowed me to speak freely.

He opened his door at my knock. Arched eyebrows as he saw me, but stood aside to let me enter. Shut the door behind me, then waited quietly as I glanced blindly around the chambers, wondering if I should go even though I wanted to stay.

"You may sit," he said. "Or pace, if you prefer."

I looked at him sharply. "You know me too well, *su'fali*—do you know why I have come?"

He smiled and sat down in an X-legged chair. "No. But I know you are Cheysuli, even without the color . . . and I know how these walls can chafe us. How they bind our souls too taut."

"*Is* it the walls?" I asked. "Or the prison of our duty?"

Ian's smile died. "Both," he told me quietly. "Have you only just come to know it?"

I stared at him. "Do you mean—*you*—? You, *su'fali*? But—I thought—"

"—that as liege man to the Mujhar, I could only relish the duty?" He shook his head. "No, Keely . . . I am as troubled as you by the burdens of honor-bound oaths, by the demands of the prophecy."

"Is that why you supported my bid for another sword fight?"

He stroked his bottom lip with a negligent finger. "Oh, partly. And partly because you deserve a second chance." He gestured to a second chair. "Why not sit, Keely? Pacing wears down the knees."

I sat. Stretched out my legs, knees intact, and frowned at him pensively. *"Su'fali—"*

Quietly, he overrode the beginnings of my question. "Keely, what I told you outside was the truth. The union is necessary, which makes Niall's caution understandable. He has no wish to curb your spirit, but he must. You are too impulsive at times, inviting accident." He gestured a little. "Today, as an example; you might have been hurt. You might have been killed."

I shook my head. "Not with Brennan, *su'fali*. Nor with any of Mujhara, they all know who I am. And besides, I know how to fight."

Ian sighed. "Arrogance born of ignorance . . . aye, well, Niall was as guilty of it when he was young. It is why I do not approve of the royal fledglings being kept so close to the mews." He smiled a little and shifted. "Keep-raised children know better; they have learned to trust no one at all, until that trust is earned. 'Solde and I grew up in Clankeep, but Niall did not. It left him unprepared for the world."

I stared at him in shock. "My *jehan?* But he went by himself to Valgaard and faced Strahan alone."

Ian shrugged a little. "Well, he went with me, but I fell ill . . . aye, in the end, he did face Strahan alone. And that is what shaped him, Keely . . . Strahan, Lillith, the plague, the loss of a *jehan*, also a war with Solinde." He looked at me intently. "It was much the same with your *rujholli*. Before they came back from Valgaard, none of them were men. Warriors only in name, even with the training. Because until they faced the demands of their *tahlmorras*, they were nothing but lumps of clay. Strahan fired each of them in the kiln of Asar-Suti."

I felt oddly cold, disliking intensely the prickling of my scalp. "Are you saying I, too, must face Strahan?"

"By the gods, I *hope* not!" He thrust himself upright in the chair. "I would wish Strahan on no one, and never on one of our House; do you think I am a fool?"

His intensity took me aback. "But—you just said—"

Ian sighed and slumped back again. "It was an example, Keely. I was pointing out how loss and hardship can shape a soul. Carry a boy from childhood to manhood." He waved off the beginnings of my question. "I mean only that you too readily assume no danger can befall you. You are Keely of Homana, Cheysuli, and daughter to the Mujhar. Your power is greater than most, which intensifies your belief that nothing can ever harm you." He touched a finger to his head. "In here, or without—" The finger moved to his heart, "—and certainly never here. Where it can hurt the most."

I drew in a deep breath, then expelled it slowly. In its place fear crept in. "I am afraid, *su'fali*."

"Something I well understand." There was distance in his eyes that spoke of private things. Things he would not divulge in words, but revealed all the same in posture and eloquent eyes.

"But you dealt with it," I told him.

"Did I? *Do* I? Or do I simply ignore it?" He shook his head slowly. "I sired a child on Lillith. An Ihlini-Cheysuli child, who serves Asar-Suti. *Abomination*, Keely; she should not be allowed to live. I should have hunted her down. Should have made sure of her death. But I did not, ignoring it; believing, somehow, that such a course would alter her aim . . . gods, I was a fool—" he sighed, "—and Brennan paid the price. Now *another* such child, bred for Strahan's amusement, for Strahan's purposes." For a long moment he was silent, then shook his head again. "The Wheel of Life keeps turning, too often repeating itself."

I looked at him without blinking, transfixed by his

eyes. "I could stop it," I told him. "I could stop the Wheel."

"How?" my uncle asked, when he saw I did not jest.

"By not marrying Sean of Erinn."

He frowned. "Oh, I hardly think—"

"*I* do. If Aidan dies, and he might, it all comes down to me. And what if I refused?"

He sat like a stone in the chair, not even so much as blinking. And then he blinked, and smiled. "You will not," he said gently. "You are not that selfish."

Am I not? I wondered. *Oh, but I think I am . . . gods, but I think I could be.*

Given reason enough.

But for now, I was not selfish, looking at my uncle. "*Su'fali,*" I said, "is there nothing to bring you peace?"

After a moment, he nodded. "Her death," he said, "or mine."

"Rhiannon is your daughter."

"She is a servant of the Seker."

"Blood of your blood, *su'fali.*"

The flesh of his face was taut. "I think not, Keely. I think it has been replaced with the excrement of the Seker."

Relentlessly, I went on. "And when Rhiannon came here, clad in the garments of subterfuge, you welcomed her. I recall it clearly, *su'fali.* I was in the room."

"Unknowing, I welcomed her. Ignorant of the truth."

"And had she come to you begging for mercy? Asking for your protection? Throwing off her *jehana's* designs?" I paused, sensing his pain; the anguish of grief denied. "Would you have felt the same?"

His tone belied the pain. "What do you want, Keely? Why do you ask these things?"

"Blood," I told him simply. "We hold it in such esteem, this blood of our ancestors. And yet when it comes to Ihlini blood mixed with our own—*the blood of our ancestors*—you say it should be spilled."

"And so it should," he answered, "when the Ihlini try to spill ours."

"But not all Ihlini," I said. "There are those who desire peace as much as we do, turning their backs on Asar-Suti. Does it make them enemy?"

"Keely—"

"There are those of the Cheysuli who no longer serve the prophecy. Does it make them enemy? Does it make them servants of Strahan, or merely of themselves?"

Ian shut his eyes and slumped. Wearily, he said, "Teir has been at you, then."

"Not *at* me . . . he spoke to me, aye, and explained how he feels . . . how the *a'saii* feel, who fear to lose their *lir*."

Ian's eyes snapped open. "Is that what he told you? Is that the lever he used?"

I felt the flare of resentment, waited until it abated. "He came to me and told me why they feel the way they do. Why it is impossible for them to work toward an end that will be the end of *us*."

"And he suggested you not marry Sean." The intensity of his anger was as startling as it was sudden. "By the gods, girl, I gave you more credit for sense . . . how can you be so blind? How can you be such a lackwit?" He rose and stood before me, no more the tolerant kinsman but liege man to the Mujhar, and an angry Cheysuli warrior. "Teirnan wants the Lion. Teirnan has *always* wanted the Lion . . . and this is how he gets it. Because if Aidan dies, it does come to you—as you yourself have said." He drew in a steadying breath. "If you refuse to marry Sean, there will be no proper heir . . . there will be no proper blood—"

"I know," I said. "I know very well what it means: Teir will inherit the Lion."

"Then if you *know*—"

I stood and faced him squarely, strung so tight I nearly trembled. "What if he is right? What if the *lir* do go? What does it leave us, *su'fali?* What does it make the Cheysuli?"

"Teirnan is an ambitious, avaricious fool."

"I know all that!" I shouted. "But *what if he is right?*"

Ian looked at Tasha, sprawled in his bed with her cubs. She stared fixedly back at him, but the link was conspicuously empty of conversation, empty of what she felt.

Blankly, he said, "I asked her once before—asked her if it were true—if the *lir* were meant to leave us—"

Fear stirred sluggishly. "What did she say?"

"Nothing," he said, "as now. Tasha holds her silence. Tasha keeps her secrets."

Something inside me broke. "Oh, gods, *su'fali*—oh, *gods*—what happens if Sean is dead?"

His head snapped around. *"What?"*

"What happens if Sean is dead? Does it end? Is it over? Does Teir win after all? Or do the Ihlini win?"

Frowning, he shook his head. "Keely, there is no reason to believe—"

"Oh, there is," I said hollowly. "Sean may indeed be dead."

He said nothing at all, asking no questions at once, demanding nothing of me. He merely put his hands on my shoulders, guided me into the chair, sat me down again. Then knelt in front of me quietly, holding my hands in his. "I think you had better tell me."

I told him all I knew. Of stolen colts and knives; of Liam's bastard son. Knowing now, better, the weight of possibilities; the promise of things undone.

I *could* stop the Wheel. If Rory had not himself.

Three

Ian released my hands and stood up, staring hard into distances though he looked directly at me. "Niall must be told."

"No!" I said sharply. Then, more quietly, "Promise me, *su'fali* . . . say nothing to *jehan*."

He shook his head. "This concerns him, Keely. This concerns us all."

I drew in a deep breath and tried to remain calm, knowing too much emotion would tip him away from me. "But we cannot be certain Sean is dead. It is only a possibility." I sat very upright on the edge of the chair, hoping the reasonable tone of voice was enough to keep him bound, if only for the moment. I needed time to think. "If you tell *jehan* that Sean is dead, murdered in a tavern brawl by his bastard *rujholli*, you may well set in motion events that could cause us harm."

He said nothing, patently unimpressed. Watching me and other things, distant things. Things I could not see.

I needed something more. Another reason, a *better* reason—and then it came to me. The reason Rory himself had used to win the promise from me. "How would Aileen feel? Or Deirdre, hearing news that may or may not be true, and not knowing which to believe?" I shook my head. "It would cause Aileen much grief, and she needs none of it just now. What she needs is her ignorance, until the truth is known."

Now he was frowning, clearly perturbed. "Keely,

we have no time to waste. If we sit here waiting for news from Erinn that may or may not come—"

"But we must," I insisted quietly. "If Sean is dead, it will come. And then you know what *jehan* will do." I grimaced and pushed myself back in the chair. "Open the bidding again."

Gone was the wry amusement. He was deadly serious now. "There is far more to this than your likes and dislikes."

Guilt flickered briefly. "Aye," I agreed. "But if you tell him, and he, in his Mujharish wisdom, sees fit to betroth me to someone else without knowing the truth of the matter, what happens if Sean is *alive?*" I spread my hands in a questioning gesture. "I am then promised to two men. And you know as well as I what broken betrothals can cause."

In view of our history, it was a telling blow. Had it not been for Homanan Lindir's repudiation of Ellic of Solinde in favor of a Cheysuli, there would have been no *qu'mahlin*. And the threads of prophecy would have been knotted that much sooner, leaving Teirnan with nothing to use as a means to rebel.

Ian, thinking deeply, turned away from me and paced absently to a table. He paused, gathered up the silver prophecy bones, began to pour them, chiming, from one hand to the other. "Time," he said softly. "That is the key to the truth."

I drew in a deep breath. *"Su'fali—"*

He swung around once more, cutting me off intently. "How long has Rory Redbeard been in Homana?"

I shook my head. "He did not say. Not long, I think—" I shrugged. "I could not say, either."

"And did he tell you when this tavern brawl occurred? Three months ago? A sixth-month?"

Again, I shook my head. *"Su'fali—"*

"Time," he repeated, pouring the bones again, back and forth, back and forth. "The first thing Liam would do is send word to Niall, as well as to

Aileen and Deirdre. That means if this tavern brawl occurred a sixth-month ago, the likelihood is that Sean is alive. We would know by now if he had been killed."

Numbly I said, "Messages go astray."

Bones chimed. "Aye, so they do. Which means it might be wise for us to send to Liam ourselves."

Tension knotted my belly. "Then you *will* tell *jehan*—"

Ian shook his head, still frowning a little. "No. Not yet. I think it might be better if we kept this between us, at least until the truth can be discovered." He watched the bones a moment, then looked at me. "You should have told me sooner, but I understand your apprehension. No, I will say nothing for the moment. It seems likely if something befell Sean just before this Redbeard sailed, we should hear very soon. If not, we must assume Sean survived."

Wearily, I sighed. "I would prefer to know."

"It is necessary to know, for the safety of Homana." His expression was unyielding. "Do you know where he is?"

I shrugged. "In the wood. But he is not a stupid man; he moves his camp about."

"Could you find him?"

"I did before. In *lir*-shape, it should be a simple task." I looked at him sharply. "But I am to go to Joyenne with Brennan and Aileen, and you have no recourse to *lir*-shape while Tasha has her cubs."

His decision was quickly made. "Go to Joyenne," he said quietly. "I will send a message there, asking you to come back on one pretext or another. It will content Brennan, who might question it if you decided to go on your own. Niall will believe you are at Joyenne, Brennan that you are here. No one will question your absence from either place. It will give you an opportunity to find the Erinnish outlaw."

An honorable man, my *su'fali*, oathbound to his brother. And yet now he served another, forsaking the other he owed. I drew in a deep breath. "You would do this for me?"

The smile was slight, but present, hooking down at one corner. "For you, Keely? Perhaps. But also for Homana—"

"—and for the fate of the prophecy." I smiled back, matching his irony. "Oh, aye, of course."

"Find him," Ian said. "Be certain of what he says; it will give us the answer we need." He paused a moment, significantly. "And then you will take that answer immediately to the Mujhar and tell him, in detail, everything you know. Everything you *think*."

His price, plain and simple. All I could do was nod.

Joyenne ordinarily is only half a day's ride from Mujhara, less than that in *lir*-shape. But Erinnish Aileen was hardly strong enough to ride so far, and the bulky horse-borne litter used to transport her in comfort made the journey twice as long. I went with her, lolling languidly on bolsters, forgoing a mount to give her closer company.

Brennan rode Bane, his black stallion, accompanied by Lio and a small detachment of the Mujharan Guard. We expected no trouble between Mujhara and Joyenne, but the escort lent us as much prestige as protection. Before us all rode the young man with the banner of the Prince of Homana: black rampant lion on a field of scarlet, very similar in nature to our father's device, but smaller, and lacking the crown signifying the Mujhar's royal personage. I had thought blazons and banners ostentatious and altogether unnecessary, until Brennan pointed out such things were little different from the *lir*-bands and earring each warrior wore so proudly. The Homanans, he said pointedly, were no less hesitant about displaying their pride in heritage as we were; the banner was thus carried about the countryside whenever the

Mujhar or his heir went anywhere officially. This visit to Joyenne was not precisely official, but Brennan wanted to give Aileen as much honor as possible, in hopes of shoring up her confidence.

Riding with her in the litter, warded from road dust by gauzy hangings, I thought it unlikely a royal banner would accomplish much toward buttressing her confidence. For one, I thought her confidence unshaken; Aileen is strong and stubborn and plainspoken, needing nothing of ceremony to convince her of her worth. She was understandably depressed by the loss of the babies, but in no danger, I felt, of falling prey to a permanent affliction of her spirits.

We spent most of the journey engaged in idle conversation. The motion of the litter was relentlessly monotonous, lulling even me toward drowsiness in the late afternoon sun. I yawned, stretched, resettled myself against the cushions and contemplated the vision beyond the loose-woven fabric. Lazily, I smiled, liking what I saw.

Late spring, almost summer: thick grass was vividly lush, providing a carpet for scattered skeins of brilliant flowers, while distant trees formed a smudgy hedge of greenery against the blinding blue of the sky. All around us was meadowland cradled by undulating hills. Hedgerows formed the warp and weft of crofter holdings. Here and there, nestled within a fold of hill, was a gray stone croft with thatched roof, or a cluster of two or three whitewashed with lime. Low rock walls flowed across the land, meeting and dividing, forming boundaries. Moss carpeted the unmortared stones, binding each in place. Ivy and other vegetation took root in cracks and crevices. Some bloomed, scattering loose gemstones against the green velvet gown.

Aileen's tone was slow and soft, reflective. " 'Tis beautiful, Homana. Far more gentle than Erinn, so buffeted by the sea . . . the colors here are brighter, more vivid, like cloth newly dyed. In Erinn colors are muted, softened by mist and fog . . . everything is salty, like the sea—it soaks our wood, our sheep, our wool . . . and the wind has teeth in it, sharp teeth, biting the land, the folk . . ." She sighed, stroking back a strand of hair. "But there is power in the wind, and magic in the soul of the land . . . 'tis what gives us our strength, our pride—" Then she broke off, laughing. "Gods, but I sound like a widow grieving over a new-dead husband!"

I shook my head. "You sound like a woman who misses her home."

Aileen sighed. "Aye, well, I do, though there's no sense in it. Homana is my home now."

"There is sense in missing what you prefer," I said. "You are of the House of Eagles, Aileen, born to the Aerie of Erinn. Daughter of Liam, of Ierne, shaped by wind and sea and the soul of a wild land." I paused. "And we have clipped your wings."

"Ye *skilfin*," she said crossly, "you've done nothing of the sort. 'Tis only you're so bound up in your Cheysuliness and your own desires you can't see what others are wanting."

"I know what you want." I kept my tone inoffensive. "You want Corin."

Though she sat perfectly still, too still, something moved in her eyes. "No."

I nearly laughed. "No?"

Aileen shook her head. "I miss him, aye. I think of him often. I wonder how he fares in Atvia, trying to replace Lillith's influence with his own, dealing daily with the madwoman who is his—and your—mother . . . but no, I'm not *wanting* him. Not as I did." Her tone was oddly compassionate, as if I was the one who required comforting. "Things have changed, Keely. I took vows, made promises. 'Tis another man I'm wed to—and I've borne that man a child."

I frowned. "Does a child make that much difference?"

Aileen's eyes widened. "Oh, *aye*, Keely! Every difference there can be." Clearly, I had surprised her; she struggled to explain in terms I, childless and unmarried, could understand. 'Tis one thing to lie down with a man—'tis no burden at all when you give one another pleasure ... but another thing entirely when you bear that man a child. When you *know*, looking at that man, that he's given you his seed, and that seed has taken root—" She broke off, frowning, and shook her head. " 'Tis hard, Keely ... all I can say is aye, it makes that much difference. 'Tis the Wheel of Life, turning; the promise of things to come." Finally, she said, " 'Tis *magic*, Keely ... a sacred, perfect power far greater than any other."

Something deep inside twisted. "You might have borne Corin a child."

After a moment, she nodded. "Aye. I wanted it. I wanted to be everything to him a woman should be: wife, bedmate, mother." Briefly, she smiled. "In the Old Tongue, I've been told, the words are *cheysula, meijha, jehana*." Aileen shrugged thoughtfully. "But 'twasn't to be, Keely. I was intended for Brennan, and Brennan it was I wed."

"You might have said no."

"I did." Aileen laughed at my expression. "Keely, you're not the first woman promised to a man she isn't wanting. And hardly the first to be saying no when it comes to making the vows." Absently she touched the neckline of her russet gown. Beneath the fabric lay the *lir*-torque Brennan had, Cheysuli-fashion, given her as a token of their marriage. "But when I said no, Corin said aye; he refused to steal his brother's betrothed."

Once, he might have. But Corin had changed. He had gone away to Erinn on the way to Atvia, where he had met his brother's betrothed, whom he wanted for himself as much as he wanted the Lion. And then he had gone to Valgaard and met himself, his *true* self, at the Gate of Asar-Suti. The Corin of old was banished.

The Corin I knew was gone; the boy replaced by a man.

Quietly, I said, "He would be worth more now."

"Aye. But so am I. I am *cheysula, meijha, jehana*—and I'd be changing nothing."

Impulsively I asked it, knowing I should not. "Do you love Brennan?"

"No," she answered steadily. "Not as I should."

Unexpectedly, it hurt. "But he cares deeply for you. I know it, now—I have seen it."

After a moment, she nodded. " 'Tis what grieves me most."

"But you yourself said it: you bore him a child!"

"And would again, if I could." Aileen shut her eyes, slumping against her cushions. "What do you want me to say? That I hate him? No. That I dislike him? *No*—Brennan is dear to me in many different ways. But—there is a difference. I don't love him the way I should. Not as much as I'm wanting to—" She stopped. Opened her eyes and met mine. They were hard and bright and piercing, allowing me no escape. "Not as much as you're wanting—no, I think, *needing*—to love my brother."

It shocked me utterly. *"What?"*

"You are afraid," she said gently. "Afraid to give up that part of yourself no one else has known. More than merely virginity, which is all too often a burden—" Aileen's smile was wry, "—but much, much more. No man can understand. No man can ever comprehend that a woman, bedded the first time, surrenders more than virginity. She also surrenders *self*."

Struck dumb, I merely stared.

Aileen smiled sadly. "How can I know, you're thinking. Well, we're not so different as that."

"But we are," I said numbly. "You accepted what you were given, regardless of your reasons. While I continue to fight against what they want to give me."

"Aye. You're very like Corin in that; he hated living up to expectations, although now he's far surpassed them." She smiled, bright of eyes. " 'Tis not so bad as you might think, Keely ... there's no question that in marriage you lose a part of yourself, but so does the man. And if you're wise, you work together toward making a new life, one born of both."

Grimly, I shook my head. "I have yet to meet a man willing to let me be me ... except, perhaps, for Ian, and he may give me my freedom merely because he is in no position to take it away."

Aileen smoothed the coverlet over her knees. Her tone was quiet, but with an underlying note of compassion. "I know how it's been for you, Keely. You've spent your life fighting one battle or another. You win, you lose, you compromise, dealing with each as it comes. But with a man, you're thinking there's no way you can win. That he'll *take*, not give. That he'll be stripping you of the Keely you've fought so hard to make."

Gods, how can she know—? And yet it seemed she did. She had reached in very gently and touched me in my soul, in the deepest part of my fear.

I drew up my knees and rested my forehead against them. "Aileen, I am so tired ... of losing, of winning, of compromise—of having to fight at all."

"I know," she said gently. "I understand, Keely. I know why you have to love him, and why you think you can't."

I raised my head. "How can you?"

The light was gentle on her face. Sunlight muted by gauze softened the angles of her face, dulling the vividness of her hair. "You have no reason to believe there is room for love in an arranged marriage, and why should you? You've never seen it. Not in Niall and Gisella, not in Brennan and me. There is Deirdre, aye, but she is mistress, not wife ... to you, a wife exists only to bear children, to pass on the proper blood. She is therefore unworthy of the man's love, being nothing more than a broodmare, as you've so often said."

Mutely, I nodded.

Aileen's voice was quiet. "To you, a wife is taken out of one mold and put into another, shaped to the hand of the man." Her eyes were tranquil once again, and full of empathy. "You are a proud, strong woman who's wanting nothing from that man, because whatever he can do for you, you can do for yourself."

I stared blindly at her face. "But no one will let me do it."

"And there is more, Keely. The last of all, I think, but by far the most important." She reached out and touched my hand. "For you, lacking love, lacking desire, lying with a man will be nothing more than rape."

It was not the answer I wanted. It was the only one she gave.

Four

For two days I waited at Joyenne, growing more and more restive and distracted, until at last the messenger came. I was summoned back to Homana-Mujhar, though no reason was given. Brennan thought it odd, but did nothing more than remark upon it; Aileen regretted aloud the need for me to go. I felt guilty at that, but could hardly tell her the summons was false, contrived only to learn the truth of her brother's welfare.

I made my good-byes to Aileen, then Brennan walked me out into the bailey, squinting against the noon sun. Joyenne, built of ocher-colored stone, was awash in the sunlight, a warm, welcoming patina of rich old gold. In Shaine's time it had belonged to Fergus, his brother, passing on Fergus' death to Carillon, to become the country dwelling of the Prince of Homana. Since then it had remained so, although Carillon had had little time to live in it, or Donal, or my father. Now it passed to Brennan, but he also was kept close in Homana-Mujhar. Joyenne was often empty, save for the servants keeping it in trust for absent landlords.

Brennan offered me a horse, but I declined, saying I preferred the swift freedom of *lir*-shape. My things he would send later, though I had brought little enough. I chafed to be gone, but reined in my impatience so as not to make Brennan suspicious.

"Odd," he said lightly, "but perhaps it has to do with Sean."

I glanced at him sharply, feeling the knot tie itself in my belly.

But Brennan shrugged one shoulder only, as if his curiosity was merely idle. "Liam may have sent at last, saying it is past time you and his son were wed."

"Perhaps," I agreed evenly. "Or perhaps it is Corin, saying he plans to visit."

Black brows arched up. "I would expect the message to include me as well, if that were true."

Resentment flickered briefly, then died. Lightly, I said, "Corin is *my* twin, not yours."

Brennan, understanding, merely rocked on his heels a moment, smiling wryly, locking thumbs into his belt. "Oh, aye, of course . . . but we shared something, he and I, in Valgaard, fighting Strahan. We are not the enemies we once were."

Again the resentment flickered. Corin had always been mine, in a manner of speaking, linked by birth and temperament. He and Brennan had never been close because Corin had long wanted the Homanan title and the promise of the Lion; later, he had even wanted Brennan's bride. Brennan had always claimed Hart as a boon companion, twin-born even as Corin and I were, which left the Mujhar's legitimate children evenly divided by habit as well as birth.

But Brennan spoke the truth: in Valgaard, battling Strahan, he and Corin had indeed shared something. Out of resentment and jealousy a new respect had been born.

I waited a moment, seemingly idle, then shrugged. "Aye, well, perhaps it is something entirely different . . . it may have something to do with Sean, or not. The best way to discover it is to go."

He put a hand on my shoulder, holding me back. "Keely—" He broke it off, frowning, then sighed and went ahead as I waited. "You and I have shared nearly as many misunderstandings as Corin and I . . . and I regret them. Too many times we argue for the sake of argument, trying by force of will to alter opinions, convictions, ideas . . . I think we would do better if we simply agreed to disagree, and let each of us do as he—or she—will."

I laughed at him. "I see Aileen has been at you."

He smiled, but there remained a trace of solemnity in his eyes. "She has said a thing or two, aye, but that is not what prompts me to speak now. We are very different, you and I, in temperament as well as desires and ambitions, but it does not mean we must be wrong, either of us." He sighed, shaking his head. "I think you are less selfish than I so often believe when you make noise about women being forced this way and that. I begin to think your concerns are legitimate, some of them, and that indeed women *are* made to do this or that, even against their own wishes."

I was astonished to hear such things from him, but said nothing at all for fear he would withdraw them, and his understanding. Instead, I waited in silence for him to finish, wondering how much of his new belief came from proximity to Aileen.

Brennan touched his left ear, absently fingering the remains of his lobe. Once, it had borne an earring of solid gold, shaped to mirror Sleeta, as his *lir*-bands did. But he had lost the earring and lobe to a Solindishman masquerading as Homanan, in service to the Ihlini. Not so much, I thought; he had nearly lost his life.

"It is not a Cheysuli way to make decisions for our women," he said intently, "and yet all too often I see those decisions being made for you. It is unfair; Maeve is free to do as she pleases, to wed whomever she desires to wed—though the gods know I pray those desires no longer include Teirnan—and yet you are made to wed into Erinn merely to satisfy a prophecy that *some* Cheysuli no longer believe or serve."

"Birth," I told him flatly. "Do you think for one moment that if Maeve were legitimate, she would be allowed that freedom?" I shook my head. "No indeed ... and I would be willing to wager *she* would be wed to Sean in my place, leaving me to be whatever I desired to be."

"And so now you will resent her for that as well." Brennan's tone was clipped and cool, betraying his favoritism. Save for Hart he was closest to Maeve of us all, sharing her confidences—and yet I wondered how much she was willing to share after all, even with him; it was *me* she had told of the child. Teirnan's bastard halfling.

"No," I answered quietly. "Maeve has her own *tahlmorra*, even if of her own making."

Brennan sighed in weary exasperation, making a placatory gesture that swept away our brief contentiousness. "Aye, well, let us recall our agreement, Keely."

"To disagree?" I grinned, making light of it. "Is this your way of avoiding another sword fight, Brennan? Tell the woman what she wants to hear, so she will go away?" Smiling, I shook my head. "Oh, no, *rujho*, I hold you to it."

"Aye," he said absently. "Of course, Keely—I promised."

Clearly he was troubled. And though he said many of the things I had tried to make him hear from me for years, I found myself defending the practices if only to make him feel better. "Well, it has always been so in royal Houses ... it is hardly a new thing, wedding sons and daughters into foreign lands." I shrugged. "As for the Cheysuli, we hold the Lion now. Sacrifices must be made. It is not always the women who suffer, though usually it is so—there is another side to it, as well." I smiled at him. "It is easy for me to look at Aileen and see a woman forced to

marry you. But the same was required of you, *rujho*
. . . and what if you had wanted another woman?"

Brennan said nothing. My question was innocent
enough, but between us rose the specter of Rhiannon,
daughter of Ian and Lillith, and *meijha* to the Prince
of Homana. She had made her presence felt in
Homana-Mujhar, and in Brennan's bed. He had not,
I knew, loved her, but there was more to it than
simple lust.

Something stirred inside me. Something of fear
and unease. *Ensorcellment. That only. Brennan could
never truly care for an Ihlini.*

"The child—" he began, and stopped.

"Aye," I agreed. "There is a child, *rujho*. Somewhere. Probably in Valgaard, with Strahan, at the
Gate of Asar-Suti." I drew in a deep breath. "What if
it is a boy? All this talk of Aidan's fragility, the need
for me to marry Sean so as to insure the proper
bloodline . . . what if the child you sired on Rhiannon
is a boy? Ihlini, illegitimate—but still the son of the
Prince of Homana, and grandson to the Mujhar.
The gods know the Homanan rebels tried hard
enough to put forth Carillon's bastard for the Lion,
and some even say Caro had more right than our
jehan . . . according to Homanan law, a son of your
loins could petition for a hearing on the legitimacy
of his claim. Even a son gotten on an Ihlini woman."

His jaw was hard as stone. "Such a petition would
never be granted."

"No, of course not—but the claim could be made.
Look at the turmoil when Elek put forth Caro's
name . . . it nearly divided the Homanan Council. It
could have cost our *jehan* the throne."

"Teir is bad enough," he said tightly. "Gods, he is
a fool—but I would sooner deal with him than deal
with Rhiannon."

"Ian would deal with her." I looked away from
him to the sun again, lifting a hand to shield my

eyes. "You know as well as I that Strahan is not finished. He will find a way to trouble us, to destroy our House's claim to the Lion. He will use the child, Brennan . . . he will use whatever—and *who*ever—he can."

"Gods," Brennan muttered, "I curse that Ihlini witch."

"Ihlini *and* Cheysuli." I glanced at him in concern, disliking the look in his eyes. Not knowing what to say. "I must go, *rujho*. Tend Aileen well. She is worth the care."

I left him then, before he could answer. Into the earth I went, sliding through all the layers, to tap the power that lies so unquietly in the depths of Homana's soul, waiting for release, answering instantly with an upsurging welcome that nearly hurled me free again, bereft of the wings I wanted.

—up—up—

—unfurling feathers, stretching wings, screaming triumph to the skies—

—free—

Below me, so far below, my brother stood caged in ocher stone, staring upward, shielding human eyes. Watching the falcon mount the skies and fly, reaching toward the sun. And I knew a moment's pleasure, sharp and intense, that he was not as I. Cheysuli, aye, and therefore blessed. Capable of sloughing off human flesh for the fur of a mountain cat, to run on four legs in the deep-shadowed woods. But still he could not *fly*.

An earthbound soul, my brother's.

Mine knew no limitations.

I flew straight to the wood near Clankeep and then searched it diligently, drifting here, there, soaring and circling, until at last I found them. Such small men, little more than awkward shapes, until I banked closer, closer yet, drifting down toward the

treetops. Arms and legs became more than sticks,
faces more distinct, words distinguishable. They
shouted, did the Erinnish, calling encouragement
and insults to the two men who fought.

Rory was one; from here I could see the brilliance
of his beard, afire in the sunlight. They gathered in
a clearing unscreened by limbs and leaves: eight
King's men and their captain, exiles all, two of them
matching strength and speed and skill. In their hands
were swords.

Lower still, until I settled on a low-grown bough
on a tree near the tiny clearing. I heard the clangor
of steel, the grunts of effort expended; smelled the
tang of sweat-stained flesh and damp leather. And
laughed within my falcon shape to watch without
them knowing.

It is hardly a new trick. As children, Brennan,
Hart and Corin had vied with one another often
over who would get a *lir* first, and what that shape
would be. It had been no wager in the end; Brennan
and Hart, twin-born, firstborn, had fallen *lir*-sick
within an hour of one another, and each, at thirteen,
had gone into the woods to seek a *lir*. Brennan had
come home with Sleeta, Hart with his hawk, Rael.

Corin had not been so fortunate. It had been
three more years before he linked with the vixen,
Kiri, and until that time Brennan and Hart had
often teased him by sneaking up on him in *lir*-shape,
catching him unaware. It had not been fair, adding
substantially to Corin's resentment of Brennan in
particular, but it was a trick every newly-linked
Cheysuli child played on those who still lacked a *lir*.

It was a game *I* had played, and often, when I had
come into my own gifts. I had made Hart and Brennan pay for the tricks played on Corin. And now it
seemed I could play the game again, this time with
Rory Redbeard as the victim.

He was very good with the sword. Soon enough I

lost my private amusement and watched out of interest in technique, marking his moves, his patterns, the positioning of his feet, the distribution of his weight. I watched the opponent as well, judging him for the quality of his defense, and knew he gave Rory a good match. The man did not hold back, but neither did he get through.

But they stopped too soon for me. Neither won; they stopped. Because, Rory said, the light was dying away. It would be dangerous to continue, for fear of missing a block, or turning a feint into a genuine blow. And so they stopped, calling one another names, slapping each other's shoulder, trading friendly insults. They were close to me, very close. All I needed to do was let go and drop, to shock them into silence.

Inwardly, I laughed. Time for truths, I thought, and pushed myself off the bough.

Midway down, I changed. Traded wings for arms, feathers for flesh, talons for booted feet. I heard curses, caught breaths, muttered petitions to the gods of Erinn. By then I was on the ground, standing squarely in front of Rory. Laughing at them all, but mostly at his expression.

"Try *me* with a blade," I challenged. "Sundown means nothing to me; I can see in the dark."

Hands were on swords, on knives, but no man drew a blade. Instead they stared, mouthing things beneath their breaths, stealing glances at one another to judge the degree of shock each expressed. As for Rory, he did none of it, standing quietly before me.

Then he scratched his beard. "Lass," he said lightly, " 'tis a poor way of stealing a horse to come in so boldly as this."

I grinned. "Aye, if I wanted the horse. And if I did, I would have taken him easily; do you think a Cheysuli knows nothing of stealth?"

He arched one eyebrow beneath a tangle of brass-bright hair. "I'm hardly the one to be asking a thing about the Cheysuli. I've never met one, lass . . . unless, of course, this bit of trickery is more than an illusion."

"Oh, aye," I agreed, affecting his lilt, "a wee bit more than illusion. Would you care to see it again?" I spread my hands. "Name your animal, Redbeard . . . I can be them all."

The light was behind him, blinding me to his expression. But his tone was eloquent: disapproval, disappointment. A reassessment of me. "Lass, you lied to me."

It was not what I expected. In no way. Not from a man such as he.

I stared at him. Amusement died away. Something twisted in my belly. "There was need."

"Was there?" He sheathed his sword with a hiss and click. "*Was* there?"

I felt empty inside. "Aye. Great need."

Rory made no answer. He strode past me out of the clearing, moving into the trees. Eight men followed him, leaving me alone.

I turned. Stared hard at his back before it disappeared. And then he swung back. "Come to the fire," he said. " 'Twill be worth a drink or two, the truth. If you'll be telling it to me this time."

Part of me was angry that he, a man of no honor, of exile, could take me to task for lying. Part of me was angry. Part of me was ashamed.

I went with him to the fire.

He perched himself upon a tree stump, unearthed a wineskin, unplugged it and drank deeply, even as his men found places and did much the same. And then he replugged the skin and slung it at me. I caught it awkwardly, clutching it to my belly, and felt the heat in my face.

"Drink," he advised. " 'Tis easier to explain away a lie when the tongue is properly loosened."

Pursing my lips, I nodded. "And was it easier for you to fight Sean over a wine-girl because your tongue was properly loosened?"

Brown eyes narrowed. Lids shuttered them a moment. "Aye, well, you'd be knowing nothing of that." He gestured. "Sit. Drink. Say what you've come to say."

"Ask what I've come to ask." I glanced around, saw nothing worth sitting on, settled down on the leaf-cushioned ground. And because he had challenged me, I drank the Erinnish liquor.

Rory sat with legs spread, at ease on the stump. The sun was gone and firelight took its place, painting his bush of a beard with glorious red-bronze color, flowing together with blond hair tangling freely on wide shoulders. A true brigand, the Redbeard, with a quiet compelling strength that shouted of competence. King's man, aye, and clearly a royal hatchling as much as my brothers were, or Deirdre and Aileen. A bold-faced, bright-eyed eaglet, born of Erinn's Aerie even if out of the mews.

Is Sean dead? I asked. *Did you murder your brother, Rory?*

But I asked it of myself, afraid to hear the truth.

"Ask it, then," he said curtly.

For a moment, only a moment, I did not understand. And then I recalled why I had come. "How long?" I asked. "We need to know how long it was before you sailed, so we can judge if Liam has sent—or *will* send—a message bearing word of Sean's death." I saw the widening of his eyes, then the downward lancing of his brows, the interlocking of them. "Do you see?" I asked. "If you have been here long enough—if you sailed from Erinn at once, and have been here long enough—chances are good Sean recovered. Liam would send word at once of his death—" I shrugged, "—to the Mujhar, to Deirdre, to Aileen—"

"—and to you?" Eyes narrowed, Rory nodded. "Aye, I know you, lass, *now*—'tis not so difficult to realize you're no arms-master's daughter, not coming here with such words in your mouth." He sighed, frowned blackly at the ground, picked at a tear in his leggings. "A matter of timing, is it? To decide if 'tis time to cast a net for another fish?" His head came up slowly. His eyes were black with anger. "So soon you bury Sean and look for a new husband?"

I nearly dropped the wineskin. *"No!"*

"Well, I'll have none of it." He jerked his head in a westerly direction. "Send to Liam yourself, girl . . . see what *he* has to say. I'll give you no word of when we left or how long we've been in Homana if you'll be using it to replace my brother in your halfwitted shapechanger prophecy."

Astonished, I nearly gaped. And then I laughed aloud, disregarding the look in his eyes, the set of jaw beneath the beard. "*You* are the one who murdered him. You are the one who makes these questions necessary." I slung the wineskin back at him. "You are a fool, Erinnish, to think that is why I am here; to make certain of his death so I may seek out another husband." Slowly, I shook my head. "You know nothing about me, nothing at all . . . or surely you would know that is the very last thing I would do."

Rory unstoppered the skin and drank, then nodded idly. "Aye, lass, I know little enough . . . only that you lied."

Bitterness and arrogance warred for my tongue. Both won. "You fool," I said scathingly, "do you think it would be so easy to replace him? Are you forgetting the demands of the prophecy?"

Rory spat to the side. "Are *you* forgetting I know next to nothing about it? D'ye think I care?" He rose, still holding the wineskin. "Come with me. There's a thing I have to show you."

Suspicious, I stayed where I was. "I am not a fool."

"No, only stubborn." Rory bent, caught a wrist, pulled me to my feet. "Come with me, lass. I'm thinking you might want to see the bright boyo, to know he's well looked after."

He led me through leaves, branches, foliage, walking as one with the shadows. And showed me Brennan's colt, who snorted and sidestepped as we appeared, then settled as Rory put a soothing hand on his shoulder, whispering meaningless words of reassurance. In Erinnish, of course; the tongue was made for horses.

I moved to the colt, cupped the soft muzzle, felt hot breath on palm and fingers, heard the nicker deep in his throat. "Brennan wants him back."

"Aye, so would I if I'd lost him." Rory grinned. "But I'll be keeping him, lass."

I grunted. "Unless Brennan comes for him."

"Let him. I've fought better men than the Prince of Homana." And then his tone altered from challenge to memory. "I've fought the Prince of Erinn."

I ducked under the colt's silken neck and stood on the far side, using him as a barrier. It made the words easier. "How long?" I asked again. "We must know, Rory. It has nothing to do with casting nets for a new fish . . ." I shook my head, stroking the chestnut back. "If Sean is dead, there is no one left for me. No one at all. It is Sean or no man: we need the Erinnish blood."

"Aileen is wed to Brennan. They already have a son." His mouth jerked briefly sideways. "Liam held a feast in honor of his first grandchild's birth. I beat Sean for the right to be the bairn's champion in a sword match."

"Who won the match?"

"I did."

I stared hard at the chestnut shoulder, not knowing how better to say it. "Aidan is sickly. He may not live to adulthood."

Rory said nothing immediately. And then he sighed, muttered something briefly in Erinnish, spoke wearily. "Aye, well, if the gods want him, he'll be walking the halls of the *cileann* . . ." He drew in a breath. "Aileen is young and of healthy stock—the House of Eagles breeds true . . . there will be more children. Another heir for Brennan."

"No."

Across the colt's back, he stilled.

"No," I repeated. "Aileen miscarried of twins less than a month ago. There will be no more."

"Aileen," he said sharply, and I recalled they knew one another. Aileen herself had said so.

"Well," I answered at once. "Recovering in the country; I promise, she is well. But there will be no more children. If Aidan dies, there is no heir for Homana."

Rory's tone was taut. "Men set aside barren wives."

"Brennan has said he would not."

The flesh under his eyes twitched. "It does him credit, that."

I said nothing of Homanan law forbidding it. For one, Brennan would have refused even if it were allowed. He had made it plain.

"So," I said, expelling a breath, "you see how it is with me. We need the Erinnish blood. If Aidan dies, it leaves us with none in the House of Homana." I looked away at once, to stare at nothing, seeing his expression. "You must understand, Rory—it is more than simple lack. It could be destruction."

Doubt was plain. "How?"

I ran my hands, one by one, down the colt's spine, smoothing silken hair. It gave me something to do as I tried to explain the binding service Teirnan, and too many others, no longer were able to honor. "The prophecy says one day a man of all blood shall unite, in peace, four warring realms and two magic races. The Firstborn shall come again, a man born of all the power, all the gifts, to take precedence in the world." I shrugged, twisting my mouth. "You may believe it or not, as you wish, but it is what the Cheysuli live for. It is our sacred duty."

"Duty," he echoed. "Aye, I know something of that." His face was mostly shadowed. "And without that duty the Cheysuli are as nothing?"

"So we are taught from birth." I stroked hair out of my face and tucked it behind an ear. "Beginning, ending, continuation . . . how can I say, Erinnish? I only know that if Aidan dies, the blood is denied to us."

"Until you bear children to Sean."

I met his unyielding eyes across the colt's sleek back. "It is difficult to bear children to a dead man."

Something altered in his gaze. Something *recoiled*. With a jerk, he turned away.

And swung back, shaking his head, fighting something within himself. "Lass," he said, "lass—" He shook his head again, lips pressed together. "We sailed at once," he said, "before the blood on the floor was dry. If he died, if he did die, you'll be knowing soon."

"But not yet," I said numbly.

"Soon," he repeated. "Today, tonight, tomorrow. Or perhaps a month from now, depending on the weather." His face was stark in the moonlight. "If Sean is dead, what will you do? What is left to you?"

"Prayer," I said succinctly. "A petition to the gods that Aidan survives to sire a son."

He judged my temper a moment, then smiled a little. "Not a daughter, then?"

Sourly, I said, "The Lion requires a male."

Rory Redbeard laughed. "Only because he's not met *you*."

I hardly knew the man, and yet I felt I could trust

him. There are times when strangers give better advice than friends, than kin, who seek only to give pleasure, to say what the other wants to hear, hiding honesty behind diplomacy. Rory Redbeard, I thought, would say precisely what he thought no matter what the cost. No matter who the hearer.

I told the truth to a stranger, in hopes he would understand. In hopes I might learn to myself. "I want nothing at all of Sean; of wedding, of bedding, of children."

Between us, the colt moved, stomping, stretching his neck to sample the leaves on a tree limb. Rory stood very still, saying nothing, doing nothing, hidden in shifting shadows.

"I would never wish him *dead*," I told him, meaning it, "not even to save myself. But I have no desire to marry. I want nothing to do with children."

Considering it, Rory unplugged the wineskin. "Have a drink, my lass. I'm thinking this will take time; why do it without good liquor?"

I ducked under the colt's neck, accepted the skin, watched in silence as Rory sat himself down on the ground and rested his spine against a tree. Now I could hardly see him, but I knew he was there.

Gods—how do I start?

I stared blankly down at the wineskin clutched against my belly. "Can you understand?"

"I'm not needing to, lass. 'Tis *you* requiring it."

So, I was transparent. I drank, swallowed convulsively, nearly choked, plugged the skin again. "I have three brothers," I told him. "And each of them has, in different ways, showed me what men think women are for." I saw the reflexive squint of skepticism. "Even *you*," I pointed out, "fought Sean over a wine-girl, to decide who would take her to bed."

Rory sighed, nodding. "Aye. Aye, we did . . . but lass, there are women and there are *women*—"

I silenced him with a gesture. "Women *are* women.

Men should not distinguish us dependent upon the bedding."

Rory chewed his lip, which also included his mustache. "I'll not be saying you're wrong, lass . . . but you've never been a man. You're not knowing how it is."

I smiled wryly. "As I said, I have three brothers. One of them is my twin; Corin and I have always been frank in matters of men and women."

Rory shook his head. "Unless you've *been* a man, you can't know how it is. How much a woman is *needed*."

"No," I agreed, "no more than an unblessed man can know what it is to shapechange." I sighed, crossed to him, handed down the skin. "Aileen said it best. She said when a woman gives up her virginity she also relinquishes *self*. She has her thoughts, aye, and her feelings, and can keep all locked away—but she can never be whole again. Never be *new* again. She can never be the woman she was before the man." I gestured emptily. "You have only to hear the jests regarding a woman whose maidenhead is unbroken . . . the ridicule, the insults . . . and yet when a man means to marry, he demands virginity. Certainly a king does . . . or the heir who will be king."

"Sean," he said heavily.

I kicked at the ground, toeing out a stone. "There was a man some time ago, an Erinnish sea captain, who claimed Sean a lusty man, and hot for his shapechanger princess. Sean would, he said, have her wedded and bedded and bearing an heir, all within a year." I stopped kicking abruptly. "It has stayed with me all this time. I know he meant nothing more than crude flattery—Sean is no wilted flower, he said—but think what it was to me. A promise of *usage*, Rory. A woman duly bedded, to be shown her proper place and to do the proper service by bearing her lord an heir."

Rory stared into darkness. "Words are not enough, lass—words are never enough. They say things we're not meaning to say, and twist the truth about." He did not look at me. "Too often, I'm thinking, we say what we're expected to say, to prop up fragile pride, and hide the feelings beneath."

It stabbed deeper than expected. "You should be Cheysuli."

Rory sounded puzzled. "What are you saying, lass?"

"That for us, it is harder." I shook my head. "It is tradition within the clans that true feelings, deep feelings, never be displayed. Not in public. Not where people can see, where enemies might use them. We dare not show weaknesses, and strong emotion is one of them."

Rory's disgust was plain. "And that includes affection?"

"Cheysuli say nothing of love ... at least, those who practice the old ways." I shrugged, knowing how it sounded. "Not all of us are so strict, certainly not my House. My father keeps it no secret that he loves his Erinnish *meijha*. Things are different, now, but the old ways are hard to change."

"Lass," Rory said, "why d'ye not want bairns?"

I turned away stiffly, gritting my teeth against the sudden wrench of regret. How to tell a man? How to explain that childbed is dangerous? Surely he knew it. I had said it of Aileen.

And then the words flowed easily. I turned to face him squarely. "Babies make me uncomfortable. There is no mothering in me. I would sooner do without."

"You're not the first who's thought so, lass—"

"—but of course I will change my mind? Once I have borne a child?" I sighed wearily. "So glibly said, Rory ... and in such ignorance."

"Is it?" He pushed himself to his feet and handed me the wineskin. "I'm thinking not, lass. I'm thinking you're only afraid."

Gods—how can he know—?

"Afraid," he repeated. "Of everything, I'm thinking ... of wedding, of bedding, of bairns ... of facing what women face when they leave girlhood behind." His eyes were kind in the moonlight. His truth less so. "Not so different from men, my lass. Not so different from me."

"But you are a *man*," I said.

Rory shook his head. "No man is unafraid. The one who says so is a liar."

I hugged the wineskin to me, seeking answers, peace, security. A way to be unafraid.

"Come to the fire," he said. " 'Tis time for supper, I'm thinking. My belly's clamoring."

My belly was tied in knots. *Gods, I* am *afraid.*

I wondered if Sean was also.

Five

I was panting, laughing, too winded to speak, which
suited him well enough; it gave him time to insult
me, which he did with great skill and pleasure in his
lilting Erinnish tongue. Grinning, he eyed me, nodding to himself. He was not so winded as I, but then
he had more experience, more reason to feel at ease.

"Gods—" I said, "—you are good . . . at least as
good as Griffon, and certainly better than Brennan."
I paused, sucking air, then blew out a gusty sigh of
satisfaction. "Aye, it ought to do—I will give him a
better match."

Rory pushed back hair from the tangle near his
eyes. "Will you tell me a thing, then?"

I nodded absently, scratching a bite on my forearm.

His eyes were perfectly steady. "I'd like to know
what it is from someone who ought to know, instead
of trusting to tales."

We stood facing one another in the clearing near
the camp, where I had found him a handful of days
before, near sundown. With swords in our hands,
too; Rory had, reluctantly, agreed to show me a trick
or two, but now the reluctance was gone. He enjoyed
it as much as I. The sword I used was borrowed, too,
heavy for me and unbalanced, but it was enough for
now.

Sweat ran down my face. I wiped it away with a
leather-wrapped wrist, exhaling heavily. The match,
for now, was done, and Rory had won again. "What,
what is?"

"What it is to shapechange."

I said nothing at all, meeting his too-steady eyes, then turned from him abruptly, walked into the trees, found the sheath for the sword. Its owner took it from me as I thanked him grimly, then returned to the camp. Hard-faced, secretive men, saying little to me other than what they had to say. But not, I thought, my enemies, merely respectful of my rank. I was their lord's betrothed.

If their lord is still alive.

Rory was behind me, sheathing his own sword. I swung back to face him. "You had best know what you are asking."

He was taken aback by my attitude. "Why, lass? 'Tis not a thing, I'm thinking, no one has asked before."

No, it was not. But no one had ever asked *me*.

I told myself it was a perfectly natural question, particularly from a foreigner who had no firsthand knowledge. But I found myself strangely defensive about my *lir*-gifts, oddly reluctant to readily admit to him just how different I was. Always before I had known nothing but pride in my blood, but now I felt something else. Something very much like foreboding.

If I tell him the truth, no matter how much he protests, he will believe me unnatural . . . even if he says no, he will think I am born of beasts. The unblessed always do, no matter what they say . . . I have seen it in their eyes, in the masks they wear as faces—

I broke it off with effort. The realization hurt. It hurt much worse than expected, because I had not cared before.

Accordingly, I was brusque. "I doubt you could understand, Erinnish. Take no offense—but you are an unblessed man."

"Unblessed! Unblessed?" He shook his head. "Lass, I *am* Erinnish, born of the House of Eagles . . . 'tis more in the way of blessing than many things I know."

"No, no—that is not what I meant." Irritably I kicked a stone away, aiming it toward the clearing. "Aye, you have the right of it: people have asked before. People will always ask, being horrified by the truth while fascinated by the horror."

"Lass," he said patiently, "I'm not a man to take fright. I'm not a man to scoff. Aileen married a mountain cat, Deirdre lives with a wolf . . . and I have seen *you* change."

I looked at him levelly. "No one can understand. They hear stories, trade tales, foster untruths, all the while making ward-signs against us." I shook my head grimly. "Not all, of course, but more than enough. There are still those who prefer to hear the darker side of the magic because it makes a better tale."

"Darker side," he echoed.

I stared hard into the clearing, not looking at him. "There is a story, a tale of a man who lost control . . . a warrior who lost himself. There is always the risk, of course; *lir*-shape is seductive." I glanced at him intently. "He stayed too long and lost himself, forsaking his human form. Caught in *lir*-shape forever, but now was something in between. He lost the sense of either side, becoming a little of both."

Rory frowned. "I thought you told me there was this thing of the death-ritual."

"He was no longer human, no longer truly Cheysuli. Such things only bind those who are willing to be bound. He was not. He was beast, abomination . . . man and wolf in one."

"Wolf," he said involuntarily, recalling traditional fear.

I nodded. "But not bound by a wolf's behavior, nor by a man's humanity. He was a thing of night-mare." I shook my head, twitching shoulders to dismiss prickling flesh. "I cannot say if the tale is true, only that it exists. Only that Homanans used it—*use* it—to frighten naughty children."

Slowly, he nodded. "And yet, it might be true. Is that what you're telling me?"

I drew in a breath. "Aye, it might be true. There is such a thing as losing balance. As I have said, *lir*-shape is seductive."

All his humor was banished, replaced by solemnity. "Tell me," he said. "Let it be truth from one who knows."

I shook my head decisively. "Words are not enough. *Lir*-shape is born of magic, shaped of power . . . there are no words for that. Only the knowledge of *feeling*."

"Tell me," he repeated. "Make me feel it, lass . . . if only for a moment."

He was deadly serious, and therefore deserving of truth no matter how discomfiting. No matter how alien.

Then let him have the whole of it. "Sit," I suggested.

Rory sat, placing the sheathed sword beside him on the ground. As always, he used a tree for a back rest.

I knelt down before him, tucking heels beneath my buttocks. "Close your eyes," I told him.

"Lass," he said doubtfully.

"Close your eyes, Erinnish. Unblessed eyes are blind."

After a moment, he closed them. "Be gentle with me, lass. I only asked a question."

"And I will answer it." I drew in a deep breath. "Think of nothing," I said. "Think of *nothingness*; lose yourself in emptiness, in the utter absence of self. Banish Rory entirely; live only for the *being*."

Slowly the flesh of his eyes loosened. The line in his brow went away. His breathing was deep and even.

"There is power," I said, "much power. And if you know how, you can tap it . . . if you are Cheysuli. If you have the blood. If the power acknowledges you." I reached out, touched his hands, took them into my own. *"Sul'harai,"* I told him, "the union of man and woman. The binding of warrior to earth—or, in my case, a woman; once, it was always so."

Sweat ran down his face. Rory said nothing at all.

"Power," I repeated, "unlike any you have known. And at your call, it answers, binding flesh, blood, bone: giving back other things. Flesh. Blood. Bone. But of a different shape."

Rory's mouth slackened.

"There is a moment," I said, "when you are neither being. Neither man nor animal, nothing more than formlessness, waiting for the shape. But it comes, it always comes, and you are free, *freed,* to be what you must be, dictated by the gods. Mountain cat, fox, hawk; wolf, owl, bear. Whatever you must be, dictated by the blood." I tightened my fingers on his. "*You* are an eagle, Rory—a bright, bold eagle born of Erinn's Aerie, above the cliffs of Kilore. Below you the Dragon's Tail, smashing against the shoreline . . . below you the fishing boats, coming home on the tide . . . below you the House of Eagles, perched atop white chalk cliffs . . . below, forever below—*you are the lord of the air,* the sovereign of the skies . . . there is magic in your blood and power in your bones—the hard, bright knowledge that you are different from men, that you are *better* than men: higher than they can go, freer than they can be, able to ride the wind even as they are bound to the earth, to ships, to legs, to horses—" I gripped his hands in my own. "So much freedom, Rory—so many fetters broken—so much power loosed to fill your wings with wind . . . and you fly, *you fly,* where no one else can go . . . being what no one else can be: born of the earth but not bound to it, because it lives in your soul, your heart, your flesh, locked inside your bones. Burning in your blood." I drew in a trembling breath, as lost in the moment as he was. "*Sul'harai*, Rory: a perfect and binding union." I paused. "And like all of them, it ends."

He did not speak at once. When he could, his voice was hoarse "*Why* must it end?"

"There always must be an ending, or your true shape can be lost. The thing that makes you human."

"And if I found I preferred the other?"

I let go of his hands. "You would be beast: abomination. A thing of ancient nightmares, like the tale I told you of the warrior who lost his soul to his other form . . . or whatever was left of it."

Rory opened his eyes. He was lost also, swallowed by distances, by things he had never known. Of things he could never share, even as I had shared them; he was an unblessed man.

I had lent him a piece of my soul. Now I wanted it back.

"Lass—"

I drew in a very deep breath and gave him my innermost truth. The thing that made me different from any other woman, from any other Cheysuli, because with my gifts came a sacrifice I had acknowledged long ago. "Do you see now," I said clearly, "why I have no need of a man?"

His eyes sharpened at once. Plainly, he understood. "Oh—gods—*lass*—"

"What man can give me that? What man would even *try*?"

"I would," he told me fiercely. "Why d'ye think I asked?"

—*oh, gods—oh, no*—

Unsteadily, I rose. "You are a fool," I said tightly, "and I a fool for staying. It is time I went back to Mujhara."

He gathered his sword and stood. "Will you be taking this with you, then?"

I thought he meant the sword. Then I saw the knife. My silver Cheysuli long-knife, aglint with royal rubies. "But—you said . . . I thought—"

"Hearth-friends, aye," he agreed, "and knives to mark the bond. But there is more to us now, I'm thinking . . . whether you know it or not."

Helplessness welled up. *"Ku'reshtin,"* I muttered.

"And other things, I'm thinking. So are you, my lass."

Grimly I accepted my knife and gave him back his own. "And the colt, as well?"

Rory Redbeard laughed. "I'm thinking not, my lass . . . the bright lad stays with me."

I shoved my knife home in its sheath and took to the air as an eagle. To show him what it was. To show him what he missed.

But I knew no triumph in it. Only emptiness.

I lost *lir*-shape near Mujhara. Abruptly, unexpectedly. Full of shock and outrage I tumbled toward the ground, using wings to break my fall even as the eagle-form turned itself inside out.

Wait—oh, gods—wait . . . what is happening—how can it happen—?

There was no answer, only a cessation of the *lir*-shape. Like a ewer of water used up, the magic was gone from me.

How—?

It simply happened. One moment I was an eagle, the next something in between. And finally a woman, possessed of arms instead of wings.

I was fully human as I landed, and though it was unpleasant and painful, it was not so hard, thank the gods, as to hurt me seriously, since the wings had lasted long enough to bear me close to the track. Mostly it bruised my pride. Sprawled awkwardly and undecorously—thank the gods I wore leggings in place of skirts!—I stared hot-faced at the man on the horse and mouthed angry, embarrassed curses.

For someone who, one moment, had been riding unconcernedly down the road leading into Mujhara and the next nearly struck by a falling eagle busily resolving itself into a woman, he was remarkably unperturbed. The horse was more upset. Absently, he soothed it, speaking words in a foreign tongue.

The knowledge was sudden and ugly. I thrust myself to my feet, reaching for my knife. "Ihlini," I challenged furiously. "What else could bring me down?"

I expected some manner of reaction, some expression of his feelings, even if only in posture. Instead, he inclined his head politely in a courtesy that rankled. "My apologies," he said quietly, still soothing the spotted horse. "When the gods created their children, they might have thought of this. It is a bit disconcerting."

It was not at all what I expected. Angrily, I began, "The gods—" but let it go, thinking of other things. "Why are you here?" I asked. "Why do you come to Homana?"

"To see the Mujhar," he told me. "I have an invitation."

"*No* Ihlini—" I stopped. Looked more closely at him: white-haired, blue-eyed, exceedingly fair of face. Ancient in the eyes, young in his demeanor. Anger spilled away, replaced with realization. "You are Taliesin." Heat crept into my face as shame stung my breasts. "Oh, gods, of course you are . . . they told me what you were like. Brennan, Hart, Corin . . . even our *jehan*." Distractedly, I took my hand from the knife hilt. "I am Keely, Niall's daughter . . . I apologize for my rudeness."

"I know very well who you are, regardless of your *lir*-shape—though that, I agree, is eloquent proof of identity." Taliesin smiled. "You are very much like Corin in ways other than coloring . . . he has a tongue in his mouth, and wit enough to wag it. You, I see, do also, if in a prettier mouth."

I twisted my pretty mouth. "Harper born and bred, regardless of race . . . your own tongue is much too glib."

He laughed. Once the harper of Tynstar himself, until he chose otherwise. Until Strahan ruined his hands. "Aye, well, there is little occasion for me to flatter a woman, meaning it or not. In your case, I mean it; you have a reputation." His eyes were amused, though his tone inoffensive. "As for this thing of rudeness, I think it is certainly pardonable in view of the circumstances. The fall might have killed you. For that, *I* apologize."

I disavowed it quickly with a dismissive wave of my hand. "You are welcome among us," I told him, echoing the ritual greeting of a clan-leader. "*Jehan* will be glad to see you. He has always wished you could come." I grinned. "Ihlini or no, you have done our House many services. Even the Lion is grateful."

Memories crowded close; I could see it in his eyes. So many services, for so many of my House. First my father, who had lost an eye to Strahan's hawk . . . then to Brennan, Hart, Corin, as they escaped from Valgaard. Fleeing Strahan himself, and his noxious god. Asar-Suti, Ihlini call him: the god of the nether-world. The Seker, who made and dwells in darkness.

I swallowed painfully, recalling how each of my brothers had come home from that god, and what had been done to change them from the boys I knew into men. Especially Corin, who had left the woman he loved to go back to Atvia. I had not seen him again.

Taliesin sighed. "The Lion," he said obscurely, "knows me as well as you." And then he was smiling, if sadly, stroking a wisp of hair from his eyes with a twisted, knotted hand. "I know Hart and Corin are gone, but I will be glad to see Brennan. The news I have concerns him as well as Niall. And you as well as them; all of the House of Homana."

A chill slid down my spine. "Why are you come?" I asked. "Not for pleasure, then—it is far more serious." I wet my lips as he nodded. "What news, Taliesin, that brings you down from Solinde? That brings you down alone, without Caro to be your hands?" I took a step closer to the horse, catching one of the reins to hold him in place; realization turned my spine's chill to ice. "You are *alone*, Taliesin ... but you are never alone. What has become of Caro?"

"Caro is dead," he said. "Strahan is loose on the land."

Six

My father is not an emotional man. Perhaps he was once, in his youth—Ian had said as much—but he had changed. For as long as I have known him, he has hidden much of what he thinks. Out of habit, if not inclination; a Mujhar can say little without putting much thought to it, or suffer the consequences. I was beginning to learn that even kings are bound by expectations, as much as the folk who serve them.

When I brought Taliesin to my father in Deirdre's sunny solar, I expected some measure of joy. Some reflection of happiness. But he knew. He knew at once. And quietly bade Taliesin to give him the whole of it.

The Ihlini harper stood quietly in the solar, refusing the wine Deirdre offered, the chair Ian did. His crippled hands he thrust within the sleeves of his belted blue robe, putting them out of sight. And yet the words he said banished hiding places.

"I was wrong," he said. "I thought he would not look so hard for us, nor so close; we have been safe in the cottage for years. Under his very nose . . ." Taliesin sighed, dismissing it consciously. "He came, with others, to our cottage. He said he had grown weary of my interference, of my service to the House of Homana in place of the House of Darkness." Something twisted his face briefly. "That is what he called it: the House of Darkness. Ruled by Asar-Suti, with Strahan as his regent."

"Or his heir?" My father rubbed the flesh of his

brow beneath the leather strap. "My sons believe Strahan fully expects to trade humanity for godhood. That he serves not so much out of a genuine conviction, but out of greed, out of ambition . . . out of perverse intent to assume a place of his own in the pantheon of the Seker."

Taliesin stared at him. Slowly the color drained from his ageless face. "He—would not . . . he *could* not, unless—" He stopped.

Ian turned from a deep-silled casement. "Unless?"

Unsteadily, Taliesin sought a chair, the chair he had declined, and sat down, hunching forward, hugging hands to chest. "If he did—if he did—" Slowly he shook his head.

Standing so close to him, I had only to put out my hand to touch Taliesin's shoulder. "Please be plain with us. You have come all this way to tell us."

"Not *that*," he said. "It was not what his father wanted. Tynstar wanted Homana. He said it was his birthplace, but denied him by the gods who cast the Ihlini out into another land, while saving Homana for the Cheysuli." His eyes were stark. "Do you see? Tynstar wanted revenge. Power, aye—how else to effect revenge?—but mostly he wanted Homana. To spit at the gods themselves."

My father's voice was steady. "But Tynstar's son wants it all. Strahan wants everything. How better to spit at the gods than to make himself one of them?"

"Reward," Taliesin said. "His reward for destroying the prophecy, for keeping the Firstborn from power."

"Godhood?" Deirdre drew in a breath. "How can it be done? A man made into a *god*?"

"Power," the harper explained. "There are two kinds, lady: the power of a king—a strictly temporal thing—and the power of the earth. Power absolute, tapped by those who know how. The Cheysuli know a little . . . so do the Ihlini. But Strahan knows more than most, being liege man to the Seker." Frowning, he shook his head. "A two-fold threat to us all, I think—if Strahan destroys the prophecy, his reward will be godhood . . . but in order *to* destroy it, he may need godhood now." Taliesin closed his eyes. "Who can say what will happen? Who can say what *can*?"

"But you are saying it could." My father sat very still, as if movement would shatter the truth and show us additional possibilities none of us wanted to face. "You are telling us now there is a way to become a god."

Taliesin looked at his hands. "I am a harper," he said slowly, "and harpers know these things. Harpers hear these things; old ones hear everything." Now his hands were trembling. "The lord I served was Tynstar in the halls of Valgaard itself; how could I not hear things? How could I drink the blood of the god without comprehending what I did, and what was left to do?" He steadied his voice with effort. "Like Corin, I overcame it. Like Corin, I suffered for it. But I never thought it would come so far; that Strahan could want so *much*."

My father's eyes did not waver. "Can it be done, Taliesin? Or is this a harper's tale, made of style instead of substance?"

The ageless face was old. "Anything can be done with the blessing of the Seker. Am I not proof of that?" He sighed. "Nearly two hundred years old."

My father rose. He walked away from us to one of the casements and stared out into the bailey. What he saw I could not say. "How did Caro die?"

"Strahan put his hand upon him."

The Mujhar swung around. "He did no more than that?"

"Nothing more was required. A man grows old, and he dies."

My father was taken aback. "Aye, over a span of *years*."

Taliesin shrugged. "With Strahan's hand upon him, a moment was all it took."

I shivered in the sunlight. *Strahan did that to him— what could he do to us?*

Ian shifted from his casual stance against one wall. "There are stories that Tynstar stole twenty years from Carillon by putting his hand upon him."

Taliesin nodded. "It is one of the darker gifts."

"And yet he gave no such gift to you." My father's tone was resolute. "Forgive me, but it seems odd he would kill Caro and yet leave you alive. You are the one he wanted, surely; Caro was innocent."

"*Jehan!*" I said sharply. "You cannot believe after all he has done that *Taliesin*—"

"No," my father said. "Not willingly; never. But Strahan is powerful. No man can stand against him."

"*Three* men did," I said. "Four, counting yourself."

The flesh near his ruined eye twitched. "The asking was required."

Taliesin nodded. "Your father is right, Keely—no man comes away from Strahan's presence unscathed, unless Strahan intends him to. None of your brothers did, nor did your father. So, you see, he is right to question my loyalty."

"Not that," my father said quickly. "Never, from you—you know that. After what you have done for me and my sons?" He shook his head slowly, recalling private things, private feelings, showing only the edges to us. "No. I only question Strahan's purpose."

"In leaving me alive?" The Ihlini harper sighed. "With death the punishment ends . . . he left me alive to suffer." He raised twisted, dessicated, trembling hands. "He did not kill me when he might have, all those years ago—instead he gave me *these* . . . and all the days of forever to suffer the destruction of my soul. Not my talent, no—music still lives in me—but my true gift was the harp, and that he took from me."

No one said a word. No one dared to breathe.

The harper's voice was unsteady. "Now, again, he takes, if only to punish me for the services I have done you. Killing is too easy, too transient for me . . . he wants me to live forever, knowing myself alone." With effort, he stilled his hands. "He killed Caro," he said. "He killed the man I loved."

It was Deirdre who went to him. Deirdre who bent to him; who held him against her so his anguish was seen by no one. In Erinnish words she soothed him, and put me in mind of Rory. It put me in mind of Sean, for whom I should but could not grieve, not knowing if he were dead.

Not knowing if I cared.

Ian made a sound. Startled, I glanced at him, thinking him unsettled by Taliesin and the truth of his preferences, which are unknown within the clans. But he did not look at the harper. He was looking out the casement into the bailey beyond.

"Niall," he said, "is it? By the gods, I think it is!"

"Is what?" I frowned, went to Ian's casement, stared out. Commotion raged below: horses, litters, bodies, shouting. "Who—?"

And then I saw the face upturned to my own, showing white teeth in a grin. A dark face framed by raven hair, with gold glinting from one ear.

"*Hart*," my father said disbelievingly. "By the gods, it *is!*"

Deirdre looked at him over her shoulder. "Were you expecting him?"

"No. No message ever arrived."

"By the gods," I said crossly, "does he require an invitation?"

And then I was gone from the solar, running down the hallway. *Gods—I wish it was Corin—*

But Hart would do well enough.

*   *   *

I met him on the steps before he could come inside, and fetched him a hard buffet on his bare right arm above the *lir*-band. *"Ku'reshtin,"* I cried, grinning, "have you spent your allowance so soon that you must come and beg for more?"

He rubbed his arm, of course, and said something about my strength being greater than his own, then patted me on the head. It was a habit I had abhorred for all of my life; now I welcomed it.

"No, no," he demurred, "I have not come seeking coin, not from the Homanan treasury." His grin was warm and wide, self-mocking as well as winsome; he could charm the maidenhead from an oath-bound virgin, and she not regret it. "Why should I? I have the Solindish treasury now, and the jewel of Solinde as well."

"Well, no doubt you will wager it." I grinned again, intensely pleased, and shook my head at him. "Have you wagered away your title?"

"I am reformed," he explained solemnly, but the glint in his eyes was pronounced. Sky-eyed, silk-tongued Hart, born but moments after Brennan and yet so very different. "Now I only wager the allowance Ilsa gives me, which is little enough, I fear." He sighed. "She is a termagant."

"Am I?" the lady asked. "I thought I was something else; the jewel of Solinde, you said?"

Hart, smiling, turned automatically, moving just enough to leave my view unobstructed. I saw Ilsa getting out of a cloth-swathed litter, settling lavender skirts over the tops of white-dyed slippers. And again, as had happened more than a year before, I was struck by the magnificence of her. Ice-eyed, pale-haired Ilsa, whose beauty was legendary. A manifest incandescence.

We are not twins, Hart and I, as he and Brennan are, but we are closely linked by blood, and as closely bound by emotions. I looked from Ilsa to him, sensing instinctively he was no longer the man I had known. It had nothing to do with rank or race—he was the Prince of Solinde, now in fact as well as title—nor to do with the realization all over again that he lacked his left hand. No. It was a consuming and focused intensity directed solely in Ilsa's direction.

He had married her for Solinde. He had gotten considerably more. Much more, I think, than he knew; certainly more than expected.

Hart? I asked inwardly. *Has the world turned upside down?*

And Rael was in my head with his liquid, golden tone. *Right side up,* the hawk said. *What you sense is happiness, and the elation of satisfaction with what has become of his life.*

I looked into the sky, squinting against the sun, and saw the lazy spiral as he drifted toward the bailey. He was pleased to be home again; I could sense it in the link.

The hawk's comment surprised me. Hart's life before had not been so bad, though filled with the inconstancies of wagering and a clearly defined reluctance to assume personal responsibility for anything else at all, least of all his title. Hart had always been supremely good-natured, untouched by Brennan's solemnity or Corin's moodiness. He had been, I had believed, the most satisfied of us all even when he had very little.

Now, in eminent clarity, he had more than any of us.

Ilsa smiled at us both, then turned back to the litter and took from someone inside a linen-wrapped bundle. From the folds emerged a wail.

"Wet," she said succinctly, "and too long a time in the heat. But at least she has Hart's coloring . . . with mine, she would be sunburned."

For a distinct, startled moment, all I could do was

stare. And then I turned on Hart. "You sent no word of a *baby!*"

Black brows arched in feigned innocence. "Did I not? I thought I did . . ." He shrugged it away easily, seemingly unperturbed, and then the grin came back. "I wanted to surprise *jehan*."

"*Jehan*, me, everyone else," I agreed dryly. "I suppose it is natural enough, but I think even you will admit you make an unlikely father."

Ilsa laughed, resettling the fabric-swathed infant. "He is a fool for the girl, worse than I am myself. You would think *he* had borne her, the way he mothers her."

Her Homanan was still accented, but less so than before. Because of Hart, I thought, and wondered about his Solindish. Bedtalk, I had heard, was good for improving language. His Homanan—and Erinnish—had always been superb.

"Is Brennan—?" he started to ask, but then *jehan* and the rest arrived, laughing, exclaiming, asking questions, and I was no longer consulted. Hart had others to talk with.

"Keely." It was Ilsa, climbing the stairs to stand beside me. "I have brought the baby's wet-nurse—is there a place we might be private?"

"Hart's old rooms, perhaps. . . ?" And I laughed, marking the bloom in her cheeks. "Aye, of course— the nursery. There is room for more than Aidan."

I led her there, Ilsa and her retinue, through halls and winding staircases, conscious of change, of *difference;* of the turning of the Wheel. But two years before, Homana-Mujhar had been full of the Mujhar's children, each of us concerned with the passage of time in a detached sort of way. Our lives had been the same for so long it was impossible to imagine anything changing them, even though we knew it would come. And it had, unexpectedly, when an accident caused by the Mujhar's sons had resulted in the deaths of thirty-two people.

Punishment had been swift: Hart was sent to Solinde, Corin to Atvia. Aileen was summoned from Erinn so that she and Brennan could marry.

And then Strahan had intervened. He had stolen each of my brothers and practiced his arts upon them. That any of them had come out of the captivity with mind and soul intact was solely due to Corin, who had come of age in Strahan's fortress.

They had changed, each of them, or had been forced to change in ways none of them ever mentioned. Some were obvious: Hart had lost a hand. But Hart had also gained Ilsa and the baby she held in her arms.

Not so different from Brennan . . . and yet nothing is the same.

"Here." I pushed open the door to the nursery and let all the Solindish in. That, too, had changed; once they were enemy, usurping Homana-Mujhar.

The chamber filled with women. Aidan's wet-nurse, his attendants, Ilsa and all of her ladies. I found myself standing close to the door, recoiling from all the noise, the chatter of women's concerns. Baby this, baby that; who wanted changing and feeding? It was nothing I had heard before, having avoided Aidan's routine. Aileen had known better than to speak of such things to me, since my interests lay most distinctly in other directions.

They stripped the girl bare and cleaned her, disposing of soiled wrappings. Then swaddled her again, but not before I had seen her. Not before I had seen tiny feet and tiny hands, the taut, rounded belly. Such pink, soft helplessness, unaccustomed to reality. Hostage to the world.

The wet-nurse bared a breast. I saw engorged flesh, swollen nipple, blue ropes beneath fair skin.

But I also saw the woman's face as she put the baby to her breast.

Gods—how can she like it—how can she shackle herself to such binding, consuming service—?

But there was peace in her face, not resentment. An abiding satisfaction.

The baby is Ilsa's, not hers—how can she be so content?

Aidan also had a wet-nurse, but I had never watched him feed. I had never asked anything of it, being disposed to avoid such things.

Ilsa looked at me. "Keely—are you all right?"

The gods know what my face showed. "Aye . . . aye, of course."

She smiled, setting the chamber alight. "When she is done, would you care to hold her?"

The immediate response was instinctive. "Have you gone mad?"

Ilsa laughed. "If you fear you will drop her, be certain you will not. It is a fear all of us have. You should have seen Hart the first time I put her into his arms."

I shook my head. "I have no desire to hold her. It has nothing to do with fear."

Ilsa said nothing at once, being more concerned with the baby. She tucked in a fallen fold of linen, then traced the fuzzy black hair as the baby sucked greedily. The wet-nurse murmured something in Solindish, crooning to the child.

"Did you want her?" I asked abruptly, heedless of the others.

Ilsa looked at me in shock. "Did I—? Of course I wanted her! How could I not?"

"Did you *want* her?" I repeated. "Not because you hoped for an heir—no need to speak of that to me—but because you desired a baby . . . for yourself as well as for Hart, the throne, the title . . . were you willing to let your body be used so simply to bring a child into the world?"

Ilsa stood very still. Then she turned to the wet-nurse, said something in Solindish and took the sated baby from her. In silence, she crossed the chamber to me.

"You will hold this child," she commanded. "You will hold this tiny girl who is the flesh and bones and spirit of all our ancestors, and then you will tell me there is no room in your heart for compassion, for love, for empathy, for awe and tenderness . . . even, I know, for fear, because fear is what every woman feels." She thrust the baby into my arms. "You will hold her," she said fiercely, "and I promise, you will *know*."

I recoiled as far as I dared. "Ilsa—I beg you—"

"*Hold* her," she said. "Do you think you are the only woman in the world who believes she cannot want a child?"

I shivered, chilled to the bone. I had not thought it so obvious.

Desperation welled. "But it is true," I told her rigidly, feeling the baby squirm. "Take her back . . . take her *back*—"

Ilsa turned from me and looked at the others in the room. She said a single word. As one, all of them left. All. Even Ilsa. Leaving me clutching Hart's tiny daughter.

And *knowing*, as she had promised.

All of it, and more.

Seven

Alone, in the darkness, I went to see the Lion. To see the mythical beast shaped in wood to form a throne, and to ask him for the answers. Surely he had *one*.

I lighted a torch, thrust it into a bracket. It was hardly enough to fill the Great Hall with light, but sufficient for what I required. I left it near the silver doors and made my way toward the dais.

Out of gilded, ancient eyes it watched me as I walked. Such a huge, gape-mouthed beast, rearing up from the marble dais on bunched, wooden legs. No one knew who had made it, or even how old it was. For century upon century it had crouched in Homana-Mujhar, holding sovereignty in the Great Hall as the Mujhar held Homana. Cheysuli-made, I thought, like the rest of my father's palace.

I stopped short of the dais. The flame far down the hall danced on its pitch-soaked wick, distorting light into darkness, darkness into light. The Lion seemed to yawn, displaying ivory teeth. Giltwork gleamed, lending depth to the woodcarver's skill. Lending the Lion life.

"You," I said quietly, "are a selfish, demanding beast, requiring too much of us. Stealing our freedom from us, denying us free will . . . warping us to *your* will in the name of a vanished race."

Silence from the mouth. From the eyes, emptiness.

A wave of frustration rose to lap at my accusations, driving them shoreward toward the Lion. "For how many decades—how many *centuries*—have you sat here on the dais, secure in your power and pride, your absolute *arrogance*, knowing us faithful, dutiful children too honor-bound to even consider turning our backs on your demands? To reconsider our place in the tapestry of selfish gods, weaving us this way and that?"

Yet again, no answer. Nor did I expect it; it was only a beast of wood. Nothing more than a symbol, yet binding a race regardless. Locking shackles around our souls.

I climbed the marble steps. Faced the Lion squarely. Then, without thought, swung around and sat myself down on the cushion. Settled hands over the paw-shaped wooden armrests and thrust myself back, back, into the depths of the Lion Throne, feeling the head looming over my own, sensing the weight of years, of strength, of *power*. Acknowledging what it was even against my will.

Ambience. The trappings of heritage, shaping my heart, my will, my beliefs. I could deny it no more than myself.

And I wondered: *Is this what Teir has done? Denied himself in his quest to free our race from gods-made iron?*

Far down the hall silver flashed. The hinges were oiled so the door made no sound as it was opened, but the glint of torchlight on hammered silver gave the visitor away.

For a moment, it was Brennan. The height, the weight, the posture ... everything was Brennan, except for the missing hand. And then he let the door fall closed and stepped into the guttering torchlight, and I saw clearly it was Hart.

Wrapped in the Lion, I waited. He came, slowly, as if in audience to our father, and paused, smiling a little, knowing what I did; possibly even why. Before the dais he halted, and inclined his black-haired head.

"It suits you," he said, "the Lion."

I grunted briefly; eloquent skepticism.

He grinned. "But it does. You have the pride for it—" lightly, "—and the arrogance."

I sighed, propping an elbow against the arm and resting my jaw in a hand. "Aye, aye, I know ... others of my kin have labored to tell me much the same." I shifted, trying to find a comfortable position. "But I find the beast too demanding; I would prefer my freedom."

Hart turned from me in seeming idleness: head tipped, lips pursed, brows arched, appraising the Great Hall. It had been very nearly two years since he had been in it. Life for him had changed utterly.

His back was to me, which pitched his comment toward the firepit instead of at me. Which was, I realized, precisely what he wanted, to make his approach of the topic easier. "Ilsa told me what happened earlier today, with Blythe."

Blythe. I had not even asked. "She should not have done it, Hart. What if something had happened?"

He shrugged, still looking around the hall. "She felt it necessary. Ilsa is—intuitive. And also immensely compassionate." He swung back almost abruptly, reassessment duly completed. "Are you forgetting one of the foremost tenets of the clans?" he asked intently. "Something you, of all people, should know: *If one is afraid, one can only become unafraid by facing that which causes the fear.*' "

I tensed against the Lion. "And you think I am afraid of a *baby*?"

"I know you are. I know you, Keely: you are terrified."

I drew in a slow breath, to keep my tone light. He wanted me to lose my temper, so he could play the part of peacemaker, of compassionate older brother. "If I had dropped her—"

A flick of his only hand dismissed the beginnings of my retort. "Not of dropping her; that is natural.

No. You are afraid of the baby itself, *your* baby, and what it represents." He climbed the bottom step of the dais and stopped, arms tucked behind his back. So casual, my middle brother; so nonchalantly intent. "You are afraid to leave the womb, Keely . . . afraid to set free your emotions for fear of losing yourself."

Denial snapped me upright. "I hardly think a *baby—*"

"I *do.* You forget: I was the most irresponsible of us all, the least likely to be trapped by the demands of my *tahlmorra.*" He climbed another step. "I was the middle son, the *wastrel* son, whose only concern was how to win the game, how to take a chance and win; to risk myself, my *lir,* my title, all on the fall of a rune-stick." His twisted grimace was self-mocking. "Aye, what I did made no difference at all, *I thought,* which left me free to conduct myself as I chose. And I chose to wager away Solinde, Ilsa . . . my hand."

Instantly, I denied it. "Oh, Hart—"

His tone was perfectly steady. "I wagered it, Keely. And it was easy, *easy—*" he thrust his left arm out in front of his body, between himself and me, "—so easy, Keely, because I thought I did not matter. Because I thought I could *win.*" He took the third and final step. Now he stood on the dais, level with the Lion, and held me with his eyes, his posture; with the intensity of his being. "I have been afraid of many things, and I have been afraid of nothing. Neither is comfortable, though ignorance makes a better bedmate." He shook his head; the earring glinted. "Your fear is not misplaced, but it can be overcome. The gods know you have the strength and courage for it, Keely . . . I know it, too. We all do—" he grinned, "—which is why you drive us half mad with the violence of your passions."

I swore without heat or intent, slumping back in the wooden embrace. "You are a fool," I said wearily, "all of you. You undervalue my convictions, thinking my opinions are born out of female contrariness—"

"Not at all," he said flatly. "Gods, Keely, do you forget the power in your blood? We do not; we *can*not. You are more gifted than any of us, and such power carries a price. I know what *I* feel in *lir*-shape . . . I know the overwhelming allure, the draw and danger of the link. And that is with only one *lir*, Keely—do you think none of us knows how difficult it is for you, with recourse to *any* shape? How strong you have to be to maintain your balance while lured by so many possibilities?" He shook his head slowly, sympathetically. "You are afraid, *rujholla*; that I promise you. You are afraid you will lose the 'Keely' the power has shaped. Wed to Sean, you are *cheysula*. With a child you are *jehana*." He paused, speaking still more quietly, more gently. "But what becomes of Keely? What becomes of the avatar of our race?"

I stared blindly into the darkness, shrouded by the Lion. "She is buried," I whispered thickly. "Swallowed by the expectations, the hopes—the *needs*—of all the others, *so many* others." I swallowed painfully. "Kin, clan, husband." My mouth was dry. "Child."

"Who could well embody more of what we were than you." Hart smiled as, startled, I snapped my head up to stare at him. "Aye. Have you not thought of that? Your child, your *children*, may be forged of stronger iron than even the *jehana*. And they, too, will be required to find the proper path. No matter how difficult." He was close to me now, so close. He put out his hand, his only hand, and touched my head, smoothing tangled hair. "You are not alone, Keely . . . not while any of us live. Not while your children live."

I shut my eyes tightly. "I am tired," I said, "so tired."

"I know, Keely. Nothing for us is easy, least of all for you." He sighed. "So much—*too* much—is at stake."

I thought of Teirnan again. Of Maeve and the child in her belly.

"Hostages," I told him. "Every single one."

Hart frowned. "Who?"

"The children. Born, unborn . . . does it matter? Hostages to the gods. Prisoners of tradition." I pulled myself out of the Lion. "She is a lovely girl, *rujho* . . . a lovely little Cheysuli. I hope the gods are kind to her."

Ian caught me as I went down the corridor to my chambers. In the hall we met one another, knowing things no one else did, and came face to face with reality.

"Well?" he asked.

"I found him," I said grimly. "I asked him. He sailed from Erinn immediately after the brawl in the tavern, and did not stay to discover if Sean survived or not."

Ian's face was solemn. "How long ago?"

I drew in a breath. "He said we should hear, as he put it, today, tonight or tomorrow . . . or perhaps a month from now." I shrugged. "We remain in ignorance, *su'fali*, and no way of knowing. All we can do is wait."

"And tell Niall, which is what you agreed to do."

I stiffened. "Now? At this moment? But—"

"No, not at this moment; he is closeted with Taliesin. Tomorrow, I think . . . or perhaps the day after." He shook his head. "There is Strahan to think about, and now that Hart is come—"

"—he will want nothing to do with questions of Sean's health." I nodded. "We have waited this long . . . a little longer will not hurt."

"A little longer, and you will be an old woman."
He smiled, brows arched, as I glared. "Well? You are
nearly twenty-three, are you not? Niall had five children by this age."

"And you, *su'fali*?" I asked sweetly. "You are—forty-
five? Forty-six? And there is frost in your hair . . ." I
grinned, turning toward my chamber. "I think you
had best go look in the polished plate before we
speak of age."

Eight

Hart set the bowl on the table and poured into it a collection of flattened, bone-white stones. Frowning, I saw nearly every one was marked with some sort of symbol. I picked one up, studied it, saw the etched design.

"A scythe?"

Hart nodded. "It portrays a generous harvest. A good stone, in Bezat." He showed me a handful of others. "Each carries its weight in meaning, but when drawn in conjunction with others, it can alter everything. Except, of course, for this one." He showed me both sides: blank. "The death-stone," he said. "Bezat. Draw this and the game is over."

I grunted. "I can see why you would like a game like this, Hart ... the risk is greater than in the fortune-game."

The late afternoon sun slanted through the casements, cutting the chamber into a lattice of shadow and light. We sat in Deirdre's solar, hunching over a low table on which rested a flagon of wine, a cluster of cups, the Solindish game. Ilsa and Deirdre worked together on the massive tapestry of lions I had grown sick of seeing, talking quietly of things such as childbearing, the preservation of certain foods, the need for new dyes to freshen wardrobes grown outdated. I was, as usual, uninterested, and therefore ignored them completely.

Ian, my father, and Taliesin were still meeting with the Homanan Council, discussing Strahan and

the need to send forces to the northern borders in
order to reinforce them against any incursions the
Ihlini might make into Homana. The harper re-
ported loss of life near the border, though as yet on
the Solindish side, across the Molon Pass; nonetheless, it underscored our need to keep close guard on
the borders. If Strahan was killing Solindish he considered disloyal, I doubted little would stop him from
crossing the border to kill Homanans or Cheysuli,
who were more traditional enemies.

I wondered why Hart was not in the meeting, said
so, and was told by the Prince of Solinde that he had
already dispatched patrols to the far north. Valgaard,
he explained, was in a pocket of Solinde that was
and had always been steadfastly loyal to Strahan, as
it had been loyal to Tynstar before him. While osten-
sibly part of Hart's holdings, Strahan held the real
power. And until Hart had won the loyalty of the
Solindish who still preferred Solindish rule, he could
hardly expect the entire realm to rise up against the
Ihlini, who did, he said dryly, have more right to the
realm than we, Solinde being the home of the Ihlini.
And not all of them were as Strahan.

And so Hart, having discharged his duty, sat with
me at the table, rattling runestones and urging me to
wager all the coin I had, even to my last copper
penny.

"Why?" I asked suspiciously. "Is it that you *have*
wagered away your allowance? Now you want mine?"

His smile was slow and sweet, his eyes, guileless;
gods, but he was good! "Without risk, there is no
point to playing."

"Without risk, there is no loss." I smiled back at
him with equal sweetness; I am, after all, his sister. "I
thought Ilsa had reformed you."

The lady herself laughed. "Only to the point of
keeping him home to wager on small games such as
this one."

Hart chewed on his thumb, the only one he could. "Will you play?"

"Only if *I* name the stakes." I thought it over. "I think—"

But what I thought remained unsaid, because Hart was paying no attention to me at all. "Brennan," he said intently. "Aye, it *is*—"

And so it was, coming through the door, but Hart had said it before he was in sight, and Rael, in the link, was silent. Hart had simply *known.*

Their grins were identical, though set in different faces. Black-haired and dark-skinned, both of them, with very similar bones, but more than the eyes were different. Their thoughts worked differently; although, at this moment, what they thought was the same, and there for everyone to see.

Hart was standing now. Sleeta, flowing through the door next to her *lir*, went immediately to Hart and threaded herself around his legs, butting his knees with her head. Through the link I felt her contentment, her greeting, though Hart heard nothing at all except the purr that was nearly a growl. To him, she was merely giving him catlike welcome. To me, and to Brennan, she was giving him honor as well.

Brennan took two long steps and stopped. Appraised Hart solemnly. Opened his mouth to speak.

But Hart, doing much the same, beat him to it. "You have grown fat," he announced.

"You *ku'reshtin*, I am nothing of the sort!"

"Soft," Hart added, nodding. "Fat and soft. Lazy, too, no doubt . . . domesticity ruins a man such as you."

Brennan's eyes narrowed. "Then I suggest we find ourselves a friendly tavern and discuss my domesticity—and various other shortcomings—over a jug of wine."

"*Usca*," Hart said promptly. "And a fortune-game."

Ilsa's head came up. Smoothly, I stepped between her husband and his brother. "I will come as well, to keep you both from trouble. I recall what it was like the last time you went drinking and gaming in Mujhara."

Clearly, so did they. Just as clearly, they preferred to go without me. But they said nothing of the sort, perhaps Hart out of deference to Ilsa; Brennan, I thought, because he knew better than to argue. If they did not take me with them, I would follow on my own.

Corin had taught me that.

The tavern was called The Rampant Lion. Its walls were whitewashed, its lion-shaped sign freshly painted. Lighted lanterns hung from posts. Altogether it was an attractive place, but instead of going in we stood outside in the street, looking at it.

"Well," Hart said finally, "I imagine they have replaced the benches and tables we broke."

"Undoubtedly," Brennan agreed, "and undoubtedly they have replaced the owner and wine-girl as well." He touched his lobeless ear, then took his hand away with effort. "Let us go in."

Hart and I followed as Brennan shouldered open the door. The interior was as clean as the exterior, well-lighted, with hardwood floor. Hart sat himself down at the first open table and called for *usca*. I joined him, but Brennan, looking around, did not at once sit. He seemed to be searching for something, and when the girl came with the jug of *usca* and cups he looked at her closely. She was young, blonde, blue-eyed; he relaxed almost at once, and paid her. Then pressed a gratuity into her hand.

"A silver royal?" I was astonished. "That is enough to buy us ten meals and all the *usca* we want, *rujho*— and you give it to a wine-girl?"

"My choice," he said quietly, and sat down next to me.

Hart's expression was uncharacteristically blank. "There is *i'toshaa-ni*," he remarked with carefully measured neutrality. "If it will give you peace again—"

Brennan cut him off with a raised finger. "I know that, Hart. But I do not notice it has done our *su'fali* any good."

"Ah," I said, "Rhiannon. Aye, it was here, was it not, that you met her?" Like Hart, I kept my tone empty of challenge; Brennan is a fair man, and even-handed, but he is all Cheysuli beneath the Homanan manners, with prickly Cheysuli pride. "And was it not here that you two and Corin fought that pompous fool, Reynald of Caledon?" I grinned. "You near destroyed his escort, as well as the tavern itself—"

"Aye." Brennan's tone was severe. "Keely, we did not come here to speak of old times."

"No?" I made my surprise elaborate. "Then why come here at all? Another tavern would do as well."

Brennan poured a mug full of *usca* and pushed it across to me. "Drink," he said succinctly. "You have come to drink, so drink . . . my business is my own, and I would rather spend the time talking with Hart than with you."

Hart's gaze on me was briefly sympathetic—he had been the subject of Brennan's irritation more often than I, and knew how it felt—then he turned to call for a fortune-game. I marked how he had adapted to using his right hand for everything, keeping the cuffed left stump away from the edge of the table. I wondered if it still hurt, as our father's empty eyesocket did when he was tired or worried. I wondered how he felt recalling how he had lost it in Solinde, to Dar, Ilsa's Solindish suitor, who served Strahan for personal gain.

And who had, I knew, been executed for it. But it did not bring back Hart's hand, which he had himself thrown into the Gate of Asar-Suti to keep Strahan from buying his service with the only thing that might: his reinstatement within the clans as a full-fledged Cheysuli warrior.

Kin-wrecked. An old custom, but still in force. Brennan had tried to have it changed, but there was as yet opposition in the clans. Already we lost traditions, the old ones said, including the *shar tahls*, because our assumption of the Lion was making us into Homanans. If we severed all ties with the old ways we would no longer be Cheysuli. A Cheysuli warrior needed *all* his limbs to be whole—otherwise how could he defend his clan?

So, for now, the custom was retained. And Hart, regardless of his title, was cut off from his clan, enjoying none of the things rightfully his by birth, by blood, by the *lir*-link with Rael.

Feckless, irresponsible Hart, who seemed the least likely of us all to care about the loss of clan-rights, since it did not affect the *lir*-gifts, nor his taste for gambling. But who, oddly enough, seemed to feel the loss the most.

Aye, Strahan had changed him. Strahan had changed them all.

We drank, played, talked. Mostly *they* talked, my brothers, renewing the link of shared birth, reconfirming the strength of their special bond.

It was different from the *lir*-link. And in many ways, more powerful. I shared my own with Corin, so I understood . . . but he was far away. Much too far away, leaving me with no one.

I drank *usca*, cursing the need for responsibility. It was, I thought, a curse Hart himself must have sworn, and often, being what he was; and yet he had changed. He had learned. He had done what was required, in the end, to maintain the delicate balance.

Even Corin, so slow to let grudges die; my angry, rebellious *rujholli*, who had resented Brennan for nearly everything, overlooking what he himself had in abundance. Even Corin had succumbed to the call of his *tahlmorra*. Now he lived in Atvia, putting his House to rights. Ridding himself of Lillith, I hoped, and dealing firmly with our mother, Mad Gisella, who would hag-ride him to his death, if he let her.

I shivered briefly. I had no memory of our mother, who had been sent in exile to Atvia before I was six months old. But I heard the tales, the whispers, the comments. I sensed the unease in our father whenever her name was spoken, because she was truly Queen of Homana, his wife by Homanan law, *cheysula* by Cheysuli; if she came back to Homana, she would have to be properly received before he sent her away again. She had borne him sons. She had given him the means to hold the Lion, the means to further the prophecy, merely by bearing boys.

Deirdre was our mother in everything but name. But Deirdre, some said, was a whore, regardless of her blood.

If Gisella ever came back to Homana to petition for permanent residence, Deirdre would have to go. There were proprieties, customs, manners . . . she would go, be *sent*, and leave our father bereft of happiness.

It was all I had known in him, happiness, in childhood and adulthood. Because of Deirdre. Because they were content with one another.

I sucked down gulps of fiery *usca*, letting it burn out my temper. Letting it let *me* admit to possibilities.

If it could be that way with jehan and Deirdre after so many—twenty-two!—*years . . . if it can be that way with Hart and Ilsa—* I gritted my teeth and swallowed liquor—*then why not with Sean and I?*

It was not impossible. If I opened my eyes, I could see it. If I could shake off my stubbornness, suppress my pride, my frustration, renounce my hostility. . . .

If.
It was not impossible. But only if Sean were alive.
And then what would become of Rory?
—oh, gods, what am I thinking—?

Nine

"Keely."

It took a very long time for me to make sense of the word. Or what it portended. Or might.

"Keely."

Aye, of course: my name. But who—? Oh, aye, Brennan; of course, Brennan, who else? It was always Brennan hag-riding me to death . . . no, no, it was Corin who would be hag-ridden—

"Keely!"

No . . . not Brennan after all, at least, not this time . . . perhaps it had been the first time, or the second, or the first time *and* the second . . . but who now—? Oh, gods, *Hart*—of course, I had forgotten. Hart was here from Solinde, with Ilsa . . . Ilsa and a baby.

I looked first at Brennan, then at Hart, and sighed. "Both of you: babies . . . babies and *cheysulas* . . . gods, I think I will be sick—you make me *sick*—"

"If you are sick," Brennan observed, "it has nothing to do with us. You are too far gone in your cups, Keely . . . and *usca* is powerful."

"*Every*one having babies." I shook my head in despair. "You, Hart, Maeve—gods, it will be Corin next, or *me*—"

Brennan went very still. "What do you mean, 'Maeve'?"

"—such a fool, such a *lack*wit! You would think she had learned her lesson after what Teirnan did . . . but *no,* he claps his hands and she runs to him, like a dog—like a *bitch,* offering herself to the hound—"

Brennan's hand came down on mine, pinning it to the table. "Keely, that is enough. It is the *usca* talking, not you—but you are, it seems, the one with all the secrets. What is this of Maeve and Teirnan—and a *baby?*"

"She went to him," I said plainly, over the *usca*-blur in my head. "She went to him, lay with him, and now she will bear his child."

Brennan's eyes were startled. "Is *that* why—"

I overrode him rudely. "Aye, of course it is—why do you think?" I scowled at him blackly. "That is why she keeps herself to Clankeep. She is ashamed. Afraid. She thinks *jehan* will be angry."

Hart, frowning, poured the stones into the bowl and began to stir them around. "Is Teir still with the *a'saii?*"

I grunted. "With them, of them, leading them . . . he has founded a new clan, and he is the clan-leader." I sat more upright on my stool. The *usca*-haze remained, mixing with candlelight to fuddle my eyes, but I knew what I was saying. "And I am not entirely certain what he claims is false."

Brennan made a sound of disgust and shoved the jug at me. "Have more *usca,* Keely . . . it improves your imagination."

"Is it my imagination that we risk losing the *lir?*" Aye, that got their attention. "Teir has pointed out that if the Firstborn come again, there will be little need for us. Or even the Ihlini. Both will be redundant. And since the Firstborn shall have all the power, why not let them have all the *lir?*"

"Because it makes no sense," Brennan retorted. "We have always had the *lir*—why would we lose them? What reason for the gods to take them from us?"

I leaned forward intently. "Because the Firstborn

are their favorites. *You* should understand that, being favored yourself—" I smiled without amusement "—and generally reaping the rewards, you and Maeve both—" But I cut it off with a chop of my hand. "It does not matter, none of it, only that I wonder again if Teirnan has the right of it ... he said the Ihlini fight us the way they do because they understand what it means ... they understand that if the prophecy comes to fruition, they will be destroyed." I swallowed heavily, tasting sour liquor. "Perhaps we will suffer the same fate, being discarded like soiled wrappings ..." I put my hands over my eyes. "Gods, it is too bright in here—I swear, I will go *blind*—"

"We should take her home," Hart said uneasily. "She will be sick right here at the table."

Brennan sighed. "Better to let her be sick outside." I heard stools scraping. "Well enough, Keely, we will take you home. Where, I daresay, someone will be delegated to put you to bed, since I doubt you are able to do it yourself."

Hands were under my arms, lifting me. The common room reeled. "Agh—*gods*—" But I bit my lip and let them escort me out of the tavern into darkness; was it evening, then? Already?

"Just as well we walked," Hart remarked in dry amusement. "I doubt she could sit a horse."

"I doubt she can *keep* a horse." Brennan's tone was bitter. "I entrusted her with my fleetest colt, and she lost him—she *lost* him ... she let thieves take him from her, and then was too frightened to lead me to where they stole him. I did not require her to come *with* me, only to tell me where—"

I stopped dead and jerked my arms from their grasps. "*I* know where," I told him. "I *know* where, and who, and how to go about it ... and I am *not afraid!* Not of him. Not of Rory. He would never harm me." I swung my head from side to side. "Not Rory Redbeard."

"*Who?*" came in unison.

Then, from Brennan, pointedly, "You said the outlaws were Erinnish. But you did not say you *knew* them."

I was hot. Sweating. "Gods—" I gasped. "—oh, *rujho*— "

Hart's voice was urgent. "In the alley—*there* . . ."

"Let her go." Brennan's tone was less friendly. Most distinctly lacking compassion. "She drank all of it without our assistance . . . let her be quit of it that way, too."

An alley . . . I caught a wall, tried to hang on, felt it spill out from under me. On my knees I paid homage to the darkness, as well as to all the *usca*.

It was Hart, eventually, who helped me up and held me, making certain I could stand. Brennan was a shadow in the darkness, silhouetted against lantern light, muttering something beneath his breath. I saw gold on his arms and in his eyes; in Hart's I saw compassion. But his were blue, after all . . . not fierce Cheysuli yellow.

I drew in a gut-deep breath. "I am sorry, *rujho* . . . I have shamed you, shamed myself—"

"Hush," Hart said gently. "No more, Keely—not now. Now is the time for you to be still, be silent . . . *usca* is not always a boon companion."

I looked past him. "Neither is *he*."

Hart smiled a little. "Aye, well, you and Brennan have always played grinding wheel to the other's steel." He sighed, smoothing tangled hair from my face. "One day, perhaps, the grinding wheel will stop turning and allow the steel to be put away."

I looked down at his other hand; no, at the stump. Carefully I reached out and caught his forearm, making certain I did not touch the wrist or the leather cuff. I brought it up into the light and stared at the emptiness. At the absence of a hand.

"They are fools," I told him, "all of them. Blind

old fools, keeping to customs no longer needed." I looked at his rigid face, at the recoiling in his eyes. "*Fools*, Hart . . . each and every one—" I stopped, fighting back tears. "And I never said—I never told you . . . I was sorry."

"I know," he said. "I knew."

"I never *told* you."

He hooked the handless arm around my neck and pulled me close. "I knew, *rujha* . . . I always knew. You wear everything on your face."

A sob caught on a laugh. "Aye. Like now?" I touched my cheek. "No doubt there is more on my face than I would care to admit."

"Aye, well . . ." He grinned. "We shall go home and wash it off."

I drew in a deep breath. "Gods—I wish Corin were here."

"I know," he said, "so do I."

"But you have Ilsa—and now the baby, too."

"Aye, and I love them both. But there is still room in my heart for others . . . for everyone else I might want. Brennan, my *lir*, you . . . did you think the space predetermined?"

"Corin," I said again, as Brennan came into the alley. "Corin—and a *jehana*."

Brennan, annoyed, sighed. "Oh, Keely—"

But Hart cut him off. "She is sick," he said. "Drunk and sick and unhappy. Have you been none of those?"

Something moved in Brennan's face. "All of them," he answered at last. "All of them, and worse." And then he came to me, to step in beside me and curve one arm around my back as Hart did much the same.

A brother on either side. But neither of them was Corin.

It was Deirdre who told me. I sat bolt upright in bed and instantly wished I had not.

"Oh, *Keely,*" she said.

I stared at her in mounting alarm, then hastily bent over the edge of the bed. Deirdre pushed the empty chamber pot into my groping hands and I promptly rid myself of more *usca*; the last of it, I hoped.

I was hot, shivering, humiliated, belly-down on the bed. Lank hair, still in its braid but coming loose, dangled over the edge. My spirit, I discovered, was as flaccid as my belly.

"Gods," I muttered, "what a *fool.*"

Deirdre shook her head. "They did not say it was *this* bad." She sighed, moving to help me clean my face with a damp linen cloth. "I will send for hot broth, something to settle your belly."

"No." I pushed myself up again, waved her away and did my very best to ignore the thumping in my head as well as the aftertaste in my mouth. "You said they went *where?*"

Dutifully, she repeated it. "To find Brennan's colt."

"Gods—they *cannot*—" I threw back the bedclothes, checked, swallowed back bile. "I think—I think I had better go—"

Deirdre shook her head. "You'll be going nowhere in such a state. Have you lost your wits as well as your belly?"

I balanced myself carefully on the edge of the bed, squinting against the morning light. "How long ago did they leave?"

"Not long." She shrugged, not really caring. "But you'll not be catching them—oh, lass, don't. You'd do better staying in bed."

The "lass" only firmed my resolve. "I have to go, Deirdre. Another time, I will explain." I stood up, began to dress carefully in the leathers I had worn the night before, since they were at hand, and I lacked the strength or inclination to look for fresh ones. "Did they go in *lir*-shape?" If they had, I needed to hurry.

"No." She was frowning, plainly troubled. "No, not with Hart lacking a hand—he says it makes flying distances too difficult. They rode."

"Better," I said, nodding, "I can beat them in the air."

Deirdre shook her head. "You're too ill to hold *lir*-shape. But if you *must* try, at least keep to the ground. I'd not be wanting you to fall."

Thinking of Taliesin—and my embarrassing landing —I answered her truthfully. "I have done it before."

She said nothing as I pulled on my boots, cursing, buckled on my belt with its sheathed Cheysuli long-knife, and rinsed my mouth with water from the pitcher on my dressing table. She said nothing as I paused long enough before the polished silver to mutter over the state of my hair, the death's-head look of my face; neither did *I* say a word. I simply headed toward the door.

"Keely," she said as I reached it, "why did you say nothing of Rory Redbeard?"

I stopped short of the door and turned. "You *know*?"

"Brennan said you mentioned the name." Deirdre's tone was intent. "Is it truly Rory Redbeard, or a stranger using the name?"

"He is Erinnish," I answered, "and he named himself Liam's bastard."

Blankly, she shook her head. "Why is he here?" she asked. "Without Sean? In secret? Stealing Brennan's *horse*?"

"I have to go," I muttered, pulling open the door.

"Why is he *here*, Keely?"

"I have to go," I repeated, and went out of the chamber as swiftly as my aching head would let me.

Neither Brennan nor Hart knew where Rory was hiding, which would slow them down. Hart would send Rael to seek the Erinnish brigand out, but it would take time. Going horseback slowed them further; I knew I had a chance.

Outside, I paused on the marble steps and gave myself to the magic, to the shapechange, to the power that made me different, as Hart had pointed out. Except this time the power was sluggish, and left me feeling drained.

I drew in two breaths and began again, trying to ignore my headache, my belly, the shakiness of my limbs. And again, the shapechange failed; I lacked the concentration.

"Lady . . . are you all right?"

I opened my eyes, squinting. Lio. Pale-haired, pale-eyed Lio, wearing my father's too-bright crimson livery and staring at me in alarm.

"No," I told him truthfully.

"Is—can I help?" Such an earnest tone and face.

I scowled at him, disliking him for his health, his lack of sour spirits. "Unless you can tap the earth magic for me and feed it into my bones, I think not." I rubbed at gritty eyes. "Can you do that, Lio?"

"No. I could try, if you want me to."

It earned him a wry smile, which was more than I had expected to give. "No, no—*leijhana tu'sai* for offering . . . no, I will have to manage alone." I sighed. "Why do people drink so much when it makes the next day so bad?"

"*Ah.*" He understood instantly. "It takes practice, lady—I think you are too new at it."

"And so I shall remain." I squinted past him to the gates. "Perhaps I should give up trying to fly, which takes more effort, and go on four feet instead."

Lio, obviously uncomfortable, shrugged awkwardly. Plainly he could not conceive of changing shapes to suit purposes. "Aye, well . . . you could."

I shut my eyes again, tried to relax, to let the discomfort ebb away.

I need you, I told the power. *I need you now, today, this moment . . . I cannot account for the actions of my rujholli, and the Erinnish is deserving of my aid. He helped me, once . . . it is the least I can do, to repay him. Good manners, if nothing else.*

Something paused, listened, answered.

I smiled, feeling immeasurably better. Certainly stronger. *Leijhana tu'sai—*

My mind cleared. I thought of flowing along the track effortlessly . . . of giving myself to the day . . . of striking an endless singing rhythm within the sinews of my body . . . my fleet, magnificent body—

"*Lady*—" Lio said, and I knew the change complete.

As a cat, I left the bailey. As a cat I was lord of the world.

Rory, I said, *here I am—*

Ten

Rory was, as I arrived, preparing to mount the colt in question. One foot was in the stirrup, the other in mid-swing; the tableau abruptly altered as I arrived because I was still in cat-shape, and the sudden appearance of a large mountain cat leaping through the woodlands, yowling loudly, is enough to upset any horse, even one accustomed to Sleeta.

Thus upset, the chestnut deposited an equally startled Rory Redbeard unceremoniously on the ground.

His roar brought everyone running, except the colt, who retreated with alacrity. I found myself surrounded by eight men more than a little shocked to discover their prey feline rather than human, but who nonetheless exhibited a perfect willingness to show Erinnish steel.

Overhead came the cry of a hunting hawk.

I shed my assumed shape and faced him as Keely again, ignoring the uneasy comments and oaths from Rory's men as they rubbed eyes and winced against the unsettling disorientation of my transformation. I wasted no time on them, but peered upward through the screening of tight-knit limbs. "Rael," I said briefly. "It means they are very close."

Rory's brows, which had been knit in a black-faced scowl, disappeared high beneath his hair. "Who, lass?"

"Hart and Brennan—"

And then they, too, were crashing through the brush, if on horseback, to join us, and Rory's men spread out to include two more Cheysuli in their thinning net of steel.

Eight men—nine, counting Rory—and two warriors with *lir*. Not enough, I knew, not *nearly* enough.

It made me proud; it made me uneasy. It made me frustrated.

"No," I told my brothers.

I had, I knew, succeeded in astonishing them as well as Rory and his men, which amused me—or would have, had I the time—but all it got me was a reassessment of circumstances.

And then Brennan was glaring at me, much as Rory had. "What are you doing here?"

"More right than you," I retorted. "I know this man; do you?"

Brennan's glare was replaced by a certain familiar grimness. "Aye," he said, "I do. He is a thief. He is the man who stole my horse. That is enough, I think; the situation hardly warrants an introduction."

In the shadows, Sleeta growled. The sound climbed from deep in her throat, rising in pitch and promise. There is nothing, even to me, quite so unsettling as a mountain cat expressing hostile intentions. I saw Rory's men come to an abrupt and unhappy realization that what they faced required something more than they had assumed. Men are one thing, even Cheysuli; a mountain cat is another.

Rael shrieked overhead and came smashing down through branches to settle on Hart's outstretched arm. Not a stoop, but close enough; enough to startle them all. Enough to make them realize, yet again, what manner of men they faced.

The white hawk bated, stretching wide black-etched wings, then lifted and flew through the clearing to settle in a tree very near a still-recumbent Rory.

Are you quite finished? I asked sourly.

Rael said he was.

Hart glanced at me, eyes amused, but swallowed.

the crooked smile. He was trying to look very fierce; laughing would not help.

"No," I said again.

"No, *what?*" Brennan was irritated. "No, this is not the man; no, this is not the horse; no, these are not bandits?" He shook his head. "Decide on one, Keely, or we will be here all day."

Hart's tone was less annoyed, being more intrigued than anything else. "How are you here?" he asked. "I thought you would be abed most of the day, after all that *usca* you drank." He grinned. "Drank *and* lost."

It was not precisely what I wanted to hear—or to have heard by others, particularly Rory—but trust Hart to say it. I shot him a disgusted glance. "I am here," I said plainly, "to make certain you do no harm to a man who gave me aid when I needed it."

"The man," Rory announced, "can speak for himself, lass." He got to his feet, ignoring Sleeta's accompanying rumble, and brushed his leathers free of clinging leaves and debris as he fixed his gaze on Brennan. "Your colt, is it, then? The fine bright lad?" He pursed lips as Brennan nodded. "So, then, I am addressing the Prince of Homana?"

Brennan, as always, was precise. "As well as the Prince of Solinde."

"*Two* princes!" Rory showed irreverent teeth through the bush of his beard. "Then I'll be thanking the gods for this day, and telling my children about it."

I gritted my teeth. "Rory."

"What, lass? Am I to bow down to them? Am I to kneel here in the dirt and leaves? Am I to swear fealty?" He laughed aloud, patently unimpressed by the exalted presence of my brothers. "Lass, lass . . . they're only men! *Men!* D'ye expect me to give them a respect they haven't earned?" He shook his head. "No, I'm thinking not. I'm thinking my lord Brennan has more horses than a single man can ride, and me with none at all—except, of course, the bright boyo."

I glared. "You at least owe them *courtesy!* Have you no manners at all?"

He grinned. "Oh, aye, lass, I do . . . but I'm for showing them only to those who are deserving. This man called me a thief."

"You are," Brennan said coolly.

Rory's brows slid up. "Am I? Am I, then? And I was thinking I got him in payment for saving the lass' life."

Hart frowned. "What do you mean?" His attention was now on me. "What is he saying, Keely?"

I was heartily sick of the subject. "Nothing," I said impatiently. "He did me a service, aye . . . some thieves—*other* thieves . . ." I scowled at Brennan. "I told *you* this already."

"A little," he agreed. And then he looked past Rory to the colt, who had recovered himself enough to wander back into the clearing. "But—did you really give him in payment?" His tone sounded uncharacteristically forlorn.

Hart snorted inelegantly. "If she did, *rujho*, surely she is worth the price."

Brennan's mouth hooked down. "Perhaps. Sometimes. Not today." He looked at me pointedly. "Nor last night." Then his attention focused itself on Rory again. "My thanks for aiding Keely—*leijhana tu'sai*, in the Old Tongue—but I will make the payment in coin."

Hart, oddly, was watching me instead of his brother. "Let him go, *rujho*."

Brennan shot him an unappreciative scowl. "Who— the colt or the thief?"

Hart's gaze was unwavering. "Both, I think."

I was hot, suddenly, and strangely unsettled. Lighthearted, good-natured Hart was more perceptive than I appreciated.

Brennan glanced at me briefly, sensing something in Hart's studied lightness, but apparently learned nothing from my red-faced expression. He shook his head, swung a leg across his saddle and jumped down. "No. I came to fetch home my colt, and so I shall."

Behind me, Rory shifted.

I thought of Brennan in Sean's place, dead of a broken skull. And also I thought of Rory, dead of a shredded throat. Swiftly I moved between them.

In the Old Tongue, Brennan told me to get out of his way. He also called me a fool and a dithering female, which I did not particularly care for, and suggested I might do better to differentiate between my possessions and his, before I was so generous with their disposition.

Equally glib, I called him a pompous, humorless *ku'reshtin* and suggested he give his *cheysula* a large portion of the respect and affection he reserved for his precious horses . . . which was not fair and did little to soothe his temper, but made me feel better nonetheless, if only briefly. Then I felt guilty.

Brennan is a fair man, and even-tempered most of the time, and does not react rashly to the provocations others, and I, give him. Usually. But he is Cheysuli, and none of us are made of stone; he had, upon occasion, lost his temper entirely, and people suffered for it.

Certainly Rory might.

Brennan put his hands on my shoulders. I pulled out of his grasp, spun, jerked my knife free of the sheath and pressed the hilt into Rory's hands.

"Lass—"

"Take it!" I hissed, and swung back to face Brennan.

Hart, I saw, was nodding, surprised by none of it. But Brennan clearly was.

He looked at Rory, who cradled the long-knife in his hands. He looked at the knife itself, as if he needed to assure himself it was what he thought it was. And then, white-faced, he looked at me.

I said nothing at all, knowing there was no need. Not for Brennan's benefit; who was Cheysuli, and knew.

He swallowed tightly, reining in the shock, the dull anger, the sudden hostility. The latter puzzled me until he spoke. "Keep your mouth from Maeve."

I was, suddenly, hot, so hot I was wet with it. I wanted to tell him he was wrong, *wrong,* but to do so revoked the gesture, diluting its purpose entirely. Destroying the meaning altogether, and therefore the protection.

Maeve, who was his favorite of the Mujhar's daughters. Whom I baited to her face and ridiculed behind her back, even before the brother who most loved her of us all.

"Aye," I agreed hoarsely.

Brennan turned back to Bane, his fidgety black stallion. He swung up, gathered reins, stared hard at me down the blade of his aristocratic nose. "Sean," he said tightly, "may be a bit discommoded."

Hart let Brennan go, holding his own bay gelding back. He looked at Rory, looked at me. "Or not," he said clearly, and swung the bay to follow his brother.

I watched Sleeta, mute, melt back into the shadows, making no sound with her passing. I watched Rael, also silent, lift from the branch and go. And Rory's men, saying nothing, disappeared into the trees.

Rory put the knife back into my sheath. "Lass," he said, "you smell."

It took effort to close my mouth.

"And your hair wants combing," he noted.

Aye, well, it did. But now, so did my temper.

Rory merely grinned, crinkling the flesh by his eyes. "Come to the fire," he said. "What you're needing *most* is a mug of Erinnish liquor."

I put my hand to my mouth. "None of that," I told him unevenly, speaking through muffling fingers.

"Aye." His hand was turning me, guiding me, pushing me through the vines and branches. "Aye, lass, you do . . . 'tis the only thing 'twill help the thumping in your head and the ocean chop in your belly."

His words made it worse. "Rory—I have to go back."

"Aye. After." He plopped me down on his favorite tree stump, then retrieved a wineskin and poured a pewter mug full. "Here, lass. Drink it all. 'Tis better than anything a leech might give you."

I clutched the mug, staring blankly over its rim. The pungent smell evoked The Rampant Lion. Candlelight, smoke, the aroma of fresh-carved meat. Shadows. Laughter and curses and shouts of victory; the rattle of rune-sticks and dice.

Brennan: searching for Rhiannon in the face of the Homanan wine-girl. *Hart*: rolling stones, explaining about Bezat. And me; of course, *me*: drinking cup after cup of *usca* for no reason at all I could think of except a need to escape.

"Sean," I said, remembering, and then I looked at Rory.

He sat down close by, arranging his bulk comfortably. Across the ash-filled fire cairn his men with averted faces quietly played an Erinnish wagering game, giving us the only privacy they could short of leaving the tiny camp.

Rory drank liquor straight out of the skin. His eyes were very calm, mostly shielded beneath lowered lashes. A strong, tough, proud man, made for better than outlawry. Made for a throne, I thought, as much as Brennan or Hart or Corin.

But he is bastard-born. Even if Sean were dead—

The liquor stilled my belly. It also cleared my head and gave me an odd, bright courage. "Why not you?" I asked. "You said Liam had acknowledged you—

that your paternity was no secret from anyone in
Erinn . . ." I drew in a deep breath. "Why not *you?*"

Rory's lashes lifted, showing me hard bright eyes.
"Me, lass . . . for what?"

"The throne," I said clearly. "I am the last to wish
harm to Sean—I promise you that, Rory—but I am
also the first, here, at this moment, to be completely
practical in things such as successions . . . I am, perhaps, more my *jehan's* daughter than I thought." I
shrugged a little, gripping the cool pewter, pressing
it hard against my breastbone. "If Sean *is* dead, Liam
will need an heir."

Lowered lids once again shuttered his eyes. He hid
thoughts behind thick lashes.

I wet drying lips. "When kings have no sons, no
heirs, they make shift where they can."

His tone was oddly flat. "I said much the same to
you of Brennan and Aileen."

"Aye, and I told you what Brennan would—or
would not—do." I paused, wishing I could be delicate; knowing it was not a particular gift of mine.
"Do you mean Liam would turn from Ierne and wed
another woman in hopes of getting a new son—an
infant—rather than make legitimate a full-grown,
proven man?"

Rory sucked down wine, squeezing the skin more
firmly than was required. It sent a broad, tight stream
shooting into his mouth to splash against teeth. Drop-
lets jeweled his beard.

I became aware of silence across the way. Eight
men watched him, watched me, waiting. Mute. Un-
moving. Waiting.

*They would serve him . . . by the gods, they would serve
him, as prince, as king, as bastard . . . to them it does not
matter. It is the man they honor, not the coincidence of
birth.*

I looked at Rory again. He had less right, perhaps,
than Teirnan to a throne, being born out of the line

of succession, and yet I believed him far more worthy. And far more dangerous, if he set his mind to have it.

Liam could have him killed—

Kings had done it before.

Rory looked straight at me. "D'ye think I'm fit for it?"

"Aye." I did not hesitate.

"You hardly know me, lass."

"Enough," I said. "Enough."

The line of his mouth hardened. "Do you, now, I'm wondering . . . *and* I'm wondering how."

I shrugged, frowning, scowling into the pewter mug. "I know," I said. "I can tell. I can *feel* it—" I shook my head, avoiding his eyes for fear of what I would see. "I grew up with brothers, Rory . . . boys who were raised to be kings. They are all of them fit, I think . . . and you no less than them."

Rory's gaze was unwavering. "If I'm fit for a throne, lass, am I also fit for you?"

I nearly dropped the mug. "What?"

Deliberately, he said, "The heir to the House of Eagles is betrothed to Keely of Homana."

Something stirred sluggishly within me. Not anger. Not fear. Something like—*anticipation.*

I was curiously light-headed. "So he is," I said.

Rory's eyes changed. "No," he said abruptly, and I felt the tension snap.

"What?" I asked. "What?"

"I'll take nothing not offered, lass . . . neither a woman nor a throne."

A blurt of bittersweet laughter scraped my throat. "In Brennan's eyes, I am."

"What d'ye—?" And then, comprehending, "Oh, lass, *no.*"

"Cheysuli custom," I explained. "The gift of a knife from woman to man is similar to your custom of hearth-friends, but with a substantial difference. In the clans, the guest *does* share the host's bed."

Rory's eyes were steady. "Only if invited. And the other, I think, knew better . . . he said something of the sort."

I lifted one heavy shoulder. "*Brennan* thinks you were. By giving you my knife I was extending Cheysuli protection to you." I swallowed tightly. "I was offering you my clan-rights."

I could not judge if he comprehended the nuances of what I had told him. The language, to me, was well known, but to a foreigner the words had different meanings, different intentions. Yet I did not know how else to say it without stripping myself naked, without baring my true feelings.

Rory smiled faintly. "You did it to keep us from fighting."

"Aye."

"To keep him from getting hurt."

"*And* you," I retorted. "Do you think Brennan would be so easy?"

He chewed his lip, considering. "Depending," he decided, "on whether he was cat or man."

I scowled blackly. "*You* are sure of yourself."

Rory's smile was benign. "I'm Erinnish, lass . . . born of the House of Eagles."

And so we returned to the beginning. In my mind's eye I placed him on the Lion, because it was the only throne I knew. And then flinched away from it, retreating onto ground that gave me comfort.

"What you are," I told him, "is an arrogant, puffed-up fool." I set down the mug and rose.

Rory caught a wrist as I turned, holding me back. "Will you stay for meat, lass? And more of the liquor you're in need of?"

Gods, I am so weary— I rubbed gritty eyes. "What I am in need of is a bed."

The bearded grin was broad. "I've that as well, my lass."

"Ku'reshtin," I said half-heartedly, catching the skin as he tossed it to me.

Eleven

In the morning, Rory brought Brennan's colt to me. "Take him, lass," he said. "I'll not be responsible for setting you and your brother at odds."

I made a face. "Oh, Brennan is just—*Brennan*."

Rory shrugged, putting the reins into my hands. "Take him anyway. I stole him from you, lass. 'Tis time he went home again."

"But—what you said to Brennan—" I frowned. "I thought you meant to keep him."

What I could see of his mouth was pulled down into a wry curl. "Aye, well, 'tisn't always a woman saying one thing and meaning another ..." He grinned. "Take him, lass. He's a bright, fine lad, deserving of better care and stables than I can give him, I'm thinking."

"And yourself?" I asked.

For a moment he was baffled. And then the brows unknitted, the frown disappeared, the lashes briefly veiled his eyes. When he looked at me again, he wore the mask I had seen before. On him and on the others.

"Go home," I suggested quietly. "You are no good to your House here."

Rory jeered at me. "Neither are you to yours. You're supposed to be in Erinn, wed to my royal brother and whelping him lad after lad." He paused in silent consideration. "And perchance a few lasses ... one or two might do, to wed into other Houses."

"Blathering fool," I said sweetly, and swung up.

into the saddle. "My thanks for the meat and drink, *and* the empty bed." I grinned at his sour expression. "*Leijhana tu'sai*, Erinnish—and may the next horse you steal belong to an Ihlini."

Rory slapped the chestnut rump. With effort I hung on, and was gone much too quickly to even say good-bye.

This time, I felt him. I sensed his presence obscuring the link as I approached Homana-Mujhar. It was hardly noticeable, but so close to the palace I was also close to *lir* such as Sleeta, Rael, Tasha and Serri. It did not matter that I reached for none of them. They were always present, and I was always aware of them. It was my task to screen them out, so as not to lose my mind.

But now the link was warped, and growing worse. Weakening. A warning of Ihlini; thank the gods it was Taliesin.

He came into the outer bailey as I rode through the big gate, turning toward the stable. He smiled, gave me good welcome, added news of my brothers. "Hart has won his wager."

I pulled the chestnut to a halt, ignoring his pleas to go on. He knew he was nearly home. "I should have known," I sighed. "Do you know what it was?"

The harper laughed and nodded. "He believed you would stay the night. Brennan said no, that your pride would prevent you."

I scowled at the colt's bright mane. "My pride has nothing to do with it." And then I looked sharply at Taliesin. "Do the others know?"

"That you spent the night with Erinnish outlaws?" Taliesin nodded. "The wager was made before witnesses, including myself. Also the Mujhar."

"*Also the M—*" I cut off the incredulous echo. "By the gods, I swear they have no sense. Either of them. Hart is no surprise, but *Brennan* . . ." I shook my head in disbelief. "He must be very angry with me, to traffic in such dealings."

The harper's voice was dry. "He suggested the wager."

It snapped my head up. "Brennan—?" But I nodded almost at once. "Oh, aye, of course . . . his way of telling *jehan* without actually bearing the tale." I sighed heavily and picked at a knot in the colt's mane. "So, everyone knows of Rory. But then, Deirdre already did, after The Rampant Lion; it comes as no surprise." I flicked him a glance. "Was *jehan* very angry?"

Taliesin considered it. "He said it was behavior most unlike you in some ways, and very like you in others."

I brightened. "But you are sure he was not angry?"

He tucked hands inside his sleeves. "I think he wanted to be. But Hart said there was no cause. That he knows you better than Brennan, who sees only what you show him."

Absently I unhooked a foot from the stirrup, swung the leg over, slithered down the colt's firm side until I stood on cobbles. "I gave him my knife," I said slowly. "There was more to it than merely staying the night—they are accustomed to me spending time away from Mujhara, when I visit Clankeep." I avoided the harper's eyes, looking instead at the chestnut's hooves. "I gave the man my knife."

Clearly, he knew what it meant. "You must make your own integrity," he said gently. "And then you may keep it or discard it, depending on your desires."

I turned, clutching reins, ignoring the colt's nose planted in my spine even as he nudged. "You are saying no one could—or *should*—do it for me."

Taliesin's eyes were oddly serene. "You must not allow them to, if you are to know true freedom."

There came a clatter of hooves behind us. I glanced

over, saw a rider come into the bailey from the city, looked again at Taliesin. "No matter who you are?"

"Perhaps because of it." He put out a twisted hand, and I saw what he waited for. Not me, but for the horse-boy who brought his spotted gelding and provisions for a journey.

It startled me. "Are you going?"

Taliesin accepted the horse, thanked the boy, hooked the reins through twisted hands. "Aye. I have given Niall my news. I did not intend to stay."

The rider clattered by us, bound for the inner bailey. He was a stranger to me, wearing livery I did not know.

I looked back at Taliesin. "I wish you would stay," I told him. "You have only just come, and you yourself said Strahan destroyed your cottage."

Taliesin smiled. "Then it is time I built a new one."

Beyond the white-haired harper, the rider was stopped at the gate to the inner bailey. Lio had the duty, asking the rider's business. When he had his answer, he gestured the man to pass. And then, seeing me, checked the rider abruptly by catching his horse's rein.

I frowned. Lio was pointing to me, or perhaps to Taliesin. I saw the rider bend down to hear better, then he looked at us, nodded, rode back the way he had come.

Reaching us, he reined in. He was brown-haired, brown-eyed, dressed in road-stained green wool, dark leather. The braided messenger's baldric stretched diagonally across his chest. Its shoulder boss was massive silver, shaped like a leaping hound.

He had the courtesy of a trained messenger, but the undertone was startled. "The Princess Royal of Homana?"

Taliesin and I exchanged an amused glance. "Aye," I agreed, knowing precisely what he saw.

He jumped down from his horse at once and presented me with a flat sealed packet he took from inside his doublet. "Lady," he said, "from my lord. He's wishing you good health, and hopes to join you soon."

The accent was unmistakable. "Erinn," I said numbly.

The young man grinned. "Aye, from Kilore. Prince's man, lady, come to serve you as well as my lord."

Alive, alive . . . he is alive after all . . . Rory, you did not kill him, you did not break his head.

Oh, gods. Rory.

The packet was heavy in slack fingers. "Serve me—?" I echoed dully.

Brown eyes were shrewdly judgmental, but what he thought I could not tell, not being disposed to try. "I'll be taking your message back to Hondarth, where my lord waits at The Red Stag Inn." He paused delicately. "If you'll be sending one, lady."

I stared hard at the silver hound on his baldric. Then at the identical impression made in green wax sealing the packet closed. "How is his health?" I asked.

The messenger was clearly startled. "Of good health, he is, lady . . . and of great good spirits, now that he's to wed." His smile was slight and private; he was, I thought, altogether too discerning for my taste. "Will you be sending a message?"

I signed for him to wait, then broke open the seal and unfolded the parchment. A blunt, inelegant message, in a blunt, inelegant hand; had he no clerk to write it for him?

It lacked salutation or honorific, beginning simply:

Keely—
Past time the marriage was made, so we may get the heirs needed for Erinn. I am my father's only son, and

*Erinn must be secured. Enough time has passed, I
think, why waste any more? We are both of us more
than old enough, and the betrothal long made. Let us
wed as soon as possible, so the bairns may be begun.*

Even Rory, I thought, had more eloquence than
this. I read the message again, noting the signature
in its bold, black hand. And yet a third time, aware
now of rising anger and a cold hostility.

With great care I folded the parchment. Clearly
the messenger knew what his lord had written; I
could see it in his eyes. "A message?" I said. "Aye,
indeed I have one ... but I will give it to him
myself."

It startled him. "Lady?"

"Are you deaf?" I asked coolly, aware of my rudeness and, in an odd, clear detachment, not caring in
the least. "I said I will give it to him myself." I
gestured briefly. "You may take yourself to the kitchens, where you will be given food and wine. Stay the
night, if you wish; I require nothing from you save
your immediate absence."

His face was white, but he said nothing more.
Simply bowed stiffly, turned his horse, walked smartly
toward the gate to the inner bailey.

Taliesin's disapproval was manifest, though little
of it showed in his expression. Saying nothing, I
handed the parchment to him and bade him read it.

When he had finished, I saw comprehension in his
eyes. "Sean," he said delicately, "is prince, not
diplomat."

"Even princes learn better," I said curtly. "Are
there no tutors in Erinn? Has he no one to write a
better hand, *and* with better words?"

The harper folded the parchment again, though
the task was awkward for him. "Are you angry because of what he has written, and how—or because
your freedom is at an end?"

"All of it," I said flatly. "By the gods, who does he think he is? To write me such things when he has never written before!"

"Perhaps this is why." Taliesin's tone was gentle. "Instead of dwelling on his crudeness, think instead that he wrote it himself. He did not delegate it to a clerk, who indeed would choose softer words, but wrote it in his own hand, speaking of private things to the woman he must marry. Some men find it difficult, much more so than women do. Perhaps he felt hideously awkward, and took no time about it." His smile was empathetic. "He wrote in Homanan, after all, which is hardly his firstborn language. Think of the man in place of the message. Judge Sean when you have met him."

The note *had* been in Homanan, not in Erinnish, though I could read it well enough after years spent with Deirdre. It showed he had taken the time to put it in my own tongue. It was something, I supposed . . . but I could wish—and *did* wish—he had spent his care on the content instead of on the tongue.

I looked at Taliesin, seeing Rory's face before me. Blunt-spoken, forthright Rory, yet a man nearer my own heart than the prince more concerned with heirs.

His father's only son? No, I think not. What I think, my Erinnish eaglet, is you had better count again.

Perversely, Taliesin's last words came back to me: *Judge Sean when you have met him.* "Aye," I agreed, "so I shall. I am going at once to do so."

"To Hondarth?" Taliesin, like the messenger, showed his surprise openly. "Why not send word he is welcome here, instead? Have him come to you." He made a simple placatory gesture. "It is, after all, what he must intend . . . he would not expect you to come to him."

I smiled slowly, savoring the moment, anticipating what was to come. "Then he will learn, and soon, that I never do what is expected, by him or by anyone else." I took the parchment back from Taliesin, crushed it in trembling hands. "I have to do this thing. Sean must know what I am."

"Do *you*?" the harper asked.

I stared blindly at the crumpled parchment. "Not any more."

After a moment, he nodded. "Then I will come with you."

In shock, I stared at him. "To Hondarth? But— you said you meant to go north . . . to rebuild your cottage."

He shrugged. "That can wait. If you truly mean to go, I will accompany you."

I would welcome him ordinarily, but his presence now would interfere. "I meant to go in *lir*-shape. A horse will slow me down, and with you I cannot fly."

"Fly, and have Sean think you too eager?" Taliesin smiled. "If you must go, Keely, do it with a measure of decorum. Or you will surely have him thinking you are hot to share his bed."

I smiled grimly. "That, I assure you, is the last thing I am—and I will see he knows it."

Taliesin watched in growing alarm as I prepared to mount Brennan's colt. "Do you mean to go now? As you are? Without telling Niall or the others?"

I swung up on the colt. "I have coin," I told him, "and you a few provisions. We can buy more on the road, and in Hondarth we can bathe. I am not entirely blind to the appearance I present; I will take pains to change it, though not as much, perhaps, as Deirdre would have me do." I grinned, envisioning her expression; also envisioning Sean's. "As for telling the others, let the Prince of Erinn's royal messenger spread the word. They will know what I have done." I gathered reins. "And, probably, why."

Twelve

Very slowly, with infinite care—much more than is my custom, which is dictated by impatience—I braided heavy waist-length hair into a single tawny rope plaited more loosely than usual. Not because I particularly desired to make myself beautiful for Sean, but because it gave me time.

My silent curse was self-mocking. Beautiful. Oh, *aye*.

I stopped short, swearing, and ripped out half the braid. Started over, forcing treble sections into a twisted rope, weaving it smooth and sleek, taming the stubborn wave of my hair into something controllable.

And will Sean try the same with me? Yet again I stopped, fingers clutching hair. *Gods, what am I doing?*

I was going to Sean.

The tap on the door was soft. Taliesin, I knew; he had come to escort me to The Red Stag Inn. It was but one street over, close by the sea. We had stopped at another inn to rest the night and to buy a bath, so I would not offend a princely nose with the stink of a two-week journey.

"Come." Quickly I finished braiding my hair, tying it off with leather.

He entered and shut the door, then paused with his back to it. His blue robe was freshly brushed, his white hair newly combed, silver harper's circlet in place. He was, as always, elegant, with a quiet, uncluttered grace. The only movement he had not mastered was the awkwardness of his hands.

Taliesin smiled. "I thought you might refuse the skirt, even after you bought it."

I scowled at him darkly. "Aye, well, I was wrong to think I might wear it. It was a waste of coin." I rose from the edge of the cot, bent to pull on boots. "I refuse to be what I am not; Sean must take me as I am."

"In leggings, jerkin, long-knife." His voice was quietly amused. "It will do, Keely . . . I promise, it will do."

I tugged on the second boot, settled my foot as I straightened. "I am not Ilsa," I snapped. "I am not a beautiful woman."

"No," he agreed.

Hands went to hips. Elbows stuck out from my sides. "You might have *disagreed*, if only for courtesy's sake."

"Why? You value honesty above all else, do you not? And, not being a vain woman, you have no patience for empty flattery." His tone, as always, was polite and inoffensive, while stripping bare the truth more eloquently than a blade. "Beautiful women rely on their beauty; you rely on *you*."

I sat myself down again, lacking the Ihlini's grace. But then I had never had it; grace or beauty. "Gods, I am *afraid*—"

"Of course you are," he agreed. "But as for your appearance, there is nothing to be ashamed of. You are not beautiful, no, not as I have seen women beautiful, women such as Ilsa, but there is a wondrous strength and courage in your face, in your carriage, in the set of your head, the way you unerringly seek out the truth in a man's soul." He smiled warmly. "Your spirit was bred in your bones."

"Another way of saying I am plain." I sighed, clapping a hand to either side of my face. "Why am I saying these things? I never cared before. I sound like *Maeve*, now, staring into her polished plate!"

Taliesin crossed the tiny room to me and pulled my hands away. His candor, as always, was couched in courtesy, but lacked no point for all of that. "Your nose is too straight," he said, "your cheekbones high and too sharply cut, lending the set of your eyes a slant. Your jaw is masculine rather than feminine, and your mouth too wide and bold for the accepted style in employing feminine wiles." He saw my expression and laughed. "You use your eyes for seeing, not for luring men, and your tongue you use as a sword, not for promises." Gently, he cradled my chin in warped, knotted fingers. "You are not a great beauty, no, but most definitely a Cheysuli ... with pride and power intact."

"But not the color," I said hollowly. "Blonde hair in place of black, blue eyes in place of yellow. And my skin is much too fair."

"Does it matter so very much?"

"Aye." I stared down at my boots as he took his hand away. "Aye, indeed it does. You have only to look at Brennan to see what I should be ... to see what I am not."

"What I see," he said plainly, "is a frightened, unhappy woman. I thought I came with Keely."

Something pinched my belly. I stared back at him bleakly, silenced, and then drew in a belly-deep breath that filled my head with light. "Aye, so you did." I rose, pulled my jerkin straight, resettled belt and buckle. "Shall we go, then? Shall we amaze the Prince of Erinn?"

Taliesin smiled. "Indeed, I think we shall."

I am accustomed to being stared at when I walk into a tavern or the common room of an inn, because women rarely enter either, being content to go to tamer places for food and drink and company. But I have never been one for avoiding a hospitable place, regardless of the behavior of its patrons and the thoughts they might care to think.

What the men in The Red Stag Inn thought, I could not say. They said nothing to me, none of them, being disposed only to watch, and with a quiet courtesy I had no reason to question. The common room was mostly empty save for a handful of strangers, and they kept to themselves in a private corner. They ate, drank, wagered, but did it nearly in silence, clearly knowing each other so well they had no need of words.

Much like Rory's men—

I broke it off at once. I was here for Sean, not Rory; it would do none of us any good if I set one brother against the other, even inside my head. Out of it was more dangerous; they had already proved themselves more than willing to fight over a wine-girl. What of the Mujhar's daughter?

"Here." Taliesin indicated a table near the wooden stairway. "We will send word through the tapster, and take our time over wine."

I hooked out a stool and sat down. "More delay for the sake of decorum?"

"There is no need to *run*." He seated himself, signaled the tapster, smiled at me kindly. "I know it is your way to rush headlong at things you wish to confront, but in this case it may be wisest to wait. You are to *marry*, Keely, and live your lives together . . . give yourselves time to learn how the other thinks, before accusing one another of being blind to needs and desires."

"*My* needs—" But I cut it off voluntarily as the tapster hastened over.

Taliesin ordered wine and cheese and then quietly, so very quietly, suggested the tapster take word to his royal guest that someone was here to see him. He said nothing at all of names, knowing there was no need; the tapster would describe both of us in detail, and Sean would know at once.

I sensed attentiveness from the other side of the common room as the tapster hastened away. I thought it more than likely they were Sean's royal escort, being clothed in Erinnish green and bearing hound-shaped bosses on leather tabards, much as the messenger had. I cast them a sidelong glance, saw them talking among themselves, and then one of them rose.

Not Sean. I knew it. Aileen had described him—blond, brown-eyed, big—and this man did not fit.

He paused at our table. His smile was tentative, but not his courtesy. "Forgive me," he said, "but would you be the Princess Royal of Homana?"

"Why?" I asked bluntly.

His grin widened. He had a good face, and green eyes glinted. "Because my lord sent a message somewhat lacking in diplomacy, and we wagered you might come if only to set him to rights." Sandy brows arched up. "You *would* be her, would ye not? Come to set him to rights?"

I exchanged glances with Taliesin. "If I were not," I said, "would you still be so free telling your lord's business to a stranger?"

"Oh, aye. He's not a man much troubled by appearances, being made for other things." He touched two fingers to the wolfhound brooch. "Lady, have you come? Will I win my wager?"

I sighed, disliking intensely that I was so predictable, especially to a man—*and* men—I had not met. "You wagered I would come?"

His eyes brightened, acknowledging my concession. "Aye, lady, I did . . . only a few of us did not. Your reputation—" But he checked instantly, turning red, knowing he had transgressed. "Lady . . . oh, *lady*—"

I shook my head. "It makes no difference. I know.

what I am; so, it appears, do you. Well, it will save me time making myself clear to your lord." I looked past him to the tapster. "No doubt he knows by now."

The tapster took that for permission to come forward, and did so. "Lady, the Prince of Erinn knows. But he sends to tell you he is in his bath. Will you wait?"

Dryly, I answered, "Rather than walking in on his nakedness? Aye, I will wait. There will be time for that later."

It amused the young Erinnishman, who told me his name was Galen and ordered The Red Stag's best wine for his lord's lady. Taliesin he all but ignored, though his manner was above reproach. He was simply more taken with me, since I would become his mistress once the vows were made and was therefore worth more attention.

Taliesin was unperturbed, but equally amused. He said nothing as the Erinnish slowly came over one by one, to pay me their respects in nearly inaudible Homanan. Homanan, not Erinnish; their accents were quite bad. I answered them in their own tongue and saw subtle glances exchanged, silent secrets passed, just like Rory's men. Were all Erinnish so?

When the wine came, Galen poured it and proposed a toast to the Princess Royal of Homana, wishing her perfect health. Again, in bad Homanan, making an effort to please me. I answered again in Erinnish and saw them, one by one, drink the wine left in their cups even as I drank my own.

And then I was poured a second, this time drinking to Sean. I thought it only polite to do so, since I had already been honored. They were pleasant men, and courteous, lacking the slyness I had seen in the messenger's eyes, knowing what he carried. It seemed they all knew, but none was amused by it at my expense. Plainly, they had thought Sean's words less

than tactful, even in Homanan, which was why most
had wagered on me.

As bad as Hart, all of them—

"Lady." It was the tapster at my side. "Lady, will
you come up? The prince has sent to ask it."

Oh, gods. I swallowed down more wine, trying not
to gulp. Over the tankard I looked at Taliesin, be-
seeching him with my eyes.

He gave me nothing back save grave courtesy. He
would not come, I knew; it was for me to do. He had
come this far with me, but Sean was my *tahlmorra*.
Taliesin had his own.

I set down the tankard with careful precision. The
others melted away, leaving only Galen with his green
Erinnish eyes, waiting silently to escort me to his
lord.

A litany ran in my head. *Tell Sean the truth. Tell him
how you feel. You told Rory the whole of it—well, nearly
the whole of it—now you must tell Sean. He is Aileen's
brother—he cannot be so bad.*

Galen escorted me to a room, opened the door,
stepped aside to let me through. I swung back in
surprise. "No one is here."

He shook his head. "No, lady . . . 'tis Sheehan's
room, not the prince's. He'll be with him now, helping him to dress . . . shall I send Sheehan to you, or
would you prefer I stay?"

A third voice intruded. "No need," it said. "I am
here now. You may go, Galen."

Galen melted away at once, going back down the
stairs as the other came into the room. For a moment only I thought it might be Sean, but I knew at
once it was not. Sheehan, then. Whose room I was
in.

He smiled, closed the door, spread his hands as he
leaned against it. His expression was rueful. "Lady, I
must apologize. We've not been completely truthful
with you concerning my lord's condition."

"Condition?" I echoed. "I thought he was taking a bath."

"So he is," Sheehan agreed, "but only because we put him in it to settle his wine-soaked head. And, I fear, his wits. He drank too much last night."

"*Did* he?"

"Aye." He attempted to mask his amusement, but the rueful smile crept out. "I'm afraid 'twas your fault."

"*My* fault!"

"Aye. It was in your honor, lady . . . he was drinking to good fortune, good health, strong sons and daughters . . ." He spread his hands again. "He was singing your praises, lady—and making up whatever he could of those he doesn't know."

I slanted Sheehan a glance of wry disgust. "Oh, aye . . . did he drink to a wine-girl, too? Did he drink to his banished brother?"

Sheehan pushed himself off the door and paced slowly away from it, showing me his back. He was tall, inherently graceful, lacking Rory's bulk but none of Rory's presence.

He turned. "My lord says nothing of his brother."

"Perhaps it is time he did." Sheehan, I thought, would be worth cultivating. He had the look of a man accustomed to learning the truth, even though he divulged none of it until it suited his—or his lord's—purposes. "Is he often in his cups?"

Sheehan's mouth was taut. "Since his brother left."

So, it meant something. That I could respect. "He could ask him back."

He frowned minutely. "You know his brother?"

"Rory?" I grinned. "Aye, I know the Redbeard. He came here in his exile. I had occasion to meet him."

Sheehan gestured to the tiny table by the window. "Wine? Sean should not be long . . . we've set four men to making him presentable. 'Tis why so few were downstairs to pay you honor. You'll forgive them, I hope?"

I smiled, thinking of my own experience with too much liquor. "Better you should ask if I will forgive *him*."

He turned from pouring wine. "But why? Sean is a man, lady . . . he does as he pleases. If it includes drinking overmuch, 'tis his choice. And it *was* in your honor."

"Aye, of course, that excuses it." I took the cup he offered, sipped out of courtesy, found the wine to my taste. "I will wed no drunkard, Sheehan. No matter who he is."

"You might reform him, lady." He smiled, drank, gestured toward a stool. "Will you sit? 'Tis but a poor room, but my lord was in no mood to go farther. We took what we could find in the way of accommodations."

I sat down, sipped wine, contemplated Sean's man across the rim of the pewter mug. "What are you to the prince? Not a soldier, I think . . . you have not the manner for it." I studied him more closely. "Nor much of an accent, either, for a man born in Erinn."

Sheehan smiled. "What accent I have is due to my circumstances. Erinnish-born I may be, but I grew up in Falia."

"Falia!" It astonished me. "How did you come to be *there*? We have trade with Falia, but little more than that. I have met no one who lives there."

He did not sit, being disposed to pace the room idly, indolent as a cat. He sipped wine, thought private thoughts, turned at last to me. "My father is Falian. A merchant. He came to Erinn for trade, and there he met and lay with my mother. He went back to Falia before I was born." He shrugged a little, as if dismissing the pain he must have felt once. "When I was eight my mother sent me to him, to Bortall, the High King's city, where he had his business. He knew I was his by looking at me. He accepted me, acknowledged me; I grew up there, and came back to Erinn twelve years later. I have been here—*there*—ever since." He smiled. "A poor tale, I fear—my life has been uneventful."

"But you serve a prince now."

"Sean is a good master. I could ask for no better." He stood at the table again, and again he did not sit. His voice was very soft. "You say nothing of my eye."

I smiled. "My father lacks an eye. I am accustomed to seeing a patch."

He raised dark brows, one mostly obscured by the strap that held the patch in place over the left eye. "That would explain, of course. You have tact, lady . . . a wondrous sense of discretion."

I laughed at him. "I? Oh, no, Sheehan, that I do not have. Anyone can tell you. Anyone *will*."

He smiled warmly. A handsome man, Sheehan, even lacking an eye. He was black-haired, bearded, showing good white teeth. Thick hair was cropped to his shoulders, where it curled against the drape of a soft leather doublet dyed blue. The color matched his eye.

"What else are you?" he asked. "If lacking in tact, in discretion, what do you *have*?"

He was due the truth, asking such of me. "Power," I told him succinctly. "Magic in my blood."

"Aye, of course: the shapechange." His beard was trimmed short and neat, unlike Rory's bush. I could see his mouth clearly as it moved into a smile. A polite, skeptical smile, telling me what he thought. "I have heard the tales."

"More," I said, "much more. Is there no magic in Falia? I know there is much in Erinn. How can you disbelieve?"

"Show me," he said lightly.

Over the cup, I stared at him. And then I set the

cup down. "I think it is time you saw to your lord, Sheehan. I am content to wait alone."

"Show me." More intently.

Sluggish anger rose. "I am not a trained dog, performing at your whim. What I am is—"

"*Show* me," he hissed. "Or is it all a lie?"

I stood up. "Do you think—" I caught myself against the table, trying to blink sudden weakness away. "Sheehan—"

"No," he said plainly. "*Stra*han." And stripped the patch from his perfect brown eye.

The wine . . . of course, *the wine*—

I turned to run, but fell. Nothing was right any more. The floor had become the roof—the roof was beneath my feet—the walls were closing in—

"Keely," he said gently, "running will not help. By now you can barely crawl."

His Erinnish accent was banished. Now he spoke fluent Homanan with a faint Solindish undertone, precisely as Strahan would. As my brothers said he did.

I pulled the table over, spilling wine as the jug broke. Shards littered the floor; wine stained my hands, my face, my leathers. I picked up the cup and threw it.

It did not so much as go near him. He guided it aside with a subtle gesture from a single negligent finger.

—numb—

Strahan came to me, knelt down, caught me in both hands. I tried to spit in his face but could not raise the saliva.

"Much too late," he said. "Do you think me a foolish man? I prepared well for this . . . it took me all of two years." Hands tightened against my bare arms. "Ever since I lost your brothers."

Taliesin. If I could reach the door somehow, or shout his name, or summon the magic to me—

"Try," he suggested. "*Try.* It will please me to see you fail. It will please me to see you cry."

—gods—so numb—too *numb*—

"Come up with me," he whispered. "Come up with me from the floor . . . we are both of us due better. It does not become you, Keely. Cheysuli never kneel. Cheysuli never *grovel*—"

He dragged me up from the floor, set me on my feet, laughed when I would have fallen. Only his hands kept me up.

"Where is the magic?" he asked. "Where is the power now? Where is your Old Blood, Keely . . . your legacy from Alix?" His face was so close, *too* close. "What has become of your spirit? Your famous sword-sharp tongue? Your vaunted warrior prowess?"

I tipped back my head and screamed, but nothing came out of my throat.

"Too late," he said sadly. "Much too late, Keely. Taliesin, too, I have taken, and this time I will keep him. This time I will kill him."

Bodily, Strahan turned me. Pressed my back against the wall. I hung there in his arms. My bones had turned to water.

"You *need* me," he said, and stepped away from me.

I fell. Down the wall to the floor, legs tangling with my arms. My head thumped against the wood.

He left me lying there, helpless in my own flesh. "I need *you*," he told me, "to bear the Firstborn children. I have begun already, with Rhiannon, with Sidra, but I require the proper blood, the proper body. Yours will do, I think."

I twitched. Rolled my head. It was the only protest I could make.

Strahan knelt once more. His hands were gentle on my wrists as he pulled me upright from the floor. He leaned me against the wall, legs sprawled in two directions, and made shift to put them right, as if to give me back some decorum.

Decorum, when he had stolen my dignity.

Spasms set arms and legs to twitching. In his hands, I shuddered.

"I know," Strahan said gently. "The first effects are unpleasant, but I promise you it will get better. This will not last long."

I was hot.

I was cold.

Cramps bound up my belly.

Strahan gripped my wrists. "Let it take you," he said. "There is nothing you can do. Let it change the blood in your veins, and then you will feel no pain."

—my *blood*—?

I writhed away from him.

"Here," he said, "I will show you."

Strahan took my knife. Turned over one of my arms to bare my wrist. And cut deeply into the flesh.

There was nothing. Nothing at all. No rush of bright red blood. No spillage across my flesh. Just a deep, clean cut, enough to kill me if left untended.

But I did not *bleed.*

Fingers were locked on my wrist. "There," he said. "There."

And so it was. There. Sluggish, but *there.* Welling slowly out of the wound to creep across my flesh.

At last I made a sound. Not much more than a whimper.

Black. My blood was *black.*

Strahan's eyes were intent. "Not forever," he promised. "For only as long as I need you. But I need you without your *lir*-gifts, and this is the only way."

The room was too bright. I shut my eyes against the light; against the mismatched eyes. One blue. One brown. In a face of incredible beauty, if muted by the beard.

He had cut his hair. Grown a beard. Worn a patch-over one telltale eye. He had set and baited the trap, and I had put myself in it.

I felt his hand sliding my knife back home in its sheath. Aye, and why not? I could do nothing against him. I could not open my eyes.

Tenderly, he stroked a strand of hair out of my lashes. "I will get a child on you, and I will use it against your kin. Your father, your uncle, your sister, your brothers ... I will destroy the House of Homana, and all with the aid of our child."

Not mine. Not his. *Ours.*

His voice was very gentle. "Do not fret, I beg. It will bring no pain to you. I am not a cruel man, Keely, to cause pain for pleasure's sake. I am a simple, devout man, no different from any other, save I am sworn to serve my god, even as the Cheysuli are sworn to theirs. What I do is *required*, not a perverted whim. So I will make it easy for you."

I forced my eyes open and stared.

Strahan's smile was sweet. "There will be no dishonor in it, no besmirching of your race. By morning, Keely, I promise, you will have forgotten you were ever Cheysuli."

PART III

One

Her memories began coming back in bits and pieces, slowly. Carefully she hoarded each one like the rarest of gems, gathering them one by one to her breast until she could judge each stone for flaws; finding none, she named it good and put it into safekeeping.

Slowly her hoard grew until she had a double handful of bright stones. Looking at them all she saw the colors of the rainbow. The colors of the world so long, too long, denied her.

Looking at them all she saw a reflection of herself. And knew herself again, after a timeless, endless space and place where she had known nothing at all. Nothing, nothing at all, except the man who used her body.

The open casement in her room was high and narrow, but by pulling over a bench she could see what lay beyond. Heathered hills and tangled forests; beaches blushed silver by moonlight, blinding white by the light of day; slate-gray ocean and endless skies. Sea-spray and mist hung over the island like a veil: the breath of the gods themselves; thick by morning, thicker by night, burning bronze in afternoons.

A faint breeze blown in from the sea caught tawny hair. She wore it unbound now, unbraided, falling freely to her waist. Because Strahan preferred it so.

She stood on the bench and hugged the stone sill, pressing cold cheek against colder stone. Staring past beaches, past mists, trying to see Homana.

"A caged bird," said his quiet, vibrant voice. "A linnet, I think, or a sparrow . . . . certainly not the fleet falcon, who would never condone it, nor the fierce Homanan hawk, who knows how to avoid the hunter."

She did not turn. She remained on the bench, at the casement, driving fingers into stone with such force her nails splintered.

And his hands were on her, lifting her down, turning her to face him, to look on his remarkable face. Bearded now, but beautiful, in the way of perfect sculpture. "You must not grieve." A tender, beguiling sympathy. "Women who grieve do not suit the men who want them." His tone softened yet again. "And I want you, Keely."

She closed her eyes as his hand slid between the folds of her loose robe to caress her breasts. His touch, as always, raised her flesh into prickles.

He smiled with infinite tenderness, with contentment, sharing with her his pleasure, his satisfaction at her response. He was pleased by the reaction, as if to kindle any response in her at all, even revulsion, was enough to arouse him.

He withdrew his hand and wove spread fingers into the loosened hair, dragging it forward over her shoulders to be gathered and caressed, pressed possessively against his mouth. "I will keep you as long as it takes," he whispered into her hair. "If you begin to age before me, I will keep you young, until the child is conceived. Until the child is born. And still after, perhaps, if you please me."

She refused to look into the eerie eyes that had a power of their own; to do so admitted defeat. She had learned not to fight him when he took her to bed because to fight gave him reason to use sorcery on her, and that she hated worse than his intimacy.

Her hair was freed at last. "Keely," he said quietly, "I have brought someone to you."

She did not answer. When she eventually opened her eyes she saw only the white-haired harper, whom she had not seen for—

—how long?

Now, at last, she could cry.

* * *

He rocked me in his arms, as if I were a child. He sang me a lullaby, as if I were a child. And I feared perhaps I had gone much too far to come all the way back to myself.

"So *long*," I whispered. "How long has it been?"

He did not answer at once. And so I asked him again.

Taliesin sighed. "Three months, Keely. We are on the Crystal Isle."

I pulled away unsteadily, turning again to the casement. The mists were heavy beyond, but at least they were gone from my head.

"How do you fare?" he asked.

I stared out blindly. Shivered. When I could, I told him. "I have food and drink and excellent health. He makes certain of that."

Taliesin came up next to me. For a moment, only a moment, I recoiled out of habit. And then bit my lip in shame.

He took my hand in his twisted ones and sat me down on the bench even as he sat himself. He said nothing at all to me, knowing, perhaps instinctively, I needed the time to adjust. *Three months*, he had said; three months with only Strahan. His mouth, his hands, his manhood.

Bile rose into my throat. I swallowed it back with effort, and bit my lip again.

"What of you?" I asked. "What has he done to you?"

"Fed me, as he has you. Given me wine to drink. Left me quite alone. But he has also taken my lifestone." The harper smiled wearily. "So many times before, I thought he would do it. He has threatened, certainly, but only to trouble me, to *tease* me. Now, at last, he has, and I find, to my surprise, I am very afraid to die."

"Lifestone," I echoed blankly.

He put his hands away into his sleeves. "Those of

us who choose to serve Asar-Suti are initiated through ritual. Corin himself began it, though he escaped before he could be taken by the god. As for me, there was a time I served Tynstar, and a time I served the Seker." His tone was oddly brittle. "It was Tynstar who required the ritual of me so I would live forever, and witness what he had wrought. I did what I was made to do, and so death as you know it is denied me."

My voice did not sound natural, though I labored to make it so. "Strahan told me he meant to kill you."

"Oh, he can. I am not immortal. I can be *killed*, certainly, but I cannot die of sickness or old age. Much like a *lir*, who lives far past a normal lifespan until the warrior dies, or until the *lir* is killed." He sighed. "The lifestone is the physical embodiment of an Ihlini's oath to the Seker and the ritual he performs, much as the *lir* are the physical embodiment of a Cheysuli's service to his gods. It is heart, soul, *power*. Without it, we die. Even those sworn to the Seker."

Prickles rose on my flesh. "He can kill you through the lifestone?"

Taliesin looked back at me squarely, avoiding nothing, not even the truth. "Strahan need only destroy it. And this time, I think he will."

The pain was sudden and absolute. "Oh, gods— gods—it was me he wanted, not you . . . you should not even *be* here!"

He caught my hands in his own. "Keely, I swear—I would sooner be here with you than have you bear this alone. That I promise you. I do not regret my presence, only my inability to stop him." Twisted hands tightened. "To keep him from you. To get us *free* of him."

"Free," I echoed scornfully, trying to swallow the pain. And then I asked him for the buckle of his belt.

After a moment he complied, stripping it free of leather. A simple round bronze buckle with a prong to keep it in place, hooked through a loop of leather. It was the prong I wanted.

I shut my right hand around the buckle. Gripped it tightly, feeling the flesh protest. Turned my left arm over, baring my wrist, and showed him the delicate tracery of scars in pale, translucent flesh. Taliesin was plainly baffled, staring at my wrist, until I thrust the prong deeply into the flesh.

He cried out, grabbing my hand to tear the clasp from me. I let him have it, saying nothing, and watched the blood, too slowly, begin to flow at last.

It welled gradually out of the gash and crept down my arm, leaving a track of glistening blackness like the slime-trail of a slug. The excrescence of the god.

Quietly, I asked, "Have you seen its like before?"

Taliesin was trembling. He closed both hands around my wrist, shutting off the blood.

"Have you seen its like before?"

"Aye," he answered harshly. "In my own veins."

Slowly, I nodded. "He calls it the blood of the god. He says it replaces my own, until my own is strong again, and only then will I be free."

His face was very pale. He knew more than he was saying, knowing Strahan better than I.

I smiled, but only a little, and none too steadily. "I have done this before, as you see, though when he learned of it he took everything from me that could be used to cut." I stared hard at the blackened blood. It bore only a tinge of red.

"Keely—"

"I am tainted," I said. *"Unclean."*

"Oh, Keely, *no*—"

I overrode his protest, his attempt to silence me. For my sake as much as his own; he wanted me to forget, so I could live with myself. "Each night he takes me to bed. Spills his seed into me. And promises me the child I bear will bring down the House of Homana."

He stared blindly at my arm, then took his hands away. Aye, he knew. Being once Seker-sworn, he knew. The gash was already closing, sealed by blackened blood. The god looks after his own.

"If he knows *I* know," I told him, "he will make me forget again. Say nothing, Taliesin, when I play my part too well."

His voice was nearly shut off. "You should play no part—you should be required to play no part—" He shook his head, trembling. "Not *you,* so blessed, born of ancient blood—"

"I think it is why," I said. "Clearly Strahan does not expect it. He thinks I am still ensorcelled."

"Then *why*—"

"Because I have conceived."

I saw him age before me, though it was impossible.

"He will take it from me," I told him. "He will pervert it. He will make it a reflection of himself. He will use it to pull down the Lion." Firmly, I shook my head. "If I tell him, he will have won. I will not let him win."

"Keely." He took himself in hand. "Keely, if you tell him, if you admit you have conceived, you will save yourself from his bed. He will not trouble you now, not expecting a child. He wants it too badly."

Fiercely, I promised, *"I will not let him win."*

Taliesin shook his head. "You cannot hide it forever. He will know very soon."

Strahan's voice intruded. "Sooner than you may wish."

I recoiled violently. Usually he uses the door. This time he did not. Out of lilac smoke he appeared, to smile benignly at us both.

"Leijhana tu'sai, harper, as the Cheysuli would say. You have served your purpose. I have the truth out of her."

I pressed myself into the wall, knowing all my secrets laid bare. The child, my memory . . . gods, he would steal them both!

Strahan smiled at me. "Linen must be washed. Did you think you could keep it from me?"

"Then why—" I broke it off, sinking teeth into my lip. *Say nothing—nothing at all, to him—show him no fear, no weakness—let him think you are strong—*

"Because I wanted to hear you say it. To Taliesin, you would. To me, you would not . . . . and so now you see the result." His hands were eloquent. "Less than six months, I believe . . . and then I shall have the child."

"Take it now!" I shouted. "Do you think I will let it live? Do you think I will bear an abomination? An Ihlini-Cheysuli halfling?"

"Rhiannon did," he said. "So has Sidra, though it lacks the Cheysuli blood. And so, I think, will you. You have no choice in the matter." Strahan smiled serenely. "No more than bitch or mare."

I still held Taliesin's buckle. Such a poor little thing, meant only to clasp a belt. But I held it, and I used it, thrusting it toward his face.

—an eye—take an eye—his hawk took one of jehan's—

But I was stopped. Simply. Eloquently. He put out a hand and held me.

It was not a hand made of flesh.

Strahan stood very still in the place from which he had issued out of air. He smiled. Flesh crinkled by his eyes. Teeth split his beard, and he laughed. He *laughed*, as the hand caught my wrist.

Not his. Something made of nothingness, conjured out of ice.

Hands. One stripped the buckle from me and threw it down, where it rang against the stone. Another touched my breasts and pushed me back and back again, until I stood pressed against the wall.

"Strahan!" the harper cried. "By the gods, let her be!"

"Why?" he asked coolly. "Because she is a woman? No. No, indeed . . . I respect her too much for that. Keely would never countenance special treatment because of her sex. She has made it very clear." The Ihlini's smile was serene. "I give her what she wants. I give her equality."

He did not touch me, Strahan. He had sorcery to serve him.

The hands were in my hair, stroking it back from my face. Insinuating themselves in strands, in waves, in tangles, loosening all the knots. Combing it into silk.

"So much," Strahan said, "and yet so very little. Would you like more? I can conjure for your pleasure much more than hands, Keely. Mouth. Tongue. *More.*"

I pressed my hand against my mouth to keep myself from vomiting. I would not give him the pleasure.

One of the hands stripped mine away.

Strahan looked at Taliesin. "Shall I make you watch?"

There was nothing he could do with twisted, ruined hands. And Strahan held his lifestone.

"*Go—*" I cried. "Oh, *go*—he will do as he pleases—he always does as he pleases—but it will be worse if you are here." And cursed myself as I said it, for I had given Strahan a weapon. A means to make me beg.

"Then watch," Strahan said, and replaced conjured hands with his own.

Taliesin sought his escape the only way he had left, shutting his eyes, losing himself, giving me what little privacy he could summon. Little enough, but much. He had his own share of magic.

As Strahan took me there on the stones, the harper began to sing.

Two

I sat on the floor near the casement, huddled against the wall. Light spilled into the chamber, but I saw none of it. Blind, deaf and dumb, focused solely on the child. On the abomination Strahan had put in my womb.

I spread hands across my belly, showing nothing of the child. Still flat. Still firm. Still mine. Still hiding its treacherous secret. It housed the seed of the Ihlini, the downfall of my race.

I dug fingers into my flesh. "You will get no kindness from me."

It was the first time I had spoken to it, aloud. The first time I had acknowledged it as a living being. Boy, girl, it hardly mattered; what mattered was that if I allowed it to live, it would destroy its heritage.

"*No* kindness," I repeated.

Cheysuli, and so much more. Solindish, Atvian, Homanan. Also Ihlini. So close to the Firstborn, but made to serve another. Begotten of an Ihlini to serve Asar-Suti.

"You will die, first," I told it. "I will do what I can to kill you."

I thought of Ian, who had sired abomination on an Ihlini woman. Of Brennan, who had done the same. But they were men, both of them. This was different. This was not the same. They had spilled their seed into the womb, no more; *I* was left to bear it. To harvest Strahan's crop.

This is so very different.

I thought of Aileen, nearly dying in the effort, who truly regretted she could not try again. Of Ilsa, glorious Ilsa, who risked beauty and life, and would again, to give my brother a son to inherit the throne of Solinde.

Of women through the ages, bearing and burying children. Accepting what the gods gave them, while I cursed them for what they gave me.

"You have to die," I told it. "There is no place in the world for you. No place in my heart for you."

I drew up my legs and hugged them, staring at my cell. A fine room, large and airy, filled with bright bronze light. A huge draperied bed. Tables. Chairs. Fireplace. Worthy of my station, worthy of my name. Certainly worthy of my blood: it was Cheysuli-built. This was the Crystal Isle, birthplace of my people.

But now it was Strahan's lair.

I hugged my legs tightly and put my head down on my knees. "I have to kill you," I whispered. "There is no place for you here."

The shutters were snatched from the casement and slammed against the wall, banging, breaking, falling. The storm swept into my room.

I sat bolt upright in my bed and stared blindly into the blackness. It was dark, so *dark*—had the gods stolen the moon? Had Strahan perverted the light?

Wind roared into the chamber and stripped my hair from my face. With it came rain and leaves, scattered across my bed. It dampened the linen of my nightshift and made it a second skin, clinging like funeral wrappings and smelling of the grave.

I was wet, cold and wet, and astonished by the storm. It filled my chamber with fury, hammering at the palace, hammering at my ears. Lightning lit up the casement and invited the thunder in.

I flinched from the sound, and then knew it was.

more than thunder. It was the crash of wood on stone; the dull ring of iron unbolted.

Taliesin stood in my room. "Keely," he said, "*come.*"

I went, and at once, dragging the weight of clinging linen up around my knees. "Where is he?" I asked as we shut the door behind us. "Where has he gone? He cannot be *here*—he would know."

Taliesin bolted the door so it looked the same as before. "The violence of the storm has drawn their attention, interfering with a rite of obeisance to the Seker. Strahan has set all the guards to searching for damage. My own, so abruptly summoned, forgot to set a watch-ward; it was easy for me to unlock my door with a bit of the old magic." Wryly, he smiled. "I had put away such things because of how it has been perverted by Strahan and others like him. I was not certain I could summon it, but a little of it came. Enough to get me free."

"*And* me."

"And you. There was a watch-ward on your lock, but it was easy enough to break. Strahan expected no trouble from an Ihlini; it was set against Cheysuli." Frowning, he stretched out a gnarled hand. "I shall have to make one myself, so no one knows you have gone. Step back, Keely . . . your nearness may warp the power."

Aye, so it might. We were too close to one another, our magic neutralized. I had no recourse to *lir*-shape or any of the gifts, he could barely summon the *godfire* to make his crude little rune.

I moved away, scraping along the wall. The wind had torn open all the shutters and come in uninvited, blowing out candles, lamps, torches. It filled the palace with darkness. It filled me with trepidation: Strahan could be near.

"Hurry," I whispered urgently, as he summoned his share of *godfire*.

I saw light, tiny light, dancing on fingernails. Such

fragile, twisted hands conjuring fragile, twisted light. It glowed purple in the darkness and set his eyes aglitter.

He knitted the individual flames together into one, forming a knotted rune. Its brilliance made me squint—and then it began to gutter.

The strain was plain in his face. His flesh was damp with it. "Farther," he urged. "Only a little, Keely . . . you are still too close to me. It is a watch-ward against Cheysuli—if it senses you, it can kill you, or at least bring Strahan to us."

I might be too close even outside the walls. And even then, it might not matter; this was the Crystal Isle. As sacred to the Cheysuli as Valgaard to the Ihlini.

"Farther," he whispered urgently, as the rune intensified.

It leaned toward me, like a hunting hound catching a scent. And it *knew* me, just as Taliesin had promised. It tasted Cheysuli in my blood.

Taliesin whispered something to it, soothing as father to child. I did not know the words, having learned no Ihlini. But clearly the rune understood. It bathed his face with light, then bowed in the palm of his hand.

The harper turned. He placed his forefinger against the lock, shut his eyes, sent the fire from flesh to iron. I saw it begin to glow.

"Weak," he muttered, "too weak . . . but it will have to do."

He turned, saw me waiting, came away down the corridor. Took my hand, squeezed it, led me down a winding stairway to a low, arched door. Beyond howled the storm.

"There is a bailey," he said, "and gates. He will have set watch-wards there as well, to keep us in—if I can, I will break them. If not, we shall have to find another way."

Taliesin pushed open the door and let the storm inside the palace. It soaked us both at once, pasting the linen to me and flattening hair against scalp and shoulders.

We waited for the lightning, huddling in the doorway. And then, when it came, he pointed a twisted finger. "There," he said, "the gate." It was just visible through the rain, blackness tarnished silver by a necklace of lightning clinging to the sky.

I ran, squinting and mouthing curses, clutching sodden linen now heavy and cumbersome. I was barefoot and cold, nearly knocked down by the force of the wind. Now I cursed aloud; Strahan would never hear me. Only the roar of the storm.

Wet cobbles were slick and treacherous under my feet. Moss softened as did mud, turning the bailey into a morass. The palace had been too long unattended, and the lack of care showed. It made the place dangerous.

"Here—" Taliesin caught my arm, pulled me close. We had reached the massive gate and huddled at its foot.

"Watch-wards." A trace of Ihlini *godfire* clung to iron crossbars. "Can you break them?"

"If not, we are trapped. This is the only way out." He stood in the wind and the rain, trembling from the effort it took to stand upright against the storm. "Stay down," he said, "stay down. This will take time, and I fear we have little left. Strahan is not stupid."

I hunched down at the foot of the gate, craning my head to watch. Rain filled my eyes again and again even against an upraised hand.

How he labored, Taliesin, drawing on self-exiled power, on his tremendous strength of will. I stared fixedly at his face and saw the tension there, the enormous effort expended, and all on my behalf. An Ihlini serving Cheysuli, risking his life to do it.

His alien, Ihlini face, so very much like my own. It

is the color that makes us different. They are so
often black-haired, even as we are, but there the
sameness in color ends. Fair-skinned, the Ihlini; we
are, for the most part, dark. And they lack yellow
eyes. But the pride is the same, and the arrogance,
the single-minded determination. You have only to
look at the faces, at the shapes of distinctive bones
and the fit of the flesh over them.

For too long we have been blind. For too long we
have not looked, afraid to admit the truth.

Strahan was kin, I knew, in spirit as well as blood.
He was Teirnan in different flesh, striving for different goals, but serving the same dark end. The
end of the prophecy.

I stared blindly across the bailey, lashes beat down
by the rain. *Why do we have to be one? Why not leave us
divided? Sharing power equally, not fighting for all of it
. . . not risking lir and lifestones. Both children of the
gods—*

"Keely," Taliesin gasped, "I cannot. I am too long
out of practice . . . the wards are too strong for
me—" He bent over, coughing, and I saw how he
cradled his hands. The tips of his fingers were burned.
"Strahan holds my lifestone at this very moment . . .
I can sense it, I can *feel* it. Keely—Strahan *knows*—"

I stood back from the gate and stared up. "If I
could only take *lir*-shape—" But I cut it off at once.
There is no sense in wishing aloud for what you
cannot have. "We will climb," I said firmly. "There is
no other choice."

He interlaced ruined fingers to form a step. "Then
allow me to be your servant. It is you he wants, not
me . . . you must go first, Keely. Promise me you
will."

I reached out to catch a shoulder. "Taliesin—"

His tone, for him, was curt. "Say '*leijhana tu'sai*'
later."

I kilted up linen as best I could, lacking a belt, and .

lifted a wet, bare foot. Taliesin set his hands beneath it, braced himself, thrust me upward toward the gate. Higher, higher, stretching to lift me as high as he could, pushing me toward the top.

I reached, stretched, caught the top hinge of the massive right leaf. Hung there, gritting teeth, hating the wind and the rain. Scraped toes across wet wood, colder iron, caught the crossbar with my left foot. Hooked my toes as best I could, using the brackets to balance.

Something touched my foot. Cold, lethal fire, spilling out to embrace my flesh.

—*gods, it is the watch-ward*—

"Keely," he cried, "hold on!"

Taliesin no longer held me. My weight hung from my arms. My right foot I hooked in the niche between gate and wall, jamming my ankle to brace myself, sprawling very nearly spread-eagle across the gate leaf.

I tried to tear my left foot free of the crossbeam, but the *godfire* held me too tightly. It crept from toes to heel to ankle, seeping through flesh into muscle and blood.

"Climb!" Taliesin cried.

Rain beat into my head and ran continually into my eyes. The thin fabric of my nightshift snagged on splintered wood, tore, gaped open. The gate scraped my breasts, chafing tender nipples.

"Taliesin—the watch-ward—"

I saw him look. He saw then how the *godfire* had spilled from iron onto flesh, trapping me easily. It ran uphill to shin and to knee, crisping the tattered hem of rain-soaked, muddy nightshift.

He put out his hands and touched the iron. I saw the *godfire* waver, reassert itself, then abruptly flow out of my flesh into iron again, and then into Taliesin. He was afire in the darkness, burning unabated in wind and rain.

"Climb!"

"Up—" I whispered. "—*up*—"

The wood was studded. Clinging carefully, I toed out from the crossbar and felt for the iron nails. Aye, here and there, in regimental lines. If I could find one not so flush, having worked itself out of the wood . . . just enough to provide me purchase—

There. My toes caught, curled, clung. Carefully I worked my right foot out of the niche, freeing my aching ankle, then lunged upward toward the top. Leaving the hinge behind, with only the lip above me.

—caught it. Used my momentum to pull myself up, *up*—

—gasping, wheezing, swearing, flogging myself with words—

oh—gods—up— Is it so much to ask?

The wood was wet with rain. Flesh could find no purchase.

"—gods—" I grunted, "—*up*—"

I jammed my right foot into the slot again, bracing myself unsteadily. Then I used it, shoving upward, chinning myself on the top.

—*almost—almost*—

I jerked, lifted, hooked an elbow over the top. Swung my left leg up as high as I could, felt the heel catch briefly on the iron-bound lip. Swung it again, grunting, felt it catch, and hold.

—*up*—

My right ankle came out of the slot, leaving skin on hinge and wall.

—hold *on*—

I was up, up . . . balancing so precariously, one leg hooked over the lip. Clinging with rain-slick hands and praying with rain-slick mouth.

I looked down at Taliesin, face upturned to mine. He was smiling against the rain, hiding his pain from me. Luminous in the darkness, ablaze like a funeral.

pyre. But alive, so *alive*, repudiating the man who had so carelessly repudiated the gods-given gift of the harpsong.

O gods, I thank you for Taliesin . . . leijhana tu'sai for this harper . . .

I grinned back and called out his name—

—and saw him changed into dust.

Taliesin?

I clung to the gate and stared.

Taliesin?

Water washed dust away. There was nothing of Taliesin.

Oh, gods, not Taliesin—

Rain beat me into wood.

I sang him a keening funeral song on an anguished, muted wail, not believing what I had seen. Not believing I saw nothing in the place of a living man.

Never *Taliesin*.

"Strahan," I said aloud, though it was lost in a crash of thunder.

Escape was what he had died for. Failure would dishonor the death.

I scraped myself over the lip of the gate and dropped.

Three

I scraped elbows, chin, breasts and knees. Bruised feet when I landed, and more yet when, overbalanced, I fell backward awkwardly to plant buttocks solidly on hard, cold cobblestones.

Instinctively, one hand spread itself across my belly. *Are you dead yet, abomination? Has this killed you yet?*

As if an answer, *godfire* crept through cracks in the massive gates and set the darkness alight.

I was up at once, and running, snatching wet linen from ankles and knees, cursing my lack of boots. The cobbles were slick, cracked, unsteady, turning from under my feet. And then it was earth, not stone; mud and slime and water. A rope of soggy vine fell out of the trees to snare me.

I tore it from me, cursing, beating away the net. It was gods-made, not human, but serving Strahan in ignorance. I was off the path through the forest, fleeing more deeply into the wood, with nothing to cut my way.

I tripped, fell, lunged up, tripped and fell again. The light was bad, but better; each time lightning netted the sky I could judge the way to go, even with no marked path. I could not help but think of Brennan with his superior night vision. It was the animal in him; I lack the yellow eyes.

Foliage crowded my way. I shredded it and ran on.

—far enough, no farther—far enough from Strahan, and lir-shape will defeat him—

An exposed root tripped me. I fell hard, gasping, feeling blood spill out of my lip. It tasted of salt and copper.

Behind me, Strahan laughed.

I lunged forward on hands and knees, thrust myself up, turned with my back against a tree. Hung there, panting noisily, conscious of pain in chest, in bone, in flesh. I wanted badly to spit at him but had no strength with which to do it.

He wore a circlet on his brow, rune-wrought, glinting silver, alive with alien shapes. And a blood-red, *true*-red robe, belted with silver bosses. The folds of the robe washed purple.

Strahan smiled his seductive smile within the shadow of his beard. *Godfire* flickered in eyes, in mouth, in nostrils, setting fingertips ablaze. "You," he said serenely, "are most direly in need of a bath."

Now I did spit.

Strahan's smile widened. Teeth parted the clipped beard. "A bedraggled, cast-off kitten thrown down a well to drown, then pulled out unexpectedly by a very thirsty man." He paused for effect, lifting winged brows. Wrought silver gleamed on his brow. A painter, transfixed by beauty, would make Strahan a king. The Seker would make him a god. "Shall I drink you, then?"

I told him what he could do in succinct, explicit Old Tongue.

Clearly he understood. "*Reshta-ni*," he answered, equally at home in the Old Tongue as he was in Homanan. He held his ground even as I did, making no effort to move in my direction. Ten long paces lay between us. "You may run," Strahan said quietly, linking hands behind him, "for as long and as far as you like. I will not move to stop you, only to recover you when you fail. This is an *island*, Keely . . . there is no place you can go. *Lir*-shape is denied you, even with your Old Blood . . . and I am stronger now than ever before, less subject to the bindings other gods have put upon us."

Rain ran down my face, washing the blood from my chin. "This is the Crystal Isle, the birthplace of the Firstborn. We hold dominance here, even as Ihlini do in Valgaard."

"Once, aye, with me, and over others, still. But things have changed, Keely . . . even as *I* have changed."

I bared my teeth. "Are you a godling, now? Has the Seker taken your manhood and given you back divinity?"

Strahan raised one brow. "As to the state of my manhood, surely you can tell me. You have reason to know if I am made castrate by greater power, giving up one for the other."

My belly clenched within me. "Is it the only reason?" I cried. "For godhood, for reward, you try to tear down Homana?" I braced against the tree and drew in a gulping breath. "You have always claimed before to do it because of your race. Salvation, you have said—salvation out of destruction."

"It is precisely that," he agreed, "and indeed, I do it for my race."

"Strahan—"

He overrode me. "What I have said before is true: the completion of the prophecy will destroy Ihlini *and* Cheysuli. Stopping that completion will void the extermination of my race, which is what we all face. You. I. All of us." He shrugged, frowning a little, then banished it with a wry twist of his mouth. "You name me demon, I know, and the servant of even worse . . . well, I will not stop you; you may call me whatever you like. No doubt there is some truth in it, when viewed through Cheysuli eyes." Strahan no longer smiled. "But the blade is two-edged, Keely. You and the rest of your House are doing everything you can to harm my race. To stop it, I must .

harm yours." He grinned slowly, disarmingly, astounding me with humanity: man in place of demon. "It was, after all, what I was bred to do, being born to Tynstar and Electra. I was reared in Valgaard, not Homana-Mujhar. The Seker is my lord, not the pantheon you serve." The mismatched eyes were eerie, reflecting self-made *godfire*. "I honored my *jehan* and *jehana* as much as you honor Niall. Are we so very different?"

Beguilement was part of his magic. I shook my head firmly. "But you want more. Much more even than Tynstar."

Strahan considered it, and nodded. "I want more."

"Why?" I cried. "Why make yourself into a god? Is this not enough?" I flung out my hands. "You are Ihlini, and powerful . . . you have more magic than any man I know. Why trade it for something else?"

Winged brows rose to touch silver, as if he considered the question ludicrous. "Because I want to," he answered. "What I want, I get. What I want, I take. And occasionally, if I must, what I want I *make*."

My hands clutched my belly. "You made this child. Against my will, you made it . . . you made abomination."

He shook his head. "Not against your will . . . you *had* no will. Now, of course, you do—I shall have to do something about that. If I cage you up with your mind intact, you will beat your wings against the bars until you burst your heart. And that I cannot allow. A dead woman bears no children."

I turned into the darkness and ran.

Yet again, I ran from him. As long and as far as I could.

You will get no children from me, Ihlini . . . this one or any other.

In the deepwood, I was sheltered from much of the storm. Close-grown trees and self-woven boughs set a ceiling over my head, shunting water and wind

to other places. Lightning still laced the sky, but the
storm was dying away.

*Run as far and as long as I like, he says—well, so I
shall, godling ... I will run all the way to Homana,
regardless of the sea—*

I ran. I *ran.* But I did not reach Homana. What I
reached was something, some*where* older. A place of
ancient and binding power, though lost to long disuse.

It loomed before me, made of stones atumble one
against the other; a small, private place, shining wetly
in the lightning, washed black and silver by rain.
Old, ancient stones, set in a crumbling circle. Time
had toppled them, spread them, knocked their heads
together like drunken soldiers in a tavern, while
their bodies slid slowly apart.

The light of the storm was fading. In its place was
darkness, the deep, heavy darkness of a spent storm
only sluggishly giving back the world the moon and
the stars it has stolen.

Light came up from behind me. A cold, spectral,
purplish light, cast in the form of nightfog rolling
low against the ground. I had seen its like before. I
knew it all too well.

Five steps only, and I was inside the tumbled chapel.
It smelled of mold, of age, wet stone, mud. But
more: it smelled of *power.*

I swung back and faced the fog. "Well, then, will
you come?"

It came. It flowed like Sleeta, hunting; like Brennan running with her; like me, in sleek strong cat-
shape, flowing smoothly under the sun. It came now
hunting *me,* throwing itself forward to enter the
chapel, but found it could not do so. I stood back
and laughed as it tried, splashing against an old and
abiding magic it had no power to break.

Splashed and fell back, like waves against a shoreline. It hovered just before the crooked doorway,
stirring sluggishly at the threshhold. Then flowed to .

either side, encircling the ruined chapel with an ankle-deep mire of *godfire*.

The roof of the chapel was gone. I could see traces of old beamwork, though most was tumbled against the ground inside the chapel walls. Timbers leaned haphazardly against broken stone. Part of the interior was still sheltered by a woodfall of ancient beams, but most lay open to the elements.

Wet walls gleamed. I looked up, up past the broken beams, and saw the moon scudding out from behind the clouds. And stars, heralding it. The storm at last was gone, giving me light to see by.

A shaft of new moonlight lay upon the remains of an altar. It tilted precariously sideways, pedestal plinth shattered, propped up by another stone. It was choked with vines and lichen, but beneath them I saw runes.

I crept forward slowly and knelt down before the altar in wet, leaf-strewn earth. I put out a scraped, muddy hand and tore away the lace of ivy, the soft cloak of bronze-green moss. Beneath my fingers were runes, grown smooth over the years, but depressions nonetheless. I let my fingertips linger, following the shapes. Old Tongue, and very formal. The form only infrequently used in the clans, and then mostly by the *shar tahls*. We have grown too far away from the old language, and the years have altered our tongue into a mixture of Cheysuli and Homanan. This language humbled me. This made me feel unworthy.

This language put me in *awe*.

I traced out the runes I could reach, then pushed more foliage out of the way. Shadows shifted, sliding aside, showing me deeper secrets. Someone had been here before me. Someone who knew the ritual forms for asking *lir*-grace of the gods, and sacred, binding blessings for a warrior gone out of life and entering into death, in honor, on his way to the afterworld.

The step was loud behind me. "Petitioning for salvation?"

It brought me upright, swinging around to face him. The altar was at my back. He was at the doorway. *At* it, not in it. Much like the glowing *godfire* that clung to his booted feet, so close to the rune-warded entrance.

He wore no knife, no sword. He needed neither of them. Strahan was power incarnate.

But here, I thought my own might do.

"Still bedraggled," he sighed. "Still in need of a bath."

I raised my chin and smiled. "Come in and give me it *here*."

He laughed. But he lingered. It was enough to tell me the truth. "If you lose the child through this night's folly, be assured there will be another. You are young and strong and healthy; a child a year, I think, will be a good beginning."

I touched my still-flat belly. "Then make another *now*. Surely this one will not mind. And I am twin-born, Strahan—perhaps there will even be two."

He said nothing in answer at once, being disposed only to reassess me. I had been too long benumbed, and he had never truly known me. Only my father, my brothers. Never had he known *me*.

Strahan reassessed me. Light glittered in his eyes and sparked off rune-wrought silver.

"What if I die?" I asked. "Women do, bearing children. Or what if, in losing it, I become barren? Women do, Strahan. And our House is full of it . . . how is your own, I wonder? There is you, and Lillith . . . Rhiannon? How many of you are left? How many Ihlini like you inhabit the House of Darkness?" I paused. "There are others, Strahan . . . others like Taliesin. Your House is a minority—how many of you are there?" Again I waited a beat, altering emphasis. "How *few* of you are there, Strahan, beloved of Asar-Suti?"

His tone was very quiet. "If you think to stay, to thwart me, remember you must eat."

It was confirmation: he could not enter the chapel. But neither could I go out. It was, I thought, annoyed, a bittersweet victory.

Until Strahan drew a five-pointed star and stepped through it into the chapel.

My back slammed hard into stone as I lurched away from him. The altar shifted, slid, toppled, taking my balance with it. I fell awkwardly and painfully, sprawled across the remains of the pedestal.

I pressed hands into damp earth to steady myself, to find purchase, to scrabble away, and felt metal bite my fingers. Something sharp. Dangerous. Something I could use.

I clutched it and came up, twisting from the ground. The litany ran in my head: *When in danger use any weapon at hand, even that which is not a weapon.*

But this one was a weapon. This one was a *knife*.

I thrust it home in his heart, clean to the twisted gold hilt.

Four

I sat in the ruined chapel with Strahan's blood on my hands. Black, viscid blood, stinking of the Seker.

I sat in the midst of stormwrack and looked on my handiwork.

The knife stood up in his chest. Moonlight gilded the hilt, setting the gold to glowing. Setting the rubies to blazing as if they might banish the *godfire*. Thus banished, it flowed away, tearing like tombrotted linen.

I stared fixedly at the knife. Not mine, but very like it, hilted in gold and rubies, with the face of a snarling lion swelling out of the satiny grip. The Lion of Homana. I had seen its like before, carved into the marble of royal sarcophogi deep in the vaults of Homana-Mujhar.

And now Strahan's body profaned it.

At last I could move. And I moved, lunging forward, kneeling close to the body, settling both hands around the hilt and jerking the blade from the cage of Strahan's ribs. It stuck, held firm, came free. Blood fouled the blade.

"No," I said aloud, and caught a corner of crimson robe, now free of clinging *godfire*, to swab the blood from the blade.

Clean, good steel, burning brightly in the moonlight. I cradled it to my breast. "*Tu'sai, leijhana tu'sai—*" And then abruptly I broke off, recalling the more recent runes carved into the ancient altar.

I turned to it, creeping forward, and knelt again

before it. It was chipped, cracked, blemished. Many of the runes were destroyed. But I saw the newer ones, the ones I had meant to read before, denied by Strahan's arrival. Now I had the time. Now I had the chance.

I traced them out carefully, reading them aloud. It was a Cheysuli birthline, naming the generations, the lineage of the warrior gone ahead to the afterworld. The names were all familiar, being of my clan. Being also of my House; he had been brother to my great-grandsire.

I sat very still for a long time. And then I reached beneath the broken altar, scrubbed away the debris of decades, brought out the armbands and earring.

Metal chimed. I saw in the bands, now dulled by dirt, the shape of a wolf running. In motion in the metal. Nose to tail, nose to tail, sweeping around the curves.

Homanan knife. Cheysuli *lir*-gold. Only one man with both.

"Gods—" I said in wonder, and then I began to laugh. *"Gods—"* I said again, this time through the tears, and clutched the gold to my breasts: knife, armbands, earring. Only one man with all. *"Leijhana tu'sai*, Finn. Your murderer is dead!"

I knew better than to tarry. Strahan was dead, but there were still Ihlini on the island. If I did not leave now they would catch me and they would keep me, to bear a dead man's child.

Carefully I set down the knife and the *lir*-gold, laying all aside until I could tend them again. Then, with great determination and even greater distaste, I went to Strahan's body and caught handfuls of heavy wet wool, refusing to touch his flesh. Slowly, muttering charms against the taint, I dragged him from the chapel.

It would have been easier to leave him. But the

chapel was Cheysuli, built to honor gods, not pre-
tenders; I wanted no profanation. Neither did I desire to trespass upon Finn's spirit, which surely
watched from somewhere.

The body was slack and heavy, utterly graceless in
death. It was, I thought, an obscene parody of what
he had been in life. I paused, hunching beside him,
looking on his face. Wasting a moment to look, because he commanded it. Even in death, there was
beauty.

He had died in shock, in disbelief. It showed in
the set of his mouth, in the staring of his eyes. One
blue. One brown. Set obliquely above the cheekbones so very like a Cheysuli's, if housed in fairer
flesh.

Bile rose in my throat. It was all I could do to
swallow it back. "So," I said aloud, "you win after all.
No prince of a royal House will take to wife a de-
spoiled woman. Even *without* the child . . . virginity is
a necessity, and I no longer suit."

Strahan made no answer. If he could, he would
have laughed.

I looked down at myself, at scraped and muddy
arms, at torn and soiled nightshift. I could hardly go
to Hondarth in such a disreputable state, or I would
be rudely received, dismissed as a beggar-girl, or
worse. I had no coin, nor a pouch to carry it in. All I
had was the *lir*-gold, and that I would not spend.

I looked again at the body, sprawled outside the
chapel. And in the end, ironically, it was Strahan
who served me. He wore no belt-purse, providing
me with no coin, but he did wear silver on brow and
hips and a soft wool robe over leathers, even wet and
muddy. It was better than what I had.

I looked grimly at the body, "*Leijhana tu'sai*," I
muttered, and bent to strip the robe from him.

It took all my strength, all my control to make
myself touch him, to touch the body that had, in

living flesh, stolen mind and will and *self*. I worked in haste, unfastening the belt, bending arms still flexible. And then I touched a hand and felt the last vestige of warmth in his flesh.

Fear stung tender breasts. *Is he alive after all?* I bit my lip to keep from vomiting, from surrendering my purpose. If I did not complete the task he would have a final victory, even after death.

Like a nightmare, it faded slowly: *No, of course he is not.* And I tugged the belt free at last.

With Finn's knife I cut the hem shorter and also the belt, tying the extra silver bosses into a corner of the robe. The touch of his clothing swaddling my body wracked me briefly with revulsion, but I set it all aside to think of escape instead. Now I was clothed enough to go into the city. Now I had enough silver to buy me food, drink, rest, and herbs to loosen the child.

But even for its value, I could not touch the rune-wrought circlet. It rested against his brow, tangled in fallen hair; a crown for the Seker's heir. I wanted none of it. His minions could have it back; or the skeleton itself.

In the chapel again, I knelt briefly at the altar. Not in the name of gods, but in the name of my long-dead kinsman. I held the knife and *lir*-gold to my breast, cradling deliverance, and in Old Tongue and Homanan thanked him for intercession.

"Kinsman, I honor you for your care. But Carillon gave you this knife when you swore yourself to his service, and I will not take it from you. Not after all these years."

Next, the *lir*-gold, glinting dully in thin moonlight. I passed my thumb over the image of the wolf, smiling a little. "I am a woman, and therefore have no *lir*. But I honor yours, knowing who he was, and give him back to you. Storr's name will be remembered."

. I tucked the earring and armbands into shadow

beside the knife, pressing all into the mud. Scraped debris over the glint, then packed it down to form a seal. It was not my place to determine if the weapon and *lir*-gold should ever be found again, or used. My place only to return it, to let Finn make the decision for another Cheysuli in need.

I turned to go, but halted. Knelt there still on leaves and mold and mud, staring at my hands. At the scrapes and cuts and grime.

Strahan's blood was gone; I had wiped it from my body. But my own remained, a little, in a cut, a scrape, a welt. Red, watery blood, no longer thick and black. Red as the robe I wore, and without the sorcerer's taint.

For a long moment all I could do was stare blindly at my arms. And then I recalled my lip, my swollen, bitten lip, and bit into it again.

Blood welled. I tasted the salt-copper tang. Rolled it across my tongue and then lifted the back of my hand to my mouth. Pressed it against my lip and stared at the result.

"Red," I said intently, and then laughed out loud for the joy of it, to know myself set free.

At once I reached for *lir*-shape, summoning the magic. It came instantly, and powerfully, spilling into my weakness and making me strong again. It stripped away the exhaustion, the grief, the lassitude of long imprisonment, and gave me back my life again, replenishing me with my magic.

Strahan's power was banished. In its place was my own. "A hawk," I said intently, "not a linnet or a sparrow. A fierce Homanan hunting hawk, whose freedom is the skies."

It came with a rush, like a river in full spate. It washed over me, sucked me down, tumbled me against rocks. There was no kindness in it, no soft welcome or gentle comfort. Power knows nothing of flesh, only the blood that summons it.

—*drowning*—

I gasped, sucked air, tried to breathe again. Felt the shift in muscle and viscera, the shrinking of my flesh, then the twisting of the bones. Power was sucking me down, taking me back, wrenching my shape from me. I had offered and it had accepted; no longer was I wholly Keely, but neither was I a hawk.

—such *pain*—

Power rearranged me. Took the "*me*" from me and made me something else.

—*too* strong—

The shape of the world was different, and all the colors in it.

"—gods—" I croaked, "you will kill me with your kindness—"

Something heard, and listened. Power receded a little. Enough to give me respite.

I lifted twisted limbs. Saw them ripple, twitch, then blur. Flesh melted into feathers.

The shape of the world was different, and all the colors in it; as different as I myself, and viewed from altered eyes.

Screaming of joy, of victory, I hurled myself into the sky.

—*surely this is the best form of all, superior to any other*—*surely every warrior must long for flight, all of those men with earthbound souls, earthbound lir; the women with nothing at all . . . oh, gods, I thank you*—*leijhana tu'sai for this gift!*—*gods, there is nothing like it, nothing to touch the exhilaration, the joyousness of flight . . . surely nothing can fill mind or body with such a perfect satisfaction*—*oh, gods, Rory, I wish you knew how to fly*—

And then, abruptly, I fell.

—*down*—

—*down*—

—*DOWN*—

Thinking, as I fell, —*but a hawk knows nothing of swimming*—

Five

Strahan's robe. Wet wool is heavy; wool in water, worse. Strahan's robe would drown me.

I fought the weight, the water, trying to reach the surface. But I had no breath, no breath at all, having come back to myself too late. Sinking even now.

Gods, am I to drown? Is this how the child dies?

I had meant to kill it, but not myself as well.

Kicking, kicking and sinking . . . I tried to unhook the belt of bosses to free myself of the robe, but my fingers were swollen and sore, too clumsy to undo the hooks.

Inwardly, I laughed. *Is this how he takes his revenge?*

Something snagged my hair. Was I so near the bottom already?

Snagged, caught, held. Dragging me toward the surface.

I let it take me, praying for air, petitioning for a rescue—

—and broke into air, choking, with an arm around my neck.

The forearm was under my chin, forcing my face out of the water. "A rope!" my rescuer cried, and I blessed him for his Homanan.

Something came down and struck my face, scratching mouth and cheek. It slapped water, was dragged down and looped around my ribs, then knotted beneath my breasts.

"Up!" the voice shouted, and I felt the rope snap taut.

Rough hemp bit through wool and linen, chafing skin already tender. The knot rolled beneath my breasts, pinching; I clutched it with both hands as I fell upward into darkness.

A boat. More than that: a ship. Well, Hondarth was a seaport; I was a fool to be surprised. I clung to the rope with all my strength and used my feet to steady my ascent.

I was pulled up and over the taffrail, lifted by many hands: large hands, toughened hands, the hands of sailors and soldiers. None of them kind or gentle, but infinitely welcome. They lay me upon the deck and took the rope from me, throwing it over the rail again to pull up my rescuer.

Men talking, shouting, laughing, calling comments to the one coming up the side. The rest knelt around me. Then one put his hands on the belt, as if he meant to strip me.

Power had left me before. Now it came rushing back.

—cat—

Claws unsheathed, I slashed, and cut somebody's hand. Blood welled, dripping; fear-scent fill my nose. I screamed and slashed again, giving rein to the magic in me.

They fell back from me at once, offering no threat. But they were men, all of them men, and one had put his hands upon me.

Acrouch upon the deck, I held my ground and snarled, showing them my teeth. I smelled blood and fear and shock, all mingled together with man-smell, the musk of an animal equally deadly as myself. Hands were on knives, on swords, but none of them drew steel. Instead, all they did was stare.

I saw the man, my rescuer, climb over the rail and drop to the deck. Wet wool stuck to his body and hair to his face. Water pooled on wood, running down to taint my paws. He flung back head and hair and showed me eyes I knew. Eyes as blue as my own, in a face, except for the beard, almost too familiar.

In shock, I banished *lir*-shape, still crouching on the deck. "*Rujho*," I blurted hoarsely, "when did you learn to swim?"

And then I sat down all at once, legs asprawl, one hand over my mouth. My belly expelled seawater with abrupt efficiency.

He came forward at once, saying something in shock, but I heard none of it. I retched and brought up seawater, retched and did again. Wondering if the baby would try to climb out as well.

He touched me. I lurched back, then cursed myself for my folly. It was Corin, *Corin*, not Strahan. But the body, at first, was blind, reacting only to what it remembered; what it needed to forget.

The spasms died. The cramping passed. I looked at him through ropes of hair and saw the tears in his eyes.

"Keely," he said softly. This time I suffered his touch.

"Get it off," I said thickly, "get it *off*—" I clawed at the belt, at the robe, trying to tear it from my body. "Corin—get it *off*—throw it into the sea . . . better yet, *burn* it, so the taint is gone from the world . . . gods, oh, *gods*, take it—take it *off* me, Corin—"

"Keely. Keely, stop."

"Corin—Corin *do* it—do it *now* . . ." I saw the men staring, eyes shining in the moonlight. "Do you think I care?" I cried. "Do you think I care about them? Let them see, let them *see* . . . after Strahan does it matter? Do you think I care anymore? Do you think modesty worth the trouble when I have been in Strahan's bed—?"

"Keely, *stop*—"

His hands were on my wrists, holding them tightly, like shackles; trapping human claws. The robe hung awry from my shoulders, baring the remains of linen.

nightshift shredded nearly to nothingness. Blood showed through the rents: I had scratched myself in my frenzy, and reopened other scrapes won in my escape. Sea-salt and wind were corrosive.

Beyond him, I saw the others, clustered at the railing. Strangers all, to me, staring with watchful eyes. The gods knew I had given them cause.

I recalled what I had said for everyone to hear. Recalled what had been done, and whose child lived in my body.

I looked from them to Corin. "You should have let me drown."

His eyes were full of questions but he asked none of them, which was a change from the old Corin, the one I had known so well. This Corin simply ignored the things I mumbled, too exhausted now to make sense, and pulled me up from the deck into his arms, to carry me below.

It was the new Corin who, taking me into a private cabin, stripped the hated belt and robe from my body, and also the shredded nightshift, then made me sit on the edge of a bunk while he washed me, cleansing salt residue from cuts and scrapes, and all done in comforting silence.

At first I protested, wanting him to see none of me. But we had been children together, and though during the difficult years of adolescence we had been modest, it had passed with adulthood. I had seen him naked and he had seen me more times than I could count; I would have thought nothing of it had it not been for Strahan's intimacy and the results in breasts and belly.

Then he put me in a nightshirt, wrapped a soft blanket around me and held a cup of wine to my mouth. "Only a little," he said, "and beware your lip as you drink."

I sipped carefully, only dimly noticing the sting of it in my cut lip. My hands shook on the cup, but his steadied me. I drank half, then shook my head, and he set the cup aside.

He asked nothing of me, which I was prepared to give. In silence we sat on the bunk, side by side, sharing nothing of what we thought and felt because it was not necessary. Born of the same labor, we often require no words.

I shivered with a sudden chill and he put an arm around me, pulling me close against his side. And then as the shivers deepened into convulsive shuddering, he wrapped me up in both arms and pressed my head against his shoulder, rocking me back and forth.

"*Shansu*," he said, "*shansu*. I am here for you. I promise, unless you ask it, you will not be left alone."

All I could do was shake.

"*Shansu*," he said, "*shansu*. There is no dishonor in tears. Drown me if you like; I think I will survive. I have learned how to swim."

It did not matter to me that he was wet, or that his hair dripped into my own. It did not matter that his beard dampened my face, or that the power of his embrace set bruised flesh to aching. All that mattered was who he was: Corin, my twin-born *rujho*, who knew me better than any.

But there was something I could not tell him, no matter who he was.

"*Shansu*," he said yet again, with a manifest gentleness I had never heard in Corin, so often given to intolerance born of a powerful impatience. Atvia had changed him. She had taken my brother from me and given me back a different man.

After a while he stopped rocking. I shut my eyes and slept.

*   *   *

Warmth. Incredible warmth. It crept throughout my body and undid the knots in all my muscles,.

leeched the worst of the soreness from my flesh. I burrowed toward the warmth, wanting more of it, and felt the damp nose press itself against my neck.

Startled, I opened my eyes. Kiri gazed back at me, so close as to make me cross-eyed.

I drew back my head a little, blinking, smiling, reaching out to touch the warm, plush fur. Corin's russet vixen was snugged up against my body. It was her warmth I felt, and an abiding empathy.

Awake, she said, *at last. They thought you might sleep forever, but none cared to disturb you. My lir has been most solicitous; he will be relieved to know you are better.*

Am I? I asked. *Is the child gone, then? Or do I carry it still?*

Kiri hesitated. *Still,* she told me at last. *You were ill, but not from that. The child has taken root and will not be easily dislodged, certainly not without risk.*

Her tone was eloquent. I gritted my teeth against it. *You think I should not take that risk.*

You will do what you will do; it is your perpetual habit. But you should consider carefully what the attempt might do to you.

Kill me, do you mean? Or make me barren, like Aileen? I sighed; the warmth was receding as I came farther out of sleep. *What does it matter, Kiri? No man will have me now, so barrenness makes no difference; it might even prove a blessing, in view of my preferences. And while I have no desire to die, I have even less to bear this abomination. I think the risk is worth it.*

So everyone thinks of everything until the risk is faced. Kiri pressed her nose against me again. *You are not a lackwit, liren, but too often a headstrong fool. Human desires, even Cheysuli, are often shaped out of ignorance, out of needs too often too small. Do what you must do, but consider it carefully, first.*

"Aye," I agreed wearily, and felt her withdrawal from me in the link. It meant she wanted privacy; all *lir* can close themselves to me, just as I can close myself to them. I knew she was talking to Corin.

He came, as expected, almost immediately, ducking to enter the tiny cabin. He smiled when he saw me watching him, turned briefly to say something to someone outside the door, then shut and latched it, coming over to the bunk.

How he has changed, my rujho . . . the others will be amazed.

It was more than just the beard, which I had forgotten he wore. He was taller, broader, harder, more significantly a man. There was no boy left in him, and I found I missed my Corin.

He grinned at me, reading my expression. Teeth split the beard, reminding me of Rory. Equally tall, equally broad, equally thick of hair, though his was darker than Rory's and the beard blond in place of red.

Corin perched himself on the edge as I sat up and made room for him. Kiri took herself to the end of the bunk and curled against one of his legs. "Hungry?" he asked. "I have sent for food and ale."

I nodded, reaching out to touch his hand. Briefly our fingers locked, squeezed, then fell away again. We would say nothing of it again, though what had been said was in silence.

He pushed back a lock of my tangled hair, then put a comb into my hand. "Here. And there is clothing for you as well; we are anchored just off Hondarth, and I bought them for you."

"Clothes?" I waited as he rose, fetched them, brought them over to me. "Smallclothes," I said dryly, "and a tunic and a *skirt*?"

Corin grinned. "I could hardly buy you Cheysuli leggings and jerkin. You will have to wait until we are home again for that."

I examined the tunic and skirt, holding each up. Nubby, soft-combed wool, summerweight; the weave was russet and cream. Also a belt, and thin leather slippers. "No boots, then?"

His tone was firm. "These will do."

"Aye, so I suppose." I dropped everything into my lap. "I had best begin on my hair. The clothing, I think, can wait."

Corin pulled a small stool from under the bunk and perched himself upon it, watching idly as I began working on the worst of the knots in my hair. But his tone was far from idle, being clipped and tightly reined in. "How did Strahan catch you?"

"With cunning, guile, and patience." I picked at a stubborn tangle, looking at it instead of at him. "He was clever, *rujho*, and much too knowledgeable of me . . . he knew what inducements to use. He knew what would bring me running all the way to Hondarth."

"Strahan has always been clever . . ." His tone was reminiscent; he was recalling, I knew, his own entrapment in Atvia, and the inducements Strahan had used to lure him from lifelong beliefs. It had very nearly worked.

"He came out of Valgaard," I explained, "first. And then, with seeming intent, he began killing those who did not serve him. Ihlini, only Ihlini, but creeping closer to Homana." I drew in a breath, took up another section of hair. "He killed Caro, but not Taliesin, because he knew what the harper would do: go straight to the Mujhar." I tightened sore lips, then wished I had not. "Because, of course, it would draw *jehan's* attention all the way north, leaving the south to Strahan." I tore mats out of my hair with more violence than was needed. "And it worked. *Jehan* sent patrols across the Bluetooth. Hart sent Solindish troops. All of us thought of the northern borders, not of Hondarth, or of the Crystal Isle, though he has used it before."

"Decoy," he murmured.

"He knew me too well, *rujho* . . . he knew how to

bait the trap." That, most of all, cut deeply. I shredded more hair, starting a pile in my lap. "He lured
me to Hondarth, caught me, took me to the Crystal
Isle. *South,* not north; if anyone looked for me, it was
in the wrong direction." I thought bitterly back to
the messenger: Solindish, not Erinnish; Strahan had
planned well. Undoubtedly the "Erinnishman" had
told no one my direction. Or, if he said anything, he
told them the wrong one. "Taliesin came with me.
Strahan caught us both."

I had, I hoped, kept my tone free of inflection.
But Corin heard something regardless. "Where is
he?" he asked intently, but I think he knew the
answer.

*—on the gate again, rain beating into my face—in wind
and rain and despair, staring down on the crystallized
dust—*

I clutched the comb in my hand. "Strahan had
Taliesin's lifestone. He destroyed it when we escaped."

Corin stared hard at the floor. Beneath tawny hair
his brow was deeply furrowed, reflecting the grief he
fought so hard to keep from showing. "Again," he
muttered, "*again!* How many lives does he take? How
many more will he—"

"None," I said flatly. "I have always said, if given no
choice, I could kill a man."

Corin's mouth opened. "*Strahan* is dead?"

"In the chapel," I told him, "though I pulled him
out of it."

His eyes were full of blindness, glazed with the
realization of deliverance and the disbelief it could
happen. "*Strahan,*" he said.

I had thought to rejoice. Surely there was relief,
curling deep in my belly, but not a trace of satisfaction. Strahan was dead, but his child lived on in me.
And there was also Sidra's, somewhere in the world.

"Dead," I agreed.

"Do you know what you have *done?*" He was up

from his tiny stool, standing rigidly before me. "Do you *know* what you have done?"

His intensity amused me. "I have some idea."

He paced back and forth, rubbing upper arms as if he was cold. "Keely—oh, gods, *Keely*—do you know? Do you have *any* idea—" He broke off, staring at me. "No more Strahan . . . no more proxy for the Seker . . . gods, I think we are *free!*"

Amusement disappeared. "The House of Darkness still stands."

It stopped him with a jerk. "What?"

"The House of Darkness," I repeated. "There is Lillith, and Rhiannon, and Brennan's bastard on her." I drew in a steadying breath. "Also a child by Sidra, who bears Strahan's blood." I shook my head. "Tynstar left us Strahan as his heir. Strahan left one as well."

"Unless it died." Corin shrugged as I looked sharply at him. "It could have. Babies die. Women die in childbed. It is possible Strahan has no heir at all, in which case we are free."

I thought of the child in my belly. *Are we, then?*

Corin frowned, still considering. "There is Lillith, aye—and Rhiannon . . . but they have been followers, not leaders. With Strahan dead, we may be free of them both."

"Perhaps." *Perhaps not.* It would take hours to untangle my hair, and I preferred another subject. "How long will you be staying? Is it for pleasure, or for business?" I glanced up abruptly. "Is it *jehana*? Had Mad Gisella driven her son out of Atvia?"

"No," he said curtly, then, sighing, sat down on the stool again. "No, not *jehana* . . . she lacks the wits to try."

I might have asked more, but something else intruded. "Is Lillith still there?"

"I sent her away. I assume she went home to Solinde. There has been no word of her in Atvia."

He shook his head. "No, Keely, I am not here for myself. I came for you."

"Me?" I gaped. "There was not time to get you word of my disappearance and have you be here by now—"

He shook his head again. "No, no, of course not . . . it had nothing to do with that." He chewed his lip a moment, purposely delaying. His eyes avoided mine. "It has to do with Sean."

"Sean," I echoed blankly. *So, Rory, here is the truth at last.* I knotted my fingers together. "Is he dead, then? Are you bringing word from Liam?"

Corin's brows ran up beneath his hair. "Dead? Sean? No." He frowned. "Why would you think he is dead?"

I opened my mouth to tell him, but shut it almost at once. Not now. In silence I began to comb my hair again, simply for something to do. "Then he is alive."

"Aye, of course. Very much so. This is his ship we are on."

The comb snagged a tangle. "*Sean's* ship? This ship? Sean is on this ship?"

Corin nodded his head.

Oh, gods. Oh, *gods.* "Sean is on this ship?"

"Come to pay suit to his bride."

I clutched the comb in one hand. The other was full of hair. "Was he on the deck? When you rescued me—was he on the deck?"

"It was Sean who pulled you up."

I remembered little of it, merely hands and faces, all jumbled together, nothing of one man. Only noise and pain and hands.

"Then he knows," I said dully. "He *knows,* and all his men. How could he not? I shrieked it at everybody." I looked straight at Corin. "Tell him to go home."

"Keely—"

—and the cat, crouched on the deck, showing them teeth and claws, screaming her rage and fear—

Humiliation set me afire. "Tell him to go *home.*"

Six

Rory grinned down at me. "You're a daft lass," he said, "to be loving the sword so much. But I'll not take you to task for it; I'm fond of the blade myself."

I grinned back, content; I had learned a new trick. "Show me again, Rory. I will need it against Brennan."

Heavy brows arched up behind the bright forelock of curling hair. "'Tis the only reason, then? You want to beat your brother?"

I shrugged, still grinning. "That, and more. I have to prove myself. I have to prove my sex."

The Erinnish brigand laughed. "That's not needing proof, my lass . . . I have eyes in my head, I'm thinking."

"Now," I said succinctly, and preceded him into the clearing.

"Now," I said aloud, and then realized I was awake.

Oh, gods: awake. It meant I had only dreamed him.

I lay swaddled in blankets, alone at last; not even Kiri was near. It was the first time since my rescue, and I had requested it.

The ship swayed gently, bobbing against her anchor rope. I heard creaks and groans and thumping, though none of it was human. The ship was singing her song.

"No more," I said aloud, and got out of the bunk to dress.

It did not take me long. Smallclothes, skirt, tunic and belt; lastly, detested slippers. I combed and braided my hair, then went out onto the deck.

She was, I thought, deserted, left behind while her men went ashore. Even Kiri was gone, accompanying Corin. I did not mind the solitude; it was better than meeting their eyes, their looks, their murmuring, the ward-signs against the shapechange.

We lay anchored just off Hondarth, too big to tie up dockside. Wind blew off the ocean, beating wavelets shoreward and causing the ship to bow and curtsy. The city shone in sunlight, all limewashed white with bleached gray thatching, and heather all over the hills. But the trees were beginning to turn and I smelled autumn in the air. Strahan had kept me through summer. I had missed a whole season.

I heard a sound and turned sharply, wishing I had my knife. A single step some distance behind me, not so close as to offer threat. A tall, quiet man, unperturbed by my awkward stiffness. He hitched one hip against the rail and leaned there, waiting in silence.

It angered me intensely, that I should be so frightened; that I should show it so readily. I said nothing at first, clenching the rail, willing the fear to go.

And, at last, it did, giving me leave to speak. "Aye," I said, "of course. Who else would stay behind?"

Wind ruffled his hair. Blond, as I expected, though lighter than Deirdre's or Rory's. Aileen had said there was red in his hair, though only a tinge of it, but the voyage had bleached it fair. It curled, too, as she had said, tangling against wide shoulders and falling into his eyes, brown eyes; Rory's, too, his eyes, and long-lashed like a woman's.

He wore no beard at all, which bared a strong, firm jaw too prominent for beauty. Big of bone and squarely built, with power in his posture. The House of Eagles is very strong; her men are often giants.

In shock, I looked away, thinking: *You are more like him than I thought.*

He said nothing at all. I made myself look back.

"Do you like what you see, my lord? Am I better or worse than expected?"

Still he leaned against the rail, idly hipshot, riding the ship easily. The breeze combed hair from his face. "Lass," he said finally, "there's no secret to what became of you, so I'm not blaming you for the hostility . . . but what have *I* done to you save come out to share the day?"

Even the voices were similar, though his a trifle deeper. He did not have quite the same air of casual negligence, or Rory's quickness of laughter; although, as he had pointed out, I had given him little reason to laugh.

I drew breath so deep as to make me light-headed and turned to face him squarely, planting feet on wooden planking. "Our business is finished, I think. The sooner I leave, the better, so you may go back to Erinn."

"And court another lass?" He folded heavy forearms, bared by the length of his tunic sleeves, dark green, which barely touched his elbows. He wore thick copper armlets twined like snakes around his wrists, and a matching torque at his throat, shining in the sun. Sean was, I thought, more bear than man, though lacking the hair, bigger of bone than the men of my race. We have the height, but not the weight. Aileen had warned me he was large, but this was unexpected. "You're quick to settle my future, lass, when you're supposed to be part of it."

"But you *know*—"

He nodded once. "And better than you think." He displayed the back of his hand; I saw the scratch across it.

"You," I said bleakly. "Oh, gods, for that I am sorry. I meant to hurt no one, but . . . but—" I checked. There was nothing left to say, to him or to anyone else.

"I know," he said quietly. "Lass, there's no need

for explaining. I have eyes; I saw what happened. I have ears; I heard what you said. And I also have understanding: Strahan took you captive. Should I be blaming you for that, when you had no choice in it?"

"Men would," I said bitterly. "Why not you?"

He spat over the rail. "I'm not much like other men, being born to the Aerie of Erinn."

And cognizant of it, too. "So much for humbleness."

He narrowed long-lashed eyes. "Is that what you're wanting, then? Humbleness, from me? Lass, I'm thinking you're daft, or blind . . . you're hardly humble yourself, being an animal when you choose. With such power, how could you?"

"Are you afraid of it?"

He spat again over the rail. "You were a frightened, half-drowned pup of a girl, bruised and scratched and bloody. What was there to fear?"

His arrogance was astonishing. "I was a *mountain cat*," I said pointedly. "Did that mean nothing to you?"

He grinned, tugging an ear. There was copper in it as well, and shining on his belt. "It meant something, aye: it earned me a new sort of battle scar, *and* the sort, I'm thinking, few other men can claim."

I stood very stiffly, holding onto the rail. "And does it mean nothing that I can be a wolf? A hawk? A bear? Or anything I choose?"

He put on a face of false amazement. "*Can* you, lass? Anything at all?"

Through my teeth, I promised, "Anything at all."

He considered it. Fingered his lip. Gravely, he nodded. "Then I'll be watching my place with you, or be naught but a scratching tree."

"You *ku'reshtin*," I said scornfully, "you are as bad as *he* is."

Blond brows arched up. "He? He who? Have I a rival already?"

Something twisted deep in my belly. I thought it was the child, then recognized it as a new and increasing despair. We had spoken so often of Sean, of death and life and the past, that we had ignored the future, and now it stood before me.

Sean, Prince of Erinn, whom I was supposed to marry. And wanting no part of it.

"Rory," I said blankly.

He stood off the rail at once, solidly braced against wind and sea. His thighs were hidden in trews, the calves in drooping boots, but neither wool nor leather hid anything of the size. "Rory," he echoed. "Rory Redbeard is *here*?"

"He was afraid he had killed you."

Sean stared past me, toward the shore, brown eyes oddly transfixed. His hand rose to his head, pushed back hair from his face, fingered the hairline. "No," he said distantly, "all I did was bleed. And not enough to be dying; he didn't break my head."

"He thought so. He feared it. And he feared Liam's retribution."

He swung toward the rail slowly, ponderously, gripping it with both hands. It creaked beneath his weight. "Liam loves us both. There'd have been no retribution."

I shrugged. "Obviously he believed otherwise, or he never would have come."

"More like he feared he'd be named in my place, if my head proved broken." His smile was a trifle twisted. "Rory Redbeard is not a man who cherishes the throne, being content with what he has."

"A captaincy in the prince's royal guard?"

He heard the irony in my tone and swung abruptly to face me again. "Aye. Bastards have known worse. 'Tis enough for Rory. He's *said* so, lass."

I nodded. "So, there *was* a chance he might have been named heir if you died . . . he said there was not."

He shrugged, folding his arms, setting his weight

on the rail again. I waited for it to snap. "I've no doubt Liam expected to have more boys. He got me, and Aileen—nothing more. Rory, so far as we're knowing, is his only bastard son, which makes it likely, I'm thinking, he'd stand to take my place. If there was a need." His expression was oddly masked. "Why, lass? Is it what you wished? Rory in my place?"

I opened my mouth to say no, of course not; how could he ask such a thing? But nothing at all came out.

Sean's eyes narrowed. "Has he stolen away your affection? *Your* affection, lass? I thought 'twas nigh impossible; 'tis said you cannot love."

"*Who* says that?"

"Stories. Tales. Rumors." He shrugged. "Enough to make a man wonder."

"Lies," I said bitterly. "But what else?—I am Cheysuli."

"Has nothing to do with that, my girl. Has to do with what's in here." Briefly, he touched his chest.

I might have laughed, once. Or I might have shouted at him, or coldly denounced the stories. But now I did none of those things, being disposed only to stare at the face so much like another man's.

"So," he said at last, "I'm seeing they were lies."

I shrugged. "Some of them, aye. Perhaps not all."

"So," he said again, "you're thinking it's done between us, that no marriage can made. Because of Strahan, then . . . or is it because of Rory?"

"After what has happened, even Rory would not take me."

"D'ye want to be taken, lass? I'd heard you wanted no man."

"No man," I agreed. "Needed, or necessary."

He sighed heavily, stripping hair out of his eyes with large, blunt fingers. "Lass, I'm no woman, and I can't be knowing what you feel, but I'm thinking we're not so many of us much like the Ihlini."

"Corin told you who—and what—he was. Strahan."

"A little, aye . . . I'd heard the name before, him being brother to Lillith, Alaric of Atvia's leman. But Corin has since chased her off, so we'll hear no more of her." He watched me with quiet sympathy. "Aye, I know a little, and a little is all that's needed. A man like that should be butchered."

"Oh, I killed him. But a clean, straight thrust. Like any man would do." I turned to face him squarely. "*That* is why, my lord. Not because I was stolen, or made to be his *meijha*. But because I am myself, and have no need at all for a man to tell me otherwise."

Sean tried not to smile, but the skin at his eyes crinkled, and then the grin broke out. "Any man who tried is more than half a fool."

"You?" I smiled back, not meaning it. "How much of a fool are you?"

"Half, I think," he said. "But no more than half, I'm thinking . . . because I'm too wise to try."

"You bold, arrogant *ku'reshtin*."

He grinned. "No different from Rory, lass."

It was all too true. "He said you were boon companions, with similar tastes in many things, including women."

"Including lasses, aye." He sighed. "Has been trouble for us both. And always the willful lasses, never the quiet ones." His tone was purposely idle. "Deirdre was willful, too, taking to bed the Prince of Homana . . . and then going to Homana-Mujhar to be naught but a leman to him, no woman of rank there." He pursed his lips thoughtfully, leaning again against the taffrail. "And then there was Aileen, in love with the wrong prince, and knowing better, too. Oh, aye, I'm much accustomed to willful women . . . in the House of Eagles, how not?" He paused significantly. "D'ye know what I'm saying, lass?"

My mouth was dry. "Aye."

"I'd not ask you to change your ways. I'd not ask

you to be milk-mouthed. I'd not ask you to be what you're not."

"No?"

"Why would I, then? 'Tis not how a marriage is made."

But so many of them were.

I drew in a long breath and spilled it out between us.. "Strahan took me to bed. Again and again and again, for three very long months." I paused. "Need I be any plainer?"

The humor ran out of his eyes. Slowly he shook his head. "No, lass, no plainer. I'm thinking you've said enough."

Seven

Corin did not like the idea of taking me ashore even
after I swore I felt well enough. Even after I explained, with exceptional clarity, that while it was
quite true I was bruised and stiff from my escape, I
had suffered much worse falling off various horses.

He sat slumped on his bunk with Kiri beside him
and gnawed at a thumb. "You always say you are
well, even when you are not."

"But I am," I insisted. "Do you think I *want* to fall
down in a swoon in the middle of the street? Do you
think I would even risk it?"

"A good reason for staying aboard."

"*Cor*in." I glared, hands on hips. "Have you gone
deaf and dumb? Are you blind? Do I look likely to
swoon to you?"

He studied me a moment. "You look weary," he
said at last, removing his thumb. "Your color is too
pale."

I spoke very slowly. "Because I have been locked
up for three months, you fool. What do you expect?"

He sighed, slanting Kiri a glance of weary disgust.
"If there is something you need, I can fetch it for
you."

"I prefer to go myself. I need to see an apothecary."

Corin sat upright. "I thought you said—"

"—that I am well. I *am*." With studied carelessness,
I shrugged. "I am having trouble sleeping."

He blinked. "That is all?"

"That is all. I mean to ask for a medicinal tea."

"Sean has wine aboard, and a strong Erinnish liquor—"

"I have no desire to drink myself into a stupor merely to sleep," I said dryly. "I would feel worse the next day for being in my cups than I already do with no sleep." I said it feelingly, recalling how poorly I had felt after drinking *usca* with Hart and Brennan.

Corin smiled and slumped back again. "Tell me what you want and I can send someone to fetch it for you."

"Oh, gods—I swear, you will coddle me to *death*. Are you forgetting that we cannot sail to Mujhara, but must spend two weeks on the road? If I am strong enough for that, I am strong enough for this!"

He shrugged, avoiding my eyes. "I had thought of a litter for you—"

"A *litter*!" I stared at him. "I will ride, or I will fly. I want nothing to do with a litter."

"Keely—"

"No." I unlatched the door. "I go with you, or without you. It is one and the same to me."

Corin knew better. He got off the bunk scowling and preceded me out the door.

It had been two years since I had been in Hondarth, and with Corin. Clearly, he recalled it as well as I. Newly banished, in punishment, from his homeland for a year, he had come down full of fear and anger, resenting Brennan as always for having what he could not. I had joined him halfway, intending to go with him, but he was bound for Erinn first, and the thought of seeing Sean that much sooner turned me back again. And so I had watched Corin sail away, hating myself for my cowardice, for failing my twin-born brother, who had never failed me.

He frowned even as I did, walking the streets of Hondarth. Much had happened since then, to both of us, and it had altered us forever. Now he was Prince of Atvia in fact as well as title, and Sean had come for me since I would not go to him.

Corin asked directions of a passerby to the nearest apothecary. The streets were narrow and winding, turning back on one another and climbing hills up from the ocean. I felt awkward in my skirts, longing for familiar leathers.

The silence between us was heavy. And at last I asked what I had wanted to ask all along. "Do you miss her?"

Corin's smile was empty. "For you, that is tact. Why not ask what you mean to ask?"

Now there was no need; he had answered without meaning to. "Is that why you never came back?"

"Aye."

"And yet you come now."

He stared at the street as we walked, gone somewhere away from me. And then came back, quietly, but with an underlying passion that belied the casualness of his tone. "I cannot hide from it—or her—forever. Though we had never met, Sean sent word he was sailing to fetch you, and asked if I wanted to go. I thought it was time I did."

Sailing to *fetch* me, like a wandering cow. But I set it aside quickly enough, thinking of Corin instead. "They have a son."

"I know."

There has never been much need between us to speak in words. There was no need now. I sensed his pain, his awkwardness, his longing to know the truth of Aileen while fearing it as well. It would hurt him beyond bearing if I told him Aileen loved Brennan, but to do so would be a lie. I was not required to.

"And she lost twins," I said. "Now there will be no more. Aidan is the only heir, and like to ever be."

Corin caught my arm and steadied me over a fall of stone, which was unnecessary as well as unlike

him; I thought it was the skirts. "Aye, so *jehan* said in
his last letter. And since Aidan is sickly . . ." He
shook his head. "It will make things precarious, until
his health is secured." And then he laughed a little,
in startled realization, and tightened his hand on my
arm. "Except that Strahan is *dead* . . which means a
sickly heir to the Lion need not be so worrisome
anymore. The gods grant the boy's health improves,
but if not, it makes the burden lighter." He laughed
exultantly. "Gods, Keely—what you have done by
ridding us of the Ihlini!"

"Only one," I muttered.

"The only one who matters." He paused. "Here is
the shop. Shall I come in with you?"

I kept my voice lightly inflected, knowing, with
him, I needed to be on my guard. Or he would come
in with me, and I would be left with no chance. "No,
no need. It should not take me long."

I turned to go in, but Corin caught my arm again
and held me back. His eyes were very steady. "I
meant to come," he said. "I swear, I did, for you.
Gods, Keely, I missed you—but I was afraid to come
. . . afraid to see her again, knowing there was still so
much between us, and no hope for either of us . . ."
He sighed and shook his head, letting go of my arm.
"Brennan is better for her. He can give her more."

"That depends on what she wants." I touched his
shoulder briefly. "*Leijhana tu'sai*, for coming. Especially now, with Sean."

Corin shrugged, leaning back against the stone
wall of the little shop. "I remember what you told me
here two years ago, when I had booked passage to
Erinn." He paused. "Do you remember? In the tavern, in the rented room . . . you told me you were
afraid, and that you needed more time." He smiled a
little, seeing my expression. "But I know you, Keely
. . . two years is not enough. And so I came with
Sean, hoping you would still need me, so I would

have someone to tend while Aileen was near, and Brennan."

"Well," I said, "you do. Tend me as much as you like, if it will make you feel better." I grinned. "As for me, I will feel better if I can sleep." And went past him into the shop.

It was a tiny, musty place, awash with herbal effluvia. The commingled stench was so powerful I nearly went out again. But I thought of Corin, so trusting; I thought of Strahan's child.

There was a single man in the shop, tending a mortar and pestle while seated on a bench. It was to him I went.

He was not old, not young, but lingering halfway in between. He had thin, flaxen hair, and pale blue eyes. His skin was of the sort that reddens easily from drink, high temper, or sun. He pursed his lips as he worked, scraping his powders together.

"Aye?" he asked. "Forgive me, but the order is wanted at once. Tell me what you need, and when I'm finished here I'll fetch it straight away."

I opened my mouth, and lied. "My mistress has sent me."

He nodded patiently. "Aye?"

Oh, gods, how do I say it? I drew in another breath. "She has conceived an unwanted child, and desires an herb to be rid of it."

He nodded, watching his work. "Betrayed her husband, did she? And now carries a bastard? Aye, well, it happens, to the high as well as the low." He did not look at me. "Tell your mistress no."

I was willing to overlook his high-handed assumption regarding my nonexistent mistress' habits, but his outright refusal surprised me. "No?"

"Aye. Tell her no."

"But—" I broke it off, began again. "But this is a shop—you *sell* such things—"

"I do," he agreed. "But to heal, not to kill. You tell

your mistress that if she had not been so loose with her favors she'd not be in such a way . . . she may be naught but a whore, but the child deserves a life. You tell her that, now . . . I'll not be party to murder."

Frowning, I shook my head. "But if the child is not wanted— "

"Doesn't matter," he interrupted. "Unwanted or no, it should live."

I thought of the child, my child, most distinctly unwanted. I thought of what it could be if given leave to live. To come into its father's powers. "And if there is a danger?"

"No child is born without it."

His serene stubbornness amazed me. "And if it is ill-formed?"

"The will of the gods, girl . . . tell your lady to pray."

Now it was a challenge. "And if it is unloved? What then? Should the child suffer an unhappy life?"

"The will of the gods, I say . . . there is always fosterage. If the lady or her husband cannot bear to keep the child, there are men and women who will."

I felt anger replace amazement. "You fool," I said curtly, "do you have all the answers? You, who are a man, and cannot know the choice?"

"There are women who feel as I do. Good women all—" Abruptly, he stopped working. Color filled his face. "It's you," he said thickly. "It's *you*, then—" And he was up, forgetting his order, putting hands on my arms. "Girl, girl—think. *Think* what you do. There is life inside of you—"

"There is *death* inside of me." I was shaking with rage, fighting to keep my voice down so as not to alarm Corin and bring him into the shop. "What right have you to dictate my life? What right have you to tell me how to conduct myself? What right have you to usurp my freedom of choice when it does not even affect you?" I stripped his hands from my arms. "Will *you* carry this child? Will *you* bear this child? Will you feed it and raise it? Will you bury it if it dies? Bury me if *I* die? Keep it from killing others?" I drew in a noisy breath, nearly hissing in my anger. "Will you do *anything at all* except tell me what to do?"

He was nearly as angry. "A woman is *meant* to bear children . . . it's what the gods intended when they gave her the means to conceive!"

"What of a child born of rape?"

His color waned. He averted his eyes.

"It happens," I said, "oh, it happens."

He moistened his lips. "The child is not to blame."

I shook my head. "Not every woman has the patience, the willingness or the strength."

"A child will cause her to learn it."

Gods, he was driving me mad! "And what of a child whose mouth is so ill-formed it cannot even eat? Will you eat *for* it?"

"The gods—"

I did not let him finish. "What of a child," I said silkily, "who is begotten of a demon? Should we suffer *it* to live?"

And I recalled, even as I asked it, how I had challenged my own uncle to give me good reason for desiring to kill Rhiannon. Now this Homanan gave me much the same challenge, and I finally understood the shame, the anguish, the humiliation Ian felt for having sired Rhiannon.

I looked hard at the Homanan, understanding him better, but more angry than ever. He had no answer for me, gazing at me in startled silence out of watery blue eyes.

I could not hide my contempt. "So many answers," I gibed, "and born of such arrogant ignorance. The next time you petition them, ask the gods for better instruction. They have more compassion than you."

Blinded by anger, by tears, I walked out of the shop into Corin.

Except he was not Corin.

"You," I said in surprise.

Solemnly, Sean nodded. He leaned against the wall even as Corin had, big arms folded casually and displaying all their copper.

I frowned. "What are you doing here?"

"I came looking for Corin, whose direction I'd been given. I meant to invite him to a tavern . . . he said you were here, and *I* said I'd bide my time while he went on ahead to the one just down the road." His hand was on my arm, guiding me away from the shop. " 'Tis near time for food, and I could stand a dram. What of you, lass?"

I ignored his question, asking one of my own. "How much did you hear?"

"Babble," he said succinctly, "but you sounded angry, lass."

"He was a fool." I dismissed the red-faced man and his well-intentioned stupidity. "I will buy from someone else." *But who?* I wondered uneasily. *And I have so little time.*

"If you're having trouble sleeping, I could sing you a song or two." He shrugged. "Some night."

I nearly stopped dead in the street. "Sing?"

Sean grinned down at me, guiding me with elaborate consideration around a puddle of urine left by a passing horse. "You've heard nothing at all till you've heard the Prince of Erinn singing a lass to sleep."

I lifted brows. "And do you do it often?"

"I've not been celibate, lass. Nor will I lie about it." And then he laughed ruefully, pulling at an ear. "But you already know that, since Rory's told you the tale of how he near broke my head."

"And how many bastards do *you* have?"

He nearly missed a step. "D'ye dislike bastards, lass? D'ye think they're less than men?"

"Or women?" I laughed at his expression. "No, of course not . . . in the clans bastardy bears no stigma. For too long my race was very near extinction. Babies, regardless of parentage, were always warmly welcomed."

"Ah. Then you'll not be minding—"

"Oh, I might . . . if any come *after* the wedding."

Sean threw back his head and laughed aloud. "Put in my place," he said ruefully. But his long-lashed eyes were alight. "Still, I think 'twas worth it . . . you've said there will *be* a wedding. 'Tis more than you've said before."

So it was. Much more. And it made my flesh go cold. *Oh, gods, how can I? After what Strahan has done?*

"Lass," he said, "we're here. Will you allow me to buy you a cup?"

A kind man, I thought. A warm, kind man, more compassionate than I had expected, in view of my stubbornness.

"Bastards," I muttered, thinking of my own.

Sean's face closed up. " 'Tis Rory, then, after all."

I looked at him in shock.

" 'Tis Rory, then," he repeated.

"Sean—"

"I love him," he said, "he's my brother. But there are things I cannot share."

His face was masked to me, but I saw something in his eyes. Something that spoke of self-denial and constraint, of a self-control so stringent it made his voice too harsh for the throat that housed it.

He was clearly unhappy, though his manner remained almost indifferent. I had expected anger, resentment, a possessiveness typical of men who feel themselves threatened by another man; they are so often like male dogs, fighting for territory. But Sean was not, though I had given him cause. Sean loved his brother, bastard-born or not.

I owed him something, Sean. And so I gave him

the truth, albeit with difficulty. "Do you think, my lord of Erinn, that after what Strahan has done, I could ever lie down with a man?"

Realization altered his eyes.

"Bastard or trueborn, do you think it really matters?"

Sean said nothing at all.

I pushed open the tavern door. "What prince wants that sort of wife?"

He pulled it closed again. "I might, lass."

Oddly, it made me angry. "How can you? You are the Prince of Erinn, Liam's heir—any man in your position must take to wife a woman beyond reproach. A woman whose virginity is intact."

" 'Twasn't your choice that yours was lost, was it, lass?"

My face burned. "Of course not."

"Then how can I blame you?"

I stared at him, mouth agape. "Do you mean to say that you will take me regardless?"

Sean sighed heavily. " 'Tisn't my decision."

"No? Whose, then? Mine? Well, *I* say—"

"Nor yours, lass. 'Twas a thing of our fathers. 'Tis for them to say yea or nay."

I stared up at him. Such a tall, strong man, powerful in spirit. I could not believe he would so meekly turn his back on independence. "Do you mean to say you will do whatever Liam tells you to do, even if you disagree?"

Sean rubbed the bridge of his nose. "Liam and I disagree on a great number of things. Sometimes I win the argument, sometimes I lose . . . but this one, lass, *this* one—" He sighed and shook his head. " 'Twas done between Liam and Niall for the good of both our lands."

"And therefore it makes no difference what either of *us* may want?"

He shrugged. "It only makes a difference if I'm opposed to the match."

It came out dully, in shock. "And—you are not."

Sean smiled a little. "Sure as I'm standing here, I'd be a fool to tell you the truth . . . or so it's said of a woman. Never tell her the truth, they say, or she'll make it into a weapon."

I gritted teeth. "Then I will say again what I said before: after what Strahan did, do you think I could ever lie down with a man?"

Sean did not even hesitate. "Aye," he said, "you will. I'm not excusing what that beastie did, and I'm not saying 'tis a thing a woman forgets . . . but aye, you'll lie down with a man, because you're too much a woman not to."

It startled me. "Too *much*—?"

Sean pulled me aside from the door as someone stepped between us to enter the tavern. The door banged closed. "Too much," Sean repeated. "Oh, I know, men have told you you're too much a *man*, I don't doubt, because you've a liking for men's things. And no doubt they say 'tis what you'd rather be: a man in place of a woman." His mouth hooked wryly. "But I'm not a fool, Keely . . . I'm not a man for judging a woman's mettle by her liking for swords or if she favors trews over skirts. You're a braw, strong lass, full of spirit and pride and temper, and a need to be free of things such as duties required by rank." His hands were on my shoulders. "A bright and shining lass, gods-made for a man like me—" his hands tightened painfully, "—*and* for a man like him."

After a moment, I shook my head. "What if I said neither?"

He did not even hesitate. "I'm thinking both of us would lose."

Gods, what a fool. I pushed open the door and went in.

Eight

The child was a boy, born on a night with no moon. A healthy, whole child, strong of limbs and lungs. He screamed in outrage at the woman who dared expel him from his safe, dark place, and thrashed in the midwife's hands.

She cleaned him, wrapped him, put him into my arms. "Strahan's get," she said. "You have only to look at his eyes."

Tangled in blankets, I cried out, fighting to get free. I sat up, tearing at wrappings, and then hands were on me, kind hands, holding me in place.

"Keely. Keely, no." The hands tightened. "It was a dream, Keely—nothing more. A *dream.*"

I blinked into darkness, knowing the hands, the voice, the kindness. Corin. Aye, of course: *Corin.* Not Strahan. And no midwives, bringing forth the Ihlini's child. I had dreamed all of it.

I sagged, let him guide me back down into my blankets, all disarranged by my violence. And then sat up again, pushing his hands away, muttering something about being all right, being fine, being well enough, *leijhana tu'sai;* would he please leave me alone?

And so he did, saying nothing; going back to his own bedding where Kiri waited, leaving me to sit with my blankets pulled around me like grave-wrappings, staring blindly into the coals of the nearby fire ring.

We had left Hondarth the morning after my aborted efforts to get herbs to rid myself of the child, leaving me with no time to seek out another apothecary. I knew women who had purposely miscarried bastards and unwanted children, and those who waited too long died, or came near to it. I was not interested in dying, or in bringing myself close to it; I wanted the child gone, but not at the risk of my life.

Hear me? I asked it. *Hear me, abomination? I want you gone. I want you dead. I want you unborn, so there is no risk to the world because of the power that, gods know, will live in your bones. I refuse to be the woman who brought forth destruction.*

There was, as I expected, no answer. It was too soon, the child too small; yet nearly too late, the child too large, for me to rid myself of it without risk.

Unbidden came the thought: *But what if, left to live, it turns its back on the dark side of its heritage? What if, reared by Cheysuli, it pays no homage to Asar-Suti or to its father's memory?*

But what if it *did?*

I sat with elbows on blanketed knees, leaning my face into my hands. What if, what if, what if.

What if I married Sean and went to live in Erinn?

What if I refused on the grounds of banished virginity, couching the refusal in polite references to my dishonor, which I had no wish to share with Sean?

What if Aidan died and there were no heirs for Homana?

What if Aidan died, and there was no Erinnish issue from me?

No link, no blood, no prophecy.

Strahan would win. Teirnan would win.

And the *lir* would stay with us.

With a muffled groan I lay down again, yanking blankets up around my ears as I turned onto my left side. All around the fire ring were lumpy bundles of men rolled up in blankets, save for the watch Sean had set. His Erinnishmen were much like Rory's, which did not surprise me; they were the remains of Sean's personal guard, the ones who had stayed behind while Rory and the others sailed. They had grown more accustomed to me once on the road, apparently deciding I was unlikely to take *lir*-shape unless threatened. Corin they treated more familiarly, having grown used to him on the voyage, but to me they gave honor and impeccable manners. I was their lord's betrothed.

Vestiges of the dream stayed with me. It would always, I thought, until the child was gone. I tucked a hand down beneath my blankets and touched my belly, following the curve of flesh beneath skirt and tunic. Three months and more, nearly four: to me, it had become obvious.

Do you hear? I asked. *I have no choice. I cannot risk so much.*

I shut my eyes, squeezing tightly. Bit deeply into my lip. Wished myself a child again, safe in Homana-Mujhar, safe in my huge cloth-draped bed, warm beneath the covers, with all the *lir* within reach, and my father present. My strong, tall *jehan*, who could chase away the demons who preyed on his daughter's dreams.

Chase away this one, I begged. *Jehan, please . . . chase away this demon.*

But I was not in Homana-Mujhar. And even if I were, and *jehan* was present, this was a demon I would have to conquer myself.

I scrubbed away hated tears. In the darkness, from the watch, came a voice I knew. Deep, warm, soft, singing something in Erinnish. A song of peace and comfort.

The Prince of Erinn, as promised, was singing me to sleep.

*   *   *

We clattered through the massive gates of Homana-Mujhar near sundown two weeks out of Hondarth. The Mujharan Guard saluted Corin, grinning; welcomed me more moderately, but with obvious relief; paid appropriate honor to Sean and his contingent once identified. But none of us lingered, wanting to go straight into the palace. And yet at least two of us dreaded it: Corin, knowing he would see Aileen; me, knowing I would have to speak aloud of the bastard in my body.

I found myself next to Sean as we rode toward the inner bailey. Thick blond brows meshed over his bold nose as he frowned, looking around; I saw he judged the fortifications, the architecture, the width of the heavy walls, the guard manning sentry-walks and towers. In the setting sun walls glowed rosy-gold. Torchlight glittered off glass and ran, like water, across marble steps and archivolted entranceways.

" 'Tis grander," he muttered. "Kilore is a fortress, an aerie on rocky cliffs ... this is more. This is—different."

This was home. I could judge it by no other.

"Gods," Corin muttered.

I saw his face, all strained and tight; his eyes, black in the dying light. Felt the tension so close to breaking. And knew I had to say something, *do* something, so he would not shame himself with the intensity of his emotions.

"When I left, she was not here," I told him. "Brennan took her to Joyenne. She may still be there."

Sean looked at me sharply. "D'ye mean Aileen? Are you saying she isn't here?"

I was glad I was not required to look at Corin for the moment, though I meant my words for him. "After she lost the twins, Brennan thought it would do her good to spend the summer away from the city." I shrugged. "She *may* be back, but she may have stayed on. How can I say?"

"No need," Corin said harshly. "It has been two years, and there is a child between them . . . I would be a fool to expect her to feel the same."

I could not help it. "*You* do."

"I am not married to someone else." He drew up his mount in the inner bailey as horse-boys ran out from the stables, calling out startled greetings. "I should have come before; there is no sense in hiding from old demons."

Sean swung down from his horse, moved a step to mine, reached up to help me even as I told him, pointedly, I could manage on my own. But at once I regretted quick tongue and quicker temper; there was no need to give him bad manners in return for his courtesy.

"Lass," he said calmly, unperturbed, "I've no doubt you'd do well enough in leggings. But skirts are cumbersome—should I leave you to fall on your head?"

"Occasionally," Corin suggested, and grinned as I scowled at him. But the grin faded too quickly; he was staring at the entrance to Homana-Mujhar. Someone had come out in answer to the clatter and loud welcome of our arrival.

Swiftly I looked, expecting the worst. "Deirdre!" And was running across the cobbles with skirts dragged up to my knees, folds flopping as I ran.

She was laughing and crying and speaking unintelligible Erinnish mixed with Homanan as I mounted the steps, nearly tripping over my skirts, and then caught me in a hug that told me, with an eloquence unmatched by words, how very much she had missed me. How very much she cared.

I am not one for hugging women, or even men, preferring to keep deeper emotions private. But Deirdre was Deirdre, *jehana* in everything but name, and I loved her. More deeply than I had believed I could love anyone, save *jehan* and Corin.

"Oh, Keely—oh, gods—Keely . . . oh, we feared you dead . . . we thought he would kill you—"

"No. No. I am well, I promise, I *swear*—"

She was crying unabashedly. "The messenger said you had ridden out with Taliesin, to accompany him back home . . . oh *gods*, Keely—Niall was near mad with grief and rage when he realized it was a trap."

"How *did* he realize it?"

"None of the *lir* could find you. Not even when Hart sent Rael out for leagues. And we knew then it was Strahan, it *had* to be—and then no one could find a trace of you even when they went north—"

"I was south," I told her. "On the Crystal Isle." I drew back as she released me. "Is *jehan* here?"

Deirdre shook her head. "No. He and the others are still searching. Each report of your presence sends them in a new direction . . . lately they have gone south, but obviously they missed you." She swallowed heavily, fighting back more tears. "Oh, Keely, they have searched half of Homana, from here to all the way to the Solindish border, so close to Valgaard—" And abruptly she stopped, staring past me. "By the gods—Corin? And—no, not *Liam*—"

"Sean," I said dryly. "Come to fetch his reluctant bride."

Deirdre was in shock, staring at the man she had last seen more than twenty years ago. Then he had been four. Now he was—twenty-six?—and no more the small boy. Not even a small man.

"Liam," she said again, still stunned. "The height, the bone, the hair—gods, he even has Liam's mouth!"

"And uses it right well." I sighed, pushing loosened hair out of my face. "I will leave you to your greetings. There is something I must do."

She might have remonstrated; I expected it. I expected her to insist on putting me to bed, or sending me to the kitchens, or banishing me to a bath. But she did none of those things, being too distracted by the presence of her nephew, and so I left her quietly, saying nothing more. Corin, next to Sean, mounted the steps into Deirdre's arms as I went into the palace.

I wasted no time. I climbed directly to my chambers, absently greeting startled servants, and stripped out of tunic, skirt, slippers. Out of everything. And replaced it all with soft Cheysuli leather: leggings, jerkin, boots. Lastly, my favorite belt. Except that when I tried to set the buckle prong into the proper hole, I found it three inches too small.

Oh, gods.

I stared blindly at the hole, now inadequate to its purpose. I am long in the waist and narrow-hipped; on another woman, a wider woman, a child so small would not show, would not interfere so soon with her clothing. But I am too much a Cheysuli: long of bone, in muscle, carrying no excess flesh.

Now carrying excess baby.

Oh, gods—

I broke it off angrily. Found a knife, though not the one Strahan had taken; that one was gone forever. Grimly, I sat down to cut a new hole.

"Keely?" Someone thumped my door: Maeve. *Maeve?* "Keely?" she called again. "Deirdre said you are home . . . Keely, are you here?"

I told her I was, and also to come in. She did so as I worked the tip of my knife through the leather, frowning at the bluntness of the steel. It needed honing. It needed tending. It would have to take the place of the other, and I did not like the idea at all.

Maeve shut the door. "What are you doing?" There was a startled note in her voice, and something that spoke of concern.

I did not bother to look at her. "Cutting a hole in my belt."

"After nearly four months of captivity, this is the first thing you do?" She came forward. "Did you think it more important to put on leathers than to greet Ilsa and me, who have been so worried about you?"

Sighing, I glanced up to tell Maeve I had not even thought she might be present—she had been gone when I left—but I stopped in midsentence. Stopped dead, open-mouthed, and stared.

Gods. I had forgotten. Forgotten her child entirely, in the knowledge of my own.

She smoothed a hand across her belly, so much larger than my own. "Two months left," she answered, seeing the question in my eyes.

All I could do, transfixed, was stare. At the loose tunic, the skirts, the swelling of her breasts. The way her posture had altered. The texture of her skin.

In one hand hung my belt. The other clutched a knife. The hole was barely cut. "You decided to have the child."

"Aye. Teirnan knows nothing of it; the child shall be *mine*, not his." She smiled. "I will make certain it is a loyal, steadfast Cheysuli, untouched by its father's folly."

I felt so odd, so distant. "You said once that the seed was sown, but the harvest not begun . . . and asked if you should make the child proxy for Teirnan's sins."

"Did I?" Maeve shrugged. "I do not recall . . . we said many things to one another the last time we met, and most of them worth forgetting." She came closer yet, one hand resting on the bulge of her swollen belly. "You might have come to us first, Keely, before this. Ilsa and I have been worried."

I heard the faint undertone of reprimand in her voice. Too often Maeve honored me with such, playing the wiser, older sister, but this time it did not matter. This time nothing mattered.

I stared at the belt. "I had to cut a new hole."

Maeve laughed once, in disbelief. "Keely, are you

mad? Do you think the fit of your clothing—" And
she cut it off. Instantly. The silence was absolute.

I set down the belt, the knife, and placed my
hands over my belly. When I looked up at her I saw
comprehension in her eyes, and, oddly, tears. "I
have less courage than you," I told her. "I cannot
bear this child."

Maeve swallowed heavily. After a moment she came
to the bed and sat down next to me very close, but
making no effort to touch me, to soothe me, to offer
meaningless comfort. I knew better than to expect it;
she knew better than to try.

"How long has it been since you knew?"

I shrugged. "I knew at once. Within a week of my
capture. At first I hoped it was shock, the drug he
gave me . . . but when I did not bleed the second
month, I knew the truth of the matter." I sighed,
crushing leather jerkin in my hands. "Four months,
I think. Perhaps a week less."

Maeve tensed beside me, meaning to speak at once,
but forced herself to relax. To speak quietly, so as
not to stir my temper. "You know it is too late.
There is too much risk attached."

Patiently, I told her, "I will not bear this child."

"*Keely*—" But again she fought back her emotions.
"It is too late. The physicians will tell you, the midwives . . . Keely, promise me—"

"No."

Her hands, as she clasped them, shook. "Do you
want so badly to die?"

I laughed, though it had a brittle sound. "I would
much prefer to live. No, Maeve, I promise you, this
is not an attempt at suicide . . . but I cannot bear this
child. Strahan is dead—he can sire no more—and I
will not give him the pleasure, even in death, of
leaving this one to assume the father's place."

Her teeth clenched tightly. "If you think I will
allow you to do this to yourself—"

I stood up abruptly and turned to face her. "You had better! This is none of your concern, Maeve . . . this is *my* task to do. *My* child to lose. Keep your own if you like, but I will not do the same with this one. I cannot risk the chance it will follow Strahan's path."

Maeve clutched the bedclothes in impotent anger, clearly wanting to rise, to challenge me, but knowing better. Her condition would defeat the attempt. "Do you think any child of yours could even be tempted to? Gods, Keely, there is so much blind loyalty in you that you cannot even see yourself! *Your* child, a traitor? *Your* child, a servant of the Seker?" She shook her head violently, blonde hair shining. "A child born to you, shaped by your hands, could *never* be like Strahan. Not even if it tried."

I appreciated her unlooked-for sisterly loyalty and confidence, even if I did not share it. "I cannot risk it, Maeve. His child could bring us down."

"So could your death," she snapped. "Have you forgotten Aidan?"

Fear stabbed deeply. "Is he dead? Has he died? Oh, gods—"

"No. No, he lives. He is at Joyenne with Aileen." With effort, Maeve controlled her voice. "But if he dies, it leaves only you. And if *you* are dead because of this selfishness, what happens to us then?"

"How do you know Sean will even have me?" I demanded. "How do you know there will ever be a child of that union, since there may never *be* a union?" I tapped my chest, leaning forward. "I have been Strahan's whore, Maeve, sharing his bed nightly. I carry an Ihlini bastard. Am I worthy to be Sean's wife? To give him the heirs he needs, while sparing one for Homana?"

She rose slowly, steadying herself against my bed. "If you try to rid yourself of this child, and die in the effort, how will you ever know?"

"Maeve, I *have* to—"

"No," she said bitterly. "No. You will do it because you *want* to; 'tis how you live, Keely. 'Tis how you have always lived, so certain of your path." She drew in an unsteady breath. "I have hated you, and loved you . . . with neither winning the throw. But always, *always* I have envied you: your freedom, your strength, your courage." Her green eyes were bright with tears of anger. "But now, seeing this, knowing what you will do, all I feel is pity. Later, perhaps, I will grieve, when we put you in the ground."

I turned from her rigidly and walked across the chamber to a casement. It was shuttered; I threw it open to darkness. And then I swung back, facing her, and told her, with exquisite precision, what else I feared so much.

"She is mad," I said flatly. "She has been mad since her birth, they tell us, even *jehan*, who wed her. Mad Gisella, they call her, speaking in whispers of her behavior, of the bizarre things she has said. Of the treachery she has *done*." I drew in a painful breath, trying to keep my tone uninflected. "She meant to give her children—her sons—to Strahan. To serve Asar-Suti. There is no sanity in her . . . should I risk a mad child as well?"

In shock, Maeve said nothing.

I wiped sweaty hands on the leather of my jerkin, trying to still their shaking. "This child already has Strahan for a father . . . do I risk mixing the blood of the Ihlini and the blood of a madwoman? Abomination, Maeve—how can this child be normal?"

"But Keely, you can't *know*—"

"Only that there is a chance. There has always been a chance."

"Oh, *gods*," she said softly, " 'tis *this*, isn't it? The reason you've never wanted a child . . . the answer to all the questions . . ." She pressed hands against her cheeks. "*All these years, Keely* . . . this? This? *This* is why!"

"She is mad," I said again.

"Keely—"

"How can you know?" I asked. "How can you even suggest you understand? Your mother is sane. There is nothing for you to fear." I could not stop the shaking. "You know what madness means to the Cheysuli ... to a *lirless* warrior ... he must *leave*, Maeve! He sacrifices clan, kin, *life* ... do you think I could live with that? Knowing that my child, in addition to being an Ihlini halfling, might also be *mad*—" I closed my mouth with both hands, then spoke through them. "Madness is anathema to anyone of the clans. You know that. You *know* that—"

Maeve's face was white. "All this time—"

"I have to be rid of this child!"

Shock faded quickly. Maeve was angry again. "You are a fool!" she cried. "A headstrong, stubborn fool. I should go straight to Deirdre—*she* would set you straight."

I took a single step toward her. "Say nothing," I said tightly. "Say *nothing*. This is mine to do!"

Maeve turned from me and walked heavily to the door. There she paused and swung back. Clearly she was angry, very angry; now, I thought, mostly at herself. "When I came home from Clankeep, I thought surely *jehan* would know about Teirnan's child. That you had told him." She laughed a little, self-mockingly. "But you had not. You said nothing, leaving me to my own decision."

I shrugged a little. "It was not my place."

Impatiently she scrubbed tears away. "And for that, I give you my silence, much as I hate myself for it. But it is the last debt I will owe you; we are quit of anything else, regardless of our blood."

I stood mute in the center of my chamber as Maeve left the room. Then, as the door thumped closed, I went back to my bed and picked up knife and belt, meaning to finish cutting the hole.

But I did not. There would be no need for it. Once the child was gone, the belt would fit again.

Nine

The solar was full of women: Deirdre, Ilsa, Maeve, and assorted Erinnish and Solindish ladies, all helping the Mujhar's *meijha* with her massive tapestry. Uninterested, I paid scant attention to it, mostly concerned with Deirdre's reaction.

It was what I expected. "How can you?" she cried. "You've only just come home—how can you think to leave again?"

"A week, no more," I promised.

Astonishment faded quickly enough, replaced with firmness; Deirdre is accustomed to dealing with my whims. "Corin has only this morning sent Kiri out to link with Serri and the other *lir*. They will be home very soon. You would do better to stay here, until they are back."

I hung onto my patience, speaking very quietly. "I need to go, Deirdre. Only a week, and to Clankeep. Not so far this time, nor for so long. I promise."

Maeve refused to look at me, staring grimly at the tawny yarn clutched in her hands. Her face was tight and color flushed her cheeks, giving away her thoughts, but no one, thank the gods, looked at her. All stared at me.

The morning sun slanting through open casements set the whitewashed room alight. Pale-eyed Ilsa, all in white, fair hair braided and netted back from her flawless face, was an ice-witch with blood to elbows; the yarn piled in her lap was red. "Keely," she said quietly, in her accented Homanan, "I think you would do well to be aware of how worried everyone has been, and what such worry does to people: griping bellies, stealing sleep, haunting dreams." She smiled a little, though her eyes were grave. "Give them time. You will have your freedom again, I know, but for now let them feel safe again, with you here where they can see you."

I stared hard at Deirdre's ladies, at Ilsa's, and then looked at my sister, at Hart's wife, at my foster-mother, knowing I would hurt them with my cruelty; knowing also it was required, or they would never let me go.

"You are none of you Cheysuli," I said harshly. "None of you, save Maeve, but even she will tell you she has no magic in her blood." I drew in a deep breath, trying not to shout; nor to cry. "None of you," I repeated, "and therefore you cannot know what it is to be stripped of honor, of worth, of *self*—" I cut it off with a sharp Cheysuli gesture, meant more for myself than for them. "I will go, because I must. There is *i'toshaa-ni* to attend to, and other, private things. If you worry for what my *jehan* will say, and my *rujholli*, and my *su'fali* and all the *lir*, tell them I have gone to cleanse myself. They will understand. They will. I promise you they will; all of them are Cheysuli."

But Deirdre was not vanquished. "What of Sean?" she asked calmly. "Will he understand? Or will he know only that you have run from him again, as you have for so many years?"

Dull anger flickered, died. "I know him better than you." I watched the knife go home. "Sean will make shift for himself, regardless of what I do."

"Keely!" Maeve was furious. "If you think I will let you come here and speak such words to our mother—"

"No," Deirdre said quietly. "No, that will come next, will it not?" She was looking at me, not at her daughter. "You are using all your weapons, I see . . .

well, why do you wait? Maeve has said the words—
now *you* are to say that no, Deirdre is not your
mother, but your father's light woman. *Meijha*, in
your tongue." Her brows rose. "Well, why do you
wait? Why not say the words, Keely, so you may cut
yourself free of us all?"

Tears welled up before I could stop them. *Gods, I
am grown so weak because of this thing in my belly—crying
all the time—* "No," I said tightly, "I will say no such
thing. I will *do* no such thing ... all I want is a week
to myself at Clankeep, for *i'toshaa-ni*—" I stared hard
at a blurred Deirdre, swallowing painfully. "How can
you think I would say such a thing? To you? How
could I? Even in anger, I would not—oh, *gods*, Deirdre, do you think me so cruel as that? Do you think I
am Strahan, preying on weaknesses—"

She rose, dropped forgotten yarn, came to me at
once. Closed her arms around me as tightly as she
had the evening before, if for a different reason.

"*Shansu*," she said in Cheysuli, having learned her
share of the tongue in twenty-two years with my
father. "Oh, Keely, forgive us ... we have been so
worried, all of us—and now that you are back, we're
not wanting to lose you again, even for so brief a
time as a week." She smoothed her hand against the
crown of my head, whispering quiet words first in
Erinnish, then in Homanan. "It has been so difficult
for all of us, over the long years ... Gisella in Atvia,
Niall's light woman here in her place ... you never
had a mother, not as I had; as Maeve has, and
others. Only me in her place, and no one able to
admit it for fear of damaging proprieties, foolish
Homanan proprieties, reserving a place for a banished queen and never letting you or your brothers
forget it—"

I held onto to her very tightly. "She was never my
mother. Never. Always, it was you."

Deirdre clung to me. "*Leijhana tu'sai*," she whispered, and then stood back from me. "Go. Go. Take what time you need."

For Deirdre, I wanted to stay. But Deirdre had set me free.

I went mutely out of the solar, unable to say what I felt. Hoping she knew it anyway; Deirdre knows so very much.

*   *   *

I went to Clankeep, spoke to the *shar tahl,* set about my ritual. I fasted; built a small, lopsided shelter of saplings, twigs and vines in the center of a clearing swept free of all save sand; sweated impurities from my flesh. Lost myself in memories, in imaginings, in things too private to tell. Bathed in smoke, water and sand; cleansed soul, self, mind; within and without, according to the ritual my uncle still observed.

Three days. On the fourth, I would eat. On the fifth, return to Clankeep and request aid in losing the child.

But on the fifth, Teirnan came.

I crawled out of the tiny shelter, burning stick in hand, and stared at him, struck dumb. Amazed at his transgression; at the audacity of his appearance.

He was alone, save for his *lir,* the small-eyed boar named Vaii. It has been said before that often the *lir* reflects the personality of the warrior; in Teir's case, I agreed. Small-minded, selfish man, equally unpredictable and dangerous when trapped.

Teirnan smiled. "Finish."

The stick in my hand smoked. "You should not be here. This is private. Personal. You should go at once."

"Before I profane your atonement?" Teir shrugged, dismissing it with an eloquent wave of one hand. "Too late, Keely . . . Strahan has already profaned you more than *i'toshaa-ni* can cleanse."

I wanted nothing more than to thrust the burning stick into his face. But he would slap it aside, and I would have betrayed my instability, which would please him. Instead, I turned calmly and set my shelter afire. It smoked, crisped, caught; I threw the stick inside.

"So." I turned back to my cousin. "What do you want from me?"

"The answer to my question. Or, better, the answer to my proposal."

Behind me the heat increased as greenwood was slowly consumed. "What proposal, Teir? What business is there between us?"

He gazed past me, watched the fire, then reached out and caught my wrist, pulling me forward. "If you remain where you are you will burn. Keely—" But he broke it off, pulling me farther yet from the fire, then let go and squatted on his haunches. He made a gesture, and after a moment I sat down. "We feel the same way," he said. "I know we do, we *must* . . . you know what I told you is true, that we stand to lose the *lir*—"

"Not everyone believes that. Very few, in fact."

His eyes were very steady. "Are you going to marry the Prince of Erinn?"

Months trickled away. Once again I faced Teir, but in another time and place, with *a'saii* gathered around, flanked by all their *lir*. He had told me to refuse Sean, to bear Sean no children, to bring down the prophecy by denying it the blood so necessary for completion.

Then, there had been no reason, other than my own intransigence, yet I knew better. It was not enough; more would be required. And so I was given it, by Strahan. Now I had sound reason: a bastard in my belly. Heir to Strahan's power. More than enough reason to refuse the marriage, and no one could name me wrong.

But Teir did not know it.

I pushed myself up from the ground. Standing, I stared down at him, aware of rising apprehension; the comprehension of his intentions, and his dedication to them. "How far?" I asked. "How far are you willing to go?"

Teirnan spread his hands, as if to promote innocence. "A thing worth doing is worth doing well. So we are taught in the clans."

"How far?" I repeated. "If I refuse to wed Sean, it guarantees nothing. There is still Aidan. The Lion has an heir."

His eyes were shuttered by lids. Then he looked up again. "He is a sickly child."

"But *alive* . . . unless you take pains to kill him."

He is good, very good. But I have learned from Strahan to judge by things other than what a man says, or even by his silence.

"So," I said quietly, "first you come to me. To persuade me, with guile and skill, not to marry Sean. And so I do not. Part of the prophecy dies." I smiled my tribute. "And then there is Aidan—small, sickly Aidan. He may die any day . . . he may be *helped* to die, and so only Brennan is left. Brennan, heir to the Lion . . . the only one in your way."

So very cool, is Teirnan. I almost believed him. "I am not interested in the Lion. This is a far greater service."

"Destroying the prophecy?" I shook my head. "First me, then Aidan, then Brennan. And, perhaps, the Mujhar? Hart is Prince of Solinde; he inherits the kingship on *jehan's* death, and will have no time for Homana. Corin inherits Atvia; the same applies to him." To mock, I inclined my head. "Leaving the Lion with no heir, and only one man close enough to lay claim in his own name. Son of the Mujhar's dead sister, your claim is quickly granted."

Teirnan's voice was very quiet. He did not look at

me, but at his loose-linked hands. "If Aidan lives to wed and sire a son, completion is nearly accomplished. If he dies, and Brennan lives to marry another Erinnish girl and get a son on *her*, completion is nearly accomplished. And if you wed Sean and bear a son to take dead Aidan's place, completion is nearly accomplished." Now he looked up from his hands. His eyes were intensely feral, consumed by dedication. It is the bedmate of obsession and often pleasurable, but this, I knew, was not. "To destroy the prophecy, I must stop all of you."

I looked at the strength of his face, the determination so valued by someone who required it; so feared by someone who knew what it could mean. Teirnan had passed the point of reasoning. His commitment was commendable for its exactitude, but the results of it would destroy my family.

And yet I dared not show him the edge of my tongue. He had needed me before; now he did not, and I was expendable as anyone else unwilling to serve his purposes.

Behind me the sticks which were my shelter snapped and blazed. Quietly, I said, "Brennan will never set Aileen aside."

Teirnan pursed lips. "So he says. But men have said things before, and have had their intentions changed. Why should he be different? If anything, he is all the more dangerous because of his loyalty—he will do what he has to do to preserve the dynasty."

"Are you forgetting Corin?" I asked. "He is unwed . . . he could well take to wife an Erinnish girl, and all your plans laid waste."

Teirnan smiled. "Corin is in love with Aileen. He will wed no other. And if Brennan is prevailed upon to set her aside, as is possible, Corin will marry her. Barren, she is no threat. No, Keely . . . Corin is no danger. Nor is he *in* danger."

"But the rest of us are." I kept my voice steady

with effort. "If I say no to you—if I say I will wed Sean—what do you do then? Kill me?"

Teirnan rose in silence. "No need," he answered quietly. "I have other means."

Once, I might have—*would* have—laughed, taunted, denied, but I knew better now. Strahan had showed me very well how dangerous is arrogance; how deadly is misplaced pride.

"Teir," I said quietly, reaching for patience and, to my surprise, finding it in abundance, "we are not enemies in this. What you have said regarding the loss of the *lir* frightens me, and badly, because I begin to think you may be right. And so you are right to question it, to bring the topic before Clan Council and all the *shar tahls*—"

"Keely, it is too late."

I tried again. "You know very well that if you try to bring down those close to the Lion by violent means—"

"There need be no violence."

I hated him for his quietude. "Teirnan, think of Maeve—"

"I have. And of you, and Niall, and even Brennan, whom neither of us has much cause to love—though I have, I think, less cause than any of us." He smiled. "Keely, you know as well as I you have come to terms with your *tahlmorra* . . . you know as well as I you will do what you feel is required to keep the prophecy whole. Lying now alters nothing. So why not simply allow me to do what must be done—"

I reached for the magic, intending to flee, but nothing came in answer.

Teirnan smiled a little. "I have an ally, Keely. Someone who needs to destroy the prophecy as much as the *a'saii*."

Behind me, the shelter collapsed. From the ruin came Rhiannon.

No time to waste—

I spun back. In two strides I braced Teirnan, lifting my knee to thrust it home where it would do the most damage. But Vaii knew my intentions nearly as quickly as I did, charging to rake tusk through boot leather into the ankle beneath.

Teirnan caught both wrists and held them firmly, unperturbed by my struggles, by the curses I heaped on him. My ankle bled and burned.

"Let me see her," Rhiannon said.

Teirnan turned me forcibly, twisting my arms behind me. I was weak from the fasting and my ankle was afire. I could not believe Vaii had attacked me. A *lir* attacking a Cheysuli?

But Vaii was Teirnan's *lir*, equally committed to treachery.

I had not seen Rhiannon for more than two years. Then, she had been Brennan's *meijha*, masquerading as a sweet-mouthed Homanan girl madly in love with the Prince of Homana. I knew better, now; she had given herself away on the day she stole Brennan for Strahan. Ian's Ihlini daughter, born of Strahan's sister, Lillith.

Black-haired, black-eyed, as so many Ihlini are, but with skin fair as Ilsa's. A lovely, striking woman, now more so than ever, who had borne my brother a child to be matched with Strahan's own, bred on his *meijha*, Sidra. Such a twisted, tangled birthline, now firmly entwined with mine.

She wore leathers, which shocked me. And gold at her throat, dangling from her ears, hooking her belt in place. Slim, deadly Rhiannon, half Cheysuli, half Ihlini, with no *lir* but all the power.

She held up a silver chain, displaying it. From it depended a ring: sapphire set in silver. It was, I knew, a trinket Brennan had once given her; she had kept it well since then, using it to augment her spells. Because it had been Brennan's, she could use it as a shield. It was why I had not known of her presence. It was why my magic was useless.

She tucked the ring and chain away. "Call me *a'saii*," she said, "it will do as well as another."

"Strahan is dead," I told her, hoping it would hurt.

Rhiannon merely nodded. "Some of us die younger than others. He is a great loss, aye, and we grieve for his absence, but there are things to do. Life must continue, and so must the duty, until our task is finished."

She had known. That much was clear. And since she was here, aiding Teirnan, I knew very well Corin's hopes for waning Ihlini influence would not come true.

"You and Lillith," I said.

"Lillith, me, the children." Rhiannon smiled slowly. "And yours as well, Keely. Did you think we did not know?"

Teirnan's hands tightened. I felt his breath against my hair. "Are you saying he got her with child?"

"A potent man, my uncle . . . in his children, his name lives on." Behind her the shelter burned low; little was left but smoke and ash. "Have her kneel, Teirnan . . . ah, better, aye. Hold her. *Hold* her. She is weak from fasting, and angry, and the child affects her power. Hold her so, Teirnan—aye, better . . . it will not be so awkward after all."

Shoulders burned from the tension of their entrapment. Teirnan stood behind me, knees pressed into my back. My own were on the ground, much as I longed to stand.

"Teir . . . she is *Ihlini*."

"I know what she is," he said, "and I know also that we want the same thing: destruction of the prophecy."

"She will destroy more than that—" I broke off as he twisted my arms.

"No more noise," he said. "For once in your life, *listen.*"

Rhiannon stood before me. "Listen," she echoed softly, "and I will tell you a tale. Of a proud Cheysuli woman with Old Blood in her veins, and the thing she had to do."

I hissed as Teirnan twisted my arms, denying me escape.

"—the thing she had to do—"

Oh, gods, stop her . . . she is coming inside my head.

"—*the thing she had to do*—"

Deep inside, something broke. Gave way before her power.

First Strahan, now Rhiannon. First body invaded, now mind.

Gods. Which is worse?

"A little thing," she said, "and well within your means."

Deep inside, the child moved. As if it knew who she was.

Rhiannon's hands were in my hair, holding my head still. Her face was close to mine. "First you will do this thing, and then you will bear the baby. A strong, healthy baby, worthy of Strahan's name. Of the blessings of the Seker."

No, I will *not*—

But the world I knew winked out. In its place was Rhiannon.

And the thing I had to do.

Ten

They were back, all of them. I could hear the low rumble of male voices, lighter-pitched female ones, laughter, the dry tones of jests once played on one another, now repeated for the entertainment of others. And such a sense of well-being and joy flooded through me that I ran up the last few steps, grateful for leggings instead of cumbersome skirts. The door to Deirdre's solar was ajar; I pushed it two-handed and grinned as it slammed against the wall, serving to silence them all.

I set one shoulder against the door and leaned, folding my arms. "Aye," I observed dryly, "I can tell you were worried. Such long faces, furrowed brows, tears of grief and anguish." I grinned at staring faces trapped in myriad expressions of astonishment. "Aye, well, I am back, and none the worse for wear. You may celebrate; I intend to, myself."

I strode into the room, caught the cup of wine from Corin's hand, drank it down. Then gave it back, laughing, as his surprise shapechanged to a scowl.

They were scattered about the solar like a handful of prophecy bones: *lir* here and there, sprawled on rugs—Rael perched on a chair; Hart with Ilsa beside him, tiny Blythe snugged into his chest; Deirdre with *jehan*, perched on the arm of his chair; Corin nearest the door, feet propped up on a stool; Brennan by a casement, but looking at me instead; Ian slouching in the sill of another; Maeve sitting

328

with yarn in her hands and Sean holding a cup of wine.

Sean.

Oh, gods, *Sean*.

"When did you get back?" I asked into the silence.

"This morning," my father answered. "Quite early, just at dawn . . . we came in *lir*-shape through the night, once Kiri passed the message." With quiet deliberation he rose. "Keely—"

I thrust my arms out from my side, as if a seamstress worked to fit my gown, and displayed myself. "I am well. Well, *jehan*—I promise. See?" I turned. "No need to fret. He left me both eyes, both hands—no scars to remember him by. He had no interest in harming me." I let my arms flop down. "Instead, I harmed him." I smiled. "He is dead, *jehan* . . . or did Corin already tell you?"

My father's face was stark. "He told me."

"Good. No need for me to repeat it, then . . . old stories bore me." I went to the low table nearest my father, found a cup amidst the jumble of yarns, poured myself what wine remained in the jug. "So, what do you think of Sean, Liam's son? Is he so much like his father? Will he be a fitting prince? A fitting husband for your daughter?"

"Keely," my father said.

I saw his face. Stood very still a moment, then with an awkward rush set down the cup and went into his arms. "Hold me," I whispered. "*Hold* me."

He said nothing, merely holding. It was all I needed from him. And all, I think, *he* needed, holding me so hard.

"I am well," I told him, "I promise."

"I never learn," he murmured. "So many times Strahan has lured my children into captivity—"

"No," I said firmly. "Enough. He is dead; we need never concern ourselves with him again." I stepped out of his arms, picked up my cup yet again, and drank. Then smiled at them all, but my face felt brittle. "So much silence! I would sooner have you trading jests—even at my expense—than gaping at me like motley-fools at a Summerfair!" I raised my cup. "Drink. Celebrate my homecoming, and Corin's, and give good welcome to Sean, Prince of Erinn, come to collect his wayward bride."

"Oh?" Sean's thick brows rose. "And is the wayward lass willing to be a bride at last, after so many years?"

I shrugged. "It matters less at this point what she is willing to do . . . more if you will have her, after what has happened. And more yet what the Mujhar says. So *you* said, aboard your ship."

Sean frowned, baffled. "Lass—"

I turned abruptly to face my father, though I swept a glance around the solar. "You are all of you kin, by blood and marriage . . . there is no sense in hiding the truth. We all know why Strahan wanted me, why he took me, and what he did while he had me: Keely, Princess Royal of Homana, is no longer the virgin she was." I clutched the cup in both hands, seeing the withdrawal in their eyes; the pain, the grief, the empathy. "Well, I can live with that, and I will—what choice have I . . . but what of Sean? Should he be expected to? Should my dishonor be his?" I looked at him briefly, then at the Mujhar. "Should the Prince of Erinn be expected to take a ravished woman to wife? To hear the gibes, the jests, the comments . . . the suggestions that the new-made Princess of Erinn is not a *maid* at all, but a whore who lay down with an Ihlini? Because they *will* say so. Just as they call Deirdre whore here in Homana, and Maeve bastard, so they will call me and the first child I bear in Erinn, if it be born any time within a year of my last day with Strahan." I drew in a steadying breath. "Tell me, *jehan*. Do I become a bride? Or do

we give Sean his freedom, you and I, so he may wed
a woman worthy of him? Worthy of giving him heirs?"

"Lass, you're worthy of anyone." Sean drank more
wine, then lowered his cup and looked at the Mujhar.
"My lord, she and I did speak of this aboard my
ship. What she says has merit—there will be questions asked, and comments made—but I'm not a
man to be troubled by the maunderings of others.
She's a braw, bright lass, and I'd be a fool to look for
another." He smiled at me crookedly, brown eyes
alight. "But there's someone else to ask, I'm thinking. Someone other than your father."

"Someone *else*? Who?"

"Rory," he said evenly. "Hie yourself to the Redbeard,
lass, and hear what he'll be saying."

It took most of my breath away, as well as stun-
ning the others. I felt the stares but managed to ask,
weakly, "Why should I? What has he to do with
this?"

Sean sighed, rubbing the bridge of his nose ruefully. "More than I'd like to admit. No man likes to
say the lass he fancies is in love with another man."

"Gods," Brennan said, "I think he means the horse
thief!"

Hart smiled a little. "I never thought you a blind
man, *rujho*." The smile stretched to a grin as I turned
to glare at him. "Oh, aye, I saw it then, Keely—save
your thunder for someone else."

"He is a *horse thief*," Brennan repeated.

"Well," Sean said lightly, "once he was something
more. A bit more, lad, being bastard brother to a
prince." He laughed easily, seeing Brennan's reaction. "Have ye none of your own?"

It was a most telling question. Brennan opened his
mouth, shut it, looked at me instead. "So," he said,
"him. And where does that leave Sean?"

"Here," Sean replied, before I could think of an
answer. "Go to Rory, lass. Hear what he'll be saying.

He's a head on his shoulders, when it isn't full of liquor, and he'll be saying what he feels."

"And if he does?" I said. "What then?"

"Depends on what he says, lass . . . but I'm thinking I have an idea."

Belligerence overcame tact. "How?"

"We've the same taste in lasses, my girl . . . 'twas why he near broke my head."

Brennan shook his head. "Sean, you are mad. You must be. My stubborn *rujholla* has fought against this marriage for as long as she has had the words—and fists—to do it, and now you give her a weapon. You put it into her hands and show her how to use it." He laughed a little, in sheer disbelief. "All she has to do is come back and say Rory will have her in your place, and then when you are gone she will calmly change her mind. And she will get what *she* wants, as she has so many times, leaving the rest of us to patch together the remains of the prophecy."

Sean's face was oddly serene. "I'll not be taking a lass who loves another man. 'Tis more in *your* line, I'm thinking; how fares Aileen?"

Deirdre clearly was shocked. "Sean! 'Tis enough!"

He was unperturbed by the reprimand. "Deirdre, my lass, you're my aunt, not my mother. I'll say what there is to be said. My father taught me so."

"There are times," she said grimly, "Liam is a fool."

"And I his son, lady." Still Sean smiled.

Corin stirred, dropping his hand over the chair arm to touch Kiri's head. "Sean," he said wearily, "Aileen is not the issue."

"No. No, she is not. 'Tis Keely, I'm thinking . . . and also my brother, whom I love, trust and value as much as you do your own, all of you, even my lord Mujhar." Now he looked at my father. "You married Gisella of Atvia, but you sleep with Deirdre of Erinn.

Surely you understand, my lord, what it is to be loving someone other than your mate."

"Indeed," my father said, and sat down in his chair again. Like Corin, he touched his *lir*; Serri lay sprawled at his feet. "Well, I see this has gone far beyond the simple agreement Liam and I made so long ago, binding our Houses through marriage. Brennan for Aileen, Keely for Sean." He sighed, rubbing at scars. "Clearly, we were wrong. We should have done it another way."

"But it *was* done, and for good reason," Brennan said irritably. "Aidan may die. Aileen is barren. The marriage between Keely and Sean may be the only alternative we have to get the blood for the prophecy."

Sean merely shrugged. "Rory is Erinnish. Rory is Liam's son. 'Tis the proper blood, I'm thinking, if got from another man."

Brennan's eyes narrowed. "Why are you so eager to be rid of my *rujholla*? Is it that you *are* shamed by what Strahan did, and think to cast her off on some byblow of Liam's so you may go home and seek another?"

I had not thought of it. Now I did, as all the others did, and I stared even as they did, as one, and hard, at Sean, who had the grace to color.

" 'Tis not that at all, ye *skilfin*! I'm thinking of the lass. I'm thinking of my brother. *And* I'm thinking of me." He took a stride forward. "If you like, I'll wed her tomorrow." A hand was thrust toward the door, wrist aglint with copper. "Have the priest called; I'll not shirk the chance. But if you have any decency in you, you'll let her see Rory. She can't be told what to do, or turned this way and that. She'll make up her own mind, my lad, or she'll go to her grave unhappy. D'ye think I want an unwilling wife? D'ye think I'm wanting a cold bed, where she dreams of someone else?"

Brennan's face was ashen. I have seen that look

before on him, when he is terribly angry or terribly shaken. If Sean had tried harder, he could not have found a more deadly weapon. "I think," he said quietly, "we should settle this argument elsewhere."

Hart scooped up Blythe and handed her to Ilsa, rising so rapidly he upset Rael, who bated on the chairback. "Brennan."

Brennan simply ignored him, looking only at Sean. "Are you any good with a sword?"

Sean grinned broadly. "I'm thinking better than you."

Deirdre looked at my father. "Stop them."

He shook his head. "They are men, not boys, *meijha*. This will be settled between themselves."

Now Maeve was standing awkwardly, hands spread over her belly. "Brennan, no! What do you care what Keely does, or whom she marries? *She* doesn't. She doesn't care if she lives or—"

"Enough," I said sharply.

Sean grinned at Brennan. "A bit of sparring, then, to see which one is better? Shall we name the stakes?"

Brennan glanced at me. "If I win, she stays here. If you win, she goes to the horse thief."

"Wait—" I began, but Sean's agreement overrode my protest.

Ian slid off the casement sill, stepping over now-cubless Tasha. "A bright day," he said lightly. "Shall we go outside?"

Outside, it was very bright. The Mujhar and assorted kinfolk went into the bailey, where Brennan and I had sparred before. He carried a sword, as did Sean, given one from Griffon, who came to arbitrate. It was a match, no more, but the forms must be followed.

It did not take long for word to spread. Within moments others gathered. Sean, seeing how many, grinned. Brennan's face was masked, hiding what he felt, though I had a good idea.

Sean stripped out of green velvet doublet and tossed it aside. It left him in linen shirtsleeves, with the ties undone at throat and wrists, baring copper necklet and broad, furred chest clear to his belt. He rolled up sleeves to elbows, flexed muscled forearms, considered stripping off wristlets. But did not, smiling a little, seeing Brennan and his gold.

I grinned at him, then stepped up as if to wish him good fortune. Instead, I took his sword. "First, there is something else to be done." I turned, ignoring his blurt of surprise, and crossed the cobbles to Brennan. "Months ago, you made a promise. Now I hold you to it. *Su'fali* served as witness; you promised a match to me. I say now."

"Not *now*," he protested. "This is for Sean and me."

"You promised." I glanced at Ian. "Did he not, *su'fali*?"

Ian's expression was rueful. "Aye. He did. But—"

I turned back to Brennan. "Well? You will beat me, of course . . . it should not take long, nor much of your strength, and you will be able to turn to Sean once you are done with me."

Brennan looked past me to our father. "*Jehan*—"

"Did you promise?"

"Aye, but—" Brennan shrugged, frustrated.

He was not happy, our father, but would not allow his heir to renege on a promise, even to his sister, of whom he was not overly fond. "Then fulfill it."

I laughed at my brother. "Your chance, *rujho*, to show me up before the others. Surely you will enjoy it."

He waved a hand. "Then go. Move away. Let this be done properly."

"Oh. Aye, of course." I turned and took a single

pace away, then swung back, still in range of his blade, and he in range of mine. "Far enough, *rujho*?"

Brennan scowled. "Gods, Keely, must you overplay this? It is a travesty, no more . . . why do you want to do this?"

I grinned. "Because you promised. Because I want to. Because I have learned a trick or two since the last time we met."

"From whom? Not Griffon."

"Not Griffon, no. A little from the horse thief, who has a way with steel."

Brennan's mouth tightened. He cast a glare at Sean, who merely laughed, showing teeth.

I grinned and waved the sword under my oldest brother's aristocratic nose. The blade was one of Griffon's, not mine, and was therefore too heavy for me, but I knew it would do. I would not need it for long.

"Keely!" Brennan ducked aside. "Gods, Keely, take care—do you wish to slice off my nose?"

"It might improve your looks." I smiled sweetly. "Why are you waiting, *rujho*? Are you afraid to begin?"

"We are still too close," he said curtly, and turned to move away.

I let him go a pace, then ran my blade through his back.

Eleven

It was Corin who smashed me down, face down, grinding me into the cobbles. The sword lay beneath me, trapped in my hands. I felt the steel cut. I felt the blood flow. I heard the people screaming.

It hurt. I was hurt. I was *bleeding*—

Everyone was shouting.

I squirmed, thrashed, trying to pull away, to drag myself from beneath him. His weight was crushing me, pushing the breath from me, jamming my hands against sharp steel.

Why is he hurting me?

Why are people shouting?

I kicked, and caught a boot. "Let me go—" I gasped. "Let me *go*—"

He dragged me up from the cobbles, pulling me to my knees. The sword clanged out of my hands, rolled, rang against the cobbles. I saw blood on the blade. Blood on the stones. Blood on *me*—

"Leave her to me!" he shouted as bodies crowded around. "Gods—leave her to *me*—"

"—bleeding," I said raggedly. "Corin—all the *blood*—"

Maeve was in my face, sobbing aloud and shouting. Over the bulge of her belly she bent, then smashed her hand across my cheek and mouth. My lip split on teeth.

Someone pulled her away. Ian. Ian, pulling Maeve away, guiding her toward the palace.

Sleeta's keening wail carried throughout the bailey.

I spat blood. Stared at my hands. Blood *everywhere*.

Someone was on the cobbles. Not me; Corin held me. Someone else on the cobbles, sprawled across the stone. One arm was twisted beneath him, legs sprawled obscenely . . . it was all I could see. Too many other people, gathered around. So many *people*.

Deirdre was crying.

"What is it?" I asked. "What is it?"

So much noise and confusion.

Corin held me up. He bundled me like a bedroll; only my hands were free.

They moved the man on the ground. Turned him over onto his back, and then I saw his face.

"Brennan!" I cried. "Not *Brennan*—"

Corin's tone was choked. "Keely, hush. Say nothing. You will make it worse."

"But—*Brennan*—"

"Keely, I beg you—"

"Let me *go*, Corin! By the gods, are you blind? Why are you holding me? Why not let me go to him?"

They were strangers all around me, though their faces were familiar. "Take her inside," someone said. "Lock her up if you must . . . we will need everyone for the healing."

"Lock me up? Lock me up? Why are you locking me up?"

"Keely, *hush*," Corin begged.

"Take her inside!" someone shouted.

Corin dragged me to my feet. "Come. No, no— Keely, I beg you, save your struggles—"

"Brennan is hurt," I told him. "Let me go—let me see—Corin, *let me go*—"

He dragged me toward the palace.

"Corin, *please*—"

Up the steps, through the open doors, past staring, white-faced servants.

"Corin, where are you taking me? Why are you locking me up? Why are you hurting me?"

Down stairs, around and around, into a shadowed corridor.

"Corin—Brennan is *hurt*—"

He held me up as I tripped. Then pulled me to a halt in front of a door, slammed it open, pushed me bodily into the chamber.

"Corin—Corin, *no*—"

He shut the door in my face. I heard the bolt go home.

Locked in.

"Corin!"

No answer.

"Is it Brennan? Is it Brennan? Has someone killed Brennan?"

He was gone.

I sagged against the door, leaving bloody handprints. "Have I done something wrong?"

A cold, dark room, stinking of disuse. No window. Only a door, and locked.

I stared at the walls. Tasted blood in my mouth. Spat it out, and looked at the cuts in my hands. Spread fingers and saw the cuts pull apart; blood sprang up afresh.

Confusion.

Who has hurt me? Who has cut me?

Oh, gods, is Brennan dead?

I sat down on the ground, hard. Crossed my arms at the wrists, palm up, warding hands against further pain.

And waited, wrapped in silence, seeing Brennan's battered, bloodied face as they turned him onto his back.

Gods, what did I *do*?

*   *   *

Three of them came, and I knew them: Ian, Hart, Corin. They bent, knelt, squatted. Pushed hair out

of my face, cleaned the blood from my lip, offered
me water. I wanted none of it.

"Keely, drink," Corin said.

I drank. Hart touched a hand; I hissed.

"She is cut," he said. "Both hands—see?"

Corin shut his eyes. "She still held the sword when
I took her down. It was beneath her . . . I should
have kicked it away."

Ian shook his head. "You had more than enough
to do." He touched my head again, smoothing fingers across my brow. "No lumps. I thought she might
have struck her head . . . but this is more, I think.
Much more . . . well, we will do what we can to set
her to rights. Keely—"

"Is he dead?" I asked intently. "Did I kill Brennan?"

It silenced all of them.

Ian's tone was quiet. "Do you remember everything?"

"Is Brennan dead?"

He shook his head. "I promise."

"But nearly."

"Nearly. Without so many of us there to tap the
earth magic, he would have died."

I stared at my hands. "I am mad, then. Like my
jehana. Like Mad Gisella. The tainted blood runs
true."

Corin's voice was strained. "Keely, *jehana's* madness has nothing to do with blood—"

Hart shook his head. "Leave it. Tell her later. For
now, we should take her to her own room—"

"No," I told him. "Leave me here. Lock me up."

"—gods," Corin choked.

Ian's voice was quiet and infinitely soothing. "Corin,
she is confused—and, I am sure, tampered with.
Here, let me move in." I looked into yellow eyes.
"Keely," he said gently, "you went to Clankeep for
i'toshaa-ni. What happened?"

"I completed the ritual."

"Then what did you do?"

"I completed the ritual. But Teir came—Teir was there—Teir profaned the cleansing—" I lurched up into hands. "Teir—Teir—Teir . . . it was Teirnan and *Rhiannon*—"

"Trap-link," Corin blurted. "Oh, gods, Rhiannon—"

Hart swore softly. "Strahan may be dead, but there are others in the world who will assume his place. Lillith. Now Rhiannon?"

Ian gave me more water. "Keely, can you remember? Can you remember what she told you?"

I mopped my chin with the back of a hand, careful of the lip Maeve's blow had cut open. "That—there was something I had to do. A task. A thing I had to do." I shivered and shut up my hands, then hissed from the pain of salt and dirt in the cuts. "I was—I was to *kill* him . . . I was to kill *Brennan* . . . and then Aidan would die—there would be no one for the Lion." I frowned, remembering. "Hart in Solinde. Corin in Atvia. No one left for the Lion—"

Hart's face was taut. "Except Teir. Of course."

"I was to kill Brennan, and then—" But I shut it off. I could not tell them that; not about the child. "I was to kill Brennan."

Ian nodded. "All right. All right, Keely . . . time to leave this place. We will stand you up—aye, *harana*, stand—and we will take you up from the dungeons— aye, *harana*, I know you are unsteady; lean against me—and put you in your room, in your bed, and let you sleep the night through. In the morning you will be rested, and so will all of us. We can deal with the trap-link then. Aye, Keely—come. Through the door and up the stairs—aye, *aye*—see? Not so very hard."

"It hurts," I said intently.

"Aye, Keely, I know."

"It *hurts*," I said again.

"*Shansu*," Ian whispered. "Not so far—a few more stairs—"

I began to laugh. "—bleeding," I gasped raggedly. "Oh, *leijhana tu'sai*—"

"Keely—" Corin began.

Warmth flooded my thighs. "*Su'fali*, wait—oh wait
. . . gods—the child is *coming* . . . no more abomination—" I sagged, unable to stand, to climb, to do
anything but grind my teeth together, trying to bite
back a moan.

Ian scooped me up. My leggings were wet with
blood.

"Corin," I said through the pain, "is Brennan really
alive?"

"Aye, Keely—I promise." And then, on a rising
note of fear: "What is wrong with her?"

"Miscarriage," Ian said grimly. "Strahan got her
with child."

Spasmodic pains wracked my belly. "—gods—put
me *down*—"

Ian lunged up the stairs.

No more abomination . . . but—oh gods—it *hurts*—

*It gives me a perverse satisfaction to miscarry Strahan's
get. Child of rape, of sorcery, bred to be our downfall. The
destruction of Homana.*

*Now, it dies so easily, spilled out onto the sheets. Gender
unknown, or untold; they will spare me what they can.
Knowing, as they spare me, that in the dying of the child
the fragility of my own precarious hold on life increases.*

—so easy to die—

"Keely . . . Keely fight it—"

*And I laugh, knowing myself caught at last. Trapped by
tahlmorra, by gender, by self. Acknowledging the capriciousness of the gods; the vulnerability of the prophecy, only
as strong as those who serve it. Until now, this moment,
here, incredibly strong, served by sons and daughters of the
Lion, who lived and died in the names of ancient oaths and
older gods, in bondage to themselves.*

"Fight the pain, Keely . . . you are much too strong
for it."

Teir has the right of it; we are deaf and dumb and blind.

Bound by the swaddling clothes of honor, the grave soil of tradition. We are a dead race living, cloaking our lack of self-purpose in the trappings of prophecy, depending on gods to give us direction, to show us the proper road. And always a single road, when so many lie before us. The world is full of roads—but we choose only one. Always. Forever. Until the end is reached, stripping us of purpose, of ambition; even of our lir.

Will the gods even bother to thank us?

Or will they pat us on the head and send us off to bed?

Turning to smile paternally on the ancient cradle called Homana, holding the Firstborn child. The child of true and abiding power; of Ihlini and Cheysuli, and all the other bloodlines.

Will they call him Mujhar?

Or will they call him god?

"Promise me, Keely, you will not give in to this."

Jehan? Are you there?

"You are the daughter of the Lion, who relishes a fight. A braw, bright lass, as Sean himself as said . . . oh, gods, Keely, do not give up now."

—dying is not so easy . . . too many things undone—too many fates unknown—

Knowing, if I die, Strahan may win after all.

Twelve

Someone sat next to my bed. I heard shallow breathing, the slight alteration of posture, the scrape of leather against wood. Someone sat in a chair beside me, smelling of leather and gold; the musk of a mountain cat.

I mouthed it. *Su'fali*. Then opened my eyes to see him; saw Brennan instead.

Oh, gods.

Not Brennan.

I shut my eyes again.

"Keely."

Humiliation bathed me. "Go away," I told him.

"Keely, this is nonsense. I am alive. I am well. Weak, aye, and sore, but all of that will pass. Keely—I am *alive*."

"And, being Brennan, full of forgiveness for me."

His tone was odd. "Let us say, full of comprehension. I understand what happened."

I opened eyes. "Then you are *not* going to forgive me?"

Brennan's smile was slight. "You would hate me if I did. What you want from me is accusation and disapproval, so you can get angry. Anger is always your best defense; it allows you the chance to climb up on the highest of your horses. But if I forgive you for running four feet of steel through my body— and I am told a foot of it came out the other side—I take away the anger, the guilt, your sense of humiliation, leaving you only with resentment. The gods know there has been that and more between us, for a variety of reasons—good *and* bad—and I am weary of it. So no, I do not forgive you . . . you nearly killed me, Keely."

"*Ku'reshtin*," I said weakly. "You always have the answers."

"Is that enough reason to kill a man?"

I was aware of weakness, of lassitude; of a strange apathy. No more pain, but discomfort. My belly felt oddly empty. "They told you about the baby."

"Aye. Teirnan, Rhiannon, the trap-link . . . also the baby, Keely. But why—" He broke it off. "No. Now is not the time, nor is it my place—"

I answered him anyway. "Because I could tell no one. Only Maeve, and she guessed. I meant to tell no one at all. I meant only to rid myself of it." I grimaced. "It rid itself of me."

He shifted again in the chair, settling his back carefully. For a man who had been run through with, as he had said, four feet of steel, he looked surprisingly hale, if pale of face and bruised. But it was earth magic, not normal healing, and such power takes its toll. Of the healed as well as the healers. "Keely—"

"Go to bed," I told him. "I see indeed you have survived, but there is no more need for you to sit here beside me and taunt me with such magnanimous empathy. It is what I expect of you, being you; go to bed, rest . . . and tell me you forgive me when I am best able to mount my highest of horses." I smiled weakly. "*Leijhana tu'sai, rujho* . . . as you say, disliking you for having all the answers is not reason enough to kill you. I shall have to find one better."

He smiled. His color had worsened, which made the bruises down the left side of his face all the more ugly, and he rose with a wince he tried but failed to suppress. "I sent for Aileen. She will be delayed—Aidan has a fever—but she should be back within a five-day. I think perhaps there are things you two may share that no one else can understand."

"And surely I more than most am in grave need of understanding." I grinned briefly as he opened his mouth to respond, and waved him away with a limp hand. "Go. Go. Before Deirdre comes to fetch you and tuck you into bed, or Maeve—most likely Maeve! —and strips you of all your dignity."

He rubbed his midriff tentatively. "The gods know they stripped me of everything else, for the healing—" He grinned. "Rest you well, *rujholla*. When you are strong again—when *both* of us are strong again—we shall have to meet a final time to decide which of us is better with a blade."

I waited until he was at the open door. "You would risk that?"

Brennan shrugged, then winced. "Why not? The trap-link is gone, banished days ago by *su'fali*, who has some knowledge of them . . . I think there is no danger."

"No . . . I meant would you risk *losing* in front of so many people?"

Brennan laughed in genuine amusement, which did not particularly please me, and took himself out of my chamber before I could respond.

They came in couples, in trios, alone, wishing me well, asking after my health, apologizing for harsh words and the roughness with which they had treated me. Maeve cried prettily over the blow she had fetched my face, but I knew she would not hesitate to repeat it, or worse, if I ever again threatened her beloved Brennan. Well, I did not expect her to do otherwise; it was the same with Corin and me.

And yet Corin was the worst, apologizing for throwing me to the cobbles and for locking me away; he was convinced his roughness had caused the loss of the baby. Perhaps it had, or perhaps ill-wishing it had, or perhaps the gods themselves had intervened. I did not care and told him so; also that I had intended to be rid of it one way or another, and he had saved me some trouble.

He was unconvinced, so I cursed him crossly and sent him away, telling him to leave me alone until he could bear to see me without apologizing.

Corin went away. Into his place came Ian.

He was uncomfortable. I saw it at once, and was astonished. I had never seen him so ill at ease.

And then I thought I knew.

"No," I said flatly, before he could open his mouth. "I will not have it. Do you think for one moment I will blame you?"

"She is my daughter. If I had not lain with Lillith in Atvia, regardless of the sorcery, Rhiannon would not exist." His face was very stiff. "She would not have come to Homana, to seduce Brennan and bear his child, who even now grows up with the tending of Ihlini . . . and she would not have been able to set a trap-link to murder him, using you as her weapon."

"Teirnan's as much as hers." I shook my head at him. "How many times have you told me we must not live in the past, but look forward to the future? Rhiannon exists; short of killing her, we cannot change it. The child exists; nor can we kill *it*, not knowing where—or who—it is. But mine does not survive, for which I thank the gods . . . Strahan will have no heir of *me*."

He made a slight banishing gesture with his hand, and I knew the topic closed. "I came also to get honesty from you. Will you give it?"

Plainly, he wanted no jest. I nodded.

"Strahan forced you," he said, "much as Lillith forced me. I know what that does to a soul."

"And you want to know how I feel."

"I know how you feel, Keely. Dirty. Soiled. Be-

smirched. Entirely worthless as a person, as a Cheysuli
. . . as part of the House of Homana."

Painfully, I swallowed. "I fulfilled *i'toshaa-ni*."

His eyes were oddly intense. "And was it enough
for you?"

I opened my mouth to say aye, of course it was; it
was a cleansing ritual, and I was now purified . . .
but I said nothing. I bit into my lip to keep from
crying and slowly shook my head.

Ian smiled, though it was an odd, bittersweet smile.
And then he put his hand on my head, cupping my
skull with his fingers. "You and I," he said. "You and
I, *harana* . . . together, we will defeat it."

Quietly, he went away, leaving me gazing at his
absence.

I slept. And then awakened, aware of a presence,
and saw another man in my room, his face grown
old before me.

"*Jehan?*" I pushed myself upright against piled
bolsters.

He made a staying gesture. "Keely—no. Stay as
you are." And he sat down in the empty chair, reaching out to catch my hand. "Listen to me. Say nothing, Keely: *listen*."

After a moment, I nodded.

He closed my hand in both of his, gripping it very
firmly. "She is mad, Keely, not because of anything
in the blood . . . not because of anything gotten from
ancestors—but because *her* mother fell while carrying her; the fall injured Gisella, who was born immediately after. She is mad because of that—and *only*
because of that; you cannot inherit it. You cannot
pass it on. You are sane and will always be sane . . .
and so will all your children."

My hand clenched spasmodically.

"I promise you, Keely. I swear on the life on my
lir."

Through my tears, I smiled. "It took you too long to get him."

He nodded gravely, though his single eye was bright. "Which serves, I think, to make the oath all the more impressive."

I held onto his fingers. "All my life I have been afraid."

"For *nothing*."

"All my life, once I was old enough to understand, I feared I might go mad; that my children might be born mad."

"Keely, we have never hidden the truth from you. You know the story of how Bronwyn in raven-shape was shot out of the sky. She died of her injuries just after Gisella was born."

I stared blindly at the coverlet. "She tried to give her sons to Strahan."

"She was made to do that. What do you expect of a woman reared by an Ihlini? Lillith was foster-mother, and Alaric—her true father—turned a blind eye. Gisella was mad already. She would have done anything and believed it expected of her." He sat back in the chair, releasing my hand; the memories, for him, were still painful. "She gave me four fine children; for that I am very grateful."

I looked up into his face. "But you will not have her here."

He shook his head. "There is no place for her here. She is better off in Atvia."

"Where Corin must deal with her, while Deirdre warms your bed." I caught my breath. "Ah, *jehan*, I am sorry. I have no right to say such things."

His tone was oddly calm. "The day Gisella dies, Deirdre will be my *cheysula*."

A long time to wait. I sighed. "I wish it might be tomorrow. Then Maeve becomes legitimate *and* the oldest daughter of the Mujhar of Homana. Let *her* be marriage bait; I am weary of it."

The Mujhar of Homana laughed. "So are we all, Keely. You are hardly the first." He rose, leaned down to kiss my head. "Nor will you be the last."

"*Jehan*—what will you do about Teir?"

His face aged before me. "Find him, somehow. And when we do, he will be brought before Clan Council to answer for what he has done."

"What will Council do?"

After a moment he shook his head. "No warrior has ever done as he has. Not even Ceinn, his father, who raised his son on rebellion. We are not a treacherous race, nor one in need of punishment . . . but what Teir has done is reprehensible."

"Because he believes differently? Are you so sure he is wrong?"

"Keely—"

"He could be right, *jehan* . . . we may lose the *lir*."

He rubbed again at scars. "If that is so, we must deal with it as it comes. But as for Teir—" He sighed; Teirnan was his dead sister's son. "He will have to be punished."

Mutely, I nodded.

At the door he paused. "*Leijhana tu'sai*, Keely."

I blinked at him, baffled. "Why? What have I done besides try to kill Brennan?"

His face tautened a moment as memory came back. But he banished the expression and smiled a crooked smile. "Aye, you did . . . just as I once tried to kill Deirdre, her brother and her father—if more indirectly. You used a sword. I, fire . . . a beacon-fire blazing atop the dragon's skull, setting assassins to work." He sighed and resettled his patch. "But that is done. I say thank you for killing Strahan."

In startled silence, I watched him go, wondering uneasily why he said nothing of Sean; why he said nothing of Rory. Nothing of marrying either, though surely he could have. Surely he had *meant* to, being father; Mujhar; Cheysuli. Faithful servant of the prophecy.

Or had he?

I considered it carefully, then scowled blackly at the door. "But we *need* the Erinnish blood."

And knew Teirnan had lost.

But neither had I won. Sean himself had said it: *"Rory is Erinnish. Rory is Liam's son."*

Making it all the harder.

Swearing, I got out of bed. Slowly, carefully, with infinite delicacy. I unearthed fresh leathers from a deep trunk—my belt fit now—and eased myself into them. Eased my feet into soft house boots, grunting against the effort, shutting teeth against one another in response to residual aches and weariness.

Swiftly I braided hair, ignoring my need for a comb. "You are soft, my lass ... *soft*. What would Rory say?"

Anguish blossomed. I took myself out of my room— cursing the need for deliberation—and went to find Sean.

Thirteen

The Prince of Erinn, when he saw me, did little more than raise eyebrows. And then smiled, bright-eyed, and said he had never seen even a newborn foal as wobbly as the Princess Royal of Homana.

It was, I thought, most unflattering, but at least better than the solicitude the others plagued me with. I hung onto the wall, smiled back sweetly, called him something less than the legitimate son of a woman who sold her favors to any man with coin. Or without, depending on how she felt.

He thought about it, said it would do, then caught me under both arms and plopped me, none-too-gently, in a chair. "Wine?" he asked politely.

Too many stairs— I slumped sideways, hooking an elbow over the chair arm, and let loose a breathy sigh. *Gods—I am weaker than I thought.*

"Lass—will ye do?"

Would I do? Depending. What did he want me to do?

"Stay alive," he answered succinctly, and threatened to call brothers, uncle, and father to hie me back to my bed.

"No, no." I waved a limp hand. "I will 'do,' Sean—give me time. I have been in bed for—five days?"

"Six."

"Then I *should* be weary—bed-rest wears down a body." I sighed again and pushed myself upright. "Aye, I will have wine. Unless you have *usca*; that will put me to rights."

" 'Tis *my* room, lass . . . what I have is Erinnish."

I waved again; he interpreted it as assent, and poured me a cup. I drank, choked, nodded. It was familiar fire; Rory had given it to me.

Rory.

I took the cup from my mouth. "Do you know why I am here?"

"Not to share my bed; you're a bit weak for that." He grinned, sat down in a chair that creaked beneath his weight. "D'ye make a practice of going alone into a man's bedchamber?"

"This is your *ante*chamber, not bedchamber . . . and why should it matter? We are betrothed, and I have been dishonored. What more harm can befall my name?"

The brightness faded from his eyes. "Bitterness doesn't become you."

I drank again, trying to hide my weakness. I had eaten little but broth for five—no, *six*—days, and drunk only water; the liquor warmed my belly and set my head to spinning. "I came to ask a service of you."

Something flickered briefly in his eyes. He shuttered it with lowered lids, hidden behind long lashes, and then looked at me again. " 'Tis Rory, then."

"Will you fetch him? I can hardly go myself, and this must be settled."

Sean pressed hands against chair arms and abruptly thrust himself upright in one powerful movement. He walked away from me, offering his back, and stared out the nearest casement. It was midday; sun flooded the chamber with light.

A broad, hard back. Stiff the length of the spine. And then he swung to face me. "D'ye know what you're asking?"

"You to fetch Rory."

"Here, lass. *Here*. In the household of your father. A bastard-born exile, who nearly killed his lord."

"His brother," I said calmly. "So did I, my lord."

It stopped him only a moment. "Have you decided, then?"

"No. But you were the one who said I should see him."

He swore. "Aye, I did, that. And aye, so you should. But you're a fine, strong lass, and I'd hate to be losing you."

I arched unsubtle brows. "I did not know you *had* me."

He scowled. "You know what I'm saying, lass."

"And you know which of you stands a better chance. You are the Prince of Erinn. He a bastard-born exile."

He tilted his head to one side. "I'd be taking him back with me, lass. My head's not broken, so there's no need for him to stay."

I had not thought of it. I had thought only of Rory in Homana, and me—with Sean—in Erinn.

One way or another, I will have to leave Homana.

I held the cup too tightly. "Will you do me the service?"

"If you'll be doing *me* one."

"Aye," I agreed, "of course."

"Go to bed, my lass ... you're needing it, I'm thinking."

I was too tired to nod. "You can call one of the servants, or one of my brothers—" I dropped the cup abruptly.

Sean plucked me out of the chair. "I'm thinking I'll do it myself."

When he came, he glittered with mail. I stared at him in surprise. "Are you going to war?"

His scowl was much like Sean's: brow bumping brow, hair hanging low, brown eyes nearly black. "From what my brother's been saying, I'm thinking I may have to."

"Why are you wearing *mail?*"

Injured pride was manifest. " 'Tis all I've got worthy of you."

"Worthy of *me!*" I laughed in disbelief. "By the gods, Rory, what a man wears is not what he is!"

"No?" His scowl had not abated; if anything, it deepened. "He said you were a lass mightily impressed by what a man wore, and the title before his name."

I smothered my laughter, seeing the bleakness in his eyes. "He lied," I told him gently. "I have been in your camp, Erinnish . . . I have spent a few nights with you, albeit not in your bed. You should know very well what it is I judge people by."

Behind the beard, he muttered, "I'll be breaking the *skilfin's* head."

"You tried it once, Rory . . . next time you may succeed, and where would you be then? Exiled somewhere else, and crying into your wine because the beloved brother is dead."

He smiled, then laughed, then nodded. Then glanced around the room. "Where is this, lass?"

"Deirdre's solar. I like it for its sunlight, and the comfort of its chairs." I paused. "Would you care to sit in one, or pace the room like a bear?"

"Pace," he answered succinctly, and suited action to words.

I made myself more comfortable in one of the comfortable chairs. Sean had gone, as requested, and fetched his brother to the palace. It had taken three days even with my explicit directions; now, seeing Rory, I thought the delay was to purchase assorted finery. He wore winterweight quilted wool tunic beneath the shirt of mail—Erinnish green, of course, or as near to as could be found in raven-and-red Mujhara—edged with silver-gilt braid. The trews were new as well, though the boots as I remembered: drooping, stained, nearly out in the toes; boots must be made, not bought, if they are to fit at all.

The curly hair was combed, but too long; the beard required trimming so as to prove the face beneath it. But he was clean and smelled of bathing, which was more than was offered before.

He stopped short and swung toward me. "Are ye well, lass? He said you'd been near to dying."

"Do I look near to dying?"

"Halfway near," he said seriously. "You've none of the color I recall, and there's blue beneath your eyes."

I put a hand to my face, drew it away at once. "Aye, well—did he tell you why?" No more need to avoid it.

He turned away again, stood still, then spun back and came to my chair. " 'Twas a child, he said. Strahan's Ihlini bastard."

I listened to the nuances of his tone. There was genuine concern. Anger on my behalf. Frustrated helplessness, that he had done nothing to aid me. But also an odd, almost strangled note of something I could not name.

"I miscarried it," I told him. "Does it make a difference to you? Do you think me soiled, now?"

He opened his mouth, then clamped it closed. Something glittered in his eyes. Tears, I thought in surprise, but not of anger, of shame, of futility. What he gave me was anguish, and an empathy almost palpable. "Lass," he said, "oh, *lass*—"

"Sit down," I told him plainly.

He stared hard at me, looming like a tree. And then sat down, as I had suggested, but on the pelt at my feet rather than in a chair. He spread both hands over my knees, as if in holding them prisoner he also held me. "I near went mad," he swore. "They came to me, your brothers, saying all manner of things not to my liking. They asked if I'd had the stealing of you—as if I would!—and did I care to feel their wrath? The wrath of a Cheysuli?" Rory nearly spat, but refrained out of respect for Deirdre's solar. "After they'd done with their talking, and I was done with mine, 'twas decided I'd seen none of you; that Strahan had done the taking."

"He had."

"I offered to ride with them. For free, I said, and no stealing along the way. But they refused, saying the search would be done in *lir*-shape, and I had naught of the magic." His eyes glittered angrily. "I told them no, 'twas true, but I knew a little of it because of you . . . and they laughed, as if my ignorance lessened me . . . as if my lack of magic made me less than a man! Unblessed, they called me . . . *gods*, I wanted to break their heads and teach them manners, to tear down that arrogance . . . how *dare* they show it to me! I am their equal in everything!"

"You just agreed you cannot shapechange."

It quieted him a moment. Then he showed me teeth through the blaze of his beard. "Aye, well, no . . . but the *arrogance* of them, lass!"

I sighed a little. "I have my own share. A common trait, in this House . . . *lir*-shape is mostly a blessing, but others might disagree."

"You've spirit, lass, and pride. There's a difference to those when compared with arrogance."

I laughed. "Only sometimes—Rory, you are crushing my knees."

He crushed them all the harder. "How can you ask it, lass? How can you ask it of me?"

I peeled back his fingers. "Ask you what?—Rory, let go."

"If I could think you soiled?"

I let go of his fingers. "Am I not?"

"I'll break the head of the man who says so, *and* the woman, lass!"

So *fierce*; I laughed. "Leave the heads intact."

He took his hands from me. "D'ye want my brother, then?"

I drew a breath. "Rory—"

"Do you *want* him, lass? In place of me?"

Oh, gods. "Rory—"

"Because he has a title? Because he's not a bastard? Because his sweet, lying mouth has done far more than it should have?"

"*Rory!*" At last, it shut his mouth. "Is railing at a woman the way you think to win her?"

"No," he answered quietly.

"Then why are you doing it?"

"To make you pay me mind, my girl . . . to make you hear what I'm saying."

"What have you said?"

"This." He rose to his feet, looming yet again and all aglitter with mail. "That I'm not caring about the baby. That I'm not caring about what the Ihlini did, other than wanting to break more than his head— though I heard you finished him yourself with no need for a man to do it." Very briefly, he smiled, but it faded almost instantly, replaced by intensity. "What I'm caring about is *you*, lass. Just you. Not what you are, but *who*. Not the blood you have, but simply that you have it, rich and warm and red." His smile, beard-clouded, was crooked. "And if you're not wanting bairns, I'll not insist upon it."

"Bairns often follow the bedding," I answered vaguely, thinking of Aileen. "Your sister is coming home."

Rory froze. "*Who?*"

"Aileen. Your sister. You may be bastard-born, but Liam's daughter is still your sister."

He stared at me hard a moment, then sighed and rubbed both hands over his face, ruffling beard and tangling forelock. "Agh, gods—sister and brother . . . where'd a man be without them? One will be Queen of Homana, the other—agh, *gods!*" He pulled his hands away. "Lass, there's so much I'm wanting to say. So much I'm *needing* to—"

"No." I cut him off curtly, rising. "No, say nothing more. You need to say nothing more." I laughed once, painfully. "You and Sean, both of you, should never have come to Homana. Because you and your royal brother have put me in such a coil I think I shall never unwind myself."

"Lass—"

"Aidan is sickly," I told him. "The blood must be preserved. Aileen is barren, which leaves only me . . . and the Erinnishman I marry. The blood *does* matter . . . more than you can know."

Rory jerked his knife free of its sheath and placed the blade against the underside of his wrist. "Shall I show you the color, then? Rich, red, and *Erinnish*? What more d'ye need, lass? I'm an eagle of the Aerie! No more, no less: *Erinnish!*"

Aye, so he was. As much as Sean himself.

Oh—gods—Sean.

I turned my back on Rory. Shut my eyes. Pressed both hands against my mouth.

And abruptly, spun back to face him. It was all I could do not to shake. "Do you know the Mujhar?"

Rory stared. "No."

"He looks very like Corin—no, Corin looks very like him; I must put the order right."

"Lass—"

"Go to the Mujhar."

"What?"

"Go to the Mujhar and tell him to fetch a priest to the Great Hall."

"Lass—"

"Tell him to gather the House of the Lion together —as well as *both* the eagles of the Aerie—and wait for me in the Great Hall." I drew in a breath. "With the priest, if you please."

"*Keely—*"

"And ask Deirdre to fetch me something to wear."

"Lass! I can't just take myself down to the Mujhar and his lady and tell them—"

"Why not?" I interrupted. "Open your mouth, Erinnish—the words will take care of themselves."

"But—"

"*Go*, Rory! Were you not taught never to keep a lady waiting?"

Swearing in Erinnish—which I understood too well—he took himself out of the solar. I buried my face in my hands.

Oh, gods, I am mad . . . mad as my mother is, to forswear myself so easily for the sake of Liam's son. What if Teir is right? What if we lose the lir?

But I am nothing if not loyal; the Lion requires an heir.

Deirdre arrived in my chambers just after I myself did. Her face was pink from running. "Keely—"

"Did you bring a gown?"

Her hands were empty. "No—"

"Good; I have decided to wear leathers." I dug more deeply into one of my clothing trunks. "Is the priest in the Great Hall?"

"No. Niall—he . . . *Keely—*"

"Is he having one fetched?"

"And everyone else as well." Her shock was fading quickly, replaced with comprehension. "Is this truly what you want?"

"No. It has never been what I wanted. But I have no choice, have I, if I am to be as good a Cheysuli as all three of my *rujholli*, as well as *jehan* and *su'fali*—it is a family tradition." I straightened, shaking out a soft, sleeveless jerkin dyed a deep, rich black. "I have leggings for this as well . . . Deirdre, will you look in my caskets and see if I have any rubies?"

"Rubies?"

I nodded intently. "Red ones."

Deirdre fought a smile and went to do as asked, pouring trinkets across my table.

I found my leggings and quickly stripped out of what I wore, replacing brown with black. And black boots, nearly new, but creased in all the right places, and with red tassels hanging from them.

Deirdre came with wristlets: hammered gold set with rubies. "And this," she said.

My lion's-head belt. I had forgotten it, since I so rarely dressed with any degree of elaboration. I smiled and took it from her, hearing the chime of heavy gold. Dozens of lion's-head bosses the size of a woman's fist, glaring out of gold, linked together into a rope to go around my hips. The largest was the clasp; its eyes were blood-red rubies.

"Homanan colors: black and red." I put it and the wristlets on. "Enough," I said, laughing. "More would blind them all."

"Turn," Deirdre ordered.

I swung to give her my back. She stripped leather tie from my hair and shook out the braid. "Loose," she said firmly, catching up a comb. "That much I'll have of you, if you'll not be wearing skirts."

"It will fall in my face. It always does."

"I'll make certain he sees your face."

I stood very still as she combed, suddenly afraid. "Do you know which one I will take?"

"No. But neither do you."

It hurt worse than expected. "I should have Hart throw dice!"

"It would do as well as anything else." She sectioned off more hair. "What is there to choose from, Keely? Two men. Both tall, both strong, both battle-proved. Both young, but not too young. Both Erinnish, to which I am partial—save for Niall, of course—and both of them Liam's sons. Eagles of the Aerie, bred of the *cileann* and blessed at birth on the sacred tor . . . what is there to choose from, Keely? Wealth? Health? Love? Or will the title make the difference?"

"Blood," I said numbly.

Deirdre came to stand in front of me. She caught both hands and turned them over, palm-up. "When you cut yourself on the sword, did one bleed red? The other green?" She shook her head calmly. "No. Exactly the same, from either hand; *it made no difference, Keely.*"

"No difference?"

"None."

I wish I had her innocence— I closed my hands on hers. "Ask Maeve if that is true. Ask your bastard-born daughter if the blood *does not* matter."

Deirdre's face went white. I turned to go, but she reached out and caught my arm. "Keely! Keely—wait." She scooped something up from the table, then put it into my hands. A slender gold circlet, twisted upon itself to form a slow, sinuous coil, them hammered nearly flat. "To keep your hair from your face."

Slowly, I put it on. It was cool against my brow, but warmed quickly to my flesh.

I swung from her abruptly. "They have waited long enough."

The hammered silver doors to the Great Hall were heavier than I remembered; or I weaker. I decided on the latter, grunting, and scraped one of them open even as Deirdre tried to help.

Brennan, Hart, Corin. Maeve and Ilsa, tiny Blythe. Ian. And *jehan*. And Liam's two tall sons, born of the Aerie of Erinn.

Also one priest, bewildered as everyone else.

"Oh, gods," I muttered, and strode the length of the hall to the marble dais, where the Lion of Homana crouched in mute, maleficent glory.

"Keely—" my father began.

I looked him straight in the eye. "You wanted me

wed, *jehan* So. I will wed. Have the priest take his place."

Rory was scowling at me. "Which of us is it, lass?"

I stood before the dais, the pit, the Lion; before them all, who stood in clusters, but none of them by the throne. I pointed at Rory, then at the place next to me, on my left. "You," I said firmly. And then, before he could speak, I motioned Sean to take the place at my right. "You." I then turned politely to the priest, who stood up one step but not on a level with the Lion, which was only for the Mujhar. "Will you recite the vows? And when you ask for the name of the man I am marrying, I will tell you which one."

"Keely!" My father was astounded. "If you intend this as a jest—"

"No," I told him coolly. "When the priest is done, I promise, your daughter will be wed."

Sean sounded alarmed. "Which one of us *is* it, lass? D'ye think this is fair?"

I glared back. "Is it fair to ask me to choose?"

His face was very white. He looked past me to Rory. "*I* think—"

One of the doors scraped open. Each of us turned to look, for all of us were present. All save Aileen, who came walking down the hall with Aidan in her arms.

I looked at once to Corin. His face was still and white, but he did not turn away.

She saw him. Color rose, fell. And crept back again, slowly, setting her eyes alight even as she smiled. A small, bittersweet smile meant for neither of those who loved her, but only for herself.

Aileen looked at Brennan. Then directly at Rory, frowning, until her expression cleared. "*Sean*," she said, laughing, "when did you dye your beard red?"

Fourteen

My kinfolk deserted me, they and the man I had known as Rory. They left me alone in the hall with only the Lion for company.

The Lion and Liam's eaglet.

Mail glittered as he moved. The red beard—*dyed*—was burnished by sunlight. A tall, strong man, nearly as large as the other. Alike and unalike, both bred in the Aerie's mews.

He stood very close, too close, looking down on me. And then, with no change of expression, he drew his knife and cut into his hand, tipping blood across his palm.

"Rory—" I checked. "*Sean.*"

He put his hand in front of my face, allowing the blood to run free. It rolled to his wrist, stained the cuff of his tunic, hid itself beneath mail. "Red," he said, "Erinnish. Will that do for you?"

I stretched out a single arm, bare of everything save Mujharan rubies and hammered, clan-worked gold, and pointed to the throne but three steps away from us both. "Ask that."

Blood ran from his hand. "I said something to you earlier. I'll be saying it again: *'I'm not caring what you are, but who.'* " Blood dripped onto stone. "I don't want the beastie, lass. What I want is you."

Slowly I shook my head. "With me, you get the 'beastie.' What do I get with you?"

He turned from me then, sheathing the knife, and mounted the dais steps: one, two, three. Stood beside the Lion, then put his hand upon it. Blood glistened dully; was taken into wood.

Sean sat down in the throne. I opened my mouth to protest, closed it almost at once. His House was as old as my own; I thought the Lion of Homana would not begrudge the eagle of Erinn his moment.

" 'Twas not a jest," he said. "I never meant it to hurt."

Until the last, it had not. They had fooled me utterly.

" 'Twas well known, lass, what manner of woman you were. A high-tempered, sharp-tongued lass not in mind to lie down with the lads . . . not even the Prince of Erinn." He paused. "*Especially* the Prince of Erinn."

I swept the circlet from my brow. Hair fell over shoulders.

He shifted in the Lion. "Never in my life have I had to beg a lass. We are both of us, Rory and I, accustomed to filling our beds with naught but a flick of an eyelash." He did not say it to boast; he spoke frankly and evenly, commanding more with quiet candor than anything else could do. "I was four," he said softly, "and you yet unborn. Our fathers linked us, lass, without considering what we might feel . . . without considering what we might *do*."

I clutched the circlet in both hands, but looked at him instead.

"I knew what I felt, lass, when it came time to think of wedding. And not being blind to women—no lass, I'm not—I knew what *you'd* be thinking; you with such glorious freedom and no one to understand . . . not even, I'm thinking, your brothers."

I recalled the day he had asked it: "*Make me feel it, lass*." And recalled how I had answered, showing him how to fly.

The quiet voice continued. "I thought of sending

for you. I thought of coming myself: I, the Prince of Erinn. But neither would do, I knew . . . 'twould lose you rather than win you." He sighed, chewing his lip. "And so I went to Rory, who shares with me so very many of my feelings . . . between us, thinking of you, we conjured the tale we hoped might win a Cheysuli princess."

"A thief."

"I robbed no one; the coin I spent was my own, come all the way from Erinn."

"You stole Brennan's horse."

"And gave him back, lass."

So I could lose him in Hondarth. "They were your guard, those men."

He smiled. "To keep me alive in a foreign land where shapechangers are more than myth."

"You told me you murdered your brother."

Sean's mouth hooked wryly. "I told you I *thought* I had, or might have, was more likely. I near broke his head, aye, 'twas true . . . but I made it sound worse than it was, to make the tale better. And it wasn't much of a lie, lass . . . it was the Redbeard who suffered the hurt, not me—not the Prince of Erinn. We only twisted it a bit, or traded places, in all the tales we told."

With effort, I kept myself calm. "How long was it to last?"

His mouth altered into grimness. "Not so long, lass. Rory was to come sooner, but Liam kept him back. I meant it to go on only long enough for you to be certain . . . for you to *want* the marriage—or, I hoped, want *me*—and then I'd tell the truth."

"What part had Rory to play in this?"

He smiled. "None of what I told you is a lie. He is indeed my brother, though bastard-born, and he is indeed Liam's son, freely acknowledged, a captain in my guard. The words I was saying in his place are things he's said to me . . . I used as much truth as I could, lass."

"And the two of you fought each other over a 'bonny lass.'"

"Aye, that we did." He shifted in the Lion. "We're very alike, Rory and I . . . and either of us would be killing the man who meant one or the other harm."

"So. Rory was to come as Sean and emphasize, oh so subtly, that I had an option other than marrying the man I believed I *had* to."

"It *was* subtle, lass. If you agreed to marry the Prince of Erinn, there I was. If you agreed to wed Rory Redbeard instead, exchanging duty for what you wanted, there I was." He shrugged. "It was to be a clean choice, I promise, and made soon after Rory's arrival."

"But then Strahan intervened." I drew in a very deep breath. "You know what he did. You know the result of it."

"Lass—"

"I am not fit for the Prince of Erinn, or even a royal bastard who has every right to inherit if his brother gets no sons."

His eyes were nearly black. "I'll be taking the lass who stands here before me, regardless of the Ihlini. She's a braw, bright lass, and I'd be a fool to want another."

The laughter was painful. "Rory told you that."

Sean fingered his mustache. "We're much alike, lass . . . 'tis why this was dangerous. He's a man for the lasses, my brother . . . he might have won you for himself."

"And very nearly did. That was a *priest*, Sean! What would you have done?"

"Oh, I'd have stopped it. 'Twas what Rory was asking, just before Aileen came. He knew then what we'd done, and how unfair it was." A smile crept out of the beard. "But then we're not certain which of us you meant to name."

And still was not, I knew, which suited me very well. I tossed hair out of my face. "You carried out this mummery to make certain I took the man I wanted. Not because of what he was, but who . . . and now I ask *you*, how do you know I will not wed him? Bastard-born or not, you have proved it does not matter."

Sean held up his hand. "This." Blood stained his palm.

I laughed out loud at him. "You are both of you Liam's sons."

The color drained out of his face, what of it I could see above the beard. "*Which*, then, lass? Which of us do you take?"

I placed the circlet back on my brow. "The Prince of Erinn, my lord."

Sean smiled, grinned, then laughed in triumph, thrusting himself to his feet. And then checked, staring. "To you, that is *Rory!*"

"So it is," I agreed. "I think you had better go."

He was shaking; mail glittered. He had taken himself to the edge, and I had pushed him off.

I waited. He walked stiffly to the end of the hall, all the way to the silver doors, and then swung to face me, shouting, to reach me at the Lion. A powerful, angry shout, full of unexpected anguish. "D'ye want me to fetch him, then? D'ye want me to fetch my brother the way he once fetched me?"

Satisfaction died; I did not want to hurt him. "I want you to fetch us *swords*, my lord . . . swords—and a priest! If I'm to be Princess of Erinn, it will be done the Erinnish way, after the fashion of the *cileann*."

His voice was clearly startled. "How d'ye know about that?"

"Aileen told me, ye *skilfin* . . . how else would I be knowing?"

Sean began to grin. I could see it clear to the Lion, creeping through the beard. Blond, I thought; it would dye easier.

I sighed. "Were you not taught never to keep a lady waiting?"

He went immediately out of the door, filling the hall with silence.

I watched the doors swing shut, silver glinting in the distance. Then turned slowly to face the Lion.

Fixed in wood, it glared. I glared back. "You have won," I told it, "but then, you always do."

Mute, it made no reply. But no longer did I need one; the question had been answered.

I sat down on the dais, doubling up knees and arms, perching rump on hard smooth marble. Thoughtfully, I said, "He's a braw, bright boyo, the eagle from Liam's mews . . . I think he might just do." I chewed idly on a thumbnail. "If he lets me have a sword."

THE HOUSE OF HOMANA

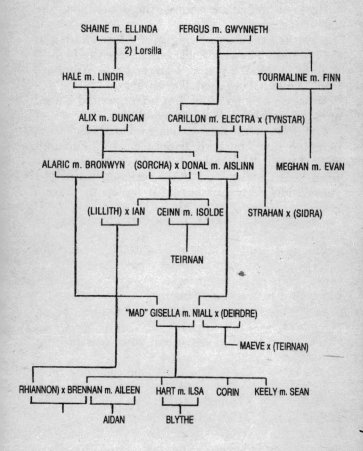

APPENDIX I

CHEYSULI/OLD TONGUE GLOSSARY
(with pronunciation guide)

a'saii (uh-SIGH) — Cheysuli zealots dedicated to pure line of descent.

bu'lasa (boo-LAH-suh) — grandson

bu'sala (boo-SAH-luh) — foster-son

cheysu (chay-SOO) — man/woman; neuter; used within phrases.

cheysul (chay-SOOL) — husband

cheysula (chay-SOO-luh) — wife

cheysuli (chay-SOO-lee) — (*literal translation*): children of the gods.

Cheysuli i'halla shansu (chay-SOO-lee i-HALLA shan-SOO) — (*lit.*): May there be Cheysuli peace upon you.

godfire (god-fire) — common manifestation of Ihlini power; cold, lurid flame; purple tones.

harana (huh-RAH-na) — niece

harani (huh-RAH-nee) — nephew

homana (ho-MAH-na) — (*literal translation*): of all blood.

i'halla (ih-HALL-uh) — upon you: used within phrases.

i'toshaa-ni (ih-tosha-NEE) — Cheysuli cleansing ceremony; atonement ritual.

ja'hai ([French *j*] zshuh-HIGH) — accept

ja'hai-na (zshuh-HIGH-nuh) — accepted

jehan (zsheh-HAHN) — father

jehana (zsheh-HAH-na) — mother

ku'reshtin (koo-RESH-tin) — epithet; name-calling

leijhana tu'sai (lay-HAHN-uh too-SIGH) — (*lit.*): thank you very much.

lir (leer) — magical animal(s) linked to individual Cheysuli; title used indiscriminately between *lir* and warriors.

meijha (MEE-hah) — Cheysuli: light woman; (*lit.*): mistress.

meijhana (mee-HAH-na) — slang: pretty one

Mujhar (moo-HAR) — king

qu'mahlin (koo-MAH-lin) — purge; extermination

Resh'ta-ni (resh-tah-NEE) — (*lit.*): As you would have it.

rujho (ROO-ho) — slang: brother (diminutive)

rujholla (roo-HALL-uh) — sister (formal)

rujholli (roo-HALL-ee) — brother (formal)

ru'maii (roo-MY-ee) — (*lit.*): in the name of

Ru'shalla-tu (roo-SHAWL-uh TOO) — (*lit.*) May it be so.

Seker (Sek-AIR) — formal title: god of the netherworld.

shansu (shan-SOO) — peace

shar tahl (shar TAHL) — priest-historian; keeper of the prophecy.

shu'maii (shoo-MY-ee) — sponsor

su'fala (soo-FALL-uh) — aunt

su'fali (soo-FALL-ee) — uncle

sul'harai (sool-hah-RYE) — moment of greatest satisfaction in union of man and woman; describes shapechange.

tahlmorra (tall-MORE-uh) — fate; destiny; kismet.

Tahlmorra lujhala mei wiccan, cheysu (tall-MORE-uh loo-HALLA may WICK-un, chay-SOO) — (*lit.*): The fate of a man rests always within the hands of the gods.

tetsu (tet-SOO) — poisonous root given to allay great pain; addictive, eventually fatal.

tu'halla dei (too-HALLA-day-EE) — (*lit.*): Lord to liege man.

usca (OOIS-kuh) — powerful liquor from the Steppes.

y'ja'hai (EE-zshuh-HIGH) — (*lit.*): I accept.